Praise for *The Meq*

"The book's blend of melancholy and optimism, synchronicity and fate, melodrama and spiritual concerns, calls to mind the work of Nicholas Christopher in such novels as *Franklin Flyer*."
—*The Washington Post Book World*

"Mesmerizing."
—*The New York Times*

"An appealing and entertaining story."
—*The Denver Post*

"A unusual and textured fantasy novel . . .
Cash has me anxiously awaiting the second installment."
—*Contra Costa Times*

"An astonishing, inventive and addictive book . . . Steve Cash's incisive storytelling runs the gamut of the emotional spectrum, touching upon love, hate, joy, loneliness and despair."
—*January Magazine*

"A surprisingly ingenious, lushly detailed story that turns fantasy on its head . . . The drama is intense, the characterizations are fully realized, and the very cadence of the language infuses a rich sense of time, place, and historical context that draws one in."
—*Booklist* (starred review)

Also by Steve Cash

THE MEQ

TIME
DANCERS

TIME
DANCERS

BOOK TWO OF THE MEQ

STEVE CASH

BALLANTINE BOOKS
NEW YORK

Time Dancers is a work of historical fiction. Apart from the well-known actual people, events, and locales that figure in the narrative, all names, characters, places, and incidents are the products of the author's imagination or are used fictitiously. Any resemblance to current events or locales, or to living persons, is entirely coincidental.

A Del Rey Trade Paperback Original

Published in the United States by Del Rey Books, an imprint of The Random House Publishing Group, a division of Random House, Inc., New York.

DEL REY is a registered trademark and the Del Rey colophon is a trademark of Random House, Inc.

Grateful acknowledgment is made to the following for permission to reprint previously published material:

Princeton University Press: Excerpt from "Ithaka" from *C. P. Cavafy: Collected Poems,* by C. P. Cavafy, translated by Edmund Keeley and Philip Sherrard, copyright © 1972 by Edmund Keeley and Philip Sherrard. Reprinted by permission of Princeton University Press.

Scribner, an imprint of Simon & Schuster Adult Publishing Group: Excerpt from *The Spirit of St. Louis* by Charles Lindbergh, copyright © 1953 by Charles Scribner's Sons, copyright renewed 1981 by Anne Morrow Lindbergh. Reprinted by permission of Scribner, an imprint of Simon & Schuster Adult Publishing Group.

ISBN 0-345-47093-1

Printed in the United States of America

www.delreybooks.com

9 8 7 6 5 4 3 2 1

For Chloe, Colin, and Zoe

ACKNOWLEDGMENTS

I want to thank Cody Cash for helping me in every way from beginning to end. I am lucky to have him as a son and know him as a friend. I also want to thank Frances Bissell for her wonderful insights and constant support, and I would like to thank Betsy Mitchell for her always accurate advice, patience, and belief in the story.

Previously, in *The Meq:*

The Meq are running out of time. World War I has ended, and in less than a hundred years they must assemble at the mystical gathering called the Gogorati, the Remembering. Within a rapidly moving twentieth century, Zianno Zezen, or Z, recounts his tale of the search for who and what the Meq truly are.

All Meq grow to the age of twelve, and are human in appearance, but this is where the similarities end. The Meq retain the physical body of a twelve-year-old for as long as they are able to survive or until they find their Ameq—their one true love and companion. Then the two must make a conscious decision whether to continue in the Itxaron, the Wait, or to "cross" in the ancient but little-understood rite known as the Zeharkatu. Those who choose the Zeharkatu become completely mortal and begin to age. They are also able to procreate, and this is how they have survived for countless millennia. Those who remain in the Wait cannot get sick or contract diseases, and they heal from all wounds and broken bones in a matter of minutes or days. They can be killed by decapitation, drowning, bleeding to death from a slashed throat, or by being—as Ray Ytuarte, one of Z's closest allies, puts it—"stomped beyond recognition by some-thin'."

The Meq experience every human emotion, but in the past they have kept human beings, known to them as the Giza, at a distance. They must. To the Meq, the Giza are greedy, dangerous, and their lives are simply too short. The ancestral home of the Meq is in the Pyrenees, and at some point in the distant past the Meq formed a symbiotic relationship with five Basque tribes, who became their protectors. Z shares this relationship with the Basque, yet he was born in the United States, and it is in St. Louis where Z begins his own history and adventures. He forms many different and lasting relationships with the Giza, most notably the inimitable Solomon J. Birnbaum and Carolina Covington Flowers. Now nearing fifty, she is Z's oldest friend and her family has become Z's family.

Unfortunately, the mysterious, murderous Meq assassin known as the Fleur-du-Mal has taunted and tortured Z for over two decades, always posing a threat to those Z cares most about in his obsession to find the elusive, mythical Sixth Stone. Five of these magical, egg-shaped black rocks are known to exist. They have been carried and passed down since prehistory, or what is called the Time of Ice, by five separate Meq families. Each Stone has a certain meaning and title, as well as possessing a curious hypnotic power. The Stone of Dreams is now carried by Z, the other four by Sailor, Geaxi, Nova (the youngest among them), and Opari, Z's Ameq. The ultimate purpose of the Stones is unknown, though the Meq are convinced it relates to their lost origins.

Thus, the story begins and continues. The Meq and their long, tangled tapestry of the past is gradually revealed, as well as their flickering present, but the future, even for the Meq, remains uncertain and unknown.

BOOK TWO

PART I

Wise as you will have become, so full of experience,
you will have understood by then what these Ithakas mean.

—C.P. CAVAFY

BIHARAMUN

(DAY AFTER TOMORROW)

Where are you looking? Through a window, from a bridge, down a well, over the rainbow, out of a mouse hole, into the light? Where are you looking? Or, rather, what are you looking for? Out there, somewhere, at some time, do you see a wish fulfilled, a dream come true, a simple affirmation and clarity of that which we cannot speak? Look closely. Can you see the day after tomorrow? Do you recognize it? Will you ever? It is approaching.

The date was March 9, 1919, and it was snowing. We were taking the train down from Chicago to St. Louis and as we crossed the bridge spanning the Mississippi, the sun's light was fading fast. The water below us looked dark, darker than I ever remembered, and deep under the low light and falling snow. I was in the aisle seat in the back row of our compartment. Opari was sitting next to me. She sat in silence with her head turned away, facing the window. Suddenly she made a trilling sound with her teeth and tongue, then whispered an ancient word in slow repetition. *"Amatxurlarru,"* she said. *"Amatxurlarru."* The word was haunting. Her careful pronunciation was hypnotic and sounded somewhere between song and prayer. I had never heard the word before, but I knew it was Meq.

"What does it mean?" I asked. I was looking past her, through the glass, speaking to her reflection.

"It is from the Time of Ice," she said. "Great rivers, like this one, were givers of all life and death. The phrase is only spoken when one crosses a river that is a Mother to many others." She paused a moment and I assumed she was returning to events, stories, people and places, adventures and wisdom, passed down to her from a time so distant I could only imagine it. She went on, "The word, both in dreams and in real life, means 'the Mother bleeds.' "

A few more seconds passed. I watched the snow while the train tracks rattled underneath us. Finally, I managed to say, "Really." It was neither question nor statement, and I was trying once again not to show my relative youth and ignorance. I know now that time and the passing of it, the difference in ages and the awareness of it, should not be a problem when you are in love, but these things have taken me a lifetime to learn, let alone accept without wonder.

Ahead, just past the western end of the bridge, the lights of downtown St. Louis were coming into view. Opari said, "This is your birth city, is it not, my love?"

"Yes," I answered. "It is that . . . and many other things." I continued staring out the window, but not at the falling snow, or St. Louis, or even the great Mississippi River. Instead, I gazed into the reflection of two beautiful black eyes, understanding then and there that I will always desire to do just that, as long as I am on this Earth. I felt the presence of her inside me the same way I had seen, for a timeless second, my own mama and papa look to and through each other, also on a train crossing a river, in 1881.

To my right, directly across the aisle, sat my oldest friend and confidante, Carolina Covington Flowers. She was almost fifty years old now, although a stranger would never guess it. She was smiling and staring through the window. Her long hair was pulled back and a few strands of silver and gold hung loose, framing her face. She wore a long black skirt and a simple white blouse buttoned to the neck. A green woolen shawl draped around her shoulders. Her only grandchild, the baby Caine, slept peacefully in her lap. As I watched, she silently wiped a single tear from her cheek. I started to ask if anything was wrong, then decided against it. There was nothing wrong and there was nothing I could do. Sad, happy, maybe both, maybe neither, it was more likely she was only experiencing the same thing I had been thinking about all day, ever since we left Chicago—*return*. And not just return to anywhere, but return to St. Louis.

The train began a slow, noisy turn to the left, preparing for our approach to Union Station. I glanced ahead at the others and a thought occurred to me that I'd been putting aside and ignoring for weeks. It concerned a situation at least four of us had always been warned to avoid, especially by Sailor. Opari, Geaxi, Nova, and I each had a Stone in our possession and we were all traveling together. The Stones carried by Geaxi and me had been stripped of their priceless gems long ago in Vancouver, but the Stones worn by Opari and Nova were still intact. Like four points on a compass, their Stones held a tiny blue diamond on the top, a star sapphire on the bottom, and lapis lazuli and pearl on each side. The Stones themselves were black and egg-shaped. Sailor had made it clear that the Gogorati, the Remembering, was much too close at hand, less than a hundred years, for any-thing awkward to happen. Accidents or errors of any sort by any one of us were unacceptable. Period. Although Sailor himself was currently unavailable and following a fear or vision only he could see, I knew he was right, and the reasoning behind his warning was still sound and significant. I made a silent promise, in deference to Sailor, to quit inviting "anything awkward."

And yet, except for the few traveling with us and a few more spread throughout the world, everyone else—all the others, the Giza—saw us only as they always had: as a troupe of twelve-year-olds, probably related. So be it. We were inside the great station already and St. Louis had never been so loud and alive, urban and big—a true city.

Within minutes we came to an abrupt and final stop. Every-one in our compartment stood at once, reaching for great coats, fedoras, mufflers, and scarves, bracing for the weather outside and filling the aisle completely, front to back. I glanced at Caro-lina and she silently mouthed the words "Let's wait." I nodded in agreement and looked up, trying to catch the eye of Willie Croft, who was sitting with Geaxi. Ahead of them, Nova and Star sat together, as they had for most of the trip since leaving England. But all were out of sight, impossible to see through the shuffling crowd.

Then Carolina shouted, "What about Nicholas and Eder?" Caine was awake and staring at her with wide-open brown eyes, startled by the sudden volume in her voice. She was concerned about her late husband, Nicholas Flowers, and Nova's mother, Eder Gaztelu. Both Nicholas and Eder were in coffins stowed away in another compartment. St. Louis would be the final stop on their final journey. I yelled back that Willie had taken care of it, but I assured her that we would check on it before we did anything else.

"Good," she said, smiling down at Caine. "Oh," she added, craning her neck so I could see her better, "then I'll tell Owen Bramley to only worry with the luggage. He and Jack will be looking for us."

Opari tugged on my arm gently and whispered in my ear, "Jack is Carolina's son, no?"

"Yes, but I've never met him."

"How many years is he?"

I thought about it for a moment, then laughed to myself. So much had happened in the last few months, I nearly forgot Opari was still learning about Carolina and her family, not to mention the entire Western world. We were both learning, especially about each other. However, there was one thing we had not yet discussed—the Wait. I always felt that once we'd arrived in St. Louis and were settled in Carolina's home, we would have to discuss it. I looked forward to it. Opari was over three thousand years old and still perfectly comfortable in a twelve-year-old body. On my next twelfth birthday, I would be fifty. Even now, I have trouble trying to articulate the intense, paradoxical, and unique power of the Itxaron, the Wait, the very essence of the Meq.

"Is the answer a laughing one?" she asked.

"Probably only to me," I said, then gave her the answer. "He's twelve, but he gets to turn thirteen in April."

After the crowd thinned out, I could finally see ahead to the front of our compartment. Geaxi, Willie Croft, Star, and Nova had also remained in their seats. Geaxi turned and caught my eye, then rose out of her seat, putting on her black beret and walking swiftly back toward me, easily avoiding everyone going the other way. Somewhere on the trip west from New York, she had begun wearing the same clothing that she had worn when I first met her in 1882—black leather leggings and a black vest held together with strips of leather attached to bone. It was unique attire for anyone, but especially so in 1919 on the body of a twelve-year-old girl. Her dark eyes shone bright and she seemed to be almost smiling.

"It is a fine feeling to be back in your city, young Zezen," she said.

"It's not *my* city, Geaxi."

"Oh, but you are mistaken, even more than you know."

"How is that?"

"Because this is a truly American city," she said, "and you, young Zezen, are truly American, agree with it or not, as you prefer. You will come to love this city, though I suspect you have this feeling within you now." She paused and smiled, then added, "Even more than you know."

I thought about what she was saying and wondered why she was saying it. Then I remembered Geaxi's birthplace. "When was the last time you visited Malta?" I asked, not knowing whether Geaxi would take offense or not.

"That is different," she replied. "My home as a real child was a simple farm with an olive grove and a few buildings, all long gone and erased from the landscape by change and circum-stance."

"But don't you want to go back, even if nothing's there?"

"Yes, I do, and I will . . . someday." She winked once, then laughed, leaning down and whispering, "When I have the time."

I glanced out the window at the bundled, busy, loud throng of people coming and going within the immense space of Union Station, and all at once everything seemed more than familiar. I laughed and said, "Then let's get off this train and go home!"

"Right you are," Carolina said. "Let's go home."

Owen Bramley, much to my surprise, was on time and already there to meet us. In fact, we almost collided with him as we stepped off the train. He had been running from car to car along the platform, looking frantically inside every window for a sign of us. Star, carrying Caine inside the old leather jacket that Willie had given her, was the most excited among us and stepped down first, leaping out with a small scream and a big smile. Owen Bramley nearly trampled her, coming hard from the other direction, but he caught himself and grabbed the handrail of the train door at the last possible moment. Star had cut her hair short on our trip west, mimicking the style of Nova, and she looked even younger than her true age of nineteen.

"My God," Owen Bramley said, astonished by what he saw in front of him. He took in a breath, then shook his head, staring into the living eyes of the daughter of Carolina. "Remarkable," he said, "simply remarkable."

Inside Star's jacket, Caine turned his head to stare at this new face and voice. "You are Owen Bramley," Star said. "I know it, I know you are. You have to be."

She stepped to the side of the stairs leading down to the platform. The rest of us fanned out behind and around her.

"Yes, I am, young lady, and I am just as sure that you are Star. I can barely believe it, but there you stand." He watched each of us gather around Star. When his eyes fell on Carolina, he said,

"My God, it is so good to see all of you." It was obvious in his eyes that he meant what he said, and clear to me that he was more than relieved to see her returning.

He wore a long trench coat with several buckles and belts, and he was hatless. Fresh snow covered his head and shoulders. His hair was still red, with only a few more streaks of gray than in New Orleans, the last time I'd seen him. His face seemed about the same, except older, of course, and he was even more freckled across his forehead, cheeks, and nose.

"Hello, Owen," I said. "You look well."

For the first time since I had known him, Owen Bramley was speechless. He had been expecting us, but the reality of seeing us in person overwhelmed him. He simply stood still, staring at all of us and shaking his head. Behind his wire-rimmed glasses, his blue eyes were bright with understanding. After a few moments, he stammered, "I . . . I don't know what to say, Z."

"Hello would be a good start, Owen." It was Carolina. She gave him a big hug and kissed him on both cheeks, then asked, "Where's Jack?"

"Why, I thought he was right here," he said, turning suddenly and looking behind him.

"Well, he's not here now."

"It's all right, Carolina," Owen said, giving her a knowing wink. "He's not alone."

"Ah . . . I see," she said with a smile. "Good."

Then Owen Bramley caught sight of Opari for the first time. She was wearing one of her ancient shawls across her shoulders and a burgundy scarf around her neck. He seemed startled, almost spellbound by her presence and natural beauty. "I don't believe I know you," he said. "I'm certain we've never met before."

"My name is Opari," she said, looking up at him. "Your name

I know from Z and Carolina." She smiled and Owen Bramley instantly became her friend and constant admirer.

"Owen," I broke in, "why don't you help the porter with the luggage while Willie and I take care of something else."

"Right, right," he said. "Let's get going then."

Willie and I left the others in order to make arrangements for the off-loading of the coffins. I played the part of the silent kid and let Willie do the talking. Months earlier at Caitlin's Ruby he'd stopped wearing his British uniform, in which he was never completely comfortable, and now, in corduroy slacks, wool sweater, and tweed jacket, he looked much more like the "real" Willie Croft. With his tousled red hair, casual charm, and soft British accent, he had helped make all our travels and troubles along the way much easier, especially through customs, which is always a little tricky for us. He was still head over heels in love with Star, which also insured his constant concern and attention to our welfare, and even though his love for her was honest and genuine, to watch him when he was around her was always comical, bordering on pathetic. However, his feelings never affected his watchful eye or awareness of our situation, whatever it might be. And he was good at directing attention away from the Meq when there were several of us traveling together, as we had been since leaving England. Individually, the Meq are excellent at blending in almost anywhere, but if we are together we draw attention from time to time for being so alike among ourselves, yet very different in cast and carriage from other children. Willie was intuitive in seeing this revelation dawn on a stranger long before they saw it themselves. His various uses of empathy and fantasy were equally and easily distributed. People were ready to give Willie all the help he needed while asking few, if any, questions. Afterward they would feel that whatever they had done to assist him must have been the right thing to do.

"Well, I suppose that's it then," he said. We were walking rapidly to catch up with the others. His tone was somber and he was looking straight ahead.

"Almost, but not quite," I answered. "Carolina wants to bury them both in the 'Honeycircle' in back of her home. I'm sure it's not legal."

"The what?"

"It's hard to explain. I think you better see it for yourself."

Willie gave me a quick glance, raising an eyebrow. "If you say so, Z . . . and don't worry about the legal bit. I'll take care of it."

"Thanks, Willie . . . for everything. I mean it."

"Nothing to it, Z. It's my pleasure."

As we hurried to catch the others, we had to pass through the Midway, a 610-foot-long, 70-foot-wide concourse that connected the train shed with the Grand Hall. Halfway through I suddenly noticed Geaxi standing by herself and staring at a poster attached to the wall. I spoke to her, but she didn't respond, so Willie and I walked over to see if anything was wrong. Of course, she had sensed our presence long before we got to her. She pivoted slowly and glanced up at Willie, as if she'd been waiting for him.

"What kind of aircraft is that?" she asked, pointing toward the poster.

Willie looked closely at the image on the poster, which was a biplane flying between clouds and banking sharply to the right. Under the image, along the bottom of the poster, were the words "Pilots needed—contact Marcellus Foose, East St. Louis, Illinois—if you can fly a Jenny, you can fly anything."

"I believe that is a Curtiss JN-4," Willie said. "The Americans like to refer to it as a 'Jenny.' Very reliable, but often difficult to handle, I'm told."

Geaxi made no reply for several moments, then said simply, "I see." She adjusted her beret slightly, and without saying another word or looking behind, started walking toward the Grand Hall. Willie turned to me for an explanation. I shrugged, then smiled and shook my head, once again realizing there is no explaining the inscrutable Geaxi Bikis.

With Geaxi in the lead, we made our way through the thinning crowd and into the Grand Hall. Willie stared up at the huge, barrel-vaulted ceiling and Romanesque architecture.

"Magnificent structure," he said. "Never seen anything like it."

"No, neither have I," I said and meant it. The building was, and is, a wonder.

"Over there," Geaxi shouted back at us, pointing toward our little troupe, all gathered around a shoeshine stand against the wall. The luggage was stacked on a large cart off to one side. Carolina was waving for us to come quickly.

When we reached them, she made the sign to keep quiet with her finger pressed to her lips, then leaned over and whispered to me, "Mitchell is teaching Jack about the shoeshine business."

I squeezed between the others to get closer. What I saw was a handsome, young black man sitting in one of the raised chairs on the stand. He was wearing a tuxedo, complete with white tie, starched white shirt, and white silk scarf around his neck. A floppy, old snap-brimmed cap rested at an angle on his head, the only incongruity in his whole wardrobe. He was looking down and carefully watching a boy about my size, who was buffing the man's patent leather shoes to a high sheen.

"You got it, Jack," the man said. "Now whip the rag in the air and wrap it around my heel. Give it a good one-two, then snap your fingers and say, 'That's all, mister. There's a shine that'll stand the test of time.' That old rhyme used to get me a tip for sure." Then, as if on cue, the black man raised his head and found my eyes, breaking into a broad and generous grin.

"Mitchell Ithaca Coates," I said.

"It's still 'Mitch' to you, Z." He paused and looked me up and down. "How you been, man? Did you get the bad guys?"

"Yes and no," I answered. "You know how it goes, Mitch—it's complicated." I smiled back at him, then turned and reached for Star's hand, pulling her forward so he could see her clearly. She held Caine, who had gone back to sleep, close to her chest. "I finally found this one, though."

Mitch removed his cap slowly and marveled at what he saw in front of him, just as Owen Bramley had. "Well, don't that beat the devil," he said. "We been waitin' for this day, but sometimes, well, sometimes I thought maybe . . . well, never mind what I thought." Then he rose out of his seat and said to Jack, "Turn around, son, and take a look at your very own sister."

For some reason the boy was slow to respond, as if he was shy or too afraid to look. Then I felt a nudge in my back and Nova pushed me aside and stepped forward. In gentle and even speech, she said, "It's all right, Jack. It's all right." When he heard Nova's voice, the boy turned immediately and gazed up at Star, the sister he had never known, the sister who had been kidnapped by the Fleur-du-Mal and taken to Africa, and the sister whose disappearance had driven their own father mad with loss and despair.

"Hello, Jack," Star said quietly. She seemed to have an intuitive understanding of his shyness and waited for him to reply.

I watched the boy carefully. We were almost the same height and weight. He was wearing a cap similar to the one Mitch wore, which he slipped off and held with both hands. He had his father's dark good looks and his mother's gray-blue eyes flecked with gold. When he saw that Star had the same eyes, his expression brightened, as if their kinship suddenly became real to him; he really did have a sister and she was living, standing right in front of him, even speaking to him. I think he made an instant and unexpected compromise with a very old and very private enemy. "Hello," he said with a half smile. "I'm Jack."

Star laughed out loud. "I know, I know. Mama told me all about you."

Mitch laughed along with her, rising out of his chair and brushing Jack softly on the back of the head. "Come on, everybody—I got two Packard Twin-6 touring cars parked outside. And I'm sorry, Miss C., about keepin' Jack from seein' you on the train, but I couldn't resist the temptation when I passed by the shoeshine stand. I mean, shoeshinin' was my life!"

"I know that, Mitch," Carolina said. I looked up at her. She was laughing and crying at the same time. "It's all right." She stepped forward and put her arms around Star and Jack, who continued blushing and trying to hide under his cap. "Let's go home," she said.

We crammed our luggage and ourselves inside the cars, slipping and sliding in the dark and the snow, which had lessened, but was still falling. After leaving the traffic of Union Station and Market Street, the trip to Carolina's house became a magical homecoming, with our own laughter and Mitch's singing filling up the silence of the snowy streets.

"How long is this snow supposed to last?" I asked Owen Bramley, just as we pulled into the long drive leading up and under the brick arch of the big house. Every window glowed from the inside. I thought of a lighthouse, seen from the sea at night, after a strange and difficult journey. Only one word came to mind—"welcome."

"They say until the day after tomorrow," Owen said, "but who really knows?"

2

PINPILIPAUXA

(BUTTERFLY)

Often when a child first catches sight of a butterfly, he or she may ask the question "Where did it come from?" Then someone, usually some-one older and presumably wiser, might relate the incredible yet true story of the humble caterpillar and its metamorphosis into the angelic, magical butterfly—dancing on air, a completely new form, shape, dream, and destiny. That part is easy. Then the child may ask, "Does the butterfly remember being the caterpillar?" After that, it is never easy.

A week later the snowstorm was already a distant memory and had been replaced by an early spring breeze, coming from the southwest and filling the bare trees with a promise of new life and new beginnings. The aftermath of the Great War, fol-lowed by the Spanish Flu, had hit St. Louis hard, with thousands of local young men lost in Europe and no one knows how many, young and old, men and women, lost to influenza at home. It seemed the whole city wanted to forget the pain and loss, and forget quickly. Our odd little family was no exception.

Perhaps the most dramatic example of this change in attitude took place upon our arrival at Carolina's that first snowy night.

We all gathered in the kitchen after unloading our luggage in the oversized living room. Owen Bramley was going to sort out who was staying in which room and save Carolina the trouble of having to deal with it. As we entered the kitchen, I noticed a familiar figure standing by the stove, though her figure was slightly fuller and her hair was now entirely gray. She turned and stared at each one of us as we sat around the long table in the center of the room. She was Ciela—premium cook and the last of Carolina's "working girls" still living in the house. She had an anxious look on her face and held a large wooden spoon in her hand. When she caught sight of Star entering the kitchen, laughing about something with Nova, Ciela did the same as Owen and Mitch had done, only she almost fainted. She dropped the spoon to the floor and backed up against the stove, putting her hand to her mouth and stifling her own exclamation, "Madre de Dios, Madre de Dios," which she couldn't stop repeating. Carolina would tell me later that for all these years, Ciela had continued to feel responsible for Star's abduction and disappearance. She kept the guilt bottled up inside, exclusively her own, a cross that God had given her to bear. In one split second it all fell away, and it was nearly too much for her.

"Ciela, please, sit down, get your breath, relax." It was Owen and he helped her into one of the chairs around the table.

"Madre de Dios," she mumbled again, staring at Star. "A miracle, a miracle," she said in English. Star walked over and knelt down next to her, taking Ciela's hand and holding it. Then the tears came and Star embraced her, letting her release fifteen years of blame and shame.

Another good and necessary change occurred three days later when we buried Eder and Nicholas in the "Honeycircle." The snow had melted away quickly and Carolina wanted to have the ceremony as soon as possible. On the day after we arrived, during a long walk together through Forest Park, she had told Jack the sad news about his father, whom he had not seen in five years. Jack took it as best he could, she said, and only mentioned a single regret—that he never got to say good-bye. She told him she felt the same way and to compensate for it, they were going to put Nicholas to rest, along with Eder, in the "Honeycircle," a place more sacred to them than any cemetery. Jack liked the idea and even asked Carolina if he could help, which he did, clearing the space and digging the graves with Owen, Willie, and me.

After our work was done and the coffins were in the ground, Carolina mouthed a silent prayer over the grave of Nicholas, and Nova stared up at the sky above where her mother lay, then walked over and kissed something standing in the center of the "Honeycircle." I had seen the object once before, far to the west of St. Louis, in a meadow high in the hills above Kepa's camp. It had been her father's most prized possession. It was Baju Gastelu's ancient Roman sundial.

Carolina, Jack, and Nova all felt a sense of completion after the informal ceremony. I could see it in their faces. It was a solemn occasion, but there was not a trace of melancholy or remorse. They had each said good-bye in the best way they knew how, and the ones they had loved were still close to them, underground in the private garden of their own backyard.

Late that same night, I asked Nova how the sundial had come to be in the "Honeycircle." She was in one of the upstairs bathrooms and the door was open. She stood in front of the mirror by the sink, washing the heavy eye makeup from her face. Her eyes were clear, but she looked surprised at the question, as if everyone knew about the sundial. I reminded her that Ray Ytuarte and I left on our long search for Star the day after she arrived, in the summer of 1904. There was no sundial in the "Honeycircle" at that time. Then, suddenly, I remembered a particular moment when Ray and I were leaving. I remembered seeing two large wooden crates, stacked together under the stone arch in the driveway. When I asked if they were his, he'd said enigmatically, "Don't ask." It had to be the sundial. Nova confirmed my theory. Eder had insisted that they bring the sundial from Kepa's camp and Owen Bramley and Ray were responsible for the dismantling, crating, and shipping.

Then Nova did something rare for her. Nova continued to be a great mystery to me. With her Egyptian-style cosmetics and mascara, eccentric dress and manner, she often seemed to be in her own world, or at least her own version of it. But just then, she looked honest, innocent, vulnerable. She turned and held both my hands, glaring at me with her dark eyes. "What about Ray?" she asked, then in a kind of whisper, "Do you think about him like I do, Z? Do you think about him at all?"

I paused and drew in a deep breath. She had touched a nerve, though I didn't want to admit it. I knew where his bowler hat was—just inside my closet—but I still had no idea where Ray was. "I think about him every day, Nova. Every single day."

"So do I," she said, turning back to the mirror and wiping away a tear, pretending it was mascara.

A few days later an early spring breeze came, bringing with it the wonderful, eternal feeling of renewal and the desire to forget and start again. We all welcomed it and it was good, but for Nova and me, there would still be one thought, one person, one question that both of us knew we would never forget.

★   ★   ★

Opari had not met anyone like Mitch Coates in all her long life. "There was one man, an Indian prince in Vishakhapatnam, he reminds me of in some ways," she said, "but Mitch has, how do you say, a 'joie de vivre' that is all his own."

"That is exactly how you say it," I told her. "And I agree, except for one man you never met—Solomon J. Birnbaum."

"Yes, Carolina has said the same."

We were in the bedroom Owen had assigned to us, on the second floor at the far end of the hall. His own unusual bedroom and living quarters were behind the door directly across from ours. It was late Saturday morning, the first day of April. "What was the prince's name?" I asked, curious because at that point in time, Opari seldom mentioned her incredible history or anyone in it.

"I do not recall the exact name, though I remember several seconds were required to pronounce his complete and formal name and title. I referred to him as 'Skylark.' He was an heir to great wealth and possessed the intellect of Pythagoras, along with a rich personality, which Pythagoras did not have."

"You knew Pythagoras?" I asked with a smile.

"Yes, briefly, however I was in flight to the East and could not linger. I recall the prince was also a 'Listener.' "

"A what?"

"A translated word for a member of a . . . *bitxi* . . . how do you say?—*strange* Hindu sect. They believed in organized, no, I should say symphonic 'listening' to the spheres for secret meanings, all of them gathering outdoors atop boulders and cliffs to the west, sitting silently for days, 'listening' for answers to the most mystical questions of the Veda. In Sanskrit they were known as Abisami, or simply the *'samupa.'* They would sit grouped, facing all directions, but in such a manner as to never catch the eye of another. Skylark was a known master in this mute music and futile prayer. Their gatherings began in the season when Sirius rises in the east. Sirius, the Dog Star, the star the *'samupa'* called 'The Leader.' According to Skylark, it was sacred to them. I have even heard rumors that remnants of the sect may still exist."

"How did you meet Skylark?"

"That answer is for another time, my love. The real matter here is that Skylark became the only true Giza friend I could trust. It may have been because he had spent time with one of us—a great deal of time, enough to learn many more things about the Meq than most Giza ever know."

"Who was the one in 'one of us'?"

"Zeru-Meq."

"Ah . . . of course." I thought back to the brief time I'd spent with him in China—not time enough to know him well, but I knew I owed him a great deal. He had led me to Opari.

She said, "Mitch makes me laugh; he is full of contradiction and surprise, yet he is a Giza I could trust. Much like Skylark."

Mitch had awakened us earlier that morning. Just before sunrise, he knocked softly on our door in a distinctive rhythm, then slipped inside, holding a lit candle and whispering, "I want to invite both y'all to a party, a tribute to someone down at my place. Tonight."

It was a surprise, but not a shock. Mitch had been coming and going at all hours, beginning the day after we arrived. In a week I learned how important he was to Jack and how indispensable he was to Carolina daily, while running his various enterprises all night. Opari was used to the random nature of Mitch's visits; still, we did wonder when, or if, he ever slept. He wore a tuxedo, which was not unusual, but what he held behind his back was. Wrapped separately in white linen handkerchiefs, he slowly brought forward two long-stemmed white roses, their petals streaked with orange and red. Each rose was about to release into full bloom.

He lifted the candle and stiffened his posture. He began reciting dramatically. *"These roses are for you, two of three, and for the rest, go seek the one who waits for thee, the one who wears the other of the three."*

His face relaxed. He winked and said, "These ain't easy to find in April," then leaned over the foot of the bed and presented the roses to Opari. "I want both of y'all to wear those on your person when you show up tonight. Then look for someone wearin' a rose just like 'em. There's a message waitin' for you. I don't know what it is." He paused. "All right, man, that's everything I was told to tell, so I did. Now, I'm real busy, Z, and I know you understand, so I'm cuttin' out of here. I got places to go yet." He started toward the door, then stopped and turned. "Miss Opari," he said, "I will see you this evening." He blew out the candle and shut the door behind him in silence. I thought I heard him talking low to someone at the end of the hall, probably Owen, then he was down the stairs and gone. Dawn was still ten minutes away.

Even for Mitchell Ithaca Coates, that was a strange and theatrical visit, which Opari thought was also charming. After she stared at the roses for a moment, she asked, "What do you think of these . . . and the speech . . . and the instructions?"

I picked up one of the beautiful and delicate roses. "I don't understand it, but there's only one way to get the answer."

It was clear why Opari trusted Mitch just as she trusted Sky-lark. I felt the same. He might surprise you, but he will never betray you. Whatever Mitch was asking us to do, I would be there and follow instructions. We were safe from the "unexpected," which I'd promised to try to avoid.

By midmorning the temperature climbed into the sixties and the sky was a bright light blue, dotted with a few ragged puffs of clouds. The breeze blew warm out of the south and I had base-ball fever. I knew I had to play catch with someone, at the very least. Baseball fever appears in the late winter or early spring and is only contracted by lovers and players of the game. Playing catch will usually scratch the itch.

I found Mama's glove and rubbed it down with oil. I wiped my fingers clean, then shoved my hand inside and pounded the pocket with my other hand. The glove was broken in well and felt perfect. Opari watched me in silence, dumbfounded. Fi-nally, she chose to ignore me altogether and asked, "Why have we not been called to breakfast? Are we late?"

I stopped pounding and thought about it. "You're right. We must be late." I glanced at the clock on the small table next to our bed. The time read at least an hour later than it should have. Almost on cue, the alarm bell sounded and Opari jumped back, shrieking something in a strange language. Opari was com-pletely unfamiliar with alarm clocks. I knew we had never set the alarm, so I knew someone else had staged this, but I had no idea who or why until we hurried downstairs to find every-one already gathered in the big kitchen. Breakfast was well under way.

Each face turned to watch us enter. Each wore a blank expression, except for Carolina, who rolled her eyes, and Jack, who was barely able to contain himself from laughing, but managed to ask, "Hey, where have you been, Z?"

Opari began to apologize and try to explain the mysteries of the alarm clock.

"Hey, Z, your shoe's untied!" Jack interrupted.

I looked down. Jack finally burst out laughing. "April Fool's! April Fool's!" he shouted.

I realized immediately who was responsible for the alarm. "That one is older than I am," I said. But he knew he'd got me, and I knew it, too. "Let's play some catch, Jack. What do you say?"

"I can't until later, Z," he said. "But I'd love to then."

I was disappointed almost as much as a real kid. Still, later was better than not at all. "Deal," I said.

"Deal," Jack answered.

Carolina was well aware of baseball fever and understood why I needed to play catch. "Why don't you have Jack show you his magazines and newspapers," she said, "so you can catch up. Jack saves everything."

And that's what I did. After breakfast and for the next several hours I was oblivious to everyone else. I sat in the long living room and read about the state of the game, the new players, the new teams, trades, rumors, and anything to do with the Cardinals, who had finished dead last in 1918, I was to find out, with a won-loss record of 51–78. In the American League the Browns had not fared much better. I found out good old Ty Cobb was still playing and tearing it up on the base paths. Branch Rickey, a man who seemed to have a lot of new ideas about everything, had been named the new manager of the Cardinals in January, replacing Jack Hendricks. I read all the articles, every statistic, every team roster, every opinion and prediction from every sportswriter in St. Louis. Opening Day for the season was April 23 and I couldn't wait. There is nothing like a real professional baseball game. Whether the outcome is a pitching duel, a slugfest, or something in between, you will disappear into the experience for however long the game lasts. It is physical chess. Carolina and Owen Bramley had box seats and season tickets, so I was looking forward to seeing as many games as possible.

Late in the afternoon with the sun low in the sky, and in a fresh breeze and freckled light, Jack and I finally played catch. Mama's glove made a familiar pop when Jack threw a hard strike. We tossed the ball back and forth, mostly in silence, until we were having trouble seeing the ball. That's when every kid wishes the sun would never set. Our arms were dog tired, and yet, only Jack and I knew how good it felt. We walked into the house talking nonstop about the art of pitching and the relevance of baseball to anything good. The itch had been scratched.

Opari, Geaxi, Nova, Star and the baby Caine, Willie, Carolina, everyone else in the house, even Ciela, spent the late afternoon in Forest Park helping Owen Bramley fly his Chinese kites. They each returned in high spirits, and along with Jack and me, we ate every morsel of food that Ciela had prepared earlier in the day. The whole meal was waiting for us, some in the oven and some in the icebox. It was delicious.

Then we all retired to our rooms to change into the tuxedos Mitch had sent over that afternoon. Each was tailored and made to fit all of us who were Meq, but since I was the only male among us, I couldn't figure why he'd sent them.

I knew he was sending his two Packard touring cars to pick us up and he had closed his club to the general public. It was to be a private party and there was no reason not to trust his judgment. We had been posing as refugees and relatives of Nova and Eder, but still, to see a group of twelve-year-old children, dressed in tuxedos, possibly sipping champagne or drinking beer, late at night in the roughest part of town, well, I had to wonder if that was wise.

Geaxi said she wanted to experience the culture and music of Mitch's world, so she thought it would be worth it. Also, she had no problem with the tuxedo. Nor did Opari, which surprised me until I remembered that they both had donned "boys' " clothing many times in many places for many reasons. Both were anxious to wear the tuxedos and Nova thought it was not only a good idea, but said she might start dressing that way in the future.

Once she was dressed, Opari added red lipstick to her lips, a red silk bow tie, and the white rose from Mitch in her lapel. The effect was stunning. She was a child-woman of uncommon beauty and presence. I understood in an instant why centuries of princes and kings, even the Empress Dowager of China, found her irresistible.

Star left Caine with Ciela and Willie helped her, along with the rest of us, into the touring cars. It was well after dark and once we'd gone a few blocks east, the trip downtown was busy and filled with the sound and lights of automobiles.

Mitch's nightclub was just off Market, near all the neighborhoods of his youth, yet I also remember never knowing exactly where he lived in those days. The entrance was a simple glass door with "Mitch's Café" painted in an arc across the glass. It was a narrow entrance, squeezed between two other businesses, a pawnshop and a barbershop, both of which Mitch also owned. The café was for real—a few tables in the front, then a counter with stools where you could order chili, barbecue sandwiches, and beer. But if you were led, as we were, around the counter and down a long, high-ceilinged hall, you would enter a room the size of a warehouse, which is exactly what it had been. The room was now transformed into a nightclub, complete with a large stage at one end, two full bars along opposite walls, tables with white linen tablecloths, and a spacious semicircular dance floor in front of the stage. Factory lights muted with green filters hung from a forty-foot gabled ceiling, and two dozen waiters in long aprons stood at the ready throughout. The music coming from the stage was the best I'd heard in years, going back to what Ray and I listened to in New Orleans. But this music had something else, a swing and syncopation I'd never heard before. People were dancing new steps and there was a raw and raucous joy everywhere in the room.

Mitch greeted us from behind the bar as soon as we emerged from the long hall. Even in his tuxedo, he leaped easily over the bar while waving to us, then motioned us toward a corner section of the big room where several tables had been pulled together to become one large table-in-the-round, covered with a banquet-sized white tablecloth. Champagne and bottles of beer sat in iced buckets placed around the table. At least six waiters stood in line, ready to act as our personal staff. Mitch made it to the table and escorted Carolina to her chair, making sure she was seated first.

"Why, thank you, Mitchell," Carolina said, sitting down and pushing up on the long formal gloves she wore on her hands and forearms. The gloves were a dark green, the same color as her dress and shoes. She was beautiful, elegant, and graceful, still commanding stares from strangers. It was hard to imagine the skinny, stringy-haired kid she had been when I first saw her, standing with her sister outside Sportsman's Park. She was now a woman completely comfortable in her own life and her own skin.

"It's my pleasure, Miss C.," Mitch said. "I want you at the head of the table. After all, you're the reason I'm able to do this."

"Nonsense," Carolina said. "And don't be modest, Mitchell. You have done what you've done on your own. I had nothing to do with it."

"Oh, yes you did. You're the one who talked to Mr. Joplin in the first place. You know what that meant to me? It meant just about everything, that's what it meant. Everything in this world started for me right then, Miss C., and I want to say thank you, thank you for everything." Mitch signaled one of the waiters, who brought a tray of glasses filled with champagne. Each glass was served and everyone but Carolina held a glass in the air. Mitch shouted, "To Miss C. and Mr. J.! May one live on and the other not be forgotten."

"Here! Here!" Owen Bramley said.

"Second that!" Willie added.

Geaxi and Opari made high-pitched trilling noises and clicked their tongues.

I looked at Mitch. "Do you mean Scott Joplin is . . . dead?"

"Yeah, Z. Mr. Joplin passed away two years ago, on the first of April." Mitch took a sip of champagne and looked around, waving his hand toward the stage. "That's why we're here tonight, Z, and I plan on doin' this every year from now on. I owe so much to the man. He taught me more than how to appreciate good music—he taught me how to appreciate *life*. He was a great man, Z."

"Indeed he was, Mitchell," Carolina said. "He will be missed." She raised her own glass to join in the toast. "And I've still got the opera packed away, Mitchell—you know where."

"Keep it safe, Miss C. Just keep it safe," Mitch said with a wink. Then he was off again, to the kitchen this time, laughing and saying over his shoulder, "I got some oysters for you. Wait until you taste 'em. They're straight from the Gulf—Apalachicola. If you need anything, these fellas in the aprons are here to get it for you. We got some other acts comin'—and the chorus line. Wait until you see that, Z," he said to me and winked again, then pointed to the lapel of his tuxedo, the buttonhole where the white rose was pinned to my tuxedo. He turned and made his way through the crowd, shaking hands and making toasts along the way. I glanced at Opari and she nodded, acknowledging she'd seen the same thing.

To our wonder and delight, both on and off the stage, it was the dancing that most fascinated all of us, especially Geaxi and Opari. Geaxi leaned over the table and asked Opari, "Have you ever seen such freedom and rhythm of movement? When you crossed through Persia, perhaps?"

"No, no," Opari said. "Never have I seen such passion and grace together. They are . . . *trebe*?"

"Skilled," Geaxi translated.

"Yes, skilled. They are skilled and still exploring."

Willie was absorbed by the sheer energy in the music and the dancers. "Bloody damn good, Z," he blared across the table more than once.

Star surprised everyone by not only listening and watching, but also joining in. Several times she jumped out of her seat and ran to the dance floor, mimicking the moves and dancing alongside the black women, who clapped and shouted and helped Star learn the steps.

During a slow blues song, even Owen Bramley and Carolina made their way to the dance floor. I must say Owen stood out in the crowd like some sort of animated carrot, dancing and enjoying himself, but definitely to his own beat.

Nova was enjoying the music as well, and yet she seemed more distracted than usual, constantly staring in a kind of trance at the stage curtains hanging behind the band. At one point, I happened to catch her unconsciously grabbing for her Stone, which she was wearing under her starched shirt. I'd never seen her do anything like that before.

After two hours of continuous music and dancing, Mitch himself took the stage. He gave a short speech and tribute to Scott Joplin, then announced a break after the next tune, in honor of Mr. J., "Maple Leaf Rag." He sat down and started playing the best ragtime piano I'd ever heard, leading the band through the whole tune. By the end of the first chorus, a line of eight showgirls, dressed in matching black tuxedos, black top hats, and black masks hiding their eyes, came dancing across the stage twirling canes and kicking up their legs. They each had a rose in their lapel. Seven of the girls wore red roses, but the last one, the girl nearest us, wore a white rose streaked with orange and red. They danced a choreographed routine with the music, all pretending to be gentlemen on the town. Mitch joined them during the last chorus and the crowd went wild with jeers, whistles, and catcalls. As the song ended, the chorus line strutted with their canes back across the stage and into the wings on our side of the room. The girl with the white rose stared directly at me just before she disappeared from view, whispering two words. Then she nodded toward the door leading backstage, not ten feet from where I sat.

I turned immediately to see if Opari was watching. She was. "Did you hear that?"

"Hear what? I heard nothing but the music, then the clapping and shouting."

"Did you see her nod toward the door?"

"Yes."

"Well, before she did that she whispered something to me. I guess she was aware no one but me would hear it. But how would she know that?"

"Z, what did she whisper?"

"She said the ancient words of greeting, the formal ones— 'Egibizirik bilatu.' "

Opari fell silent for several moments. Then I noticed Nova quietly take a seat next to mine. She leaned forward, anxious to hear what we had to say. Across the table, Geaxi was talking with Carolina while still paying close attention to everything and everyone.

"What does it signify?" I asked. "That is the Meq's most secret exchange, isn't it?"

"It means the message comes from an old one, a truly old one. Only an old one would know of this. My guess could be but one—Mowsel. The greeting was used in the Time of Ice when the element of 'time' was involved and complete trust was required. A Giza was always used to deliver the message. By telling the messenger to utter our oldest exchange of greeting and farewell, the sender is ensuring the truth of the message and the messenger. The ritual is called the *'beharrezko,'* the necessity. It is necessary because in this exchange there is no written document. The message *is* the messenger."

"I saw something, I . . . felt something," Nova said suddenly. There was fear in her voice. "I felt something coming from the stage . . . from the girl. I don't know what it is."

I glanced at Opari. She shrugged her shoulders and nodded toward the stage door the girl had indicated. I looked around the room. No one seemed to be paying much attention to us. I rose out of my chair and walked to the door and slipped inside.

The girl was standing alone on the top step of a small stairwell. She'd taken off her mask and was leaning against the brick wall. Above and behind her, a single red light burned over the backstage exit to the street. I couldn't see her face completely, but she seemed to be in her early twenties with distinctive dark eyes and straight dark hair, cut at the shoulder. There was a small scar high on her left cheek. She was pretty, and she was Basque, I was sure of it. Between long, slender fingers, she held the white rose. I could see the veins standing out on the back of her hand. I took a few steps toward the stairwell and stopped in front of her.

"You were looking for me?" I asked.

"Yes, señor. I apologize for this drama and mystery. Mowsel said it was a necessity."

That proved Opari was right. It was Trumoi-Meq. "What is your name?" I asked.

"I apologize again, señor." For the first time, she turned and looked behind her. There were a few dimly lit dressing rooms in the distance. I could hear conversation inside one of them, but no one was visible. She turned back and continued. Her accent was slight and she spoke clearly. "My name is Arrosa Arginzoniz and I was sent by Mowsel to give you a message and a warning. There are three who are in danger, three of you. One is the one who wears the star sapphire on his forefinger. Mowsel said you would know who this is."

"I do. Go on."

But before she could I heard someone slip through the door behind me. It was Opari. She saw the girl and the rose, then walked over and took my hand in hers.

"You are Opari, no?" the girl asked.

"Yes," Opari answered and glanced at me.

"Mowsel has told me your name. My name is Arrosa Arginzoniz. I am the last of the tribe of Caristies, protectors of the Stone of Silence." She paused.

"Unai," Opari whispered. "That was Unai's Stone. Now it is carried by Nova Gaztelu."

"Yes," the girl said.

I turned to Opari. "Arrosa was telling me she has a message and a warning from Mowsel. She says three of us are in danger. One you know well, as did your sister."

"Ah, yes," Opari said, knowing I meant Sailor.

"Who are the other two?" I asked Arrosa.

"Unai and Usoa," she answered without hesitation.

I stared up at her for a full three seconds, then eased closer so I could see her eyes.

"You know them well, don't you, Arrosa?"

"Yes, señor. They are also my godparents. My father was Aita. He . . ." Suddenly she let out a long sigh and the white rose dropped to the floor.

"This sounds complicated," I said, "and you look tired." I glanced at Opari and she understood. "Would you be able to leave this dance troupe now, Arrosa? And I really mean now. Can you gather your things and go with us? Stay with us while you tell us everything? Also, there is someone who needs to meet you and you her. I think she has already sensed your presence anyway. Can you come with us?"

She took a deep breath and seemed to be relieved of a great burden. "Thank you, señor. I will welcome the rest and I have much to say, much to ask." She peeked behind her. "Give me one minute," she said.

She was back and carrying a single suitcase in less than a minute, more like thirty seconds. She smiled down at both of us. "Thank you again. It is my honor."

"And ours," Opari said.

We turned to leave, and from somewhere in the semidarkness, I heard Mitch's voice and a girl's voice coming toward the backstage exit. "Go ahead," I told Opari. "I'll catch up. I want to thank Mitch for the evening." Opari agreed, saying she would tell Owen of the change in plans. I turned back to wait for Mitch.

Mitch's voice was calm, yet he seemed to be almost scolding the girl, not like an employee or dancer, but like a daughter. The girl was whining and begging him to let her stay. The two of them finally got to the stage door and stood under the red light.

"You can't be hidin' in here anymore. I told you a hundred times already," Mitch said as he started to open the door. I was only twelve feet away, but neither he nor the girl had seen me yet.

"But how else will I learn? I got to learn the steps," the girl complained.

"Not yet, you don't. And not in my place." Mitch opened the door. "You got to go. I mean now, right now."

She started to leave, then spun around and leaned back into the light. That's when she and I made eye contact. She was just a kid, maybe thirteen or slightly older, and she smiled at me—a genuine, ear-to-ear grin that radiated mischief and joy. I smiled back. Mitch noticed me and gently pushed her out the door.

Without ever mentioning the girl, he walked over and asked how everything went and I told him the "white rose" was coming home with us for a few days. He then asked how I liked the club, the sound of the band, and the tribute. I told him it was a great and glorious evening and all of us appreciated his generosity. I waited for him to volunteer some information about what I had just seen, then realized he was not going to offer any, but I was too curious.

"Who was the girl, Mitch?"

"Aw, just some girl from around here. She won't stay out of my club, and I can't allow it, Z."

"What's her name?"

"I call her 'Tumpy,' " Mitch said, "but her name is Josephine." He went on to tell me she was a good kid who had probably seen too much too soon and wanted out of her home and out of St. Louis. He was trying to help her, but she was anxious and he was worried she wouldn't wait.

Fifteen minutes later we were in the Packards and on our way to Carolina's. I was riding in the same car with Carolina and Arrosa. Carolina had readily accepted and welcomed Arrosa into her home, and she was in deep discussion with her about the new music the band had been playing. What did she think of the improvisations? What was it called, or did it even have a name? Arrosa answered with a word I had never heard before. She called it "jazz."

Nova rode in the other car on purpose. She had acted nervous when Opari and I introduced the girl to everyone at the table, then I watched her consciously wait for Arrosa to step into our Packard before she scurried to the other one. I asked Geaxi to ride with her and explain to her what Sailor had explained to me years earlier when he introduced me to my Basque protectors and my Aita, Kepa Txopitea. "You come to them," he said, "they do not come to you." Nova seemed a little more like herself once we got to Carolina's, but something was still bothering her. However, it had been a long day and night and I decided to talk to her about it another time.

The size and opulence of the big house astounded Arrosa. As Owen and Carolina showed her upstairs to her room, she was genuinely humbled and thanked Carolina profusely, saying she might sleep forever in such a comfortable place. Carolina said she certainly hoped that didn't happen because Ciela would have a hearty St. Louis breakfast ready and waiting for everyone in the morning.

A short while later, Opari and I were also turning out the lights. Opari whispered, "The first day of April in America is a beautiful day, no?"

I laughed and agreed, but as I lay back on the pillow, over and over in my head, I kept hearing Jack's voice saying, "Hey, Z, your shoe's untied . . . your shoe's untied."

At breakfast we mostly made small talk. Everyone who was living in the house was present except Nova. Several times during the meal Arrosa complimented Ciela, at one point saying, "I have only tasted flavors like this in the small Cuban neighborhoods of New York." Ciela laughed and kept the food coming. "*Sí, sí,*" she said, "*es verdad, es verdad.*" After breakfast I found Nova and asked if we could talk somewhere. She said she wanted to talk to me, too, and we strolled out to the "Honeycircle," where the crocuses were still wet with dew. We walked over to Baju's sundial and within minutes I knew I'd been wrong about why Nova had acted nervous around Arrosa. Nova had *seen* something the moment Arrosa stepped onstage at Mitch's. She said when she looked at the white rose Arrosa was wearing, her real vision blurred and another reality, another vision, took its place. In this alternate vision Nova saw Arrosa's throat being cut. The knife was flashing in bright sunlight, making it difficult for her to clearly see the one with the knife, but she could make out three things: the attacker was Meq, he had green eyes, and he wore two red ruby earrings. There were other images in the vision that came into focus and blurred again, including a gold mask and eyes that never close, a bleeding rose, and torches moving through airless darkness. Nova said she snapped out of it only after Arrosa left the stage. She asked me what it might mean and before I could even respond, I felt the old prickly feeling of the net descending. I didn't know what the other images meant, but there was just one who could be the one with the knife—the Fleur-du-Mal. But what would he be doing attacking a young Basque girl, who meant nothing to him, in a vision of someone who has never seen him and probably never heard of him? I knew he was unpredictable, but it made no sense whatsoever. Also, I had to respect Nova's "ability," and yet I wondered if she could sometimes get it wrong, like Ray.

Nova's "ability" was the most baffling to me of all the varieties we possess. Even she seemed bewildered by it. Was she able to see real events to come, or did she see symbols of events; feelings and projections of her own fears and demons? And time was never part of the vision. For all I knew, each vision could be in some sort of dreamtime that has nothing to do with real events. However, if the Fleur-du-Mal was even remotely connected, I could not afford to ignore any "vision."

It was clear why Nova was avoiding Arrosa. She knew the Meq are expected to be completely forthcoming and honest with their Basque protectors, and the same is true for them. It has been that way for countless generations and it presented Nova with a dilemma. Should she tell Arrosa what she had seen? Should she remain silent?

Sailor had told me in Cornwall to serve the family. I thought this was a good time to do just that. I made the decision for her and told her to stay silent. I advised her to establish close ties with Arrosa and learn as much as she could from her, but for now, stay silent about the "vision." I told her we must first find out Mowsel's message, then we could decide about what should or shouldn't be revealed.

"Message?" Nova asked.

She was truly surprised and I realized she was unaware of Arrosa's hidden mission. "That's why she came. She has a message to deliver from Trumoi-Meq. It concerns Unai and Usoa."

"Oh . . . I see," she said, staring down at the crocuses. "And who better to deliver the message, right? The last in the line of the tribe of Caristies."

"Right," I said. I searched her eyes and their expression was enigmatic. I could read nothing, and the heavy Egyptian mascara gave her the appearance of wearing a mask. "Nova," I said quietly, "you and I—" I stopped. I made sure we were looking at each other eye to eye. "We—you and me—are the only ones to be born in the West, in America, and carry the Stone." I paused again. "We have much to learn, you and I."

"I know, Z. I'm trying."

"Get to know her, Nova. Learn from her, even though she is young. Learn the long history of your Stone and her tribe. Don't worry about what you saw in your vision."

Nova smiled and picked a few crocuses, gently shaking the dew from their long petals. "Arrosa probably needs our help," she said, almost to herself.

"Most likely. More likely my help since I was close to Unai and Usoa shortly before they crossed in the Zeharkatu. No one knows exactly why, but Opari said that makes a difference. The Zeharkatu is our deepest mystery. It is the moment and place where our bodies become like the Giza and we begin to age. It is an act of ultimate surrender to your Ameq, and it allows us to procreate."

"But—"

"I know, I remember what you said at 'the slabs'—'The old way will not work. The old Zeharkatu will not cross in the old way.'"

"I don't even know why I said that, Z."

"One thing at a time, Nova."

"Come on," Nova said and turned to leave. "Let's find out the message. I know just the place to go."

I gathered Geaxi, Opari, and Arrosa. We all followed Nova the short distance to Forest Park. It was early afternoon and the fair weather was holding. The park itself was crowded with people of all ages and descriptions. We passed around a nine-hole golf course that had been in existence for a few years, but was new to me. Several of the caddies removed their oversized caps and whistled at Arrosa, who ignored them entirely. I got the impression she had heard worse and dealt with it many times. Geaxi shouted something back to the caddies in a strange language I'd never heard and we kept on walking, laughing all the way.

Eventually, Nova steered us to Art Hill and on to a natural amphitheater nearby. Plays were performed there in the summer, she told us, with enough chairs for a thousand people. We stood at the top of the hill and below us were two large oak trees that framed the raised ground of the stage. Behind the stage there was a small bridge that spanned a creek called the River des Peres.

"Down there," Nova said, "to the bridge. It's a good place to talk."

We bounded down the slope like kids playing tag and spread out on the bridge. Nova was right—it was a good place to talk. We could speak freely and listen without interruption. Geaxi and Nova took seats atop the wooden railing on one side of the little bridge and Opari and I sat across from them on the opposite railing. Arrosa paced back and forth between us and, for the next half hour, told us Mowsel's message and warning, using his exact words whenever possible. She spoke rapidly and we learned many things in a brief amount of time, the first of which was the reason Trumoi-Meq was not with her.

Although Arrosa continued to refer to Sailor as "the one who wears the star sapphire," we learned that Mowsel was worried about his "old friend" and was off to a mysterious destination in the Canary Islands. We were all worried about Sailor and without having to say a word, all of us, even Geaxi, agreed with Trumoi-Meq's decision. Then we heard the sad and heartbreaking story of Unai and Usoa. Arrosa prefaced this part with a few personal anecdotes about both of them and how much they meant to her, especially Unai, who had saved her from despair and became her best friend following her father's death. He knew people in New York and was instrumental in her move there and introduced her to other painters and artists.

When Unai and Usoa's child, a boy, died from influenza, Arrosa didn't hear about it until Mowsel told her six months later. By that time they had disappeared into the mountains, living hand to mouth and moving daily on an endless journey in search of the haunted vision that drove Usoa—she believed their boy had been switched with another and was still alive and kept hidden from her. It was insane, but Unai loved her from a place with no boundaries and told himself he would "see" what she "saw" if that's what it took to live in this world, because he had decided long ago he would not live in this world without her.

Kepa and his family followed their movements and made sure they did not accidentally endanger themselves, but often they were hard to track because Usoa changed her mind or "found" a new direction and they would leave without warning. For a long time now they had not slept in the same place two nights in a row. Still, nothing about this worried Mowsel until he found out they had suddenly left Europe for New York.

Arrosa stopped her tale and looked at me. "And that is why I was contacted and sent to you, señor. Mowsel thinks you should be the one to be warned."

"Me?"

"Yes. His words were, 'Tell Zianno first. Go as swift as the train will take you!' "

I glanced in the eyes of Geaxi, Nova, and Opari. They gave nothing away. "Warn me of what?" I asked.

"Unai and Usoa search in vain for their child. It is fact that he died. They are helpless and pitiful and someone is using them and their unbearable grief. They were sent a letter from New York City, the New York Foundling Hospital, informing them that a young child, a boy, had been left at their doorstep and the baby could be Usoa's 'missing son.' The letter also mentioned the child had one green eye and one brown. Mowsel said there are less than five people who know this fact. Unai and Usoa left within days of receiving the letter and have not been sighted since."

"Is this unusual?" I asked. "Haven't they been duped before? Anyone that delusional and fragile in spirit will be vulnerable to almost anything."

"Yes, they have. But Mowsel sent me to talk with Reverend Bookbinder, the one who sent the letter. The child was left with a note pinned to his clothing, stating Unai's full name and the only address in Spain where he can still be reached, a small town called Barakaldo, not far from Bilbao."

"How would anyone know that?"

"There is more, señor. Mowsel said to tell you the Reverend caught a glimpse of the one who left the child. He said it was impossible to say whether the person was male or female, but the person was young, had green eyes, and wore red ruby ear-rings. Mowsel said this was necessary for you to know as soon as possible."

My heart jumped and in my mind I could see his smile, his white teeth, hear his bitter laugh. I glanced at Nova and there was fear and concern in her eyes. Geaxi groaned and cursed. Opari placed her hand on top of mine. The Fleur-du-Mal, it had to be him.

Arrosa sensed our unease with the news. "Mowsel wants me

to return to New York, either with you or without you, señor. He said you should follow your heart and choose carefully. But either way, I am to find this child and thereby find Unai and Usoa."

"Of course," I said, thinking not only of Unai and Usoa, but Carolina, Star, and the baby Caine most of all.

"Is there a danger for them, señor—Unai and Usoa?"

She waited for me to respond. Finally, I glanced up at her. I didn't realize I had been staring down at the River des Peres. It looked polluted and puny, more like an open sewer than a creek.

"Yes," I said in an even voice. "There is a danger."

"Young Zezen," Geaxi said suddenly in a firm voice. "There is no choice for you. You must stay here. I shall go with Arrosa. I know the danger well enough."

Before I could even respond, Nova said, "I am going along. I need to go with Arrosa."

I looked at Nova and she was staring hard at me, with no intention of letting me say no. Opari squeezed my hand and said, "Geaxi is right, my love. You cannot leave St. Louis now. You know this one better than anyone. You know his nature, his *obsessions*." She paused and waited for me to look at her.

I turned and Opari gasped slightly. She must have seen an old companion of mine returning behind my eyes, because I could feel it there, cold and clear. She must have seen the hate.

"Nobody knows him," I said. "Nobody."

Except for Jack's birthday on the twenty-sixth, I found little joy during the rest of April. Arrosa, Geaxi, and Nova left for New York two days after our Sunday in Forest Park. Arrosa thanked Carolina for her hospitality and kindness and promised to return in the future. Nova told Owen Bramley she was going along just to see New York, and Geaxi gave no explanation at all for her leaving. I had already decided in Forest Park not to tell Carolina the real reason for their hasty departure. I wanted to help Unai and Usoa, but it could be a ploy the Fleur-du-Mal was using to lower our guard. I still felt the guilt inside for the Meq changing her world and her life forever. Geaxi advised me that the Meq should ignore guilt when it comes to relations with the Giza. I told her this was not just the Giza, this was Carolina and her family. Geaxi understood, though she disagreed, and let the subject drop.

After the three of them were gone, I retreated into a cocoon of constant worry. Opari was worried also, but not about the byzantine and deadly Fleur-du-Mal. She was concerned for me and reminded me that I would be no help to Carolina or Star or Jack or anyone else if I was only seeing my own thoughts and fears.

It wasn't until the first of May that we finally heard something from New York. Arrosa sent a telegram saying the Reverend Bookbinder had mysteriously disappeared and no one else on the staff at New York Foundling Hospital seemed to have any knowledge of the child. She said she was "SEEKING OTHER SOURCES." Then on the fourth, my birthday, I got another telegram with news I never expected. Unai and Usoa were on board the "ORPHAN TRAIN" and headed for the Midwest. Arrosa's message ended simply with the words: "HAVE OBTAINED RELIABLE INFORMATION FROM FORMER NURSE—TWO-YEAR-OLD CHILD IS WITH THEM—WILL PASS THROUGH ST. LOUIS MAY 12."

For the next week I went over a thousand scenarios in my mind, trying to imagine what to expect and what to do about it. Without being obvious, I tried to keep a close eye on Star and the baby Caine. I told her not to go anywhere without taking Opari or me along. I said it one too many times, however, because she finally said, "Okay, okay, Z, I heard you the first time." Then she looked me squarely in the eye and asked, "Is there something wrong? Should I know something you're not telling me?"

"No, no," I lied. "Nothing is wrong, just stay close, that's all." She agreed, but I don't think she ever believed me.

I also asked Owen Bramley if he had any knowledge of an "Orphan Train." He had no idea what I was talking about, but Carolina did. She told me the Orphan Trains were exactly what their name implied and had been around since the 1850s. Foundlings, homeless children, and others abandoned by parents too poor to care for them were gathered from the streets and orphanages of New York and other eastern cities, then put aboard trains to be "placed out" to homes and families out west. If no one chose them by the end of the rail line, they were shipped back east to try again. The program had sounded good in theory, she said, but in practice was often another matter.

"Do you . . . know someone on the Orphan Train?" she asked.

"No," I said. "I mean, I might. I just wanted to know what it was, how it works."

Carolina gave me a strange look. Thankfully, she did not pursue it further.

On the morning of the eleventh, a day before the train was due to arrive, I was pacing the floor of our bedroom and mumbling under my breath, though I was unaware of it. Opari told me to relax, settle down. "Go to a baseball game," she said. I argued that it wouldn't change anything, but it was a beautiful day and I followed her advice. Carolina, Jack, and I took a taxi to Sportsman's Park that afternoon to watch the Cardinals play the Cincinnati Reds. The crowd was sparse and there was little to cheer about. Hod Eller of the Reds pitched a no-hitter, striking out eight men and walking only three. The Reds won 6–0 and played errorless baseball.

To our surprise, Mitch was waiting for us outside the ballpark in one of the big gray and brown Packards. "Get in!" he shouted through the open window. "Hurry—I'm double-parked."

We climbed inside and I told him about the no-hitter. "That ain't really a shock," he said. "Branch Rickey's got a long way to go before that club is any good." He asked who was pitching for the Cardinals and I answered, "Frank 'Jakie' May."

"Man, that cat's only got two pitches," Mitch said, then went silent.

"Well," I asked finally, "what are they?"

He turned in his seat and grinned. "Hope and pray," he said. I smiled to myself and had to agree.

I had found only one notice mentioning the Orphan Train coming through St. Louis, a piece in the *Post-Dispatch* that began, "Wanted: Homes for Children . . . These children are of various ages and sexes, having been thrown friendless upon the world . . ." The article ended with the information: ". . . train arriving at 3:00 P.M. in Delmar Station." That was encouraging because Delmar Station was small and within walking distance from Carolina's. It meant Opari and I could observe everything without the additional distractions and crowds of Union Station. Opari suggested we take Willie along, reasoning we might need an "adult" with us to explain our presence, if asked. I agreed and briefed Willie on the entire event, carefully leaving out any references to the Fleur-du-Mal.

We left Carolina's house at approximately 2:00 P.M., saying we were on our way to the park.

"It looks like rain is coming," Carolina warned.

"We've been wet before," I said and tried to avoid her eyes. Even though I had good intentions in mind, I could feel the weight of my lies piling up.

We were outside the station by 2:30.

"Spread out and walk around," I said, "and look for anything strange. Find all the entrances and exits. Let's not go inside until the last minute." I knew Opari and I carried our Stones, but if the Fleur-du-Mal was involved, I also knew they would be useless against him or any other Meq.

In a drizzling rain, the Orphan Train arrived at 3:00 sharp. A large group of people stood waiting at the platform, I suppose in order to get an early glimpse. The two dozen or so children on board were supposed to exit the train with their chaperones and then be taken to a nearby theater, where they would be lined up and looked over by families and individuals.

The three of us scanned the curious, leering crowd. "The faces of these Giza remind me of the Carthaginians," Opari said sarcastically. "And believe me," she added, "there was little welfare in their eyes."

One by one, the children stepped down from the train. Most were in oversized coats and shoes. All were tired and hungry. Only the older children bothered to see anything around them. One in particular, about my height, wearing an old black raincoat and a knit cap pulled down to the eyes, seemed to scan the crowd incessantly. Their chaperones were mostly women and all were wearing wide-brimmed hats and long dresses. They looked worn down by the miles, the job, and the hard, wooden seats on the train.

"No bloody damn good, this," Willie said quietly.

Opari leaned in close to my ear and whispered, "Why do you think Unai and Usoa have chosen such a train, my love?"

I thought back to Cornwall and Caitlin's Ruby and what Trumoi-Meq had told me. Though he hadn't been specific about location, he said Unai and Usoa crossed in the Zeharkatu in 1908. That meant they were in their early twenties now. I thought they must be acting as chaperones, probably through Reverend Bookbinder, but if Usoa had become delusional, that would be unlikely. I watched more and more children stepping down, orphans who had known no other life than scraping by on city streets. Carolina had said, in many instances the Orphan Train was the only chance those kids would have, but it didn't look like much of a chance to me.

"Maybe someone chose it for them," I said.

In any case, Unai and Usoa never departed the train. Minutes later, the chaperones had the children walking in straight lines and shuffling off to the theater to find out their fates. The crowd lingered, then drifted along behind. We waited. The two cars that comprised the Orphan Train stood empty and silent. In the distance, there was the grinding, gnashing sound of other cars being coupled and uncoupled.

"Do we want to be takin' a look inside, Z?" Willie asked.

"I think we should," I said and glanced at Opari. "But just us, Willie, okay?"

"I'll be right outside, Z." He winked and nodded toward the open door and the steps leading up to the train.

Slowly, I walked on board and turned to my right, entering

the compartment ahead of Opari. I was expecting to feel the net descending, the sensation I always felt in the presence of evil. I felt nothing. Yet, there was a foreboding, a weight in the silence. Cheap magazines and dime novels lay scattered in the otherwise empty wooden seats. Odd bits of clothing and a dozen toys were strewn through the car—chipped, broken, missing parts. We walked to the end of the aisle. Neither of us said a word nor made a sound.

We crossed to the next car and as I reached out to open the door, I paused and Opari touched my arm from behind. I heard a strange sound coming from inside the compartment. My "ability" enabled me to hear a barely audible, irregular bubbling sound, somewhere to the back of the car.

"Do you hear that?" I whispered.

Opari pressed her fingers into my shoulder. "No, my love. I hear nothing, however . . . there is something . . ."

"What?"

"I smell death."

I knew Opari's instincts and "abilities" were vast and refined over millennia. She would not be mistaken and there was no more time for caution. I pushed the door open. Inside, it was a complete change from the other car. Deep shadows and occasional bars of light crisscrossed the long compartment. Over half the window shades were drawn. Blankets were bunched in most of the seats or thrown over the backrests. This was the car used for sleeping, probably because they didn't have enough blankets for two cars.

We walked through, glancing in every seat on both sides of the aisle. Nothing. Then I heard the bubbling sound again. It was just in front of me, in the last seat on the left. I ran the few feet remaining and turned to look in the seat. What I saw made

me sick with grief and rage and broke my heart with a deep
blow.

It was Unai and Usoa. They were under a thin gray blanket.
Unai was leaning against the window and Usoa was slumped in
his lap. Unai looked asleep. On his head was a simple beret, the
kind seen anywhere in Bilbao. He resembled my papa in his
early twenties. He wore an old jacket and a white, collarless shirt
underneath that was no longer white. It was drenched in crimson blood. Unai's throat had been slashed just above the collar
line, ear to ear. I couldn't see Usoa's face. Her throat had also
been cut ear to ear, then someone turned her head at an angle
and removed the lower part of her right ear, the one in which
she wore the blue diamond. I bent over them to see if their
backs had been carved with a rose, the Fleur-du-Mal's signature.
There was nothing on their backs, but he might not have had
the time. The bubbling sound came from Usoa's neck and the
razor-thin slice across her throat.

"Lo egin bake," Opari said, then repeated as she leaned down
to turn Usoa's head back to a natural position. I wasn't sure of
the exact meaning of the phrase, but I knew it had something to
do with sleeping in peace.

Why? Why? It made no sense, no sense whatsoever. My mind
raced. I thought back to the orphans as they stepped down from
the train. I focused on every face. The kid with the knit cap and
the long raincoat, the only one who kept scanning the crowd—
it had to be him! Then another thought occurred to me—where
was the child? Arrosa had said in her telegram the two-year-old
child was with them. Even before I finished the thought, I heard
the muffled breathing coming from inside the wall of the train,
just three feet away, the very back of the compartment. I examined the wall and found the outline of a narrow door, cut to

blend in with the tongue-and-groove of the wooden slats. I pressed in on one side and the door popped open.

Inside, there was a small, shallow closet. Two axes were strapped against the back wall, along with a warning written in white paint: "FOR EMERGENCY USE ONLY!" Crouched on the floor directly below the warning, a boy about seven or eight years old stared up at me with brown eyes the size of half-dollars. His mouth was stuffed with what looked like a biscuit. It was wrapped in cloth and he held it there tightly with one hand, probably to keep from being heard. In his arms, he was cradling a two-year-old, and his other hand was over the child's mouth and face. The child was lifeless with open, fixed eyes staring blankly into space, and they were neither green nor brown, but blue. The boy had most likely witnessed the murders through the crack in the wall, and in his fear and terror, he had accidentally suffocated the child while trying to save it. The boy was unaware the child was dead. He was in shock, and yet once he searched the eyes of Opari, he relaxed, releasing his grip and his own consciousness. He fell forward and I caught the dead child in my arms, just as the boy let go his hold.

"Quickly—" Opari said without hesitation. "This boy needs our attention and protection."

"Owen Bramley," I said. "We should get to Owen as soon as possible—for the boy, for everyone. Let's find Willie. He can get us to Carolina's and Owen will know how to keep this among ourselves."

I picked up a spare blanket from one of the seats and wrapped the dead child in it, then draped another blanket over the bodies of Unai and Usoa.

Opari held the boy in her arms. He was nothing but skin and

bones, one of the poorest of all the orphans on the Orphan Train. She led the way out, but turned once and asked me a question. "Is this the way he usually does it?"

"Yes," I said. I could see the Fleur-du-Mal's face, his smile. "Yes."

Eight days later, on the twentieth of May, I was back at Sportsman's Park. The Cardinals were out of town and the Browns were taking on the Boston Red Sox. It was Carolina who talked me into going. I had been extremely morose and moody, angry and defensive, abusive to everyone for the whole week after we found Unai and Usoa. They were Egizahar Meq, friends of my own mama and papa, and had crossed in the Zeharkatu for one reason only—to be happy. They had lived long, fruitful lives, only to die in delusion and madness, betrayed by one of their own. I could not reconcile it or place it anywhere in my mind, and Opari, my Ameq, could not console me, though she tried in every way possible. I also feared greatly for the baby Caine. The Fleur-du-Mal's obsessions were too close once again, and who knows what he had in mind for tomorrow, or the next day, or the next.

Owen Bramley had, indeed, taken care of all loose ends, including the police and the newspapers. The murders, the death of the child, and the discovery of the orphan boy were never mentioned in the news or in a police report. Carolina had requested to be the orphan boy's guardian for as long as he liked, and he was to live in the big house, in Georgia's piano room if need be, whatever it took to keep him from returning to the Orphan Train. The boy was mute, as Carolina's sister Georgia had been, and whether the boy's condition was from the trauma of events, or illness, or even a genetic defect, Carolina didn't know or care—the boy was staying in St. Louis with her. Owen Bramley understood there would be no changing her mind and handled all the details involved. I thanked Owen and told him I was impressed with his "network" of people, information, and political clout. I also mentioned to him that he reminded me a little of Solomon with his talent for getting things done, one way or another. He replied, "Where do you think I learned, Z?"

Carolina finally got tired of my continued ill temper and gave me no choice. She said constant worry and expecting the worst at every moment was not healthy, not for me and not for her family. She insisted Opari and I accompany her, along with Jack, to Sportsman's Park. "Baseball is the answer," she said, and off we went.

We sat in Carolina's box seats, three rows back from the field and just beyond the dugout on the first base side. They were great seats and foul balls were a common occurrence, making Opari wonder about the intelligence of sitting so close to the action. "That's part of the thrill," I said. "Wait until you catch one."

On the mound for the Boston Red Sox was a big, lanky left-hander and he had good stuff. Dave Davenport was pitching for the Browns. It was a perfect day for baseball, sunny and warm, but my thoughts kept drifting back to the murders. Why had Unai and Usoa been duped and used in such a complex manner, then killed without mercy? It seemed unnecessary and arcane, even for the Fleur-du-Mal. It was as if they had been delivered to us, almost at the moment of death. What kind of a message was it? And again, the same question—why?

There was one thing I had resolved to take care of myself.

Unai and Usoa must be given some dignity and shown respect for their long, long lives. I was the only one to do it. Their bodies deserved to be returned to their homeland, to the Pyrenees, and buried with reverence and ceremony. However, I could not leave Carolina, Star, and Caine to whatever the Fleur-du-Mal might have in mind. Someone had to be in St. Louis to protect them, someone who could sense his presence, possibly even kill him; someone who was Meq, strong, reliable, and knowledgeable of the Fleur-du-Mal and his history. I turned and looked at the only answer to my dilemma.

"Opari," I said carefully, in a voice only she could hear. "I have a great favor to ask."

She knew exactly what I was going to ask because she put her finger to my lips and said, "Take them to Kepa. I will wait for you here and watch for him. Do not take your concerns with you. I will watch carefully, my beloved."

I kissed her finger and held it. "I know you wanted to see your home again."

"And that day will come, Z. Do not be concerned. Remember what you told me in Africa—we have the time."

I smiled and continued to watch the game, but in a distracted state of mind. Jack punched me in the arm more than once, saying, "Hey, Z, did you see that?" I would answer with "Yeah," or "Sure did," or something else just as unconvincing. I told Opari I thought I would ask Mitch to accompany me to New York instead of Willie or Owen Bramley. That would leave both of them in St. Louis, in case anything happened. She agreed and told me to try to enjoy the game—relax. I said I would, and I tried; however, I could not stop thinking about what was ahead and the problems that might arise.

"I wish I had another one of us with me," I said. "Someone I trust completely."

Almost at the same moment, before Opari could respond, I felt something—a presence, a Meq presence. I turned to look behind me and then heard the crack of a baseball being hit hard, and everyone around me leaped to their feet to follow the flight of the ball. I turned back to the field and saw the big, lanky left-hander, trotting around the bases, watching the ball sail out of the park over the fence in right field. Three runners crossed the plate ahead of him. The pitcher had hit a grand slam, the first one of his long career I was to find out later.

"Did you see that, Z?" Jack cried. "That ball went a mile!"

"Yeah, I did, Jack. Who is that player? What's his name?"

"Babe Ruth," Jack answered.

I looked at Opari to see if she had felt anything before the home run. She had, I could see it in her eyes. I started to excuse myself and motioned for Opari to follow me. I wanted to get higher up in the grandstands, where we could better scan the crowd. That's when I heard the bitter laugh. Not the evil one I was all too familiar with, but another one, one I had not heard in years. It was coming from just behind me, two rows up. I turned again and found him immediately. He was standing on the steps in the aisle. His legs were spread wide and he had his hands on his hips. His eyes were a bright green. He wore baggy black trousers and a white shirt with the sleeves rolled up. He looked good, and healthy, and the only thing missing was his bowler hat, which was stored safely away in my closet at Carolina's.

"How you doin', Z?" he asked. "You're lookin' about the same."

"How are you doing, Ray?" I said back. "I've been waiting for you."

"What do you think about that pitcher for the Sox?"

"I think he's a pretty good hitter," I said.

"Well, I think you're right," he said. "But right now all you're seein' is the caterpillar. Wait 'til you see the butterfly."

3

TXAPEL

(BERET)

A man on a train once told me the tale of a chieftain who was far from home on a perilous mission for his tribe. He came to a pass in the mountains with which he was unfamiliar. He knew there was no going back and his time was limited. False routes with bandits waiting in ambush lay ahead. Sitting on opposite sides of the trail at the head of the pass were two men about the same age. Physically, there seemed to be no difference between them, except that one was wearing a beret and the other was not. Both claimed to know the true and only safe way through the pass. The chieftain knew if he chose the wrong guide, his mission would certainly fail and he would likely be robbed, beaten, or killed. Not a single soul from his tribe would ever learn his fate. To the chieftain, there was but one choice. Laughing out loud, and without hesitation, he chose the man in the beret to be his guide. Why? Simply because a man with a beret will always have more to offer than a man without. If the "truth" is unknowable, he believed, then one should enjoy the journey, regardless of the outcome.

"What became of the chieftain?" I asked.

The man on the train turned his head toward the window and gazed out at the passing fields and farms. "No one knows," he said quietly.

Ray Ytuarte is a survivor. He never thinks of his present situation as dire, only urgent. That is the difference between those who go under in a flood of circumstance and those who find their way to shore, any shore, and survive. True survivors never look back, except to remember what not to do again, and they rarely look ahead because the future is merely a dream, a trick of the mind. They exist squarely in the present, usually with good humor and always with no illusions. And they make excellent friends.

I overheard a woman say once: "Friendship is the work of childhood." I suppose that's about as true a thing as anything there is. In Africa I had witnessed how effortless that work becomes, in the heart, in the moment when Ray saved my life, putting his own life in harm's way without a thought and delighting in it.

Ray and I embraced each other while the crowd was still standing and marveling at the distance of Babe Ruth's grand slam.

"Damn, Z," Ray said, "are you tryin' to break my ribs?"

I laughed and let go of him, but I could easily have broken something without much effort. It felt that good to see him in flesh and blood. Opari was staring at both of us. So were Carolina and Jack.

It was because the Meq remain unmarked, or changed in any way, that it was impossible to tell what Ray had been through. He looked the same. I wanted to know everything that had happened to him since Africa. I wanted to know right there in Sportsman's Park, but I also knew I would have to wait.

Carolina touched Ray's shoulder and he looked up at her. "Good to see you, Ray," she said, "we've missed you terribly."

"It's good to be back," Ray said. "It surely is."

I started to introduce Opari when Jack suddenly pulled on my sleeve. "How many more are there, Z?"

"More what, Jack?"

He hesitated, glanced at his mother, and turned back to me. "Well, you know, Z . . . how many more like you?"

Carolina seemed embarrassed, then looked at me and shrugged. Questions about the Meq almost never surfaced when we were together. I assumed we were simply a fact of life. I didn't quite know what to say.

Then with a grin and a mysterious wink in my direction, Ray answered, "More than you think, kid . . . more than you think."

As I introduced Ray to Jack, and finally to Opari, I heard the words being exchanged between them and watched their faces laughing and smiling, but I seemed to be somewhere else. I had an odd feeling, a dreamlike feeling I had experienced once before when Solomon reappeared after years of absence. I even heard the sound of a dog barking in the distance. Was it really Ray standing next to me speaking? I didn't fully realize until that moment how much I had truly missed my old friend.

"Why now, Ray? Why here?" I asked him.

"Well . . . 'here' because I stopped off at Carolina's first. I found out a few things from Owen, you know, about everything from Eder and Nicholas to that nasty business down at the train station. Even saw Star and the baby . . . man, oh, man, Z . . . you did it, you really did it. Then I thought I had better come on down directly, and here I am."

"How long have you been in the States?"

"That's the 'now' part of the answer. About two months ago, I hitched up as a batboy with a Venezuelan exhibition team while they were in Veracruz. That got me into the States through Miami. A couple days later I felt a kind of storm, but different . . . strange . . . in the direction of St. Louis. By the time I got a little closer, maybe five hundred miles or so, I knew it was something else."

He stopped talking and looked at me closely, like a doctor examining his patient, then he grinned and tapped me in the middle of my forehead with the end of his finger. He said, "I think all it was, was you worrying, Z. So, as long as I was already in the area, I thought I might as well save your ass . . . again."

"When are you going to tell me where you've been?"

"When we get gone."

"Gone where?"

"To do this thing. Owen told me, remember? You might need some help with Unai and Usoa and the trip back to Spain, to the Pyrenees. You ought to know by now two brains are better than one."

I stared at Ray and smiled. I couldn't wait to see him in his bowler again. "How was it?" I asked. "I mean, over all, how was it . . . because you look good, Ray."

"Well, let me just say I learned a few things, and I also didn't see a few things coming, like Mozart, for example."

"Mozart? The composer?"

"Yeah, same guy. I tell you, Z, I really came to love his music. Never expected that. And I like a little modern painting now and then, know what I mean, Z?"

"No," I said, shaking my head in disbelief. What could Ray, Mozart, and modern painting possibly have in common? "No, Ray, I haven't got a clue, but I can't wait for you to tell me."

"Ready to go?" It was Carolina. The game was over and the Browns had lost. Babe Ruth got the win for the Red Sox.

"Yeah," Ray yelled back. "We're ready. Ain't we, Z?"

"We're ready."

As soon as we left Sportsman's Park, Ray began peppering me with questions concerning Nova. I told him everything I knew about her current location, but he wanted to know more than her address and state of welfare. For some reason he never seemed to doubt that she was all right; he wanted to know what she was like, how she "turned out." I told him about the night Eder died, and how Nova carried a Stone now, Unai's Stone, which Sailor had thrown to her in the shadow of the "slabs" in Cornwall. I told him that Nova worried about him and added that I thought she missed him a great deal. I didn't tell him Sailor had asked Geaxi and Opari to follow Nova's progress and be patient. I didn't mention her unique dress and heavy makeup, let alone her occasionally strange behavior.

"That don't sound right," Ray said.

"What do you mean?" I asked, knowing I'd been caught. I should have realized Ray was much too streetwise to ever swallow only half the truth.

"It just don't sound like Nova," he said. "You sure you're not leavin' something out?"

So I told him about the Egyptian mascara, the semitrances, and an attitude that I admitted I never quite understood.

"Now that's my Nova!" Ray almost shouted. He leaned over and tapped me lightly on the temple. "What's the matter with you, Z? How long you think I been gone?"

Then something happened that made me even more concerned about leaving St. Louis at that point in time. It took
place not five minutes after we returned to Carolina's and it involved Ray and the orphan boy. No one saw it coming. The
boy was still healing from the traumatic events on the train and
we should have seen the possibility, but as I said, it was uninten-
tional. Nevertheless, because of it the boy confirmed a suspicion about Unai and Usoa's killer that he could not have
revealed in any other way.

Carolina had given the boy a name since there was no official
name available. She called him Oliver Bookbinder—Oliver because she said he "looked straight out of Dickens" and Bookbinder for the Reverend who sent the two-year-old the boy had
tried to save. The boy was dark and Hispanic in appearance and
I thought he might someday have a few questions for Carolina
about her choice of names. She told Ray no one was calling
him Oliver because Ciela had nicknamed him Biscuit for the
biscuit in a handkerchief that the boy would barely take out of
his mouth when we first brought him home. He had already
won everyone's heart, especially Ciela's, and Carolina thought
Ray should meet him right away.

She led us to the kitchen where the boy sat with Ciela at the
long table. They were playing checkers, sort of. The boy had
captured nearly all of Ciela's pieces. She had only two pieces left
on the board. He was sitting with his back to us, but once
he heard us, he spun around and found himself face-to-face
with Ray.

He stared into Ray's green eyes for only a second, then started
trembling head to foot, and finally he fell to the floor, dragging
the checkerboard down with him. The checkers went flying and

scattered across the kitchen. He rolled under the table and curled up in a fetal position, trying to cover his head with the checkerboard. He was still shaking all over.

Ray immediately leaned over and spoke softly to him. "It's all right, kid. I'm not going to hurt you, I promise."

But it was no use. Ciela knelt down next to Ray and motioned with her head for him to leave, then turned and waved her arm for all of us to leave. "Go," she whispered. "*Vamos!* I will take care of this."

We left the room as quickly and silently as we could. Carolina was extremely upset and so was Ray. He felt like he had been responsible and apologized over and over, to Carolina, to me, to anyone who would listen.

"It's not you, Ray," I said.

"Then what is it?" he asked.

I hesitated and glanced at Opari, who had remained mostly quiet but was observing everything carefully. The boy had never exhibited any fear of the rest of us.

"What, Z? What is it?" Ray asked again.

"Not what, Ray. It's *who*. It's someone who looks very much like you."

"The Fleur-du-Mal," Ray said, more as statement than question. I never had to answer. "He's a son of a bitch, that one," Ray said to no one in particular, "a real live son of a bitch."

An hour later Ciela had calmed the boy enough to where he fell asleep on the bed in her bedroom. Carolina told us he was breathing evenly and she tried to assure Ray that the boy would be fine. Ray did not forget the incident soon, however. Things like that affect him deeply, much more than he ever lets anyone know, and he carried the boy's terrified reaction with him for weeks, though the boy himself forgot about it and even became Ray's friend within days. Upstairs, I tried to bolster Ray's spirit. I took him to my closet where I kept his oldest possession, his bowler hat.

He smiled once as he rubbed the brim, then placed it carefully on his head. "Kept it all the way through Africa, did you, Z?"

I smiled back. "Sure did."

The next day I contacted Mitch and told him of our plan. I asked if he could accompany an old friend and me as far as New York. From there, the "white rose" would be our escort. He agreed on the spot, saying he needed the trip anyway for "business reasons." At the same time, Owen Bramley was busy making all the arrangements for the entire journey. As we were going over the names of various emergency contacts, something suddenly occurred to me, something that would have been very important to Unai. I asked Owen if he had remembered Unai's beret. "You bet, Z," Owen said. "I wouldn't forget that. It's in there with him."

I also sent Arrosa a telegram informing her of our scheduled arrival in New York and told her to contact Kepa in Spain, asking him to have someone meet us in Barcelona, where we would disembark. Arrosa still did not know the details of Unai's and Usoa's deaths. In my previous telegram I had only told her they had died. I knew she would be heartbroken with the news and I wanted to wait and tell her the rest in New York.

Ray spent most of the day getting to know Star and playing with Caine. All babies seemed to love Ray, and even though he would deny it, Ray loved all babies. Willie was enthralled with Ray, having never met any Meq quite like him. Jack had the same reaction and stayed home from school just to talk to Ray. Carolina did not object and kept herself occupied reading stories to Biscuit, which she said he enjoyed more than anything. Ciela remained in the kitchen, chopping, slicing, and singing, preparing a delicious Cuban feast in honor of our departure.

Every minute of every hour that day, Opari was by my side. She had a reserve and quietness about her that was different and mysterious. She even wore a garment I had not seen before, a deep blue Indian sari, exquisitely embroidered with mythological beasts and birds. There were ancient Meq barrettes in her hair similar to the ones Eder had shown me years earlier. And there was a faint scent of lavender on her skin, a scent I also had never known her to wear. Everything about her struck me as exotic and intoxicating. It was difficult for me to concentrate when I talked to Owen and the others.

Late in the afternoon the two of us finally found ourselves alone. We walked out to the "Honeycircle" at my suggestion. The sky was blue and clear and everything inside the lush circle was in bloom. We were holding hands and I lifted her hand to kiss her fingers and palm, then I kissed her lips. She let go my hand and put her arms around my neck. I kissed her cheeks and tasted lavender. I kissed her eyelids, then her eyebrows. They were soft black silk.

"We have not yet discussed the Wait, the Itxaron," I said.

"Yes, my love, I know." She put her hand on my chest and placed my hand on her chest, pushing aside the Stone she wore on a simple necklace. "Do you feel this pounding in our hearts?" she whispered.

"Yes."

"This is the essence, Zianno. This is the true meaning and dream of the Itxaron—not longing or waiting or wondering, but *knowing*. We are knowing our own destiny, my love. You, Zianno Zezen, are my destiny, flesh and blood, and I am yours. All else is unknown, unknowable, no longer . . . *garrantzitsu*. All else is no longer of importance, not to us and not to this pounding in our hearts. The Wait is not our enemy. The Wait is a gift from the stars." She paused and kissed my lips. "Do you know what my name means in Basque?" she asked, then answered before I could respond. "It means 'gift.' I have a gift that others before me, others who wore the Stone of Blood, also possessed. Tonight I give this gift to you, my beloved. Just as you have let me into your dreams from half a world away, I will take you into mine. Tomorrow, when you leave me, you will know this gift and you will take it with you in your mind and heart. It will sustain you on your journey and bring you back to me. Not all Meq know of this gift, but tomorrow, you will, Zianno."

"What is the gift?"

She pressed her finger to my lips and smiled. "Tonight, my love."

Carolina decided against using her formal dining area for Ciela's feast. Instead, shortly after sunset, we were all called into the kitchen and, one by one, took our seats around the long table. Wonderful Caribbean scents and aromas filled the room—grilled meat, roasted peppers, toasted marjoram, and more, wafting from a half-dozen side dishes laid out on counters and atop the stove. Inside the oven, Ciela said, was a suckling pig, cooked from a recipe as old as her village, and served with a "mojo" prepared with lard, cloves of garlic, and sour orange rind. At both ends of the table several bottles of champagne were chilling on ice. Owen said each bottle was a 1911 Perrier-Jouet, one of the finest vintages of any champagne since 1874.

Ray took one look at the array of delicious, steaming dishes and fresh-baked bread that covered the table, then summed up everyone's reaction. "Damn!" he said, looking over at Ciela with a broad grin across his face.

Carolina rose from her seat before we began eating and gave a toast and short speech that was neither somber nor joyous. She mentioned Unai and Usoa, though she had never really known them, and she thanked God, Ray, and me for bringing Star and Caine to safety. She ignored the obvious danger that could still exist and said we should be grateful for the moment, the food, and the unique family we had become. Following with a toast of his own, Owen Bramley began by recounting his and Ray's adventures and difficulties while trying to crate and haul Baju's sundial to St. Louis all those years ago. He segued into comparing our odd family with the formation of Woodrow Wilson's idea for a League of Nations and the upcoming conference in Versailles. It was typical Owen logic and rhetoric and as he rambled on, my mind drifted to thoughts of Opari. She was sitting across the table, looking at me, smiling. I no longer heard Owen's voice. I only heard the echo of her voice, her simple words, "Tonight, my love." I smiled back and lifted a silent toast to her, and the feast began.

> *Here vigor failed the towering fantasy.*
> *But yet the will rolled onward, like a wheel*
> *In even motion. By the Love impelled,*
> *That moves the sun in heaven and all the stars.*

—DANTE ALIGHIERI, *Paradise,* Canto XXXIII

It was well after midnight. Holding the inside of the frame with my hand, I leaned out one of our bedroom windows, over the sill, out far enough to look up and catch a glimpse of the great Milky Way overhead. I wanted to see if the stars were still burning. I wanted to see if they still wheeled through the sky or if they had stopped in place, because I was certain I now knew what made them move.

"Be careful, Z," Opari whispered out at me. "It is some distance to the ground."

"I couldn't fall tonight. Not now, it would be impossible."

She smiled and kissed the knuckles of my hand holding the frame. "What do you see?"

"I see what I never have before."

She laughed and turned, walking back toward the bed while removing the old barrettes from her hair. I watched her every move. She was as graceful and silent as Geaxi, with an added mystery in her step, as if she walked surrounded by a field of excited particles. I now knew one of her most intimate secrets. It is the reason kings, sultans, priests, and princes, even jealous empresses, have for centuries sought her presence and given her the same protection as their royal treasures. It is not just the Stone of Blood, nor the gems that adorn it, nothing like that. It is something much more sublime and yet overwhelming, a knowledge every Giza and Meq has within them, but very few ever experience. Opari is a vessel of this knowledge, this experience. This is her "gift." It is the most refined of all her "abilities" and in this world, in this form, her most powerful ally.

The experience lasts a little over an hour for Giza and can last two or more hours for the Meq. Beginning at approximately 10:00 P.M. and in various stages until about 12:30 A.M., through Opari's touch and guidance, I had been shown this "gift," this dance, this fugue, this impossible balance of control and surrender, and led to a sublime perimeter of possibilities and particles. I returned with a feeling of renewal I had never felt before. I felt connected to everything, to the . . . "Love impelled, that moves the sun in heaven and all the stars."

"Opari," I said, ducking my head back in the room, "does it have a name?"

She was just turning out the last of the lights and about to climb into bed. "Yes," she said through the sudden dark. "But the name is nonverbal. Do you . . . need a name, my love?"

"No, no," I said, stumbling into the room.

"Come to bed, Z. I want you next to me."

I bumped into the bed and crawled between the sheets where I found her skin.

"In the morning you leave," she said. "Tonight, come dream with me."

Not long after first light, I awoke to the voices of Owen Bramley and Mitch in the hallway. Owen seemed to be giving instructions and Mitch was saying, "I got it, I got it." Then he was bounding down the stairs and I heard the sound of a door opening and closing. I sat up and glanced out the window. The sky was blue and clear and the sun was shining. If the time had come to leave St. Louis, I thought, at least it would be on a beautiful spring day.

As I dressed, Opari sang a song in Old French, a gentle Provençal poem she had learned from a troubadour a thousand years earlier. It was called an *aubade,* she said, and told the story of lovers parting at dawn.

We said good-bye at the bedroom door. It was much easier than I anticipated and lasted only a few moments. Opari simply reminded me that I must return; otherwise she would have to come and find me. I laughed and kissed her lips, which were moist and soft against mine. To this day, partings from the ones you hold most dear are a great mystery to me. They always seem to break your heart and fill it with warmth at the same time, a nearly impossible balance of feelings and emotion. Before she closed the door, Opari touched my cheek once more, then traced every feature on my face with her fingertips. Her last words were, "Au revoir, my love, and find a good place for Unai and Usoa to rest in peace."

Owen met me at the end of the hall and handed over a packet of letters and instructions for various contacts along the train route and in New York. He had special letters written for a man in U.S. Customs and the captain of the ship on which we would be sailing, the *Iona*. He assured me that enough money to keep from worrying would be transferred to Barcelona and available to me upon arrival. He also said he had procured a private rail-car for our journey, equipped with sleeping berths and a separate storage compartment for the coffins.

I looked across the hall to the room Ray had been using. The door was wide open but the room was empty.

"Where's Ray?" I asked.

"I'm not sure," Owen said. "He knocked on my door a good twenty minutes before sunrise and informed me he wanted me to find Mitch and tell him to meet him down at Union Station early. Never gave a reason. Just told me to tell Mitch. He was packed and on his way by dawn." Owen adjusted his glasses and the two of us stood in silence for a few moments.

"Where's Carolina?" I asked.

"She's in the kitchen. She said to remind you if you didn't say good-bye this time, you couldn't come back." He picked up a fedora that lay on a side table, then pointed with it downstairs. "I'll wait outside for you."

I had said my farewells to Star and Willie and Jack the night before. I wanted to see Carolina last. "Give me five minutes, Owen."

"Take your time, Z."

Carolina was standing alone in the kitchen, caught in a beam of early light streaming in from the east. She was facing the window, kneading a loaf of bread on the counter. Her hands were covered with flour and a small cloud of flour dust surrounded her, floating in the beam of sunlight. Her freckles stood out in bright brown patches across her nose and cheeks. A strand of hair came loose and she stopped to brush it away from her face.

I stood just inside the door and spoke before she saw me. "I was told I had better come see you or else suffer the consequences."

"Z!" she cried, then relaxed. "Well, yes, that's true. There would have been consequences." She smiled once and returned to kneading the bread. "Z, I want you to come back swiftly this time. There is no requirement for you to remain after you have done what you must do. And it is not because I live in fear of that evil one, the Fleur-du-Mal. I don't give him a second thought and I don't want you to give a second thought to worrying about us. We will be fine, I promise." She stopped and turned to look at me directly. "Come back, Z, come back soon." She paused and smiled again. "And I will make sure Jack keeps your mama's glove oiled."

"That's all I could ask," I said, and started to leave, then turned back. "Don't forget, Carolina, Opari carries one of these." I held the Stone out in front of me.

"I won't forget, Z. Now go. And what did you say to me once at Union Station when you were leaving? What was the phrase . . . *egi* . . . *egibiz* . . . ?"

"Egibizirik bilatu," I finished. She was remarkable and she was my oldest friend. "I'll be back soon, Carolina. I promise."

Things went smoothly and quickly at Union Station. Owen Bramley introduced me to Caleb, a black porter who was a friend of Owen's and the first of several porters along our route who made sure we had everything we needed. Ray and Mitch were already on board and the train left exactly on time. Within minutes we were crossing the Mississippi and heading straight for the morning sun. By late afternoon we were approaching Champaign, Illinois, where we would be recoupled to another line and another train.

Mitch and Ray had become friends the first moment they met in St. Louis. They spent the entire morning and most of the afternoon exploring what they had in common, sharing stories and anecdotes about places and characters they had known in the life on the riverfront and the streets of downtown St. Louis. Mitch was fascinated with the criminal past that Ray knew personally, and Ray wanted to know all about running a nightclub. I wasn't really included or excluded, just ignored. Ray never mentioned why he left Carolina's early and Mitch never brought it up. However, I didn't mind the time alone, I welcomed it. I was still getting used to the idea of leaving St. Louis so soon and so suddenly. I watched the flat farmland pass by, corn and soybeans, one farm after another. I fell into a reverie of reliving the events from the day before, including Ciela's feast. While I was smiling to myself, recalling the way Opari looked across the table, I remembered a single moment that I didn't quite understand at the time. She was facing Ray and they were both excited, smiling, talking about something, when Ray suddenly dropped his smile and glanced at me. I think I turned to listen to Owen for a few seconds, then turned back and Ray was gone. He was absent the rest of the evening and I didn't see him again until I boarded the train. Whatever had happened in that moment with Opari had affected all his actions since. Ray's friendship meant too much to me to wait and guess. I had to find out what was wrong. Champaign, Illinois, was the place to do it.

On a sidetrack several hundred yards from the station itself, our railcar was uncoupled. While we waited for the other train, I suggested Ray and I get some fried egg sandwiches from the café inside. Mitch agreed, saying he had business with the porter, Caleb, and to make sure we brought him three sandwiches instead of one, with fried potatoes, if possible.

As Ray and I started down the long platform toward the station, we didn't speak. Ray saw a bottle cap on the platform and picked it up, then tossed it down the tracks so hard and so well, I lost sight of it completely. But it wasn't only skill that threw the bottle cap so far, it was anger. I saw it in his eyes.

I stopped walking and held back. "What happened last night, Ray? What did Opari tell you?"

Ray continued walking for another three paces, then stopped and turned slowly. There was a look on his face I will never forget and hope I never see again—a look of intense rage, anger, and profound disappointment. He slumped forward slightly, shaking his head back and forth. Quietly, he said, "Opari told me I had the same eyes as my sister." He stopped talking and laughed to himself. It was his bitter laugh. "What the hell were you thinkin', Z?" he asked. "How come you didn't tell me you had seen Zuriaa? As far back as China, goddamnit! How come you didn't tell me my sister was alive, Z?" He put his bowler back on and knelt down in a crouch, as if he couldn't or wouldn't stand up any longer. He felt betrayed and cut to the bone. And I was the only one to blame. I had no defense or excuse. Opari was not aware that I had never told Ray about his sister. At the time, I thought it was better that he not know she had changed and was not the sister he remembered; however, true friends do not keep the truth from each other. No matter what my reasons were, they were wrong.

"It was a mistake," I said. "A mistake I should never have made, Ray. And one I can never make right. I'm sorry. If you can't forgive me, I understand. I can only swear to you that I will never make that mistake again. Ever."

Ray removed his bowler one more time and held it with both hands, turning it, examining every square inch of the brim. He rose from his crouch and stood up facing me. The rage was gone. He cleared his throat and took his time. "You gonna tell me about her, tell me what you know?"

"Yes, everything, the good and the ugly. Right here, right now, if you want."

"You don't have to go overboard, Z. I forgive you. I know you probably meant well." He winked once and turned toward the station and the café. "Just don't do it again. Deal?"

"Deal."

That night as we were rolling through northern Indiana and Ohio, on our way to our next change of trains in Cleveland, I told Ray everything I knew about Zuriaa, which wasn't much. I told him how I had met her in China and recognized her immediately, exposing her as his sister and calling her by name. I told him of the shock in her eyes when I had said his name, and how she fainted on the spot in front of the Empress Dowager of China. I also told him about seeing her again in Carthage and watching her kill "Razor Eyes" without mercy, then ride away. I said Opari would be a better source of information because she and Zuriaa had traveled together for many years throughout Asia. There had been a falling out between them, the exact nature of which had never been explained to me. Lastly, I told him Zuriaa might have been in Africa doing business with or for the Fleur-du-Mal.

"What!"

"That's right, Ray. He was waiting for Zuriaa and 'Razor Eyes' to deliver Star to him."

Ray fell silent. He shook his head back and forth, then turned to me. "I ain't seen her for over a hundred years, Z. Did you know that?"

"Yeah, Ray. I know."

He paused. "A hundred years," he said again, then in a whisper I barely heard, "Anybody can change in a hundred years. Anybody." He picked up his bowler, which lay in the seat next to him, and studied it thoroughly. He shook his head again, then looked up and faced the window as our train continued east through the darkness.

"Ray?" I asked. "When are you going to tell me where you've been?"

"Later, Z," he said without turning around. "And you ain't gonna believe it."

He was nearly right. All night long, while Mitch slept peacefully in his berth, Ray told the tale of his travels and travails during the last twelve years. By the time we reached Cleveland, I could barely believe what I'd heard, and never would have if it hadn't been Ray who had done the telling.

He began by informing me his "kidnapping" had turned out to be the greatest adventure of his life—the exact opposite of what I'd been imagining since that Christmas Day in Senegal. There were no terrors or tortures, no chains, no imprisonment or being held for ransom. In fact, after boarding the German yacht we'd seen anchored in the harbor, his abductor, Cheng, or "Razor Eyes," made Ray an offer he couldn't refuse. It was not a threat, but a genuine offer of a great deal of money, along with a fee attached for Cheng and the German ship's captain to share. And he would not be required to "do" anything, other than be himself and accompany an old man on a quest through East Africa somewhere north of the Rift Valley. It was to be a search for a special one of the Magic Children, a girl the old man had known in his youth. He believed she had returned to her mythical homeland and he was determined to find it before he died. Cheng had been scouring the ports of Africa looking for one of us because the old man was positive that in order to find the girl, he needed someone of her own kind to help him. Completely by accident or providence, he had seen Ray and me coming ashore in Saint-Louis and decided to "surprise" the two of us, then make his offer. Because Ray wanted to create as much distance between Cheng and me as quickly as possible, he accepted the offer without hesitation. They set sail for East Africa, stopping along the way in the ports of Lomé, Douala, Swakopmund, and Luderitz Bay, then rounding the Cape and docking in the ancient port of Dar es Salaam, where the old man was waiting for them inside the walls of his private estate.

Ray was taken to an open courtyard covered in multicolored tile, laid in intricate geometric patterns, and introduced to Baron Ernst Rudiger von Steichen, the German-Austrian patriarch of a family and a business that spanned generations going back a thousand years or more. Their roots were in the lake country outside Salzburg. Their business was salt. The Baron seemed startled or puzzled at first, then shook his head slightly and smiled, asking Ray in English which would he prefer, tea or coffee? Ray liked the old man the instant he stared into his bright blue eyes and guessed him to be about seventy-five years old, but quick, slick, and charming as a riverboat gambler. The Baron assured Ray a considerable amount of gold would be deposited into a private account that would be established in his name, in Zurich, within a week. Ray could verify this before they ever left Dar es Salaam. After that, the Baron warned, where they were going or when they would return could not be accurately predicted. Ray said he would do it for nothing, but the Baron wouldn't have it and insisted on paying him. Ray agreed and was immediately escorted by the old man to another part of his estate where forty or fifty men were busy sorting through massive amounts of supplies that lay strewn across the grounds of a polo field. It was a fully outfitted safari on the verge of departure. The Baron turned and told Ray he'd been waiting for him.

Six months later Ray had seen Mount Kilimanjaro and heard

the sounds of the Serengeti at night. He had learned two languages and shared the campfires of warriors, herdsmen, fishermen, and kings. They had pushed on west to the shores of Lake
Victoria and north to a river with three different names. This
river and a reliable new guide would eventually lead them farther north to the remote area around Lake Turkana. From there,
and for the next seven years, Ray and the Baron chased rumors
and legends of the Meq girl's origins. They never found a trace
of her and by then the war had broken out, causing the Baron
concern for his estate in Dar es Salaam. He decided with great
reluctance to finally abandon his quest and return to protect his
property. They made their way east to the port of Djibouti,
where the Baron sold all his goods to local traders and procured
illegal passage down the coast, avoiding any confrontations or
blockades along the way.

The Baron's estate was intact and the place became a safe
haven for him and Ray during the early stages of the Great War,
as it was fought in East Africa. The Baron confessed to Ray
that he had a son and grandson who were both fighting for the
German army, somewhere in France. He tried to persuade his
friend, General von Lettow-Vorbeck, to arrange for their transfer to Africa. It never happened. When Dar es Salaam was under
siege and then bombarded, the old man's estate was destroyed.
Baron Ernst Rudiger von Steichen was hit and killed by flying
debris during one of the explosions. Ray said his own leg, arm,
and five of his ribs were broken in the blast and it took him
nearly a week to heal. Once he did, he contacted the Baron's
family in Salzburg. The Baroness Matilde, granddaughter-in-
law to the Baron, sent a long letter in return, thanking Ray
and giving him the sad news that the Baron's son and grandson

had both been killed in the war. In a postscript she asked Ray
if he could somehow bring the Baron's body back to Salzburg.
She wanted to bury them all among their own family and ancestors.

War makes pirates and strange bedfellows out of almost everybody. With his abundance of street skills and plenty of money,
Ray was able to smuggle himself and the Baron's coffin by ship
to the Black Sea, then up the Danube all the way to Linz, where
he made connections to Salzburg. The trip was a difficult and
dangerous journey, but Ray made it in less than four months.

In Salzburg, he was met and welcomed by the Baroness
Matilde. Ray said he could tell instantly that she knew he was
Meq and in thirty minutes they were driving through the gates
of the von Steichen "family spread," as Ray called it. Nestled
between a lakefront and the sheer rock face of a mountain, and
connected across an entire hillside, stood a series of castlelike
stone structures. This had been the home of the von Steichens
since the Middle Ages.

The Baroness showed Ray to his quarters deep within the
complex. Ray said there were so many buildings, most with additions and additions to the additions, it felt more like its own
village than a family home. The master bedroom of his suite was
covered in three-hundred-year-old rugs from Isfahan and even
older Venetian tapestries hanging on the walls and over an enormous fireplace with a mantel well above Ray's head. The
Baroness asked him to stay for the funeral and Ray accepted. She
was alone now in the great home. Her mother-in-law had suffered a stroke during the war, as had the last Baroness, the
Baron's own wife of fifty years. She died without ever knowing
his fate and Matilde guessed it had been the same for the Baron.

Ray told her the Baron always referred to his wife as a living person. That was comforting news to the Baroness Matilde. She then asked Ray to stay for as long as he liked, for the duration of the war if he wished. Ray told her it might be a good idea to "sit out the squabble," as he referred to waiting for World War I to end. She also hinted that she had a special place to show him, saying it was the source of the Baron's mad quest.

Ray stayed in Salzburg with the Baroness for almost a year, becoming her closest friend and acquiring in the process his newfound interest in Mozart and modern painting. At war's end, he decided to return to the city of his birth, Veracruz. The Baroness understood and they said their farewells in Salzburg at the train station. Ray then headed for Switzerland to pick up the gold the Baron had insisted on paying him. After a brief stop in Munich, where he met and talked with a character named Hess that Ray described as "a real piece of work," he found the bank and the gold waiting for him in Zurich. He traveled south to Marseille and boarded a ship sailing for Panama. From Panama, he made his way to Mexico and eventually St. Louis, in order to "save my ass," as he reminded me.

Ray stopped his tale and looked out the window. The train was slowing down and the sun was just rising in the east. We were approaching the outskirts of Cleveland. Ray smiled to himself and reached into his vest, pulling out a packet of photographs and staring down at them.

"Well?" I asked. "Did she ever show you the special place?"

"That's the part you ain't gonna believe, Z. But I want you to look at something first. The Baroness let me take some photographs before I left."

"Photographs of what?"

"Paintings—portraits painted by Vermeer and Botticelli."

"Are they rare?"

"Yeah, you could say that, only I think the word 'rare' ain't nearly enough. These are portraits of the same girl." Ray stopped talking and looked at me for a reaction, then he said, "Vermeer lived almost two centuries later than Botticelli."

"Then . . . how is that possible?"

"You mean I've gotta explain it to you, Z? You can't figure that out?"

"She's Meq?"

"You got it." Ray handed me the photographs. "Look at her, Z. The Baroness told me her name is Susheela the Ninth. She's Meq, all right, but she ain't Egipurdiko or Egizahar."

The photographs were sharp and clear, but they were not in color. Ray described the colors for me, mentioning especially the green of the girl's eyes in the portrait by Vermeer. "If you've ever seen Vermeer's blues, then you'll know what I mean," Ray said. "Her eyes are the greenest damn green I've ever looked on, Z."

I studied the portraits closely, amazed and bewildered by what I saw. The girl was Meq without a doubt; her individual features, specifically her lips, were even similar to Opari's. However, there was one very obvious and unexplainable difference, a difference unlike any other difference between us. The Meq girl in both portraits was *black*.

"So the Baron was telling the truth," I said. "She was real."

"She sure was, and is, as far as anybody knows."

Just then, our train changed tracks for the approach into the rail yard. The jolt woke Mitch and he leaned out of his sleeping berth, trying to see out the window. "Where are we, Z?"

"Cleveland," I answered. "New York by tonight."

Ray winked and said, "There's something else I want you to see, Z, but let's wait until we're on our way to Spain, what do you say?"

I gave the photographs one last glance, then handed them back to him. "Those portraits are nothing short of amazing, Ray."

Ray winked again. "Ain't life grand, Z? You never know, do you?"

New York City is not a city for the faint of heart. It is the biggest, toughest, meanest city in America, and arguably the greatest. Anything and everything has or will happen in New York. Until you have experienced for yourself the size, sounds, smells, the pace of life, you cannot imagine how overwhelming it can be. As we were pulling into Pennsylvania Station, Ray said it best: "I love this place, but it can kick your ass."

It was well past working hours on a working day, yet there were still thousands of people coming and going through the huge terminal. Arrosa was there to greet us, however, and helped with the transfer of Unai and Usoa from Pennsylvania Station to our ship, the *Iona*. I saw a trace of sadness in her eyes, but she was efficient and the whole process took less than an hour. Ray was also a little sad. After I had introduced him to Arrosa, he immediately asked about Nova. Neither she nor Geaxi were present and the disappointment was evident on his face and in his eyes. Arrosa informed him that both of them were in Ithaca, New York, having left only two days earlier.

"Ithaca? What's in Ithaca?" I asked.

"You will have to ask Nova, señor. I only have the names of the men she was to meet—Theodore and Leopold Wharton. Geaxi accompanied her and also gave no explanation." Arrosa paused, then added, "I am thinking she might have seen something, señor, in a dream or vision. She was not herself."

Ray and I exchanged puzzled glances. I knew Geaxi had gone for one reason—to watch over Nova—but I had no idea what Nova might have seen. Her visions were powerful, private enigmas that came without warning.

Suddenly Mitch spoke out. "My daddy, if he's still alive, might be livin' in Ithaca. On my way back to St. Louis, I could spend a little time there, find out what's goin' on with Nova, and maybe pay him a visit. I never have before and this is as good a time as any."

"What?" I asked, completely surprised. "I have never heard you even mention him."

"It never came up, Z. Where do you think I got my middle name? My mama wanted me to never forget where he was from, so she gave me the name Ithaca." He paused. "I might have a sister somewhere, too."

I didn't know what to say. None of this was expected. I looked at Ray and he grinned, then adjusted his bowler and said, "Let's get somethin' to eat, what do you say?"

"Good idea," Mitch said.

"This way," Arrosa said to all of us, adjusting her own black beret. Minutes later we were in a taxi, weaving our way down Fifth Avenue to Arrosa's loft apartment, three blocks from Washington Square in Greenwich Village. We were due to set sail for Barcelona in twenty-four hours. That is a blink of the eye in New York City. I had hoped for the chance of seeing a ball game at the Polo Grounds, but that would have to wait for another time. Soon, I told myself. Soon.

The next day passed even quicker than I imagined and Mitch

saw us off in the evening, looking resplendent in a black tuxedo and white silk scarf. He had an appointment later to meet a man in Harlem about investing in a nightclub, saying, "I can't resist it, Z. This town is poppin'." I told him I would cable him as soon as we reached Barcelona. I also wondered why no one was there to say farewell to Arrosa and I asked if any of her friends knew she was leaving. She answered, "No, and this is not a problem, señor. I knew this might happen. It is better this way."

The *Iona* eased her way into a crowded and busy New York harbor, then steamed out to open seas. By midnight she had set a course east and south, bound for the Canary Islands, our only scheduled port of call before Barcelona.

I turned to Ray just before we said good night. "Any strange weather ahead, Weatherman?"

Ray grinned. "Nothin' I can see, Z."

There were few women on board the *Iona*. Most of the crew were Greek and spoke a dialect none of us had heard before. However, I needed no translation to understand what they meant when Arrosa was around. She did nothing to provoke them. Her clothes were simple and she wore no makeup or jewelry. None of their words or leering glances seemed to affect her, but I was uncomfortable with it and so was Ray.

The weather held across the mid-Atlantic and even though I was already missing Opari and the others, it felt good to be at sea again. The three of us spent much of our time on deck, walking or sitting in deck chairs. The passengers generally left us alone, and for the few who inquired, Ray and I were posing as brothers and Arrosa was our aunt. We never quite explained the reason for our trip and kept every conversation confined to the trivial. On the night before we reached the Canary Islands, Ray and I found ourselves alone, leaning on the railing near the stern, staring up at the great sweep of stars from horizon to horizon. My eyes drifted up and across, then focused on the constellation Pleiades, the Seven Sisters. The more I stared, the more they seemed to be whispering, sharing their secrets with each other at the very top of the sky.

I turned to Ray. "When are you going to show me the 'something else' concerning the Meq girl?"

"Tomorrow, Z. I got it hid away in a special place in my suitcase. I'll get it out when we dock. It's kind of fragile."

The next morning we made port in the beautiful deepwater harbor of Santa Cruz de Tenerife, a place Captain Woodget and I had visited several times for several reasons as smugglers. The Canary Islands were a haven and an oasis for us, as they had been for sailors and merchants for centuries. I learned later the Meq have known and passed through the islands for millennia. Unai himself told many tales involving the Guanche, a mysterious, tall, blond, bearded tribe who inhabited the islands two thousand years before Columbus sailed anywhere.

The harbor was busy with merchant ships and container ships of all sizes, most filled with bananas or tomatoes. There were some passenger ships and private vessels, but not many. The *Iona* steered a clear path through traffic and we docked safely about midmorning. We would only be in port for the day and nearly every passenger was on deck and planning on going ashore. Ray had his white shirtsleeves rolled up and Arrosa wore a red flower print sundress and sandals. The air was hot and dry and the sky was a sharp, bright blue.

Arrosa smiled. "Are we going ashore? I have never been to this place."

"Of course," I said. "But, Arrosa, there is something I must ask you and I hope you aren't offended."

"I will not be offended. What do you ask, Zianno?"

"Only that you wait ashore for Ray and me. He has . . . he has something to show me in private."

She laughed slightly. "That is not a problem, señor." She turned and pointed toward an area on the dock that was a hundred yards from the *Iona,* away from the stream of passengers and cargo handlers and close to a tangled stack of banana crates. "I will wait for you there," she said, adjusting her black beret to the proper angle.

"We won't be long, Arrosa. I promise."

"It shouldn't take but a few minutes," Ray said.

She laughed again. "It is not a problem, believe me. I will be waiting."

She turned to leave and Ray and I watched her until she was walking down the gangway, then we went directly to his cabin. He pulled out his battered suitcase and opened it on top of the small bed. There was a false bottom in the suitcase and Ray dismantled it carefully. Underneath, hidden in a padded compartment, lay a papyrus scroll, weighted at both ends with long pieces of carved ivory and rolled into a coil. Ray lifted the scroll gently and spread it across the bed. Once he had it completely secured, he shook his head and looked over at me.

"Can't make heads or tails out of what it says, Z, but I thought you ought to see it. Especially when I found out who had it and who it was for!"

I stared down at the stained, ancient paper. At first, I saw nothing on it except a group of red dots in the upper left section, possibly made with ocher. Then, below a fold and crack in the center of the papyrus, I saw a few blurry, faint scratches in black. I leaned over, looked closer, and was astounded.

"Who had this, Ray? Where did you get it?"

"In the 'special place' the Baroness Matilde talked about. It was a room, Z, a huge room in the oldest part of the castle, right up against the mountain. It used to be the entrance to a salt mine. One of the first von Steichens sealed it off, then converted it into an enormous space attached directly to the castle. Susheela the Ninth used it as her home for a thousand years. The papyrus was hers, Z. When she left without a word, she left this behind."

A few seconds passed in silence. I was dumbfounded. "How old was, or is, Susheela the Ninth?"

"I don't know, but the Baroness said the girl always referred to herself as 'the last of her kind.' "

"You said you thought I ought to see this because you found out who had it and who it was for. What did you mean?"

"I mean there was another piece of paper with the papyrus. It was written by Susheela the Ninth and gave instructions, in German, as to exactly who was supposed to see the papyrus. The Baroness had to translate the instructions for me, but not the name."

"What was the name?"

Ray grinned and picked up his bowler, spinning and twirling it on his finger. He opened his mouth to answer and just before he spoke, I stopped him. "Wait! Hush! Do you hear that?"

Ray was startled at first, then understood immediately that I was using my "ability." "I can't hear nothin', Z," he said.

I listened again to make sure the sound was what I thought.

Then it came again, this time in panic, and I realized who it was. "No! No!" the voice shouted. "Get off me, you pig!"

"Come on," I said to Ray and took off running for the gangway, dodging several people and pushing others to the side. Ray had no difficulty keeping pace. He was right on my heels and once we were down the gangway, I could hear the shouts and curses behind us of the people who had been knocked out of the way. I paid no attention and was in a full running stride.

"Where are we going?" Ray asked casually.

"Arrosa is in trouble!" I shouted back.

Ray caught up with me. "Did you ever get that Stone back?" he asked with a wink.

"Sure did," I said, tapping my pocket and slowing down to a trot. We were getting close. Even Ray could hear the struggle now. Ahead of us a jumble of crates filled with bananas were stacked one on top of the other in front of an open warehouse. On the opposite side of the crates Arrosa was being dragged into the warehouse. She was screaming in Spanish and fighting back.

Ray grabbed my sleeve. "Let me go first," he said. "If there's more than one, then they'll all go for me, and you can do your little trick with the rock. What do you say?"

"Go," I said without hesitation, then reached in my pocket and found the Stone.

Ray ran around the stacks of bananas, which were piled twenty feet high. Within seconds there were shouts and loud curses in Greek. There seemed to be at least three men attacking Arrosa. They were screaming back and forth and Ray was shouting in English to let the girl go. Arrosa was shouting, too, asking Ray in Spanish if I was with him.

I came around the last stack of bananas and as I reached my arm out to use the Stone, two thick, bare arms encircled me from behind and held me in a viselike grip. The man who grabbed me was heavyset and stank of sweat and stale rum. He held me in the air like a doll. My arms went numb and the Stone dropped out of my hand and rolled on the ground.

"Damn," Ray said. Someone even bigger was holding him in the same manner. I thought I had seen the man on board the *Iona*.

"Are you all right?" I shouted to Arrosa. She had quit struggling and was almost out of sight, being dragged inside the warehouse by a third man. The man had a knife pressed against her throat. His undershirt had been torn to shreds by her teeth and fingernails.

"Not for long," she shouted back, trying to sound brave. The man laughed and ran one hand through her hair, grabbing a fistful and holding it. Then, in a weak and terrified voice, Arrosa said, "I am scared, Zianno." The man laughed again in the shadows, telling her in Greek and Spanish, "You will love it, my flower."

Suddenly, in the blink of an eye, something happened that did not make sense, as if everything had stopped, or slowed down, or changed dimensions. The man dragging Arrosa fell silent and let go of her. Arrosa's bare legs rose off the ground slightly and her sandals floated off her feet and then moved in a flash, by themselves, into the shadows of the warehouse. There was a slapping sound from inside, then a yelp and a scream. The man in the undershirt appeared in the sunlight, staggering forward and unable to speak because his own knife was embedded in his throat. Blood shot from the wound spraying his undershirt and arms. His eyes rolled back in his head. He took three steps, then fell forward, falling directly on top of Arrosa's black beret. In the next second, the men holding Ray and me screamed in agony, cursing in Greek and letting go their grips as if they had been burned or shocked. Then they each began a series of involuntary tumbles and back somersaults, ending in a heap at the bottom of the tallest stack of crates. Something invisible had pulled or pushed them with great force and speed.

Ray and I looked at each other. Neither of us had moved a muscle. I started to reach for the Stone I had dropped, but before I could, it came to me. At a fairly rapid pace and in a gentle arc, like a baseball toss, the Stone rose from the ground and flew over to me. I caught it softly in one hand.

"What the . . ." Ray said and never finished. His mouth was hanging open.

Behind the two men, who were barely conscious, the stacked crates full of bananas began to shake and vibrate. In ten seconds they were falling in an avalanche of wood and bananas and buried the two men where they lay.

Arrosa crawled out of the shadows of the warehouse. She was barefoot and her red dress was torn and bloodied. There were several places on her neck and arms beginning to bruise. Still, she seemed to be all right.

A shadow moved in the open space between Ray and where I was standing. It appeared to leap and dance in a diagonal line. Something or someone was on top of the stacks behind me. I turned and saw a figure bounding down from crate to crate. In the glare of the sun, I couldn't make out who or what it was, but the movements were quick, graceful, intuitive. There was no doubt or hesitation about where to land or where next to leap. In seconds the figure had dropped eighteen feet, then hit the ground with both feet and started walking toward Ray and me.

He wore loose black trousers tucked into boots laced to the knees. His shirt was a simple white cotton tunic with intricate orange stitching. He was exactly my height and weight and looked exactly the same as the last time I had seen him, except the braid behind his left ear was now weighted with black onyx. He stopped in front of me. His "ghost eye" swirled with clouds. On his forefinger he wore a ring of star sapphire set in silver. He reached out and lightly tapped my hand, the one holding the Stone.

"You should learn to hold on to that, Zianno." Then he smiled, which I had not seen in a very long time. "Sorry I missed your birthday. I was . . . preoccupied."

He turned without another word and walked over to where Arrosa still sat on the ground, bewildered and exhausted. He gave her his hand to help her stand and steady herself.

"Arrosa Arginzoniz, no? Allow me to introduce myself. I am Umla-Meq, Egizahar Meq, through the tribe of Berones, protectors of the Stone of Memory. Please, call me Sailor, if you wish."

"*Sí,* señor. I know of your name."

"Are you hurt? Do you need medical attention of any kind?"

"No, no, I am fine. I should not have been waiting in this area. I should have known better."

"Nonsense. You are completely without blame. Those men were filth and refuse. I have seen men like them on these seas for longer than I care to remember. Are you certain that you have no serious injury?"

"Yes," Arrosa answered. She was looking down at Sailor, but she could have been on her knees. "*Gracias, señor, gracias,*" she kept repeating. "*Gracias.*"

"*De nada,* my dear."

Ray had silently walked over next to me. "Did Sailor do that?" he whispered.

"He sure did."

"How?"

"You know how. In the same way you can run fast and foretell the weather; the same way I can hear things from a great distance. What Sailor does is called telekinesis." Ray's mouth finally closed. He rubbed his chin, then mumbled something. "Damn," I think he said.

"I suggest we return to your ship, and quickly," Sailor said. "Someone might have questions about this and I feel no desire to answer them. Also, I have news of which you are unaware, news I regret I must deliver." He reached for the arm of Arrosa. "Are you ready, my dear?"

They made their way out of the jumble of broken crates and bananas, Arrosa walking barefoot and Sailor kicking a clear path with his boots. Ray picked up her sandals and I retrieved her bloodstained black beret. Once again, an old one, Umla-Meq, had shown me something fundamental about the Meq and living in the moment. Never take it for granted and never despair, it will pass. Ray saw it from a little different perspective. Just as we were about to walk up the gangway of the *Iona*, Ray looked up at Sailor ahead of us and said with a wink, "Who said you can't teach an old dog new tricks?"

I laughed, then suddenly remembered what we were doing before I heard Arrosa's screams. The scratches I found on the papyrus were not scratches at all. They were words, words written in the ancient Meq script that only I could read. "Ray," I said, "whose name is on that note from Susheela the Ninth? Who was meant to see the papyrus?"

Ray grinned and looked up the gangway at Sailor and Arrosa

stepping on board. "Him," he answered. "The name on the note is Umla-Meq."

Once we were on board and away from the other passengers, Sailor wasted no time in explaining his timely arrival. It was not a lucky accident. He had been waiting for us for days, even purchasing a ticket for passage on the final leg to Barcelona. When he saw Arrosa leaving the ship, he followed her, taking a position atop the banana crates. He was about to act just as Ray and I ran blindly, without thinking, directly into the danger and nearly paid the price. Sailor glared at both of us as he recounted this and I felt scolded. The heat of embarrassment hit my cheeks, but Sailor ignored my reaction and went on to say he bore sad news, especially for Ray and me. Arrosa offered to leave, saying she longed to soak in a hot bath for at least an hour. Sailor said he understood, but this news concerned her as well. Only a week earlier, Kepa Txopitea had died of a stroke while fishing in the Pyrenees with his son, Pello. He was a chieftain and father of the western clan of the tribe of Vardules. He was also my Aita and a wise and treasured friend to all four of us.

The news was not at all expected and stunned me. Each of us stood in silence for several moments, alone with our own memories of the old man. I started to speak and nothing came out. Then I was overcome with remorse and regret that I had not gone to see him when I could have, just after the war.

Sailor said, "I would not have missed the burial of Unai and Usoa, and now, with great respect, we shall bury them all together."

Another long silence hung in the air. All of us knew what was ahead of us and it was acknowledged without a word.

Ray finally broke the silence. "I got somethin' you ought to see, Sailor."

Sailor raised one eyebrow and unconsciously rubbed the star sapphire on his forefinger. "Then I will see it," he said and paused, facing Arrosa. "Whatever it may be, you are welcome to come along, Arrosa. Unai never kept anything from you and I will always honor his judgment."

"No, señor, please," Arrosa said, then smiled weakly. "Not this time. I want to be alone for a while and I need to rest."

"I understand," Sailor said, nodding once. "Then we will see you this evening for dinner, after we set sail. *Bueno?*"

"*Bueno.*" Arrosa glanced at each of us and smiled again. Ray handed her the sandals and I gave her the beret. She stared at the bloodstains and her smile slid away and vanished. There was a faint tremble in her bottom lip and her eyes welled a bit, but that was all. She turned to leave. "Thank you, Umla-Meq. Thank all of you," she said.

After she was out of sight, we began to walk back to Ray's cabin. Sailor said he wanted to tell us why he had been "out of touch" the past several months. As we walked and he talked, the huge volcanic mountain of Pico del Teide was visible far to the southwest. Wrapped in swirling clouds, the snowy peak reminded me of Sailor's "ghost eye."

It was common knowledge among the Meq that Sailor believed there was a Sixth Stone somewhere—lost, buried, stolen, no one knew, but Sailor firmly believed it existed. So he began by stating that he had gained access to evidence, the best in centuries, he added, and the evidence proved the Stone's existence and possible whereabouts. Then he said something that made little sense to me. It was the kind of statement that had troubled Trumoi-Meq and others. Sailor said, "Finding the Sixth Stone will reveal the true reason Unai and Usoa's baby died. Everything is there, gentlemen, everything is there." But instead of it sounding delusional or obsessive, it made me remember the words on the papyrus and the reason for Umla-Meq's name on the note became clear.

I burst out, "Stop, Sailor, and come with me. You must see what Ray has discovered. Now!"

Sailor and Ray had to run to keep up with me, much to the annoyance of Sailor, who kept complaining as we were running, saying, "Zianno, please, is this absolutely necessary? I am an old man." An American on board, a fat man in his fifties, was bumped by all three of us as we ran by. He yelled after us, "Goddamn kids! Watch where you're going, goddamnit!"

As soon as Ray opened the door to his cabin, I said to Sailor, "Look at this." The papyrus was still out on the bed. Ray said, "And look at this." He handed Sailor the note he had been carrying since leaving Salzburg. The writing on the note was in a neat black script, handwritten in German and signed *"Susheela the Ninth."* Her handwriting could be mistaken for any Giza's. The name Umla-Meq was clearly visible, appearing twice in the text. Sailor needed no translator to read the note and as he read, Ray related the story of the mysterious black Meq girl who had lived outside Salzburg for a thousand years with the papyrus in her possession, then disappeared, leaving behind the papyrus and the handwritten note and instructions. Ray concluded with, "Thought I'd try and get it to you. Never thought it'd be here, though."

"These things occur," Sailor said and glanced at me with a faint grin. I didn't say anything, but I realized he was back to being the same Sailor I had always known, not the frantic, angry, crazy Sailor I had last seen in Cornwall. He set the note aside without asking Ray one question, then touched the papyrus with his fingertips, tracing the surface until he found the tiny script in faded dark ocher near the center. He leaned over and examined it, not three inches away. Slowly, he turned his head and looked at me. "This is—" he started, but I finished the sentence for him.

"The same script that is in the Meq caves. Yes. Impossible, but true."

His "ghost eye" narrowed. "What does it say, Zianno?" he asked in a low drone.

"It begins," and I had to walk around the bed once in order to read the entire text. The tiny lines and half circles were written in the shape of a nautilus shell, beginning in the center and spiraling out to the end. Nine sentences, or "Steps," each one punctuated and separated by a miniature image of a handprint. "It begins with these words: *'Nine Steps of the Six,'* then nine lines follow in a spiral—*'The First One shall not know. The Second One shall not know. The Third One shall not know. The Fourth One shall not know. The Fifth One shall not know. The Living Change shall live within the Sixth One. The Five shall be drawn unto the Source Stone. The Living Change shall be Revealed. The Five shall be Extinguished.'* "

When I finished, I looked up and Sailor was staring out one of the two tiny portholes in Ray's cabin. The *Iona* was just getting under way and our next port of call was Barcelona. The whitewashed buildings of Santa Cruz de Tenerife were only a thin white stripe against the deep blue of sea and sky. "This confirms it," Sailor said evenly, then turned and stared Ray and me in the eye, one to one and back again. He had stopped rubbing the star sapphire and his hands were still. In the light his eyes were like black diamonds. "We must find the Sixth Stone, gentlemen," he said. "And I know where to begin."

"Where?" I asked.

"Cairo, then the upper cataracts of the Nile and beyond, possibly as far as Ethiopia."

"When?"

"As soon as we bury our friends."

I looked at Ray and he shrugged, knowing what I was thinking and possibly thinking or feeling something similar about Nova.

Sailor could see the reason for my hesitation in my eyes. However, he also knew something about me that could still be summoned and stirred, and he made me an offer I could not refuse, regardless of my desire to return to St. Louis and Opari. "Do you know the reason I could not tell you I would be here?" he asked. "Why only Mowsel and Pello knew my location? It was because someone has been tracing my movements and harassing me from a distance. Someone who believes in the Sixth Stone and has a piece of the same information as I . . . someone who will surely be on the same trail, either waiting or following . . . someone I will gladly help you kill in any manner you choose, Zianno. When Mowsel told me of the savage and senseless attack on Unai and Usoa, I made my decision. Xanti Otso shall no longer be tolerated. The 'Little Wolf,' the Fleur-du-Mal, must be eliminated and a trap could be set for him with the Sixth Stone. He will chase it like a rat after cheese." Sailor paused and looked at Ray, then back to me. "I also have something to give you, Zianno, something from Kepa. It was sent to me by Pello, along with instructions that Kepa wanted you to have it." He bent down and extracted a neatly folded red beret tucked inside the top of his boot. He shook it out and handed it to me.

For some reason, I glanced at Ray's tattered and torn bowler resting on a chair. "Ray," I said, "you need a new look for this century. I want you to have Kepa's beret."

Ray took the beret and examined it, feeling the texture of the old woven wool, then looked over to his bowler. "It is a fine-looking beret, Z. And a damn nice color of red."

"Well, what do you think?"

"I think you're right. I think I need a change and I think we ought to go with Sailor. The time is right, Z."

I realized I had already made my decision and I agreed with him. I turned to Sailor. "What about Arrosa?"

"If she wishes to return to New York, she may do so, or if she wishes to remain with Pello, it will be arranged. Whatever she chooses to do, someone from Kepa's camp will watch over her."

I nodded. "All right, then. I'm in."

"Good, good," Sailor said, then added cryptically, *"Keep Ithaka always in your mind. Arriving there is what you are destined for."*

Ray and I exchanged curious glances. "How do you know about Ithaca?" I asked.

"Ithaca?" Sailor said. His "ghost eye" focused in on me. "I was quoting lines from a poem."

"Oh," I said and left it alone.

"I'm hungry," Ray blurted out. "Is it too early to find somethin' to eat on this ship?"

"Of course not," Sailor answered. "Remember, Ray, we are only children. We do not know any better."

Ray laughed and said, "Let's go." He placed Kepa's red beret on his head at a precise angle, as if he had been wearing it for centuries. He and Sailor started for the door. Before we were out of the room, Ray said, "You know, Sailor, when I was travelin' with the Baron, many times we were near the country you're talkin' about—the Blue Nile and Ethiopia and those parts." Sailor looked at Ray with surprise and admiration. Ray went on, "That's right. I nearly got my head chopped off three times and practically starved to death on several occasions. Then I got my foot stomped on by a packhorse, took a spear point in the thigh, and was poisoned four separate times. Beautiful country, though. Beautiful."

I laughed to myself and followed behind, listening to every word. After all, if the truth is, in fact, unknowable, then a wise man always follows the man with the beret.

PART II

Not to know what is in one's past
is to remain perpetually a child.

—CICERO

4

OLAGARRO

(OCTOPUS)

The dying mariner approaches land after a long and troubled journey at sea. He drifts into the shallow pools of a rocky cove with nothing left but his secret, the secret he has stolen and smuggled to this unknown, distant place. Yet, he cannot take it ashore. He must leave it and hide it carefully until the time comes when it will be needed. But where can he hide it? Who can protect it? Who can he trust? Underwater, darting through the shallows, something passes silently from rock to rock. Shy, intelligent, reclusive, with three hearts and eight arms, the octopus moves, blending into the surroundings, changing color, poisoning and paralyzing any enemy if necessary, then disappearing behind a black cloud into hidden holes, crevices, caves, dens, and grottoes, not to be seen, not to be found. Yes, the mariner decides, the octopus is the one.

Somewhere between the Balearic Islands and the harbor of Barcelona, Sailor disappeared on board the *Iona*. None of us were surprised. Ray and I were aware and Arrosa suspected that Sailor rarely entered a country or continent legally. He is as good or better than any Meq at using false papers and identities; however, he prefers not to make use of them. The risk is unnecessary and he continues the practice. He would never admit it, but I think he does it simply for the thrill.

The *Iona* slowly found her berth among the crowded waters of the old port. It was late morning and the sun was high and bright in a clear blue sky. Ray was excited. He said, "I heard this city is as wild as New Orleans." Arrosa said she had never heard that before, but she did say, "Barcelona is unique among all cities." She was very familiar with Barcelona and all of Catalonia. Her fluency in Catalan even helped speed us through customs and the stack of paperwork concerning the caskets of Unai and Usoa. We were each in a good mood, perhaps too much so. When Pello met us at the exit gate and I looked into his eyes, I saw a certain kind of pain that brought me back instantly to the true and somber reason for our visit—we were here to bury loved ones. I could see clearly that Pello had loved no one more than his father, Kepa Txopitea. The loss in his eyes was infinite.

"I . . . I am sorry, Pello," I said.

He now wore a blue beret instead of red. He was leaning on his cane and shifted his weight slightly, then removed his beret. His hair had turned completely gray in the six months since I had seen him last. "Thank you, señor," he said softly. "My father was an old man and lived a long, good life." I could still see the soldier in the back of Pello's eyes, but the shepherd was in his voice. Pello and Kepa had shared a deep and special bond. Kepa was in his nineties when he died and Pello was his youngest son. Ever since Pello was born, Kepa had given him the friendship of a brother, the love of a father, and the wisdom of a grandfather, all in one. That is a lot to lose.

Ray said, "Long time no see, Pello."

"*Sí*, señor," Pello said, and he noticed Ray was wearing Kepa's beret. He looked at me, then back to Ray, then back at me.

"I thought Ray should have it," I said simply, hoping I had not offended him.

Slowly, a smile spread across Pello's angular face. *"Sí, sí,"* he said, leaning down to give Ray a warm embrace. He welcomed Arrosa and kissed her on both cheeks several times. She told him she was glad to be home and asked about Koldo, a name I had not heard her mention before. "He is with the motor cars in Zaragoza," Pello answered. "He waits for us there."

"Who is Koldo?" I asked.

"My son, Zianno. He and Arrosa grew up together in our family's *baserri.*" Pello looked closer at Arrosa, then reached out and cupped her chin in his hand. Gently, he turned her face right and left. "You have become a beautiful woman, Arrosa. Koldo will be pleased to see you." He smiled again and looked at me. "Come, señor, all is taken care of here. Our train leaves in three hours. Is there anywhere you wish to go? Perhaps the bank, no?"

"Yes, Pello. I almost forgot." I gave him the name and address that Owen had given me. "Do you know this place?"

"Sí. It is not far, and near to where we have an appointment."

"Where is that?"

"A district that is becoming notorious, I am afraid, in the lower Raval, between Sant Pau and the sea."

"What sort of appointment?"

"Someone is waiting for us." Pello explained no further and led the way out of the waterfront, walking with a cane and a limp, but never slowing down.

We found the bank within half an hour and were lucky to arrive when we did. They were about to close for the midday meal and a siesta. Pello made sure there were no problems with the transaction and Arrosa spoke Catalan with the employees.

We were out in minutes. We walked down La Rambla until we entered the district Pello had mentioned earlier, the tiny network of alleys and avenues later known as Barrio Chino, or Chinatown. It was a haven for drifters, criminals, pimps, prostitutes, gamblers, and drug dealers.

Ray said, "Told you so, Z . . . just like New Orleans."

But as we entered an alley off the Nou de la Rambla, I thought the district felt more dangerous and sordid than New Orleans ever had. The only obvious similarity was the fact that we were ignored as children. Orphans, refugees, and runaways were no strangers here. I saw girls with faces no older than mine leaning over the balconies and standing in the doorways of several brothels. The bars and a few cabarets were open to anyone, anytime. Pello walked with one arm around Arrosa's shoulder and Arrosa welcomed it.

Finally, we paused in front of a bar and restaurant with a blue awning over the doorway. In cracked and faded gold letters across the awning were the Catalan words Las Sis Caracoles, or The Six Snails. It seemed the only pleasant odors in the whole district were emanating from inside. Pello led the way and we left the bright sunlight for the darkness of a bar lit with candles and a single lightbulb over the cash register. The bar itself ran along one side of the room and a dozen or so tables lined the other. We walked past two merchant seamen sitting at the bar and stopped in front of the last table, which was lit by a candle placed in the center. There was no tablecloth. The candle dripped and spilled over the edge of its holder and hardened in pools over the years of graffiti carved into the wood. Five stools encircled the table and we sat down on four of them. On the fifth, leaning forward, ignoring our arrival completely, and lustily consuming a steaming dish of calamari and black rice, sat Sailor.

"You are late," he said, pausing for a large gulp of cider. "Pello, it is good to see you are well. You know what your father meant to me."

"*Sí*, señor," Pello said.

Without a mention of how or when he left the *Iona*, Sailor motioned to a man behind the bar and thirty seconds later plates of olives, marinated anchovies, white asparagus, and a salad I did not recognize were brought to the table.

Arrosa seemed baffled as well. *"Que es?"* she asked the girl setting out the dishes.

"Pulpo gallego," she answered.

I looked at Sailor. "Octopus Galician style," he said, then added with a wink of his "ghost eye," "eat it, Zianno, it is delicious."

So for the next hour and a half, we ate and drank. What little we did say concerned only where we were going from Barcelona. Sailor asked Pello about the weather, the snowmelt in the upper valleys, problems with the Spanish Civil Guard, what effect the Great War had on the Basque homelands, and whether a few old fishermen that he and Kepa had known were still alive. They were not.

As we got up to leave and started for the door, Sailor grabbed my sleeve and pulled me aside. "Do you feel it, Zianno?"

"Feel what?"

"Look around, observe. Go slowly. Look with your senses; look through this place, backward and forward in time."

I did what he said and turned twice in a slow circle. After scanning every table against the wall and every stool at the bar, I noticed a room at the rear I had not seen before, dark and hidden from view behind a beaded curtain. I felt it immediately—the prickly sensation in every nerve end, the net descending.

Sailor saw my recognition. "He was here, Zianno, and not long ago. The Fleur-du-Mal was here!"

"Yes," I said, simple and dull as a heartbeat. "He was."

Ray walked to where Sailor and I were standing. He glanced at Sailor, then spoke to me. "Have we got a problem?"

"Sure do."

Ray looked around slowly, then stared directly toward the room behind the beads. He rubbed the back of his neck as if something had tickled him. "And the problem has been here, right?"

I didn't answer. He knew who it was. The three of us turned and walked out the door, hurrying to catch up with Pello and Arrosa. We had a duty and a promise to keep high in the western Pyrenees. Outside in the open air and sunshine, something else occurred to me. I looked at Sailor. "Was that an accident or did he know we would be there and feel his presence?"

Sailor kept walking. He was staring straight ahead, looking past or through a thousand faces in the street. His jaw tightened and his "ghost eye" narrowed against the light. "I do not know, Zianno." He was angry. Usoa had told me long ago: "You do not find Sailor, he finds you." The current circumstance had abused his pride as much as anything. "But we shall find out," he said, "I assure you." Because of the unpredictable nature of the Fleur-du-Mal, I wondered just how long it might be before we knew the answer. It came sooner than I expected.

Pello and Arrosa were waiting for us on the broad promenade of Las Ramblas. Pello announced we had one more appointment, not a mile away, but instead of walking toward the city, we headed back in the direction of the waterfront. Most people were off the streets taking their afternoon siesta and Pello quickly found the narrow, almost invisible alley where our meeting was to take place. At the end of the alley was a tiny bar called Agua and inside there was only one customer, a boy sitting at a little round table near the open door. The boy was about twelve years old with dark eyes and dark hair curling over and around his ears. He wore leather boots laced to the knees, baggy black trousers, a simple cotton shirt with no collar, and a blue kerchief tied loosely around his neck. He was drinking a glass of beer and as he wiped his mouth after a large slurp, he smiled. He was missing a front tooth. A French naval officer's cap lay on the table in front of him. He picked it up and tossed it to Sailor.

Sailor looked the cap over closely. "Am I to assume you are now serving the country of France?"

The boy laughed and motioned for us to sit. "I only serve the Meq, you old pirate. I thought you might like it."

"Yes, well, it was a generous thought, Mowsel."

Mowsel, or Trumoi-Meq, was the oldest living Meq. He was born before the time of Those-Who-Fled, several generations before Sailor and Opari. His independence was legendary and with his deep knowledge of our past, he seemed to me like a caretaker of all things Meq, a protector of "what was" along with great concern for "what will be." It was likely that his un-expected appearance in Barcelona had an immediate reason and purpose. He and Sailor had known each other for almost three thousand years. In that time, they had developed a kind of shorthand between them. A single nod, shrug, or remark from one could tell the other all he needed to know. Sailor understood everything in seconds and knew with certainty that the Fleur-du-Mal's presence at The Six Snails was no accident or coincidence.

"We found the room at the rear, behind the beads," Sailor said. "How long has it been?"

"Less than a week," Mowsel answered, then turned and looked at Ray, glancing briefly at Kepa's beret. "You must be Ray Ytuarte," he said. "I was told you were missing. My name is Trumoi-Meq. Call me Mowsel, Ray." He took Ray's hand in his, placed a cube of salt in his palm, and closed Ray's fingers around it. *"Egibizirik bilatu."* It was the most informal formal greeting I had ever witnessed.

Without hesitating, Ray said, "You bet."

At the same time, Pello was backing out the door with Arrosa. He was well aware that Mowsel had something to say in private. He told us they would be waiting at the entrance to the alley, then pivoted on his cane and walked away.

Trumoi-Meq turned to me and nodded. "Zianno Zezen," he said, grinning.

"Mowsel," I said, nodding back. "How are you?"

"I am well, except I think you are already missing St. Louis, no?"

"Is it that obvious?"

"It is common, it is common. Now, you must listen to me." Mowsel turned to face Sailor. "The Fleur-du-Mal was here to meet with Giles Xuereb, against Giles's wishes, according to my source. He wanted the same information Giles gave to you—the possible location of the Octopus."

"How?" Sailor almost shouted. "How was he aware that Giles had met with me?"

"You know our Xanti Otso, Sailor. He seems to have networks within networks."

"What is the Octopus?" I asked.

"A box," Sailor answered. "A very old box made of onyx and serpentine with the image of an octopus inlaid in lapis lazuli on the top. Its origin is unknown, but it was last seen on Crete in the city of Knossos, before the island of Thera exploded. After that, it disappeared. However, it is not the box, it is what the box supposedly contains that interests me . . . and the Fleur-du-Mal."

"The Sixth Stone," Ray said.

"That is correct, Ray. And, Ray, I think you should let Mowsel see those photographs you made in Salzburg. Now."

Ray handed over the small packet with the two photographs. Mowsel studied them for only a second and the color seemed to drain from his face. He looked up at Ray and stared at Sailor in disbelief. "Hail, Hadrian! Am I to understand that these are portraits of Susheela the Ninth?"

"Yes."

"Truly?"

"Yes. Truly." Sailor glanced at Ray and me. "I should have told you both on the *Iona*. Susheela the Ninth is a name I have heard before. For centuries, she was rumored to be the only Meq older than Trumoi-Meq. This is the first time there has been any proof of her existence. Also, there is a theory she is connected in some way to the Octopus, though all of this is speculation, or was, until Ray showed me the papyrus and the note."

"Now I am confused," Mowsel interrupted.

"I will explain all to you later, but tell me, Mowsel, do you know where he went from Barcelona?"

"He forced Giles to leave with him, using threats to his sister, I believe. They left for Giles's Mediterranean farm."

"Which one?"

"The one on Gozo. His 'little home above the cave,' as he calls it." Mowsel then looked out the open doorway toward the entrance to the alley, where Pello and Arrosa waited. "You will have to leave tonight, Sailor. I found a ship for you, all of you, but you must set sail tonight. The captain is a former officer in the French navy. His missions these days are of a more independent nature. He knows of us and can be trusted. The Fleur-du-Mal is sailing on a much slower vessel, a passenger ship. This man will catch him if it is possible."

Sailor followed Mowsel's gaze with his own eyes. "Does Pello know we will be leaving?"

"Yes. He is at peace with it. You will not offend him. Pello, Arrosa, and I will attend to Unai, Usoa, and Kepa. Still, it is your choice. Each of you must decide what you must do."

For Sailor there was no choice. His decision had already been made, and without asking, I knew Ray felt the same. In my heart, so did I. We were going after the Fleur-du-Mal and that was that. The guilt of breaking a promise and not saying a proper farewell to our friends would have to be the price. All paths of action have a toll. Revenge has several.

Pello and Arrosa walked with us to the docks. Awkwardly, we all embraced in a great rush. I would miss Arrosa and told her so, then thanked her for everything she had done. She smiled and said, "I think it is I, señor, who should be thanking all of you. Especially you," she added, dropping her smile and looking straight at Sailor. Sailor nodded in silence. Pello told me I would have to come to the Pyrenees when our business was concluded and I promised I would, for Kepa's memory and my own peace of mind. Mowsel said he expected to rejoin them on the train "somewhere between here and Zaragoza." Then Pello and Arrosa were gone, into the streets of Barcelona and eventually into the mountains of northern Spain.

"Come," Mowsel said, "we have much to do."

The last rays of sunlight were fading fast by the time we had transferred and loaded everything we needed onto the *Emme,* our new ship and home at sea. At first glance, she appeared to be a simple, somewhat altered, small schooner, maybe sixty-five or seventy feet in length and no more than twenty across. In reality she was something else entirely. She had been cleverly refitted on and belowdecks with hidden state-of-the-art navigation equipment, armaments, diving accoutrements, and bolted down between two central bulkheads, a specially built lightweight Rolls-Royce engine that powered two concealed propellers in the rear. She had a shallow draft and could sail close to the wind. Painted dark blue and black, and almost invisible in deep water or at night, the *Emme* was beautiful, fast, and dangerous. I was impressed, as was Sailor, who commented that his favorite vessel to sail had always been the schooner.

It was obvious the ship had experience in clandestine missions. However, it was difficult to imagine from the appearance, attitude, and manners of the ship's three-man crew and captain. The crew was young, late twenties or early thirties, and the captain looked to be only a few years older, yet they all were extremely polite and at ease around us. They each spoke softly, in English laced with varying degrees of a French accent. Two of the crew had neatly trimmed full beards, the third was clean-shaven, and the captain wore a goatee, which was sprinkled here and there with gray. Mowsel introduced him simply as "Captain B" and the others went by nicknames. Together, they made an efficient unit, practiced and precise, but relaxed.

We were given private cabins and Captain B led us on a short tour of his ship, pointing out everything we would need to know. Then he mentioned that if we got to the Balearics by midnight we might catch a good ride on a little breeze coming out of Africa. I looked at Ray to see if that could mean a storm was brewing, but he shook his head and mouthed the word "nothin'." Captain B said we should leave soon and Trumoi-Meq asked if we could have a few minutes alone before we set sail. We gathered in Sailor's cabin and Mowsel spoke to him first.

"This Giza, Captain B, is aware of who we are and can be trusted completely."

"I assumed as much," Sailor said.

Mowsel paused, staring into Sailor's "ghost eye." "I think we should attempt to contact Zeru-Meq."

"No, no, please. A waste of time, I tell you, an absolute waste of time. That tree will not bear fruit, old friend. Ask Zianno. He remembers how troublesome that can be."

I looked at Sailor, then Mowsel. "How can Zeru-Meq help?"

"Have Sailor tell you about the death of Aitor, your grandfather, Zianno."

I stared at Sailor and my mouth dropped open. "What do you know? Why have you never mentioned this before?"

"You never asked," he said flatly.

Instantly, blood came rushing to my face. I was glaring at Sailor. "That is no excuse!"

"Damn, Z," Ray interrupted. "Settle down, will you? I be-

lieve you kept a couple of things from me, if I'm not mistaken."
He grinned and tapped me on the forehead.

"You're right," I said. I felt foolish and caught. "I'm sorry,
Sailor."

"Forget it, Zianno. Apology is unnecessary. I will tell you
what I know in the next few days, then you decide for yourself
how Zeru-Meq can help."

I nodded and turned back to Trumoi-Meq. "Please get word
to Owen Bramley, as soon as you are able. Tell him everything.
They are expecting us back in St. Louis. They'll want to know."

"I will."

"Mowsel?" Ray asked in a tone unusual for him. He almost
sounded meek. "Try to find somethin' out about Nova, would
you?"

"I will." He smiled and I stared into the gap of his missing
tooth. "Hail Hadrian," he said, then laughed and turned to go
ashore. "Good luck," he added, "it will likely be in short supply.
By the way, in case you might need to know, the captain's real
name is Boutrain. And, Zianno, once you return and have the
time to teach me, I want to learn to read the 'old script.' "

I raised my hand and held it palm out, fingers slightly spread,
facing Trumoi-Meq. "I will," I said. He shut the door behind
him and in a matter of seconds was off the *Emme* and disappearing into the early evening crowds that would only increase and
swell through the night, from the waterfront all the way up Las
Ramblas until early the next morning. By then the *Emme* would
be well on her way through the Balearics and Mowsel would be
somewhere on board a train for Zaragoza. And I would have
dreamed of a young man wearing a faded red beret. He looked
exactly like my papa, but he was not. His name was Aitor and he

was reaching into a pool of water. He was reaching for the Octopus. It was the dead of night and he was not alone. Someone
was behind him, whispering his name, laughing. Something
long and shiny was in his hand.

The first four days on board the *Emme* went smoothly. We sailed
far to the south, then caught the "breeze" Captain B was expecting out of Africa. We rode it east through the Strait of Sicily
and nearly all the way to Gozo. Captain B proved to be a con-
summate sailor and it became clear his crew respected his ability
as well as his authority. I learned early when I first went to sea
with Captain Woodget that a sailor honors few things more than
good seamanship. Even Umla-Meq, an expert and veteran at
sea for centuries, watched and praised Captain B for maintaining maximum speed while exercising minimum maneuvering.
"Using this complex rigging, keeping the speed he is keeping,"
Sailor said, "one has to know what one is doing."

I kept waiting for the moment Sailor would get around to
telling me about the Fleur-du-Mal and the death of my grandfather. However, I also knew he was once again trying to teach
me patience, and I was trying to learn. I just wasn't a very good
student.

Ray enjoyed this type of ship and this way of sailing. He and
Captain B made fast friends and Ray spent most of his time
alongside him at the wheel. The air was clean, the food was
good, and the whole experience seemed to sharpen his mind
and bring out the "Weatherman." He began sensing something
in every gust of wind, change of light, or shape of cloud. He
sounded a little crazy at first, but I assured Captain B that Ray
was authentic and dependable. If Ray said we were heading into

trouble, I told Captain B he should heed Ray's advice. And that is precisely what happened.

On the fifth day out, Ray said he felt something brewing quickly, "A big blow from the south, gale force for sure." Sailor and I looked at Captain B, who did not hesitate. He stuck out his chin slightly, stroked his goatee once, and gave the orders to turn sharply north, maintaining a north-northeast heading indefinitely. In two hours we received word that a sirocco, filled with dust from northern Africa, was blowing with cyclone force winds and about to cover Malta and Gozo. Because of Ray, the *Emme* and all aboard were spared a possible catastrophe. Captain B handed out cigars for everyone and then toasted Ray for his rare gift. Unfortunately, there was one serious consequence from our escape.

Three and a half days later we anchored in Mgarr Harbor and made our way ashore. We followed a winding trail through the hills beyond until we found Giles Xuereb's "little home above the cave." Giles was there and he was alive, barely. The Fleur-du-Mal was gone. We had missed him by no more than an hour or two. None of us knew it at the time, of course, and even if we had known, none of us would have regretted Captain B's decision. It was the right one, the only one. However, those three and a half days cost us the next three and a half years and very nearly the life of a trusted friend of the Meq.

Giles Xuereb had long been considered to be many things by many people. He was the last heir to an old Maltese fortune, a dealer in illegal antiquities and semiprecious stones, a master forger, a former professor of religious philosophy at Cambridge, tall, dark, and handsome. As a result of the Fleur-du-Mal's handiwork, he would never again be considered handsome, but at least he was still alive. Giles was lying unconscious and chained to the massive oak table in the center of his kitchen. His entire face and body were covered in hundreds of bleeding cuts and slashes, carved in a distinct and complex pattern, ranging in length from half-inch "thorns" to whole "roses" in full bloom, each drawn in a single stroke with the blade of a stiletto.

Sailor found some water and let a few drops spill onto Giles's lips, which helped him regain consciousness. He tried to smile once he recognized Sailor's face. Then the pain hit. He winced, trembled, and passed out again. We dressed his wounds as best we could, but he would need a doctor as soon as possible, followed by an extended rehabilitation in the hospital. Sailor guessed the Fleur-du-Mal had been torturing Giles for information, or had already obtained it and thought Giles had lied to him, which would have been worse. "Much worse," I added. Sailor said Giles probably would have tried to trick the Fleur-du-Mal rather than betray the contract they had together. It was the way his family had conducted business affairs since the Middle Ages. Giles happened to be the last in a long bloodline of honest pirates, which was the very reason the Meq had begun a relationship with Giles's family in the first place. Sailor knew that and the Fleur-du-Mal knew that.

"There is something more, Zianno," Sailor said slowly. He stared into my eyes, making sure he had my attention. "The Fleur-du-Mal may have done this to send a message."

"A message to whom?" I asked. "The Meq?"

"No. More specific than that." He paused again. "This is the exact method the Fleur-du-Mal employed to . . . to torture and kill your grandfather, Aitor. This could be a message for you, Zianno. His aberrant mind compels him to play games when he kills. He may be saying he knows you are with me. This may only be his opening move."

"Goddamnit!" Ray shouted, stomping the stone floor and slapping his beret against his leg. "He has to go, Z! We need to take that murderin' son of a bitch out!"

"I know," I said, but Sailor's words had stunned me. Why would the Fleur-du-Mal do that? What would so possess him to do something so cruel? What did my grandfather know?

Sailor was genuinely concerned about Giles and his condition. Every day all of us would ferry over to Malta and the hospital in Valletta to visit him. He drifted in and out of consciousness for five days, then on the morning of the sixth day he was able to speak and he and Sailor spoke to each other in whispers. They used Maltese, Giles's native tongue and a language I had never heard. Even in slow, hoarse whispers, it sounded distinguished and elegant. Once we were out of the hospital, Sailor was openly relieved that Giles was going to live, but concerned about what Giles had told him.

"We shall see if he acted fearlessly or foolishly," Sailor said.

"What did he do?" I asked.

"He did indeed lie to the Fleur-du-Mal."

"We already assumed that."

"Yes, however, the Fleur-du-Mal *believed* him. That will surely be a death sentence for Giles when he realizes the truth."

"Not if we find him first," Ray said.

"Yes," Sailor said, but I could hear the doubt in his voice.

"What did Giles lie about?" I asked.

"What else? He lied about the Octopus. He told him the box was inlaid with ruby instead of lapis lazuli and the trail to find it begins in Damascus, not Cairo. That means we have an advantage in our search, but Giles will still be here, helpless and defenseless against the Fleur-du-Mal's anger when he eventually discovers the truth, and he will."

"How can we protect Giles?"

"We cannot. We must find the Octopus before the Fleur-du-Mal finds the truth. Then we shall bait the trap. It is that simple."

"That don't sound like it will be too easy," Ray said.

"No," Sailor almost whispered, "it will not."

Captain B and his crew had the *Emme* restocked, rigged, and ready to sail by noon of the following day. We would have raised anchor immediately, but Sailor and I were late returning from Valletta, where Sailor wanted to send a cable to Pello. The cable was actually a coded message to Mowsel. Translated, it read, "Find Zeru-Meq now—Giles/Aitor a fact." While we were there, I wrote and posted a quick letter to Opari in St. Louis. I told her we were on our way to Egypt and I would dream of her every night—I would dream of her face, her voice, her lips . . . her gift.

On the way back to the *Emme,* I asked Sailor why he and Mowsel thought Zeru-Meq might be able to help.

"He might be able to unravel the demented puzzle driving the Fleur-du-Mal and his aberrations," Sailor said. "After the death of Aitor, Mowsel suspected it. Now, with the mutilation of Giles, I agree with him. Aitor discovered something about the Fleur-du-Mal that evoked a vicious response. Mowsel thinks Zeru-Meq may know what it was. I have my own thoughts on the matter, but they are only speculations."

We walked a few paces in silence. I was confused. "Tell me about my grandfather," I said.

"That will take some time and make us late for our departure."

"Then make us late, Sailor. I want to know now."

"Of course. I understand." Sailor stopped walking and motioned for us to sit together on a low stone wall just to our left. From there we could see the harbor and the vast blue Mediterranean beyond. "The murder happened there," he said, pointing north across the sea, "1,739 years ago on the western coast of Italy, near a fishing village along the Gulf of Salerno. The village is where your father was born and the murder occurred on the same night as his birth, a cruel irony that was neither accident nor coincidence.

"Your grandfather and your grandmother, Itzia, before and after they crossed in the Zeharkatu, were a uniquely gifted pair. I used to visit them at least once a year, if only to hear Aitor talk for hours about how it felt, biologically and psychologically, to age. He was obsessed with the science of it. Both he and Itzia possessed keen and curious minds and both had eclectic interests that led them all across the Mediterranean, Near East, and the shores of the Black Sea. Along with being an avid fisherman, Aitor was a student of tidal pools and marine life in coastal waters. He studied every species, but after the Zeharkatu, focused his studies on the cephalopod mollusks, particularly the octopus. Itzia was an expert in the medical sciences and studied for a time under the tutelage of an odd and brilliant Giza, the Greek physician Galen. Oddly, it was Galen who gave Aitor the first bit of information that inadvertently led to his death.

"Also, you must remember, Zianno, at this time the Fleur-du-Mal was not of much concern to the Meq. We followed him from a distance, disapproving, of course, but uninvolved. Aitor had even met him on three separate occasions over the previous two hundred years. They had exchanged a few unpleasant remarks and Aitor was not impressed, being repulsed by Xanti Otso's mind and presence. During that time, the Fleur-du-Mal was extremely active and proud of it. Assassinations were rampant and he was in demand. However, to our knowledge, he had not yet killed or tortured one of us.

"Itzia said Galen knew she was Meq and became a trusted friend. He also knew of Aitor's fascination with marine biology, especially the octopus. Apparently, on one long night in front of the fire, Galen told Aitor about a nefarious man, an opium dealer, he had encountered on the island of Crete. The man told Galen about a strange green-eyed boy who never seemed to age. The boy kept his hair tied in the back with a green ribbon and he wore red ruby earrings. Galen did not know the Fleur-du-Mal. What he thought Aitor might be interested in was the fact that the boy was an addict, and in his opium stupor would always ask, "Where is the octopus? Where is the octopus?" Galen thought the story was hilarious. Aitor was intrigued. A year later, Aitor was traveling to Crete concerning another matter. By the evening of his second day there, he was in the streets of Iraklion and the surrounding countryside asking guarded questions and searching for the opium dealer. After a week of disappointment, he finally located the man. The poor fellow had sunk into the depths of addiction himself. He was emaciated, lost and hopeless, but he happened to be lucid on the afternoon Aitor visited him. Whatever secret Aitor learned about the Fleur-du-Mal was learned there. It could not have simply been the fact that the man exposed the Fleur-du-Mal as an ad-

dict. His drug use was legendary and only one of his minor de-
pravities. Much later, I discovered the opium dealer had been
brutally murdered and decapitated shortly after Aitor's conversation with him. That is when I first realized the extent of the
Fleur-du-Mal's network of information and how fast he can act
upon it. In Aitor's case, however, he did not. His confrontation
with Aitor was much more diabolical. He waited a full two
years, until Itzia became pregnant with your father, then on the
night of his birth, appeared out of the darkness unasked and
unannounced on Aitor's doorstep. Itzia told me later she was in
bed with her newborn and Aitor was sitting next to her. Aitor
rose to answer the knock at the door, kissed her on the cheek,
and walked out of the room. She never saw him again. She said
she heard a raspy voice, a boy's voice, congratulate Aitor, then
ask him something about an octopus, after which Aitor raised
his voice, saying "Outside with this!" and they left. The next
morning, Aitor was found near a tide pool in the same condition in which we found Giles, except Aitor's throat had been slit
and he had been scalped. A green ribbon was woven into the
hair and the whole scalp had been placed over Aitor's face. No
notes, no reasons, nothing. The Fleur-du-Mal disappeared."

I was stunned and sickened and speechless for several moments. Finally, I asked, "Was Zeru-Meq informed of the murder?"

"Yes."

"What was his reaction?"

"He wept," Sailor said in a flat monotone. "He wept and then
wandered into the Caucasus without a word."

"Zeru-Meq told me in China he thought the Fleur-du-Mal
was only a 'sad, dangerous pilgrim.' "

"Yes, and Zeru-Meq likes to think of himself as seeking a

higher truth, when in fact he lives a lie. He could help to end this madness and he knows it. He is aware of something about the Fleur-du-Mal that we are not, likely the truth concerning the deaths of his parents. While she was living, Zeru-Meq had always been protective of his sister, Hilargi, the Fleur-du-Mal's mother. The father I never knew. Perhaps, Zeru-Meq bears a secret guilt. It is possible. After Aitor, it is not important. Guilt was not acceptable as an excuse for his silence. He can stop this insanity and he has not, he does not." Sailor paused, then sighed. "Still, I suppose we must try again."

I let Sailor's words and images sink in permanently. Below us, the blue Mediterranean spread out in all directions. "Let's go to Cairo," I said.

Sailor unconsciously twirled the blue star sapphire on his forefinger, then stood up. "Yes," he said, "Cairo it is."

There were fair winds every day and clear skies every night on our sail south and east. I watched the stars for hours at a time, pacing the ship. I could not get the image of Aitor out of my mind and had trouble sleeping. As we approached Egypt, the summer heat became intense and oppressive, and on the night before we made landfall, I awoke after a long, strange dream. I had dreamed I was observing a card game from a distance. We were in a loud, smoke-filled saloon in the Far East, somewhere near the sea. The time was in the past, though it felt like the present. There were several men sitting around a large, round table littered with whiskey bottles, glasses, lit cigars in ashtrays, poker chips, and money. One man was shoving all his chips and gold coins across the table to another man, whom I knew quite well.

He looked up and turned his head in my direction. "Welcome, Zianno," he said. He winked once and added, "Yahweh has been good to me." The other man raised his head and looked at Solomon, then at me. He seemed older than he does now, but I was certain the man was Captain B.

I awoke suddenly. I was dripping with sweat. I reached for a towel and silently made my way on deck to dry off and get some air. Only two men were on watch—Captain B, who was at the wheel, and his first mate, a man who went by the nickname Pic. Pic was getting ready to go below and whispered a last remark to Captain B. I don't think he saw me, but even if he had, he would not have suspected I could hear him. He spoke French. Translated, he said, "If you want my opinion, I would listen to her, Antoine. She is your wife!" Then he saluted casually and disappeared belowdecks.

The night sky sparkled with stars. I walked up to Captain B, wiping the sweat from my head and arms.

"Can you not sleep, monsieur?" he asked.

I glanced at the sky. "Not tonight, Captain." I leaned over the railing to catch the sea spray on my face. The cold felt good, but the salty spray stung my eyes. I wiped them clear and found my-self staring down at the painted name on the side of our schooner—*Emme*. I thought back to the only Emme I had ever known. I wondered where she was and how she was. I turned and looked toward Africa, which was just over the horizon. She had saved my life and spent almost a decade of her own trying to help me find Star. I owed her a great deal, as well as her grandfather, PoPo.

Captain B saw me staring at the name. "Is something wrong, monsieur?"

"No, no, Captain. I was just thinking of someone I once knew, a girl named Emme. She was special in many, many ways."

"*Oui,* she is."

I turned and looked at him, wondering what he meant. He was smiling. "She has a keen mind," he said, "but her heart wanders."

My mouth dropped and I was stunned. "That can only be one person, Captain. A man named PoPo told me the same thing about her."

"And me, monsieur. I knew him well. It was I who wrote the letter informing her that he was dying."

"Knew?"

"*Oui.* He passed on not long after she returned."

I remembered the day she read that letter. We were deep in the Sahara in a desolate crossroads called In Salah. It was where we said good-bye. "You mean your ship is named after Emme Ya Ambala?"

"*Oui,* she is the same girl. Only her name is longer now, monsieur, by one name. Mine."

"Emme is your wife?"

"*Oui.*" He paused, then went on. "I see we both have this secret from the other, though this thing does not surprise me. Emme is the one who taught me of your existence. She told me you have great abilities, monsieur. Because of Emme, when Mowsel approached me three years ago, I surprised him by recognizing him as, well, what he was . . . what you are. Now, I do this work when he needs me and Emme protests my absence."

"Where is she?"

"Paris. We live in Paris, also Marseille and Corsica. My work makes it necessary to live many places. Emme wants me in Paris to live all the time, but this is still difficult for me. Do you understand this problem, monsieur?"

"Oui," I said. "I think it might be universal, Captain."

"I was waiting for the certain moment to tell you of my *petit* secret, monsieur. I hope I have not become untrustworthy. I never intended a deception."

"No, Captain, I do not feel deceived. I feel enlightened. I am more than happy to discover that Emme is alive and well. And please, call me Z. Now tell me, how long have you known her, and where and how did you meet?"

"This answer is complicated . . . Z."

"Believe me, Captain, I am familiar with complications."

Glancing up at the sails every so often, Captain B began to tell me a brief history of his life. Born out of wedlock on the island of Martinique to a French sea captain and his mistress, a woman named Isabelle, he was raised in various ports until being removed from his mother's care by his father because she had become addicted to absinthe. After that, he never saw her again. He was schooled in naval academies in France, then posted in Dakar and Saint-Louis, Senegal, where he met a young black student named Emme Ya Ambala.

They had a relationship for over a year, even discussing marriage, then for a reason Captain B did not explain, had a falling out and she left him on Christmas Day. That was the very same day she delivered the premature baby and rescued me. Many years later, in the middle of the Sahara, Emme said she had reconsidered her decision about leaving a man she only referred to as A.B. Suddenly, I remembered Pic's whisper to Captain B. "Antoine," he had called him. Captain B's name was Antoine Boutrain. Then the full meaning of my dream came to me. The coincidence was astounding. Captain B was the son of Captain Antoine Boutrain, the man in my dream, the man who had lost a small fortune to Solomon and given him the contacts Solomon needed to start his own fortune. His mother was the same woman Captain Woodget had loved and watched over for years.

I let Captain B finish talking and said nothing for several moments. The *Emme* sliced through the dark water smooth as a blade and a faint glow began to appear over the horizon to the east. In a few more hours we would part ways with Captain B and his crew, but it would not be the last time we would see each other or share a secret.

"I knew your mother," I said.

"No! Is this possible?"

"Yes. I didn't know her well, but she was a good person, Captain. There was a night when she gave me hot tea, warm blankets, and shelter during the middle of a hurricane. That was in Louisiana. An old friend of mine loved her well there. He took care of her and gave her a fine funeral when she died."

Captain B glanced up to check the wind in the sails, then scanned the horizon slowly. Minutes later, he said, "*Merci,* monsieur. Thank you, Z. I have always wondered this."

Sailor, Ray, and I left Captain B and the *Emme* behind in the harbor of the old port of Alexandria, the city founded and built by the Greeks and the capital city of Cleopatra. Once a jewel of the Mediterranean, it was no longer. Alexandria needed both restoration and modernization. People and traffic kept it busy and crowded, but to me it seemed slightly abandoned and neglected.

We were using visas Sailor had obtained while in Malta, making the three of us cousins and all Egyptian nationals whose parents lived on Maltese soil. Sailor spoke Arabic fluently and we passed into the country within minutes, legally, in a manner of speaking. We picked up some local clothing and light caftans, then walked to the train station and took the first available connection to Cairo. After a short time on board amid the heat and dust and sweat, we looked and felt as Egyptian as any other children in Egypt. By sunset, we were in the lobby of a small hotel Sailor knew well. The air was stifling. We were sipping tea and waiting for a man named Rais Hussein, who supposedly had information concerning the Octopus. He was late. We ordered *mulukhis* and *kofta* and sipped more tea. He never appeared. It had been a long day, but it was only the first of a thousand to come just like it, each seeming to end in some form of frustration or empty promise.

In Cairo, despite the heat, Sailor and Ray felt more in their element than any place we had been. Sailor because he had traveled through the city on many occasions over the centuries, staying once for a full year as a visitor in the court of Shagaret-el-Dorr (Tree of Pearls), the Mameluke former slave and wife of Al-Saleh, the last Ayyubid Sultan. And Ray because he liked the way it was now—a den of thieves and a city where anything was for sale. All you had to know was who to ask.

We spent three sweltering weeks in Cairo. The "City of a Thousand Minarets" truly did appear to have a thousand of them. We combed the narrow streets and alleys, bazaars and markets, searching for any trace of Rais Hussein. There were tens of thousands of shops, from rugs, brass, and tambourines to teashops and smoke rooms. Finally, we were given a tip, more of a rumor, that Rais and his brother Gad Hussein had moved to

Luxor in order to work under Rais Ahmed Gurger. He was the foreman for the British archaeologist, Howard Carter, who was resuming his dig in the Valley of the Kings. Carter was looking for intact tombs dating back to the Amarna period and the Eighteenth Dynasty. This, I learned, was the exact reason Giles Xuereb told Sailor to contact Rais Hussein. The Octopus could be in one of these tombs.

The assumption had been made by Giles based on an ancient legend only recently found on an inscription and translated, but not yet published, by Sir Alan Gardiner, a close friend of both Giles and Howard Carter. According to the legend, Nefertiti, the beautiful wife of Akhenaton, had once been presented with a special gift from a foreigner. Nefertiti received no other gift she treasured more. The gift was known as the Octopus. The legend says the foreigner came from Crete, but the origin of the Octopus was thought to be "near the source of the Great River, beyond the Great Convulsions." When Akhenaton died, Nefertiti lost favor with the priests in Karnak, who wanted the rebellious Pharaoh erased in every aspect. The legend mentions two possible fates for Nefertiti. In one, she escapes with the Octopus and disappears into unknown lands to the south, beyond the cataracts of the Nile, never to be seen again. In the other, she secretly returns at the death of her son, the boy king, Tutankhamen, in order to place the Octopus in his tomb. Giles preferred the second version, saying Sir Alan Gardiner had concurred, then informed him that Carter was going back to the Valley of the Kings in search of tombs. Giles reminded Sailor that the tomb of King Tutankhamen had never been found. He convinced Sailor to find Rais. The inscription was legitimate and Howard Carter was a good archaeologist. Even if Carter was not looking for the Octopus, he could lead us to it. Rais and his brother Gad would be working directly on the site. Sailor wanted any news of all discoveries on the site to come from an inside man. Rais Hussein was his man.

We took the train to Luxor, the city of temples on the east bank of the Nile, just south of Karnak. Palm trees lined the river and the temperature was ten degrees hotter. On the trip, Ray and I had marveled at the landscape and the sight of toppled ruins that were often visible from the train. Sailor casually pointed out the ones he had seen while they were still standing and in use.

In Luxor, we ate a quick meal in the train station, then made our way to the markets and shops south of Luxor Temple on Sharia al-Markez. Using various dialects, Sailor located Rais within two hours and concluded a deal between the two of them within one. Rais agreed to send Giles a letter once a month with news of how the dig was going. In return for each letter, he would receive a bank draft of twenty pounds sterling, regardless of whether any tombs were found. Sailor would contact Giles from wherever we happened to be. However, the season for any archaeological digs was still months away. None of us had even thought of that. Sailor then suggested something that neither Ray nor I could question. He thought we should immediately investigate the other possible ending to the legend. What if Nefertiti did disappear to the south, never to return, with the Octopus in her possession? Should we not do all we could do to see if it is true? The Fleur-du-Mal certainly would, and without delay. Ray and I agreed. We decided to go south, as far up the Nile as necessary, and find what we could find. Sailor still had a few contacts in various towns and villages and we could start with them. The decision must have had the same effect as breaking a small mirror, because after that our good luck vanished.

As usual, we traveled simply and often procured rides in small native boats called faluccas. We dressed the same as all boys along the Nile and tried to blend in with local populations as best we could. Near the small town of Dendur, Ray even replaced his beret with a white skullcap. We were delayed there for five weeks while waiting for a man we later found out had been dead for some time. Delay and detour became commonplace. Fifty-five miles south of Dendur, three months passed in a desolate village named Korosko, a place where caravans used to gather and prepare for the two-hundred-mile journey to Khartoum. South of Korosko, in Derr, we were held up again for six months, chasing leads and making trips by donkey to sites in the area. At every opportunity Sailor contacted Giles, only to hear the continuing news that nothing had been discovered in the Valley of the Kings. I wrote letters to Opari and sent them off with no return address. In Qasr Ibrim, the last stop before Abu Simbel, we thought we had found the information we needed and again headed south, into the Sudan and east to places not accurately mapped or recorded. Over a year had gone by before we found a village and a village elder who supposedly possessed an object that had passed down among his people for countless generations since the era of the Nubian kings. It took us three months to win his confidence because he did not trust children who wished to see such things. Finally, Ray gained the elder's favor and he eventually let us look at the object. It was a beautiful piece of work, an alabaster vase with an Egyptian queen depicted in bas-relief. The image could have represented Nefertiti, but there was no way to know for sure. One thing was certain—it was not the Octopus. Three months later our search ended abruptly because something happened that none of us could have expected or predicted. It was profound and frightening and seemed utterly impossible. Ray Ytuarte got sick.

There was no warning and we were not doing anything we had not done many times in many places. Following another lead, we were deep in the Sudan crossing a shallow river on foot. The water was only a few feet deep and the riverbed was mostly mud. The sun was setting and the whole western sky burned red and orange. On the far bank of the river, Ray stopped to clean the caked mud from his shoes and was bitten on the back of his neck by a mosquito. By the time we reached the village of Wad Rasala, where we were staying the night, Ray was shaking with chills and experiencing severe pain from head to foot. I wasn't sure what to do and neither was Sailor. I had never seen Ray even out of breath, let alone sick and in pain. He then developed a skin rash and a high fever and he began drifting in and out of consciousness. With no other alternative we sought out the local medicine man, who was a woman, a kind of shaman and midwife. She took one look at Ray and shouted something in a language I'd never heard.

Sailor spoke to her in a dialect she understood. He asked question after question and repeated one of them over and over. Each time the woman would nod and shout the word again.

I grabbed Sailor by the arm. "What are you asking her?"

"I am asking her if she is certain."

"Certain of what?"

"Certain that Ray has contracted what she calls 'Breakbone Fever,' an often fatal disease."

"That is impossible," I said, shaking my head.

Sailor knelt next to where Ray was lying and waited a full minute before he spoke. He stared down at Ray, who was sweating from every pore. Then gently, almost with the touch of a father, he wiped Ray's face and neck with a wet cloth. He looked up at me. His "ghost eye" swirled with clouds the same way it had that night in Cornwall when he told us about the death of Unai and Usoa's baby. In a bitter whisper, he said, "Apparently nothing is impossible, Zianno."

Ray survived the night, but his condition did not improve. For three days and nights he remained delirious, often breaking into cold sweats and mumbling in strange languages I had never heard, either from Ray or anyone else. The medicine woman, Dejik, said most children, if they lived, sometimes took weeks to recover. Adults could take months of recuperation and would likely suffer repeated bouts of extreme exhaustion. Sailor and I both thought of what that could mean for Ray. If it was that bad for the Giza, what would it be like for the Meq?

On the fourth night, Ray regained full consciousness, though he was so weak he could barely speak. Even the deep green of his eyes seemed pale in the candlelight. "Where are we, Z?" he asked. "In Veracruz?"

"No, Ray, we're still in Africa."

"What happened to me? I never been so damn tired and sore in my life."

"You got bit by a mosquito."

Ray looked at me without understanding, as if I had told him a joke he didn't quite catch. "What do you mean by that?"

"You got sick. You are sick. The mosquito gave you a virus, a bad one."

"I been bit before, Z."

"I know."

Sailor was standing behind me and he stepped closer, so Ray could see him. "We shall get you through this, Ray. Sleep, rest, and try to eat when you are able. Zianno, Dejik, and I shall get you well."

Ray stared back at Sailor, then turned his head and tried to focus on Dejik, who leaned forward and offered him a small amount of broth in a bowl. He turned back to me. "This don't make sense, Z."

"I know, Ray. I can't explain it. Let's just get you well, then we'll figure out why."

Ray was rapidly losing consciousness again. As his eyes were closing he asked, "What about the Fleur-du-Mal?" He fell asleep before Sailor or I said a word in reply.

After Dejik made sure Ray was comfortable, I asked Sailor to follow me outside. Ray's question could not be ignored. In the open air, under the stars, I looked over at Sailor. I was suddenly angry at the fact Ray had only contracted the virus because we were on a wild goose chase after an object that may or may not exist, for the reason that it might help us trap a madman and assassin called the Fleur-du-Mal. It made no sense. It all seemed futile and pointless. "Why does the Fleur-du-Mal want the Octopus and the Sixth Stone, if there is one? Especially when he has never wanted any of the other five. Why, Sailor, why is it important?"

"Because we are aging, Zianno. Not individually, but together as a whole, the Meq are aging. I am certain of this, as is the Fleur-du-Mal. Zeru-Meq has told me so. He believes the Sixth Stone will have different . . . characteristics, shall we say, than the ones you and I carry. He believes it may have a power over the others and will enable him to do whatever he pleases, including telekinesis. He could be right. We must find it first."

"We? Or do you mean *you*?"

"Zianno, please. You are upset and confused about what has happened to Ray. Calm down and you will realize there was no way to have foreseen this. Ray's life and health are sacred to me. We must stay here as long as it takes for him to recover. We shall worry about the Fleur-du-Mal and the Octopus once Ray regains his strength, and only then, not one day sooner." Sailor twirled the blue sapphire on his finger. "Do you understand?"

"Yes," I said, "and once again, Sailor, I apologize. I was wrong."

"Unnecessary," he answered, "and remember, Zianno, Ray is under two hundred years old. Perhaps that shall help speed his recovery."

I looked at Sailor and smiled. Only Umla-Meq and a very few other beings on the planet would consider "under two hundred years" as being young.

Dejik took meticulous care of Ray, keeping him clean, cool, and fed the best she could. She massaged his limbs daily, sang songs, and recited incantations during rough periods when he slipped back into unconsciousness. In return, Sailor and I made frequent trips to larger villages and trading centers, bringing back simple medicines such as sulphate of zinc, quinine, and carbolic acid to aid in the care of her own people. In six months, Ray was able to stand, but he was too weak to travel. A few minutes of walking would bring on total exhaustion and pain. Ray told me once, "I feel like there's nothin' but sand and grit in my joints, Z, and it's all rubbin' together every time I move."

Two more months passed with little improvement. I knew he

was starting to feel better, however, when he asked Dejik for second and third helpings of a simple dish consisting mainly of broad beans cooked in oil.

"What do you call this?" Ray asked, licking his spoon and rubbing his belly.

"Fool," Dejik answered.

Ray stared back at her. "Well, you don't have to call me names, do you?"

"No, no, no. That 'fool,' that 'fool,' " she said, pointing at his bowl of beans.

"Perfect," Ray said, "I mistook myself for a bowl of beans."

Dejik never once questioned us about who we were or what we were doing in the Sudan. Sailor had a simple explanation. "She is a shaman, Zianno. Our existence is not out of place in her world. Her reality accepts us the same way she accepts the magic in plants, spells, and dreams. To Dejik, no natural wonder is strange. This ability, this state of being, also allows her to be an excellent healer and medicine woman."

I had to agree. In two more months Ray was strong as ever and it was not because of Sailor or me. He began running for exercise and pleasure, and he told me he could now feel the weather changing in his bones as well as his mind.

"Is that good?" I asked.

"You bet, Z. Now I got a reserve system, if you know what I mean."

After thanking her in every way we could and promising to return, we said good-bye to Dejik on a beautiful October morning, leaving with a cousin of hers who accompanied us on the long journey to Khartoum. From there we traveled a short distance to Omdurman, then by donkey, boat, and train to Aswan.

In another week, we were finally approaching the outskirts of Luxor. It was a Friday. The date was November 17, 1922.

Once we were on the streets of Luxor, there was only one story being circulated. Twelve days earlier, Howard Carter had discovered a missing tomb in the Valley of the Kings, possibly with its seals still in tact. Carter was going to open the tomb as soon as he returned from Cairo with his benefactor, Lord Carnarvon. He was due back within a week.

I was speechless at the news. Ray laughed and said, "Damn!" Sailor said, "Damn, indeed."

I am batting. I have just swung and hit the ball deep into right center. I watch it fly as I run to first base. The ball seems propelled by magic and all eyes in the grandstands are following the ball. At the apex of its flight, the ball defies gravity and stops in midair. Everyone is frozen in place. The ball begins changing color and becomes a black dot growing larger, widening, then I recognize it as the moon sliding into place in front of the sun. It is a total solar eclipse, the Bitxileiho, the Strange Window. I hear steps behind me. I turn and the umpire is walking toward me, ignoring the eclipse. He takes off his mask. I know him. He has green eyes, he is familiar, but . . . something is different . . . something is wrong.

"You're out, Z!"

I opened my eyes. Ray was standing over me, blocking the sun. "What?"

"You went out like a light. You're dreaming. Wake up, we're almost there."

I looked around. We were on water, crammed in a small boat

with two dozen others, mostly men, but also several boys about
our size. Everyone, including us, wore loosely wrapped turbans,
simple linen robes, and sandals. Then I remembered.

We were crossing the Nile on our way to meet with Rais
Hussein and his brother Gad in the Valley of the Kings. It was
eight days after we arrived in Luxor. The news of Howard
Carter's discovery had spread everywhere in the country. The
Valley of the Kings was already crowded and access to the site
had become limited. It would not be long before the pompous
and the powerful appeared and took over completely. It had
taken us six days to track down Rais Hussein. At first, Sailor
tried to reach Giles Xuereb on Malta, but was unsuccessful.
Then we found out through a contact in Cairo that Giles had
gone missing. He had disappeared without a trace, leaving all his
belongings in the house and a half-eaten meal on the table. The
same thought came to each of us. More than enough time had
elapsed in order for the Fleur-du-Mal to realize Giles had deceived him. Revenge would be swift and harsh. We feared for
Giles, but we did not speak of it and kept searching for Rais.
Eventually, we located him in Gurna, not far from Howard
Carter's residence. Immediately, Sailor made Rais an offer he
could not refuse. If Rais would get us on the dig site and near
to the tomb, Sailor offered to pay Rais and his brother two hundred pounds sterling. Rais and Gad Hussein were two of Howard
Carter's most trusted workmen. They had access and they could
get us close. Rais agreed to the deal. We were to meet him at a
specified location in two days. Now, on a mild and balmy Sunday morning, we were almost there.

A nervous, skinny man wearing a fez waited for us as we disembarked. After only giving his name, he led us to another man

waiting with donkeys. We followed him on a long trek along narrow trails through rubble and rock until we found Rais and Gad resting in the shadow of a boulder at a crossroads in the trails. They both seemed relaxed and happy to see us. Sailor made the money exchange with Rais and he bowed slightly in return. He said he would take us to Rais Ahmed Gurgar, the foreman for Howard Carter at the site. Since we were small, we could be used to carry the last bits of debris and rubbish from the narrow steps leading directly down to the tomb. Gurgar would arrange it. Sailor thanked Rais, saying that would, indeed, be close enough.

With Rais and his brother in the lead, we snaked our way into the Valley of the Kings. We passed by dozens of workman and boys, some standing in small groups, but most were one behind the other in long lines with baskets of rock and debris on their heads. A few men were animated and shouting. All of them let Rais and Gad through without a question, usually greeting them with a smile or a phrase in Arabic. Sailor, Ray, and I stayed close on their heels and kept silent. Signs of earlier digs and excavations littered the valley on all sides. The tomb Howard Carter had discovered was small compared to some of the other sites. It lay directly underneath the rubble that had accumulated during the construction of the later and much larger tomb of Rameses VI. This was one of the reasons it had not been found by tomb robbers or anyone else for over three thousand years.

Rais informed us that a day earlier they had cleared the stairs, broken the seals, and opened the doorway, only to come upon another blocked descending passage filled with local stone, fragments of jars, vases, and other broken objects all of a type dating to the Eighteenth Dynasty. Today, they had already cleared nine meters of the passage.

As we approached the activity surrounding the entrance, Gurgar, the foreman, and a man Rais called Callender came forward to confront Rais and Gad.

"Are these the boys?" he asked.

"Yes," Rais replied. "These are the boys. Are they the proper size?"

The man gave us a quick glance. "Yes, yes, of course," he said. "Keep them near, Rais. We are about to open the second doorway. We are only waiting for Lord Carnarvon and his daughter, Lady Evelyn. Once they arrive, send me the boys."

Callender turned abruptly and walked over to confer with another man, an Englishman dressed in a suit. He had a neatly trimmed mustache and wore a wide-brimmed hat that kept his face in shadow. Rais was proud to tell us the man was his boss, the archaeologist Howard Carter.

Though every face of every man close to the entrance looked tense and anxious, there was little being said. The anticipation was palpable. Rais led us to a low stone wall where a few carpenters sat watching the proceedings. They had been summoned the night before by Carter and asked to build a temporary wooden grille over the first doorway to protect the tomb. Sailor, Ray, and I crouched down in the shade of the wall and waited. We said nothing.

Several minutes passed, then I heard a group of voices speaking English in the distance. They were coming toward us. Howard Carter broke away from the men around him and walked to greet them. He was smiling broadly. It was Lord Carnarvon and his party, which included several Englishmen, three men from the Egyptian Antiquities Department, and two women, one of whom was Lady Evelyn. The women wore wide hats and long full skirts. To make sure they were cool and comfortable, a boy about our age followed behind, carrying two unopened umbrellas in the event either or both of the women required shade. Lady Evelyn smiled back at Howard Carter as he approached.

And then my skin began to crawl. I lost my breath and felt a chill run down my entire body. My eyes opened wide and froze. Next to me, I thought I heard Ray growl under his breath. Sailor leaped to his feet and started forward. I grabbed his wrist and stopped him. We could not believe what was in front of us, what was walking by and smiling along with everyone else. The green eyes, the brilliant white of his teeth. The small bitter laugh behind the smile. Evil pure as light. The boy walking by, the boy holding the umbrellas, was the Fleur-du-Mal.

"Hello, *mon petit,*" he whispered, knowing only I would hear. "I have missed you."

I could feel my jaw tighten, but I made no response. Their small party passed quickly and joined Howard Carter. He led them all toward the entrance of the tomb. The Fleur-du-Mal turned once and winked at Sailor, who stood still as stone and then spit on the ground. Callender walked up to Rais, saying he would only need one of "his boys." He turned and pointed to me. "You there," he said. "Come along, come with me! Come now, boy!" I glanced at Sailor and Ray. There was no hesitation. I nodded and followed him step for step.

The workmen crowding near the entrance made way for Callender. In moments we were facing the descending stairs of the tomb. Howard Carter stood waiting at the top step. Behind him Lord Carnarvon was speaking in hushed tones to another man, followed by Lady Evelyn and another woman. And since candles are always required to check for foul gases when opening ancient subterranean tombs, the Fleur-du-Mal stood waiting behind the women, holding candles.

"Hand the boy the candles, Callender," Carter said. "Tell him to stay near the other boy. Then come along. We are about to enter."

"Done," Callender answered.

There was no time to think. I watched Howard Carter and the others begin to descend the stairs. Callender had Gurgar hand me the candles and in seconds the Fleur-du-Mal and I were shoulder to shoulder, unable to speak to each other, descending the stairs and entering the tomb. We walked past the remnants of the first doorway and down the long passage that led to the second doorway. Broken things, potsherds, and scraps of rubbish still littered the floor. Carter cleared the last of it away. Callender helped him. No one spoke. Then he and Carter began to make a hole in the top left corner of the doorway. Carter asked for the candles. All eyes in the tomb turned to us.

I glanced at the Fleur-du-Mal for the first time. He winked, then led us around the others until we flanked the ancient doorway on both sides. Carter lit the candles. He and Callender widened the breach they had started. We held the candles high in front of it. No one breathed. A moment later the candles began to flicker from the hot gases escaping.

"Hold them closer," Carter said, peering inside. No one moved. Seconds ticked and the candles danced in the light. He said nothing. I stared in the eyes of the Fleur-du-Mal. I saw something I never expected. Unconsciously, something much more common than psychopathic obsession appeared in his eyes. Something as common to the Giza as it is to the Meq, and as old. Hope. And that is the real secret of the Octopus. The power of the Octopus is and always has been that it represents the seed of Hope. In his eyes, in his face, I saw what my grandfather had seen, and I knew instantly why the Fleur-du-Mal had killed him.

Lord Carnarvon spoke first. "Well, can you see anything?"

Carter turned his head slightly. "Yes," he said. "Things . . . wonderful things."

To tell a story with words is admirable and usually adequate, but to tell a story with things, real things, is to make it come alive. The discovery of the tomb of King Tutankhamen opened a real and tactile conduit to a unique world and time that had passed three thousand two hundred years earlier. Intact, Howard Carter brought that world directly into the light of the twentieth century. The best story ever. Within forty-eight hours, the twentieth century had descended on the story and the Valley of the Kings. The site was made completely inaccessible to almost everyone. Howard Carter, Callender, Gurgar, and emissaries of the Egyptian government saw to that.

The Fleur-du-Mal had disappeared without a trace immediately after we emerged from the tomb. The general chaos and excitement had created a crowd scene, which he slipped through easily. I was reminded of a real octopus using his own black cloud for confusion and escape.

We were forced to wait another four months before we found a method for viewing the artifacts being removed, one by one, from inside the tomb. Each piece, each object being taken out, was priceless. Couches, caskets, alabaster vases, gold stools and chairs, chests of inlaid ivory ornamented with scenes of hunting and battle, golden bows, staves, and eventually exquisite jewelry and personal effects of the boy king. On and on, the list seemed endless. If the Octopus happened to be in the tomb, it would be brought out. One evening, Ray stated the obvious. He said, "I wonder what they're doing with all the loot." Sailor and I wondered the same thing.

We learned from Rais that Carter had been keeping everything in one place for cleaning and treatment before being packed and transported to Cairo. All objects were stored in the tomb of Seti II. Rais told Sailor there was a man he knew who might be able to smuggle us into the site as donkey boys, for a fee, of course. Another man in security might agree to let us have an hour or so inside the tomb of Seti II, for an added fee, of course. Rais claimed this was personally distasteful and also unavoidable. Sailor paid him well and I gave him an extra American double eagle twenty-dollar gold piece, which Rais held and coveted more than anything being removed from the tomb.

I never mentioned to Sailor or Ray what I had discovered in the eyes of the Fleur-du-Mal. I don't know why. For the entire four months, he had not been seen anywhere. He was out of sight, but not out of mind. I knew better, and on March 14, the news arrived that Lord Carnarvon had contracted blood poisoning from a mysterious mosquito bite. He was transferred immediately from Luxor to Cairo. Lord Carnarvon would die there a few weeks later and the rumor of a curse circulated instantly. I knew the truth. The Fleur-du-Mal had extracted all he needed from Lord Carnarvon and had still come up empty. Blood poisoning may have been the cause of death, but it did not come from a mosquito bite. The real insect and curse was the Fleur-du-Mal. He was angry, active, and probably very near.

The tomb of Seti II is quarried into the base of a cliff face at the head of the wadi, or dry wash, running southwest from the main Valley of the Kings. There is only one entrance and the tomb is cut in a straight line going over two hundred feet into the cliff face with no lateral rooms. Even Sailor would not have been able to get in without being seen. The bribe to the security force, one man in particular, was an absolute necessity.

The call came from Rais on the morning of April 6, the day after Lord Carnarvon died. All work at the site had been suspended in his honor. Rais said his man would give us one hour inside the tomb. We crossed to the west bank at noon and led our donkeys along the road to the Valley of the Kings. We were in place for our rendezvous just as the sun sank over the almost vertical cliff face surrounding the tomb of Seti II. The man met us at the perimeter of the temporary security. The air was cool inside the shadow of the cliff. He hurried us toward the tomb, then handed Sailor a portable gas lamp and a key to the makeshift gate across the entrance. In Arabic, he said he would be gone until his belly was full. If we were still there when he returned, he would arrest us. There was another man waiting inside. He would be our escort, our guide, and our guard. He knew by memory where every single object was stored, so behave. Without another word, he left, rolling a cigarette and whistling as he walked away. We were completely alone, ten yards from the gate. Sailor lit the lamp.

Before we took one step, I heard a sound above us. I looked up into the glare of the last rays of light coming over the cliff. Then I felt it everywhere, the net descending. The presence of the Fleur-du-Mal was coming directly toward us, down the stone wall of the cliff face at a rapid pace. There was a cloud of rocks and dust, but in his wake, as if he were skiing. In seconds we saw the reflection of his ruby earrings. We saw his white smile. He was climbing down the steep rock at an impossible speed and angle, as quick or quicker than Geaxi, and he was laughing. In a few more seconds he stood between Sailor and the lock on the gate. His legs were spread wide. He wore leather boots laced to the knees and a long black linen tunic embroidered with tiny diamonds. He was missing his green ribbon and his black hair hung long, uncut, and loose.

We said nothing. He looked at me and grinned, then glanced at Sailor, then Ray. "You are Ray Ytuarte, no?"

"Who's askin'?" Ray said without hesitation or a trace of irony, a poker player's voice.

The Fleur-du-Mal dropped his smile and stared at Ray, taking a short step toward him. Their eyes were the exact same color. "I beg your pardon?" he asked. He kept gazing at Ray as if he had never seen a Meq before. Then suddenly, he broke into a loud, bitter laugh, a roar that echoed off everything around us. "Perfect! And I must request your permission to use it myself, should the occasion arise. *'Who's askin'?'* Brilliant, absolutely brilliant, do you not agree, Sailor?" He dropped his smile again, producing a stiletto from under his tunic. He made a move and before anyone blinked, the point of the blade was pressing into Sailor's stomach, just above the navel. "Do you not agree?" he said again, whispering through his teeth.

"You are repeating yourself," Sailor said calmly.

The Fleur-du-Mal ignored the response, but released pressure on the stiletto. "Now, unlock the gate, Umla-Meq. Let us see what Monsieur Carter has stumbled on, shall we?"

"I want to know something first," I said.

"Is it not obvious, *mon petit*? I care little or not at all about what you want. Do you understand? It is meaningless what you want. You are as stupid as your father."

"Let's leave him out of it. Why kill Lord Carnarvon? Why torture and kill Giles, which I'm sure you did? Why murder Unai and Usoa? Because of what *might* be stored inside this tomb? Is that it? Is that all?"

The Fleur-du-Mal sighed deeply, dramatically. "Oh, Zezen, I am afraid you are destined for a short, miserable, frustrating life of inglorious ignorance." He paused and glanced at the point of his stiletto. "Business, *mon petit,* business," he said. "I would have thought that old fool, Solomon, had taught you about the sacredness of contracts . . . and the consequences if they are breached. I am a professional, Zezen, do you know what that means? I have a certain . . . reputation to uphold. My word is my truth. Your ideas of truth, reason, and morality are false and archaic, as they always have been, and they have nothing to do with business. And by the way, I had nothing to do with those annoying little monkeys, Unai and Usoa."

"Unai and Usoa?" Sailor broke in. "You did not murder Unai and Usoa?"

"Now it is you who are repeating yourself, Sailor, but to answer your rude query, no, I had nothing to do with it. Why should I?"

"But, then . . ." I couldn't finish my question.

"Think, *mon petit,* think. Who wanted Baju dead?"

I remembered Baju whispering to me as he was dying, "This is not about theft."

"Who was in Africa? Who hates everyone? I am certain she detests Opari and I believe the poor girl even hates me. She is riddled with envy. She also impersonates me from time to time. Once, not so long ago, I told you to ask Opari about these things. I said you had the wrong villain. There is one who was a protégée of mine and a student of Opari. She has been called many things, including the Pearl, however, her name is—"

"Zuriaa!" Ray burst out. "My sister, Zuriaa?"

The Fleur-du-Mal looked at Ray again, but this time he looked him up and down, as he would merchandise, or a victim. "She has a brother?" he asked, raising one eyebrow. "Interesting."

He glanced up at the sky, which was darkening. A quarter moon hung just above the horizon. The world seemed stopped, balanced between night and day. But there was no time to assess the truth of the Fleur-du-Mal's words. "Now, Sailor," he said, "without delay, unlock the gate." He kept the knife blade close to Sailor's ribs and nudged him forward. As the gate swung open, he motioned for Ray and me to take the lead. By the light of the portable lamp, we walked into the once empty, but now crowded tomb of Seti II.

The short entryway was stacked floor to ceiling with empty wooden crates and pallets, ready for the next load. Three long corridors followed and each was nearly filled with artifacts and furniture. A medley of colors surrounded us as we walked. Every object still shone bright and clear in the lamplight— brown, yellow, blue, amber, russet, black, and gold, lots of gold. We walked slowly through the maze until we passed into a well room that connected to a four-pillared hall, which was also nearly filled with boxes and hundreds of neatly stacked crates. Each crate held smaller, more fragile artifacts, such as vases and jewelry. Off to the side, tucked into the only niche in the wall, a tiny, balding man sat behind a desk lit by a lamp similar to ours. He stood and took off his wire-rimmed glasses. He was no taller than we were. "I have been waiting," he said in English. "What do you wish to see? To see everything is out of the question. You must be specific. All objects are undergoing notation. Everything is unsorted, except to me." He wiped his glasses with a handkerchief, then put them back on. He looked at me. "What do you wish to see?"

"A black box of onyx and serpentine, inlaid on top with lapis lazuli in the shape of an octopus."

The man paused and looked closely at each of our faces, switching rapidly from one to the other, checking for differences and similarities. Then he took off his glasses again and rubbed his bald head. Without explanation, he said, "This way."

We followed him to the other side of the hall where a burial chamber had been carved from what was intended to be another corridor, had Seti II not died when he did. The king's sarcophagus was located here. Next to it was a stack of crates. The man removed the top crate and set it carefully on the stone floor. "I will tell you lads the same thing I told the other one. I told her there is no touching until every object has been cleaned and catalogued. You may gaze, but you may not touch."

"Who was here?" Sailor interrupted.

"A girl," the man said. "Two nights ago. A girl that greatly resembled all of you, only . . ." He paused again and glanced at each of us.

"Only what?" the Fleur-du-Mal asked.

"Only the girl was black . . . black as an Ethiopian tribesman."

"Susheela the Ninth," I whispered.

"She is a myth," the Fleur-du-Mal said sarcastically. "If she existed, I would have seen her by now."

"She ain't no myth," Ray said. "I guarantee it."

"Open the crate, sir, if you please," Sailor said softly, ignoring the rest of us.

The man nodded, adjusted his glasses, and pried open the top of the crate. A tangled nest of straw and paper lay inside. There was a small indentation in the center, no bigger than my palm. Whatever had rested there was there no longer.

The man cursed in Arabic and removed his glasses, staring at the empty crate. "Impossible!" he shouted. He fumbled with the straw, searching in vain for the missing object. "She must have stolen it. It was here, I tell you, it was here and I never saw her touch it. I was watching her every second. Impossible."

Sailor looked at me, then said to the man, "Apparently nothing is impossible, sir."

"Tell me what was taken," the Fleur-du-Mal said.

"A black box," the man said, "inlaid with lapis lazuli. The most beautiful work I have ever seen. The girl called it 'the Octopus.' Carter will have my head for this." He looked over his shoulder as if Howard Carter might be watching and listening. "Quickly," he said, closing the crate. "You must leave at once, all of you. I want you out of here now. I . . . I must sort this out."

He escorted us out of the tomb, taking the key from Sailor and locking the gate behind us. Mumbling to himself, he told us never to speak of this encounter to anyone. If we did, he would deny it ever occurred. We hurried down the slope that led to the paths and roads beyond. The man veered off on an obscure trail within minutes, walking away in the darkness. The Fleur-du-Mal was still side by side with Sailor. He kept the point of his stiletto no more than an inch from Sailor's ribs. Once the man was out of sight, he began walking away himself, backward, never taking his eyes from ours. Twenty yards in the distance, I could only see his smile, then he turned and ran.

"I want you to know one more thing," I yelled. "I know what Aitor knew. I know why you want the Sixth Stone. I know why you killed my grandfather."

At least a quarter mile away, I heard the sound of a dog barking, then yelping in pain. I heard a bitter, solitary, hollow laugh. "You know nothing, Zezen," he said, and he was gone.

5

AHOTS
(VOICE)

"I'm so far separated from the earthly life I know that I accept whatever circumstance may come. In fact, these emissaries from a spirit world are quite in keeping with the night and day. They're neither intruders nor strangers. It's more like a gathering of family and friends after years of separation, as though I've known all of them before in some past reincarnation."

—CHARLES LINDBERGH, over the Atlantic, near dawn,
after twenty-four hours in the air

I awoke just after dawn from a long, startling, compelling dream. It was the kind of dream in which you are certain you are *not* dreaming. It feels too real to be illusion or fantasy. You are in another time, another place.

I was with the hunters, six men from the same clan. The clan mother had told them not to fail and her approval was vital. They took abnormal risks they would usually avoid. Now they were in trouble. The hunters had gone too far, too close to the ice. They were beyond the call of the others and still had not seen the herd of beasts they were seeking. The hunting season was short and nearing its end. Yet there was no return. Not this time. They huddled together for a meeting. The wind howled, sometimes gusting and blinding us with tiny ice crystals. They decided to make "the Voice." All six sat where they were and gathered in a tight circle, holding hands and gazing toward the invisible center between them. Then, somehow without speaking, they made a sound together I could only hear from inside my head, or my heart. The sound was one voice chanting the word "ea" over and over. The word meant "come and help" in their strange language. They did this for three days without stopping and without sleeping. It was my duty to keep them warm and out of the wind. I melted ice for water and let it drip onto their lips at regular intervals. I never spoke and their one voice never ceased. On the third day, suddenly, there was another voice answering in reply. However, it was weak and undecipherable. Just as it became louder and began to clear, I opened my eyes.

But where was I? My bed was bolted to the wall and the room seemed tiny. Then the room and everything in it tilted slightly and I remembered. It was my birthday, May 4, 1923. We were on a passenger ship, headed for the port of Southampton, where we were to meet Trumoi-Meq. I dressed in silence and left my berth to watch the dawn from on deck. The air was cool and salty. I leaned against the railing and looked out on a dull gray sea and sky. At the edge of the horizon, in half-light, the nearly featureless landscape of Southampton came slowly into view. Inside, I felt dull and gray as the sea around me and turning twelve again seemed nothing to celebrate. We had missed our chance in Egypt. There was no telling when we would get another. The Fleur-du-Mal had disappeared again without a trace, as had the Octopus and the ghostlike Susheela the Ninth. We had neither suspected nor detected her presence anywhere in Egypt at any time, yet in the end she had proven to be ahead of us all, including the Fleur-du-Mal. We spent a week in Cairo chasing down any lead, bribing every contact Sailor knew, and came up with nothing. Then I received a common tourist postcard in the mail with a blurry image of the Parthenon on the front. It was sent from Athens and addressed to me in care of our hotel. The short note on the back was written in a beautiful calligraphic script. *"Mon petit,"* it began, "so sorry we were not able to visit longer. I wanted to inquire about that little bastard son of Jisil—Caine, I believe he is named. I could not bear for him to think I had forgotten. Give him my regards, *s'il vous plaît*. You are such a dear. Wish you were here. Love, Xanti."

The next day Sailor received a telegram from Mowsel. It read: "COME TO ENGLAND WITHOUT DELAY STOP WILL MEET YOU AT THE GRAPES STOP." We assumed he had information regarding either the Fleur-du-Mal or Susheela the Ninth and booked passage almost immediately, using our Egyptian passports. The voyage was uneventful and we said little to each other for three days. Finally, over dinner on the third night, Sailor said, "Gentlemen, it has become obvious to me that it is time for us to part. Your thoughts are drifting elsewhere, and they should, it is common. But do not let your thoughts dwell for a moment in despair. Much was learned in Egypt, especially when Ray became ill."

"Thanks for remindin' me, Sailor," Ray said. "That virus nearly killed me."

"And that is my point. It *nearly* killed you, but it did not. You lived and recovered completely, Ray. That proves some Meq have resistance, even after becoming ill. Who and why is more difficult to determine. It may have something to do with being Egipurdiko. Unai and Usoa's baby was Egizahar. Perhaps it is because you are older. I do not know, I am speculating. Mowsel will have an opinion, to be sure." He paused. "I understand your yearnings, both of you. Do not apologize or defend. I know Ray wants to find the truth about Zuriaa, as do all of us."

"I have got a question or two for Opari," Ray said, giving me a wink.

I only wanted to go home and Sailor knew it.

"Zianno," he said, "I think you should visit Opari as well." His "ghost eye" closed slightly. He twirled the star sapphire around his forefinger, then added, "From England, I shall be going east. I intend to find Zeru-Meq, no matter his objections. I also have a question or two and this time I want the answers."

Now the docks of Southampton were in full view in front of me. I leaned over the railing and looked back out to open sea. It was my birthday and I knew I would be going home soon. Home with more questions than answers, but at least I would be going home. The thought was soothing and I let it extend and evolve into the belief that bad luck and bad news were behind us. I was wrong.

Once we were through the formalities of entering England, Sailor led the way to The Grapes, a pub for workingmen and sailors just beyond the dock gates. The door stood wide open and a man wearing a floor-length apron was sweeping the floor. It was still early morning and the pub was empty except for one,

Trumoi-Meq, who sat on top of the bar with his legs crossed. He wore his dark blue kerchief and a blue beret, which he removed as we entered the pub. Half in shadow, half in light, he was not smiling and there was the image of death in his eyes. "Come with me," he said, hopping down from the bar and heading for the door. The man sweeping the floor ignored us completely.

In silence, we walked at a leisurely pace through the streets of Southampton until we reached Watts Park and the stone Cenotaph honoring servicemen killed in the Great War. An overcast and windless sky gave the park a feeling of quiet grace and peace. A familiar figure stood with his back to us, reading the long list of names chiseled into the stone. He turned and smiled, but it was a weak smile and his eyes were sad. It was Willie Croft.

"Hello, boys," he said, even though he was Giza and the youngest among us.

Each of us said hello, then I asked, "Did you know many of those folks, Willie?"

"No, Z, didn't know a one. Brave lads, though, every one of them."

"Has something happened, Willie?" Sailor asked bluntly.

Willie started to answer, then turned and glanced at Mowsel. "Mowsel, why don't you tell them while I bring round the limousine."

Willie walked away in his unusual, almost stumbling gait. Mowsel waited until he was out of sight before looking at Sailor. "It took me three weeks to locate you this time, old one. No doubt due to an unexpected misfortune, I assume, but that story must come later." He paused a moment. "I am sorry to say Daphne Croft is dead, as well as Tillman Fadle. Willie did not

want to bury either of them without us present. It was a desire
Daphne had put in her will and also expressed to me years ago.
I gave her my solemn word it would be so."

Sailor let out a long sigh and said, "Yes, yes, I agree entirely.
We all owe them both a great deal."

"More than that," Mowsel replied.

Sailor looked Mowsel squarely in the eye. I could tell they
were each recalling events and situations they had experienced
at Caitlin's Ruby, not only during Daphne's lifetime, but in all
the lives of the Bramleys and Fadles going back four centuries to
Caitlin herself.

"Again," Sailor said, "I agree. We must be there."

"I never did get to know the lady," Ray said quietly.

"What happened?" I asked.

Mowsel looked up at the low gray cloud cover above us, then
toward the west and a small sliver of blue sky on the horizon.
"Apparently, about a month ago, sometime in the early morning, Daphne sat down to write a letter, a letter she never finished. While in the act of writing, she suffered a stroke. She
remained alive, but unable to move or speak. All day she lay
there. You are asking yourself, where was Tillman Fadle, no?
The great irony is he had been in the garage since dawn, breaking down the engine of the limousine for repair. Finally, sometime around dusk, Tillman discovered her lying on the kitchen
floor. He dragged her to the garage in order to drive her into
Falmouth, but of course the limousine was unavailable. In des-
peration he used Carolina's black coupe. This vehicle he had
never driven and it was missing a headlight. On a curve only
two miles from Caitlin's Ruby, he lost control. I doubt he ever
saw the rock wall approaching. They were both killed instantly.
Daphne was found still inside the coupe and Tillman had been

thrown over the wall. I was in London at the time. Once I was informed of the accident, I wired Owen immediately. He broke the news to Willie in St. Louis and Willie arrived in Cornwall ten days later. Since then we have been waiting for you." He stopped talking and rubbed his face with both hands.

"Are you ill?" Sailor asked.

"No, of course not," Mowsel said. "Are you mad, you old hound? I am tired . . . simply tired." He looked to his left, scanning the street. "Hail Hadrian, there is Willie now. Cornwall awaits us." He put his arm around Ray's shoulder and started walking toward the street and the big limousine pulling up to the curb. "Now, Ray, you must tell me what happened in Egypt."

"Do I have to?" Ray asked with a straight face.

Mowsel smiled, exposing the gap of his missing tooth. Then he slapped Ray on the back and laughed. "Make it up if you so desire, Ray. Fact or fiction, it often makes little difference, no?"

Though we were all weary from travel and disappointment, the long drive to Cornwall and Caitlin's Ruby was beautiful and relaxing. The car was loud, but solid, with good suspension and Willie drove at an even pace. It often felt more like we were in a large boat rather than a limousine. Willie made certain I rode up front with him. I found out why two hours into our journey.

An old suede jacket lay on the seat between us. Keeping one eye on the road and one hand on the wheel, Willie reached into the jacket and withdrew a letter, which he handed to me. There was no envelope and the writing only covered half the page. It was unfinished and unsigned.

"She was writing to you, Z," Willie said, giving me a quick glance.

"Do you mean Daphne?"

"Yes. She was writing to you when the stroke took her down." He paused and nodded once toward the letter. "Those were her last words, Z. I . . . I think you should read them."

I looked at the letter and read the date scrawled in the upper left corner, then the salutation underneath. I could hear Daphne's voice in my head.

My dearest Z,

Where has the time gone? I ask you this because of a lovely dream I had this morning in which my William and I were in China and still working at the mission. Nothing much happened in the dream. William and I were simply out in the garden, planting seeds with at least a dozen children. My goodness, it was a wonderful time, a wonderful dream, and after waking my thoughts passed to you and your beautiful, charming companion, Opari. What you two have is as rare as the mountain air in my dream. And I so enjoyed the days we spent together here at the Ruby. In the few years since, I have been thinking of my William more and more. Never let your thoughts drift far from Opari, Z. Everything else will fade with time, even for you marvelous children. Be grateful and never let the light dim, never let your hearts doubt, never—

There the letter broke off abruptly. In silence, I looked up and stared out the window, watching miles of rich green country pass by. I don't know how long I did this, but eventually I turned in my seat, folded the letter, and placed it back in the jacket. Willie glanced over at me. "Thanks, Willie," I said. "Thanks."

As we neared the winding gravel drive leading down to Caitlin's Ruby, a light rain began to fall and continued to fall for the following seven days. On the morning of the third day, Daphne was buried alongside her beloved William in a small cemetery behind the Anglican Church where she and William had worshipped for much of their lives. Mowsel, Sailor, Ray, and I hung in the background during the ceremony while Willie accepted condolences from old friends and members of the congregation. He held an umbrella in one hand, but his red hair still matted and clung to his forehead. He was gracious and kind to each person, most of whom he knew well. All were from families with deep roots in the community and surrounding county. He surprised everyone, including me, by announcing he would be staying put at Caitlin's Ruby. He was moving back from America. Because Willie had been so obsessively in love the last time I was around him, it made me wonder, where was Star in this plan?

On the drive back to Caitlin's Ruby, I sat up front with Willie. All I had to do was look at him and he realized what I wanted to know.

"I suppose you were wondering about Star and Caine, right?"

"Yes, I was. Has something . . . changed?"

"No, not exactly. I still love her a great deal, Z. I always will. It just seems to me I should be back here, at least until I find someone I trust to live in and look after the Ruby full-time."

"I agree, Willie, and you're right to do it. But that's not all, is it?"

"No, it isn't." He hesitated and glanced over at me, keeping both hands on the wheel. Rain continued to fall and every road was treacherous. "I think she needs to find something, Z, and at the present time, I do not know what that is."

"Is she depressed? Is she angry, what?"

"Now don't get me wrong, Z, because I'm not speaking of Opari here, but I think they've all gone bonkers—Star, Nova, Geaxi, even Carolina on occasion, maybe the whole damn country. On top of that, it is now impossible to order a pint of ale at the corner bar because of bloody Prohibition!"

I almost laughed out loud, but Willie was being earnest and I checked myself. "Bonkers? How do you mean?"

"I mean bonkers, loony, completely unpredictable and living as if there is no tomorrow. Geaxi is off in Illinois somewhere living as a 'wing walker' in a traveling air show. Nova hears 'voices' constantly and often wanders from coast to coast to find their source. She is also what is known as a 'movie star.' Yes, it's true. She is a child actress in motion pictures. Our privacy has become a ridiculous problem. Geaxi used to travel with her, but now Star is her companion. Star is obsessed with acting and her beauty is attracting the sharks. There was no place for me, Z. I'm afraid my only obsession was Star and that became quite awkward for both of us. For now, at least, it is better if I stay away. And as for my mother, I would never let Caitlin's Ruby go under, never—for Daphne, for all of us."

I watched Willie and I could see the sadness in his eyes finding a good, wise place to go. There it would settle in him, becoming a part of him just as he was a part of Caitlin's Ruby. I said, "I understand, Willie, but what did you mean when you said, 'even Carolina on occasion'?"

"Between blues players and ballplayers coming and going, taking care of Caine, Biscuit, Jack, Owen, and arguing with Ciela, she is fine, and as bonkers as the others, if you want the truth. It's a bloody zoo, Z, so be prepared."

"When was it any other way?"

Willie ran one hand through his damp red hair, brushing it

back off his forehead. He glanced across at me on the turn into Caitlin's Ruby. "Quite," he said, steering the big wheel and smiling faintly.

Later that evening Willie prepared a meal in honor of Daphne. He announced the kitchen to be off-limits to everyone while he cooked. The meal included all of her favorites, even an apricot tart. Willie made a valiant and admirable effort, but the result was slightly dangerous to the digestive system.

In three days the weather cleared and for the first time in our visit the cats of Caitlin's Ruby appeared. Moving, resting, moving again, they were on every window ledge and rock wall, dozens of silent curious witnesses in every shade and color, never making a sound, not a one. None looked the same and none came forward. They were true sentinels in a wild place.

That night, under a full moon, Mowsel, Sailor, Ray, and I took a walk along one of the many paths leading away from the main house. I told them about Nova's recent behavior and public celebrity, and both Mowsel and Sailor showed genuine concern. They seemed shocked and confounded. I agreed. It was not only that she was Meq, but through Baju's bloodline, Nova also carried the Stone of Silence.

Sailor was unable to speak for several seconds, then he took a step forward. His "ghost eye" became a hurricane of clouds, but Mowsel grabbed Sailor's shoulder and held him back. "Silence of water—" he whispered.

"We are," I finished. It was one of the lines Trumoi-Meq had written on the wall of the first Meq cave I discovered in Africa.

Finally, Sailor said, "Indeed."

"It don't surprise me, Z, not a bit," Ray said. Then he turned to Mowsel and Sailor and winked. "I don't think we seen the end of it, either."

I also informed them of Nova's "voices" and Sailor became even more agitated and concerned. "You must tell her this is of grave importance. She may be the bridge in finding the Egongela, the Living Room. Do you understand? I need not remind you we have less than one hundred years until the Remembering. And where is Geaxi? Why is she not there to watch over Nova?"

I told him what Geaxi was doing. He looked over at Mowsel, who shrugged. For a brief moment Sailor smiled, then dismissed the whole subject with a mysterious comment. "Geaxi is being seduced," he said.

We left Caitlin's Ruby early on the morning of June 24, the day before Ray and I were scheduled to depart for America. Willie drove us back to Southampton in the big limousine. From there, he and Sailor and Mowsel planned to continue on to London in order to meet a man of about twenty years of age named Douglas Douglas-Hamilton, the future fourteenth Duke of Hamilton. Willie was supposed to teach him how to fly airplanes. Sailor informed me that Mowsel had arranged the meeting and the lessons. He had been a quiet and close friend of the family for centuries, and tried to maintain a personal relationship with each generation. I knew Mowsel was looking forward to the meeting because he told me so as we were saying our farewells. We were standing dockside, not far from the memorial to the *Titanic*. The ship was still loading cargo and passengers were beginning to board. Mowsel and Willie were about to leave to find petrol for the limousine and the rest of their trip to London. After we embraced, Mowsel reminded Sailor they had an appointment with Douglas-Hamilton and asked him not to dally.

"I think I may be able to learn a great deal from this young man," he said.

As he was turning to go, I had to ask, "Mowsel, what could you possibly learn from a twenty-year-old that you do not already know?"

He glanced at Sailor, then grinned. "I cannot answer that before it happens, Zianno, but this I will tell you—I intend to listen well. I am surprised that with your 'ability' to hear beyond any of us, you still have not learned to listen well. Do this, Zianno, and you will learn many things you never imagined." He held up one hand with his palm facing out and his fingers slightly spread. "Five fingers," he said.

"One hand," I answered, holding up my hand and mirroring his.

I watched him as he walked away with Willie and even though it was a warm, clear summer day, Trumoi-Meq withdrew a long plaid woolen scarf, or muffler, and wrapped it once around his neck, letting the rest trail behind. Just before he was lost in the crowd, he turned and yelled back, "Hail Hadrian!"

I turned to Sailor. "Why does Mowsel like to praise Hadrian? What does it mean? Is it a joke?"

Sailor burst out in a rare and rowdy laugh, causing several early arriving passengers to look our way. He ignored them. "If it is a joke," he said, "I am certain it is on Hadrian. Believe me, it is no joke to Mowsel. Someday, I shall tell you the tale. It is the origin of his name 'Mowsel' and the reason he is missing a tooth." Sailor looked once toward our ship and the passengers queuing up to board. "Have a safe voyage, gentlemen. I will notify you when—"

I interrupted. "Tell me the tale now, Sailor. We've got time."

He glanced in the direction of where Willie and Mowsel had

gone. "Why not?" he said. "However, it must be a brief re-counting."

"Fine," I said.

"Damn right," Ray added. "I've always wondered about that crazy name."

Sailor smiled faintly and gazed not out to the open sea, but northward over the low horizon and beyond. "In the country of what is now Scotland, the land of Douglas-Hamilton's distant ancestors, Trumoi-Meq is a living legend, just as he is to a few precious families in Cornwall. And it all began with the Roman Emperor, Hadrian, and the construction of his infamous wall. In Cilurnum, a cavalry fort on the River Tyne, in AD 123, Trumoi-Meq was recognized as Meq and captured by a Greek slaver who arrived with the First Cohort of Vangiones from the Upper Rhineland. Trumoi-Meq had been traveling and living throughout the northern island chains studying the standing stones and ancient sea routes for hundreds of years before the Romans invaded. Being Meq, he moved easily among the many Celtic tribes, often as a messenger because of his quick understanding of their diverse dialects and customs. On one of these missions he heard reports of a slaver who had been stealing children while accompanying the cavalry on their frequent raids into the 'barbarian' north. Through Cilurnum, the slaver was shipping the children to all parts of the Empire, but if he found one particularly exotic, that child would be sent directly to the Emperor where they would usually be sacrificed in an equally exotic manner. How this slaver knew of the Meq has never been determined. What is known is that he recognized Trumoi-Meq as one of us and to prove it to the soldiers, he had one of Trumoi-Meq's front teeth forcefully extracted, boasting to the Romans that the wound would heal in minutes and another tooth would take its place by morning. Trumoi-Meq was in agony and bleeding profusely, as anyone would be, but the wound did, indeed, heal within minutes. Using that small triumph, the slaver had Trumoi-Meq chained and thrown into solitary confinement until the following day. The Roman soldiers crowded around, saying such things were impossible, and the slaver took all wagers offered. He was no charlatan—the boy would grow another tooth! He had also secretly planned to personally present Trumoi-Meq to Hadrian, thereby becoming instantly wealthy from the Emperor's abundant delight and gratitude.

"That night in the damp and dark of the tiny cell where they kept him, Trumoi-Meq did something quite extraordinary, especially for the Meq. In order to survive, he consciously willed his body, his metabolism, blood, and ancient genetic code, everything in his being, to stop his tooth from regenerating. The Meq have a word for this impossible ability, an old word rarely used—*askenameslilura,* the 'last mirage.' Only by doing this could Trumoi-Meq prove he was *not* Meq. The slaver would be discredited and forced to set him free. It might be his only chance for escape. No one had ever done this before, but Trumoi-Meq *did,* and the following morning he was inspected and released. Before running away, he turned to the slaver. Grinning like a buffoon, he displayed the great gap that is still permanently in the front of his mouth. 'Hail Hadrian,' Trumoi-Meq said, then disappeared through the soldiers and into the crowd. However, he did not leave Cilurnum right away. He was now determined to take every stolen child in the slaver's custody back to their various mothers, fathers, and tribes. Then something occurred to him instinctively. In the same manner, Zianno, as you knew how to read the old script without ever having seen it, Trumoi-Meq knew he could use his missing tooth to save the children, and he knew how. He ran swiftly to the west gate of Cilurnum and the building housing the bread ovens servicing the entire fort. The long building lay in the shadow of the west gate. Below the great brick and stone ovens, the Romans had also dug a narrow tunnel that led away from the fort a good hundred and fifty yards before surfacing in a grove of trees near a small spring. Only a few men at a time used the tunnel, normally for clandestine night raids and reconnaissance patrols. Trumoi-Meq had already befriended and easily bribed the baker in charge of the ovens, whose name was Ith. He had been born a Celt and was sympathetic to the plight of the children. When told of the plan, Ith reminded Trumoi-Meq that it must be done just before dawn, during the brief time he would be preparing the loaves. Once he lit the wood fires and the ovens were warmed, it would be too hot to enter or exit the tunnel. Trumoi-Meq told the baker not to worry, the children would all be moving in silence and without delay. The escape was set for that evening. With a crescent moon high above the fort, long after the soldiers had fallen asleep, Trumoi-Meq slipped into the area where the children were being held. Two dozen children filled the room. They were sleeping on a bare stone floor covered with straw. The smell and stench of stale urine was overwhelming. Their faces were terrified and half starving. Slowly, the children gathered around Trumoi-Meq, but none stood up. They all sat huddled together at his feet. The room was dark and he waited until each one could see his eyes and mouth. He began to speak in an even manner and tone, using a common Celtic tongue. He said, 'Look into the mouse hole, dear ones, and listen. Do not be afraid. Look and listen.' Trumoi-Meq then opened his mouth and grinned. He knelt down until his face was level with the children's faces and let each one gaze into his grin and his gap, his missing tooth, his magic mouse hole. What they saw and what they heard transported them into a suspended, hypnotic state that was not quite a trance, but more a state of infinite trust. Inside Trumoi-Meq's gap, they each found safety and sanctuary. Trumoi-Meq then used the 'voice' he had discovered and understood instinctively, the 'voice' that could save the children. 'Be silent, be swift, and do not be afraid. We are going home. Follow me.' And they did. Once he had picked the locks of their linking chains, Trumoi-Meq led the children through the darkness across the entire fort, from the barracks, past the stables, to the bread ovens and the west gate. The silent voice acted as a beacon in the dark and they arrived unseen and unheard just as Ith was ready to light his fires. 'Not yet,' Trumoi-Meq told him. 'Now open the tunnel, my friend.' In silence, one by one, the children stepped down into the narrow tunnel and none showed any fear or hesitation. 'Into the mouse hole,' Trumoi-Meq said gently as they entered. 'Do not be afraid.' After the last child had disappeared below, Trumoi-Meq followed. By dawn, all were beyond the reach of the slaver and within a week, each had returned to his or her home, though many of them discovered they were now orphans. Trumoi-Meq eventually found a home for them as well. Whenever asked how they had escaped with only another child to lead them, the stolen children always gave the same answer. 'Through the mouse hole,' they said. In the course of time, the name changed and shortened into one mystical, mythical place and person—Mowsel."

Sailor looked back through the crowd and saw something or someone he recognized in the distance. It was Trumoi-Meq. He was standing on the running board of the limousine, waving his long plaid scarf in a circular motion. "It is time," Sailor said, turning back to Ray and me. I stared into his swirling "ghost eye" and thought again about Trumoi-Meq and Sailor and how long they both had been traveling, seeking, and surviving. Sailor would never admit it, yet both of them, without exception or hesitation, still adhered to one basic principle and simple code of behavior—the "Golden Rule." "Ray," Sailor said, "I can see you have an intuitive connection with Nova. You may be the only one she can trust, the only one who may be able to unravel what is troubling her. Do you understand?"

"You bet."

"Keep her in this world, Ray. We need her."

"I'll do what I can, Sailor."

Sailor began backing away and his last comment surprised me. "Zianno, does young Caine wear the blue stone, the lapis lazuli I gave him outside Alexandria?"

"I . . . I don't know."

"Make sure that he does," Sailor said, then darted into the rush, threading his way through the stream of oncoming passengers and luggage, never slowing down, never touching anyone and barely being seen.

The America to which Ray and I returned was not the America we left, and we were given a short preview of it on our four-day passage from Southampton to New York. A large group of mostly young Americans, none older than thirty, were traveling together in what seemed to be a rambling party, constantly flirting, arguing, or laughing with each other in a shifting, never-ending exchange. They gathered in different areas of the ship or walked the decks at all hours of the day and night. None of them seemed particularly rich, yet they drank champagne to excess, often making loud obscene toasts to Prohibition, which never failed to arouse a cheer from each of them. They discussed and debated everything from politics to polyrhythmic African chants. They dressed in various styles and manners ranging from plain and sloppy to tie and tails. Their American slang was unfamiliar, and except for one name, T. S. Eliot, so were their references to current painting, poetry, and music. Many had been directly involved in the Great War and all had left it far behind. Something had changed. These were new Americans in a new age.

Ray noticed the same thing and talked to several of them whenever he got the chance. Since we were still carrying our Egyptian passports, he used that as an excuse to strike up conversations, saying he and I were brothers wishing to practice our English. Being children, we were rarely turned away. After we docked and passed through customs, Ray summed it up in a taxi on our way to Pennsylvania Station. Smoke and gas and noise surrounded us. New York seemed to have a million cars and trucks and ten times that many people, all in motion. He said, "Looks like we're a little behind the times, Z."

Inside the station we ate a delicious meal, bought our tickets, and boarded the first train through to St. Louis. Traveling on our train and sitting across the aisle from us was a young man in his early twenties who had a warm smile and gentle nod for anyone and everyone. In no time, Ray was in conversation with him about all the current news in America, especially baseball. The young man knew a great deal about baseball, more than most fans, and was impressed with Ray's questions. He finally introduced himself, which explained it. His name was Jim Bottomley, better known as Sunny Jim. He was a Major League ballplayer with the St. Louis Cardinals. He had the pleasant disposition and quiet demeanor of an accountant or store clerk, but as we witnessed later, he could play. He was traveling on his own because he had been hit in the head by a pitch in the last game of a series against the New York Giants a few days earlier. He lost consciousness and was diagnosed with a concussion. The doctor wanted him kept under observation in the hospital for at least forty-eight hours. The Cardinals were scheduled to leave New York for Pittsburgh that night. Sunny Jim stayed behind in the hospital. Now he had fully recovered and was on his way to rejoin his teammates in St. Louis. This was his first complete season in the big leagues and at the end of it he would be named Rookie of the Year in the National League. At Ebbets Field the next year, he would hit twelve RBIs in one game, a record that still stands. He would also become a close and loyal friend to Ray and me and Carolina's family.

On July 3 our train made a long stop in Akron, Ohio. It was late in the afternoon and inside the train the heat was stifling. While we waited, porters offered free lemonade outside on the platform. Sunny Jim and Ray decided to look for any bootleg cold beer that might be available for a price. Sunny Jim said all you had to do was ask the right fellow and you could find some hooch practically anywhere in America. And he didn't think it was unusual in the least that a boy like Ray might want a beer instead of lemonade. He said he grew up on the stuff. I chose the lemonade and then went to send a telegram to Owen Bramley informing him of our arrival in St. Louis the following day.

While on my way back to the train I spotted a large poster advertising a demonstration of aeronautical skills coming to Akron later that summer. Many top pilots and barnstormers were flying, including "Tex Rankin of Walla Walla," Marcellus Foose, and Bessie Coleman, or "Queen Bess," the only black licensed pilot in the world. The show also featured wing walkers and parachute jumpers and their names were listed at the bottom of the bill. The last name I hadn't seen in forty-one years. I almost laughed out loud. It said, "Also appearing by popular demand, The Great Geaxi, Spider Boy of the Pyrenees." Not far from the air show poster was another poster advertising a "double feature" motion picture extravaganza now showing downtown at the Rialto Theater. One film was titled *The Ten Commandments,* starring Richard Dix. The other was *The Daughter of Cleopatra,* starring Pearl White and Nova Gastelu, "America's little princess." Maybe Willie was right, I thought. Maybe they really have gone bonkers.

The next day we were delayed repeatedly on our way through Indiana and Illinois. Finally, well after dark, we approached the Mississippi. We could see the lights of St. Louis across the river and, all along the waterfront, fireworks. At least six different celebrations were taking place at once. Sunny Jim leaned over to watch from our side of the train.

Ray said, "Looks like they're giving me a surprise birthday party, Z."

I looked at Ray without speaking, waiting for the punch line, but none came. "Those fireworks are birthday celebrations for America, Ray. This is the Fourth of July, remember?"

"How could I forget? Me and this old country were born on the same day, only eleven years apart."

Ray was smiling, however he was not joking. He was simply telling the truth. "I never knew that," I said. "I knew the year but not the day. Why didn't you tell me before?"

"Well, it's clear as a tear, ain't it, Z? Like Sailor said, you never asked."

I started to laugh and changed my mind. "Happy Birthday, Ray."

Sunny Jim slapped Ray on the shoulder and said, "You got a great imagination, kid."

With fireworks still exploding in the distance, we said our farewells to Sunny Jim on the steps of Union Station. He invited us to a ball game, adding that he might be able to wrangle us a job as batboys for a game or two, if we were interested. Ray told him we'd be there and promised to wear his red beret through the rest of the season in honor of the Cardinals.

Our original intention was to walk the entire distance from downtown to Carolina's, just for old times' sake. Ray said it was too damn hot for that. I agreed and we caught a taxi instead. Ray grinned out the open window almost all the way. The Jazz Age was everywhere. He stared at the cars, people, clothes, and the frantic pace of life, the action. He turned to me and said, "I think I'm gonna enjoy this catchin' up, Z."

Gradually, the traffic thinned and we pulled into the lush and quiet privacy of Carolina's neighborhood. I had the driver let us out on the street in front of her house, which was dimly lit. He glanced once at the big stone mansion and told us what we owed him, looking us both up and down. "You two live here, do you?"

"You bet," Ray said. He twirled his beret on his finger, then gave the man a double eagle, which was ten times our fare. "Thank you for the ride, sir," Ray said politely. "And please keep the change." The driver started to laugh, then sped away. Ray turned and looked up the long driveway toward the house. "Let's go see some folks, what do you say, Z?"

Overhead through a canopy of oaks and elms, only a few stars were visible. There was no sound, except for occasional bursts of fireworks in the distance. A single light came from the first floor and another flickering light shone behind a window on the second. We walked under the stone arch and found the entrance leading to the kitchen. The door was open. We slipped through in silence and saw a figure with his back to us, sitting at the far end of the long kitchen table. He was a black man wearing a formal white shirt. The collar was unbuttoned and his sleeves were rolled up. He was eating a large piece of peach pie and humming a tune I had never heard, a beautiful slow ballad, which he seemed to be improvising.

After several moments, I interrupted. "Mitch?"

He turned as if he had been expecting us. "Hey, Z, man! I've been waitin' for you. Everybody already left to catch the fireworks display in Forest Park." He paused and wiped his mouth. "What kept you?"

"Trains," I said.

"Well, you look good. You, too, Ray. Good to have you back, both of you."

"You gonna eat that whole pie by yourself, Mitch?" Ray asked.

Mitch laughed. "No, man, I wouldn't do that. Get over here and have a piece. It's the best peach pie you ever had."

"So, you're all alone?" I asked.

"Well, no, not exactly," he said and hesitated.

"What do . . ."

I was about to ask what he meant, but it wasn't necessary. I heard small footsteps coming down the stairs from the second floor. Then I heard the voice that only I am able to hear—the silent touch, the Whisper, the Isilikutu. "Beloved," the voice said, "welcome home."

"Z, you all right, man?" Mitch asked.

I blinked and turned around in time to see her walk into the kitchen. I stared into her dark eyes coming out of the darkness, coming toward me. "Opari," I whispered, knowing only she would hear. I took a step to meet her. I could smell her skin. I could see her lips. "Come to me," I said.

Ray and Mitch must have been eating and talking behind us, but I never heard them. For several minutes Opari and I embraced and held each other without speaking. I kissed her eyelids and nose and lips. She wore a long cotton tunic, Berber in design, and I could feel the warmth of her body underneath. The Stone hung from her neck and I swung it aside to bring her closer. I tasted tiny beads of sweat on her forehead and neck. "I missed you more than I ever thought I would or could," I told her.

"And I you."

"I have so much to tell you."

"Tell me now."

"Now?"

She wanted to know everything I'd done, everywhere I'd been. I only wanted to sit and look at her, so I spoke in a low voice and watched her listen. I talked and rambled on. I was unaware of what I was really saying until Opari's eyes opened wide and she put her finger to my lips to stop.

"What did you say, my love? Did you say it may have been Zuriaa who murdered Unai and Usoa?"

I hesitated. "Yes . . . according to the Fleur-du-Mal. I don't know why, Opari, but I believe him. I think he is telling the truth."

Opari stood motionless, staring away, remembering something. "Yes," she said finally. "This is so and I should have seen it—the missing blue diamond in Usoa's ear—the Fleur-du-Mal might have stolen the ear but never the gem. Also, the Fleur-du-Mal would never lie about an assassination. He thinks it to be *unprofessional,* no?"

"So he says," I answered.

"I was afraid of this."

"Afraid of what?"

"Afraid of this knowledge, Zianno."

I watched her carefully. Every feature on her face seemed to change slightly and her dark eyes filled with a calm and compassion I had first seen in the eyes of Geaxi, a look of innocence drowned in experience that is only found in the eyes of an old one. "Ray wants to ask you some questions," I said. "About Zuriaa."

"And I need to speak with Ray, but first, my love, there is something I must tell you."

Just then Carolina burst through the side door and into the kitchen, followed by Ciela, Jack, Owen Bramley, a teenager I assumed was Biscuit, and a boy with dark, wavy hair about five years old—Caine. They were loud and laughing and in high spirits from watching the fireworks in Forest Park. Carolina saw Ray and me immediately and told everyone to hush. They stopped laughing long enough for her to say, "You two are late." Before I could respond, Jack, who was now almost six feet tall and beginning to look exactly like Nicholas, said, "Yeah, Z, you're late by about three and a half years." Everyone began laughing again, and for the rest of the night and throughout the summer of 1923, we did nothing but laugh, celebrate, and "catch up." Ray and I caught up with the times and we all caught up with each other. Only one day from early July to early October was filled with anything but joy and good news for everyone. It was the day after our arrival and the day Ray learned a hard truth about his sister from Opari. It was not what he wanted to hear and the decision had been mine whether he heard it at all.

The first moment we were alone, Opari told me what she knew concerning Zuriaa. Afterward, she asked if this knowledge was knowledge Ray would want to learn. She had held it back from me because she assumed the problem had been resolved. That was before she heard the Fleur-du-Mal denied murdering Unai and Usoa. Now she realized the problem had never been resolved, but had evolved and resurfaced. "Tell Ray everything you told me," I said without hesitation.

The day after our homecoming there was a doubleheader at Sportsman's Park. Carolina still had box seats, so a few of us, including Ray, decided to go see the Cardinals play the Phillies. The box was located in a perfect spot, about ten rows up, just above the Cardinal dugout. It was a hot, humid day with overcast skies and little breeze. The Cardinals' uniforms now had numbers on the back, something they'd never had before. Sunny Jim Bottomley wore number 5 and as soon as I got his attention, I waved to him. He motioned me down to the dugout and asked if I might want to be batboy for the day since their regular boy was sick. I said, "Are you kiddin'? Yeah, sure! Do I get to wear a uniform?"

"Well, sure, kid. We'll fix you up," Sunny Jim said.

A kid was exactly what I felt like. It had been a long time since I was glad to look twelve years old.

During the third inning of the first game, with the Cardinals at bat, I saw Ray and Opari talking face-to-face. Neither paid attention to the game. Opari talked and Ray listened. By the third strike of the third out, he had heard everything. His expression was blank and distant, as if he had suddenly returned from a place he had never been before. Without looking at anyone, Ray stood and turned to leave. In a few seconds he was only a blur in the crowd.

It had been a century since Ray lost touch with Zuriaa in New Orleans. She was his younger sister, barely into the Wait at the time. What Ray heard was this: Zuriaa, his sister, is a murderer. She has murdered many times in many places. She has murdered men, women, and children. She has murdered for money, revenge, and worst of all—pleasure. She was trained and taught the craft of killing by the Fleur-du-Mal until she betrayed him. She has tried to trap and kill Opari through intrigue and stealth on several occasions and failed. She is sick, lost, totally insane, and consumed with hate. The killing of Unai and Usoa means she is once again in the middle of her madness. She is psychotic and dangerous, particularly for those who wear the Stone.

Ray left St. Louis the next day. He said he wanted to visit the Ozarks, see the Buffalo River, and check out the gambling in Hot Springs a little farther south. I knew his real reason was to be alone. At first, I was surprised how hard Opari's words hit him. Then I realized it was typical of Ray to keep those kinds of feelings deep within himself. Still, there seemed to be more to it. While he was gone, Opari told me everything she knew about Zuriaa and her obsessions. At one point, she asked if I knew of anything traumatic that had happened to Zuriaa as a child, a real child. I told her I knew next to nothing about Zuriaa and Ray's early life. I did remember that Ray had said their mother was murdered, but he never shared all the details.

A week later, Ray returned from the Ozarks. He was in better spirits and wanted to talk about Zuriaa openly. The three of us took a long stroll through Carolina's "Honeycircle" and Ray wasted no time in telling us how he felt. He wanted to know if Opari thought Zuriaa could change. The healer in Opari assured Ray there was always a chance Zuriaa could be helped, but it was a small chance. Then Opari asked Ray if he would mind telling her about the murder of their mother. If he would rather not, Opari said she understood and it would not be mentioned again. Ray didn't mind and went through what the police had told him about it. He said it occurred the same year in which Zuriaa turned twelve. Opari asked where Zuriaa was when the murder took place. Ray said Zuriaa was there, in the hotel room. She was found hiding behind a curtain, but she had witnessed the whole thing. On her face there were drops of blood, blood that had spewed out from her mother as the man held her head back and slit her throat.

Opari made a trilling sound with her tongue and teeth, then said, "Iturri!"

"What does that mean?" Ray asked.

" 'Origin,' 'first,' 'beginning.' This could be the origin of the break in her mind, a place of infinite pain the Fleur-du-Mal could easily exploit." She paused and looked at me. "Remember, the Fleur-du-Mal also witnessed his mother being murdered." Opari unconsciously pressed her hand against her chest where the Stone hung inside her tunic. "It is clear now. The murder of Unai and Usoa was a message from Zuriaa delivered to us, especially to me. She is in America. She knows where we live . . . and whom we love. And she may be under the illusion that she is now the Fleur-du-Mal."

"Yeah," Ray said, "that may be true, but what if we find her first?"

"That will be difficult," Opari answered. "The Fleur-du-Mal taught her well, Ray. In China, she was known by several names. The 'Pearl' was most common, but another was the 'Shadow and the Sword.' She has never lived anywhere permanently. She is everywhere and nowhere."

"Like you for a few millennia?" I asked.

Opari raised one eyebrow, then smiled. Her black eyes flashed between Ray and me. "Yes, like me," she said.

For three days beginning on October 4, 1923, a spectacular air show was staged in St. Louis. It was a combination of trade show, swap meet, county fair, military parade, and the largest aeronautical demonstration that had ever been held anywhere in the world. There were 725,000 people watching all events on the last day. The events included an air race, the Pulitzer Trophy Race, a parachute spot landing contest, stunts of flying at Lambert Field and elsewhere, even under the Eads and Municipal bridges, and wing walking. The Great Geaxi, "Spider Boy of the Pyrenees," was one of the featured wing walkers. We had not heard from her all summer because she had been on tour with a dozen different air shows across the United States and Canada. The show in St. Louis was being heavily promoted. On one poster there was a group portrait of six wing walkers, one of whom was Geaxi. The other five had her hoisted on their shoulders. Her left hand held her beret skyward. She wore her leather leggings and boots. The others were smiling but she was not. Her hair was cut shorter than most men or boys and she now wore a false pencil-thin mustache on her upper lip. A long white scarf was wrapped around her neck and goggles were pushed up on her forehead. Her chin jutted out in false pride and her right hand was tucked inside the front of her shirt. She stared straight at the camera. She resembled a very young and thin Spanish Napoleon. Even Carolina had to laugh when she saw the poster.

The show itself was a huge success. We attended every day's events, with Ciela bringing along baskets of fruit, fried chicken, and ham sandwiches. Sunny Jim Bottomley came along with us. Caine rode on his shoulders, wearing Mama's baseball glove, which he now carried everywhere. Sunny Jim was fascinated with the glove and said he had never seen one like it. I told him there never had been one like it.

Geaxi did not arrive in St. Louis until October 6, the last day of the show, and she stayed away from Carolina's home before the events began. Perhaps she had to make preparations for her performance, but I think it was because she wanted us to see her perform before we spoke. I had no idea why she was wing walking at all; nevertheless, I couldn't wait to watch her do it. Neither could everyone else, except Opari. She was more anxious to talk with Geaxi about Zuriaa.

In the early afternoon, a sudden rainsquall over Lambert Field delayed the air show for at least an hour. Once the sky cleared, there was an announcement that the wing walkers would be next, followed by the parachute spot landing contest. Owen Bramley had found an ideal place for us to watch the proceedings. It was away from the main crowd, near one of the hangars being used to service the airplanes in the show. We sat in folding chairs with our hands over our eyes for shade and watched the sky, waiting for the Great Geaxi, Spider Boy of the Pyrenees, to appear in her stunt plane. All the wing walkers used biplanes. The crisscrossing wires between the wings made it possible for the most daring walkers to "travel" on the wing from fuselage to wing tip and back. None of the first five wing walkers attempted that stunt. The sixth biplane to fly over was painted a brilliant scarlet red. Between the wings, with goggles down and white scarf flowing behind, stood Geaxi. Her legs were spread wide. She was grabbing a wire with one hand and saluting the crowd with the other. The biplane made two passes and in that short amount of time, Geaxi almost danced from fuselage to wing tip and back, then out again, where she could not resist lifting one leg high and holding a ballet pose for several seconds.

The crowd went wild. Jack and Biscuit thought it was the best stunt they had ever seen. Ciela had her hands over her eyes, scared to death and unable to watch. Owen Bramley cleaned his glasses with a handkerchief and kept repeating, "Remarkable, simply remarkable." Ray whistled as loud as he could and waved his beret. Carolina whooped and shouted, and Caine, who sat high atop Sunny Jim's shoulders, pointed toward the sky and laughed and laughed. I turned to Opari and said, "Let's go find Geaxi as soon as she lands. I've got to tell her that was amazing, then you can talk to her."

"Yes, I agree," Opari said. "She is something, no?"

"Yes," I said, grinning and shaking my head. "She is something."

Owen arranged for Opari and me to enter the hangar where the biplane would be parked and serviced. The area was off-limits to anyone but pilots and performers connected with the show. Owen walked with us through the maze of airplanes, pilots, and mechanics clustered outside the hangar. We attracted a few passing glances, but most were too busy to notice. Owen posted himself by a side door while Opari and I slipped inside. Immediately, we were disoriented. The hangar had been partitioned into three separate areas, divided by immense curtains of sailcloth, which were billowing and moving back and forth in the cavernous space. There seemed to be only three planes inside, but it was difficult to tell. We walked around the first curtain and I caught a glimpse of brilliant red just beyond the second curtain. "That's her biplane," I said.

We walked toward it. I could hear the big engine roaring. The other two planes were silent with no one in them or working on them. The second curtain swelled and waved from the force of the propeller's blades. Opari and I slowly rounded the curtain and in a split second we were both reaching for our Stones. Ten feet from the red biplane, Geaxi's pilot lay on the hangar floor facedown. He was either dead or knocked out. Beyond him, only five feet from the powerful propeller, two men had Geaxi wrapped inside a carpet, making it impossible for her to reach for her Stone or move anything but her head. They were holding her up and level, walking her toward the propeller, head first. The men wore dark suits and looked to be Maori tribesmen. They were both over six feet tall and heavily tattooed on their faces.

Geaxi either felt us or saw us the moment we saw her. She turned her head in the carpet and smiled. "Good timing, young Zezen!" she screamed.

The two men stopped and turned to look, but before either of us could use the Stone or say the words, two other men appeared from around the curtain behind us. One of the men, tall and skinny with the face of a boy, yelled out, "Look here now! What's going on? What do you think you're doing with that boy? Put him down or I'll find the police!"

The two Maori glanced at each other, then without a word between them, put Geaxi down and walked away. They were not in a hurry and they were not frightened. They were professional killers and their plans had simply changed.

Opari ran to help Geaxi out of the rolled-up carpet. The two men and I followed and the shorter one climbed up the fuselage and jumped into the cockpit, shutting down the engine at once. As Geaxi got to her feet, the taller man asked, "Are you all right, kid?"

"Yes, I think so," Geaxi said, glancing at me.

"Do you want me to get the police?"

"No, no, that is unnecessary," Geaxi said firmly. She found her beret on the floor and quickly brushed it clean and placed it on her head.

"Are you sure?"

"Yes. Is Cooper alive?"

The other man checked on the pilot, who was regaining consciousness and groaning. "He's going to have a hell of a headache for a while, but he should be fine," the man said.

Geaxi looked up at the tall man. "I owe you one, Slim."

"That's all right, kid. Who were those fellows, anyway?"

"I have no clue," Geaxi replied, then stared at Opari and me. "Perhaps my cousins know," she said. "I will ask them."

The tall man scratched his head and said, "Well, if you want me to get some help, I will, otherwise Bud and I will take Cooper to get some first aid."

"Thank you again, Slim."

"Anytime, kid. By the way, Bud and I came back here to tell you the ballet pose was something else." He turned to me as he was leaving. "Your cousin is something else, isn't he?"

"That's for sure," I said. "He is something else."

After the two men escorted the groggy pilot away, I asked Geaxi who they were. She said the shorter man was Bud Gurney, a friend who had entered the parachute spot landing contest. The tall, skinny, boyish-looking one was his pilot. Geaxi said everyone called him "Slim," but his real name was Charles Lindbergh.

"Are you unhurt, Geaxi?" Opari asked.

"Yes, of course," Geaxi said and paused, looking into Opari's eyes. "You saw the faces of the Maori?"

"Yes."

"I know of only one tribe who tattoo their faces with such a pattern—the 'po ngaru,' the 'night wave.' " She ripped the false mustache from her upper lip. "This is true, no?"

Opari nodded in agreement.

"And there is only one who employs this tribe—the Fleur-du-Mal."

"No, there is another, Geaxi, though I am now certain she believes she is the Fleur-du-Mal."

Geaxi looked puzzled. "I do not understand. Who is trying to kill me, and why?"

I interrupted. "The same one who murdered Unai and Usoa. It was not the Fleur-du-Mal. It was Ray Ytuarte's sister, Zuriaa."

Geaxi seemed unfamiliar with the name Zuriaa.

"She is also known as the 'Pearl,' " Opari said.

"Ahhh," Geaxi sighed, recognizing the name. "The Fleur-du-Mal's rejected apprentice, no?"

"Yes, and mine in some ways, I am ashamed to say. Her mind has broken. We are all in danger."

"But I never saw or felt anyone else in the hangar," Geaxi said. "The two Maori were by themselves."

"Yes, and this is . . . larritu . . . worrisome," Opari said, glancing at me. "I am not sensing her presence; however, I am certain she is near."

"Two birds with one Stone," I said suddenly, not even realizing I said it out loud.

"You are not making sense, Zianno," Geaxi said.

"Opari?" I asked. "Could Zuriaa have always known of the Fleur-du-Mal's obsession with the 'Prophesy' and with Star?"

"Yes, it is possible. She was his shadow for many years."

"If Zuriaa's mind has . . . fractured, and part of her, or all of her, truly believes she is the Fleur-du-Mal, then that part would be in St. Louis for one reason—to kill Caine and determine his fate! That's why she is not in the hangar!"

I spun on my heels and sprinted for the corner of the giant sailcloth curtain, pulled it back, and ran through the hangar, under the wings of the second biplane, then around the second curtain and back to the side door where Owen was waiting outside talking to a promoter. Opari and Geaxi were right behind, not even breathing hard. I waved for Owen to follow. We raced through mechanics and tools and ladders, taking a shortcut back to where Carolina and Sunny Jim and the others sat with Caine. The sun was low in the sky and I had to shield my eyes to find them. Finally, fifty yards away, I could see them through the maze of people and planes. We ducked under the wing of the last plane. They were sitting in a circle and they had a blanket spread between the folding chairs. Ciela was reaching in her basket, handing out pieces of chicken to everyone. They seemed to be moving in slow motion. Caine sat in Carolina's lap and Sunny Jim sat next to them. He was showing Caine how to pound the pocket of Mama's glove. He held Caine's hands in his, guiding him. Then, in an instant, Ray leaped up in front of Caine. He screamed a name I had never heard before. He screamed, "Ikerne! Ikerne!" I looked to where Ray was looking and saw a paradox. Standing ten feet away with legs spread, facing Carolina and Caine, was the Fleur-du-Mal, except I knew it was not the Fleur-du-Mal. It was Zuriaa. She looked and dressed exactly like him, down to ruby earrings and ponytail with green ribbon. She had a stainless-steel throwing knife in one hand and her arm was cocked and ready to release. But she was frozen, mesmerized, staring at Caine and not blinking. Ray's voice held her and the name he uttered had kept her from throwing.

"Zuriaa!" Opari yelled out. "Put the knife down! Now!"

Opari's voice woke her. She blinked violently and gasped for air, then turned and stared at Opari. They locked eyes and I saw the vicious and fierce hatred in Zuriaa come alive. Her green eyes flamed with psychotic rage. Ray took a tentative step forward. She backed up instinctively, without looking at him, still focusing on Opari. Her throwing arm never moved or dropped. She took one more step back, then pivoted suddenly to find her target. She let the knife fly and it zipped past Ray's head, directly toward Caine's chest. In the same instant, Sunny Jim raised Caine's hand and caught the knife in the webbing of Mama's glove, six inches from Caine's heart. A great catch from a good first baseman.

Just then the entire crowd around Lambert Field exploded with applause and a tremendous roaring cheer. Someone had made a perfect parachute spot landing in the center ring. Zuriaa yelled a phrase or a curse in Chinese, then turned and vanished, a blur of green and black and red.

"I'm goin' after her," Ray shouted.

"It is too late, Ray," Opari told him and held his arm. "You will never find her. She has already planned her escape."

"I think it is high time we leave this place," Carolina said. She was still sitting in her chair, holding Caine to her chest with both arms around him.

"I think you're right," I said, looking directly into her eyes. I saw genuine fear and firm resolve. "I'm sorry, Carolina. You know I wish I could change things. This should never have happened."

"Yes, Z, but as Opari just said—it is too late. Besides, all of this is not anyone's *fault*. Now, let's go home, and quickly."

"Right, right," Owen added, helping Carolina to her feet. Sunny Jim removed Zuriaa's knife from Mama's glove and handed both over to me. He said, "I won't say a word about this, kid." Jack and Biscuit helped Ciela with the baskets and blanket and all of us hurried through the crowd with Owen Bramley leading the way. Ray kept scanning the crowd for his sister. I had never seen so much concern in his eyes.

"What was the name you shouted to Zuriaa, Ray?" I asked.

"Ikerne," Ray said quietly.

"Who is she?"

"Our mother."

Geaxi's wing walking "ballet" merited a small headline and story on page three of the *Post-Dispatch*. The headline read, "Spider Boy Spins Magic Over Lambert." The writer had no way of knowing it was also the Great Geaxi's final barnstorming performance. That same night, Opari, Ray, and I learned it was not a decision she made out of caution or fear of Zuriaa or her own death. Her decision to stop wing walking came from a completely different place. She said it was time for her to return to her true job—finding the Egongela, the Living Room, our "destination" as Sailor likes to call it. And she feared for Nova. Nova and Star were currently traveling in Scandinavia on a pro-

motional tour. Geaxi wanted to warn Nova of the danger from
Zuriaa in person. Nova needed to hear this information from
her, she said, otherwise Nova might not take it seriously, or even
care. Nova's "visions" had become her obsession. When Ray
heard this, he insisted on going with Geaxi. After that, he said,
he would begin searching for his sister, Zuriaa. She had to be
saved from herself, if possible . . . or stopped. Opari then insisted she accompany Ray. He would absolutely need her assistance to find Zuriaa, she said, and it was something she should
have done long ago.

Opari looked at me. "You must remain here, my love, in St.
Louis with Carolina and Caine. I am certain when Star hears of
this incident, she will be returning. You must be a good shepherd for these good people, Z. Unfortunately, the Meq have
once again brought terror and insanity into their lives. Now we
must remove it."

We were standing in the "Honeycircle." There were only a
few more minutes of daylight. I stared up at the big oaks and
maples surrounding Carolina's property. All were still in full leaf.
A few were beginning to change color, showing hints of red,
yellow, and gold.

"Zianno," Opari said, "you are agreeing, no?"

"Yes, I am agreeing."

Haste became essential. Not only had the Fleur-du-Mal proved
himself obsessed and unpredictable, but now his living ghost,
Zuriaa, had entered the equation. Nova and Star were vulnerable. They must be told as soon as possible.

Events happened quickly. Opari and I had little time to say
good-bye. Three days after the air show, Ray, Geaxi, and Opari

boarded a train in Union Station bound for New York. Geaxi wore her black beret and Ray wore Kepa's old red beret. Their Meq presence seemed to glow, at least to me. Ray and I rarely said good-bye and this was no exception. I reminded him to tell Geaxi and Opari about Susheela the Ninth and the Octopus.

Geaxi heard me and asked, "By the way, young Zezen, how was Africa?"

"Complicated," I said.

"As always, as always. There is something you must see, Zianno. I will leave it with you for study. Nova saw a clear image in one of her 'visions' and I asked her to write it down." Geaxi handed me a sheet of paper with two intersecting lines of written script in the shape of an X. The script was the old Meq script that only I could read. I translated it instantly. The lines intersected through the word "in." They read, *"The Son is in the Daughter, The Daughter is in the Son."*

"Where were these lines in her 'vision'?"

"Floating. Floating in water."

"What do you think it means?"

"I will leave that to you, and Sailor when I see him," Geaxi said, then adjusted her beret and headed for the train.

Opari and I embraced on the station platform. It was not a common embrace of twelve-year-old children, and much too passionate for a brother and sister, but we were oblivious to the comments and stares we might have caused. I wonder if there is a word for a singular force and living bond beyond lovers and friends? If so, we were there, we are always . . . there.

Early the next morning I had a dream. I was riding bicycles with Sunny Jim Bottomley and Carolina and the Fleur-du-Mal. The Fleur-du-Mal was smiling. His teeth sparkled. Carolina was twelve again and wearing a yellow dress. Her hair was blond and stringy. Sunny Jim wore his Cardinals uniform and cap. He said, "Come on! This way!" He led us into Forest Park, but it was an area I had never seen. The street signs were written in Meq. "Where are we?" I shouted ahead. The three of them were pedaling up the hill in front of me. They didn't answer and none of them turned around. They crested the hill and I put my head down, pedaling furiously, trying to catch them. My bicycle began to wobble and shake. The spokes bent and twisted and popped loose, flying in all directions. "Wait! Wait!" I yelled. "Come on, Zianno, hurry!" Sunny Jim shouted from over the hill. "Come on! We're going to Ithaca!"

I opened my eyes.

"Come on, Zano, come on! Wake up, Zano!" It was Caine. He was at eye level and shaking the bed. His dark hair was tousled and tangled from sleep. I remembered his mother waking me in just the same way to go to the World's Fair. She had called me "ZeeZee" that fateful morning.

"Pancakes," Caine said. "Granny made pancakes." He tugged on me and smiled, showing the gap between his two front teeth, which were still baby teeth.

His smile and voice brought on a wave of emptiness and sadness I could not explain or hold back. It was strange. I knew the sudden departure of everyone was not the reason. The reason was a state of mind common to many Meq, more like an infinite ennui that appears out of nowhere. Opari had warned me of it. For the Meq, she likened the experience to a "time disease." It comes on suddenly and has no focus or form, but if left unchecked, can feed like a virus on the weeks, months, and years to come.

Luckily, my spirits lifted only a few hours later. The date was October 10, 1923. The World Series was beginning in New

York between the Yankees and Giants at Yankee Stadium and it was the first time a World Series game was broadcast coast to coast on radio. We gathered in front of Carolina's big Edison radio and it seemed like magic to hear a play-by-play broadcast all the way from New York. That was the first thing to make me feel better and I knew it would. The second I never expected and it has never been explained to me since. Maybe it had something to do with Zuriaa's return, but whatever it was, it was a miracle to all of us, especially to the skinny, dark-skinned orphan, now seventeen, from the streets of New York, renamed Oliver "Biscuit" Bookbinder.

Carolina and Ciela (in Spanish) had always included and spoken to Biscuit as if he were an active part of any conversation. However, Biscuit had not spoken a word and remained mute ever since he witnessed Unai and Usoa's murder on the Orphan Train. He and Jack were best friends and went everywhere together, but Jack did all the talking. Carolina taught him a similar kind of "no speak" communication she and Georgia had developed naturally. Sunny Jim didn't speak to Biscuit at all when he visited. He didn't have to. Baseball did it for him. For a boy his age, Biscuit was one of the best fielding shortstops I had ever seen. Sunny Jim spent hours with him and taught him every fundamental of the game. Their conversations together were a pleasure to watch, full of silent power, grace, and balance.

The announcer's voice boomed out of the radio. Owen Bramley had turned up the volume in the seventh inning. We sat scattered on the floor and in chairs and cheered for the Giants. All of us, particularly Biscuit, hated the Yankees. It was the top of the ninth inning and the score was tied 4–4. There were two outs. The announcer's voice rose, then almost screamed the next play, which ended up being the winning run. A young player for the Giants named Casey Stengel hit an inside-the-park home run to left center field. While he was rounding the bases, he lost his left shoe and the announcer mentioned it. Without warning, Biscuit stood up off the floor, cheering wildly and laughing hysterically. Everyone else stopped cheering instantly and stared at Biscuit. He was not yet aware he had laughed out loud. He kept cheering and laughing until he suddenly realized he was the only one making a sound. His laughter ceased and he turned slowly, looking into each of our faces. Some were smiling, some were crying. An old invisible wall in his mind had crumbled away and disappeared. "Madre de Dios," he said.

"Madre de Dios," Ciela echoed, then crossed herself three times.

As Opari had predicted, Star cabled from Oslo as soon as she learned about Zuriaa and the events at Lambert Field. She said she was returning home at once. Alone, she set sail for New York, stopping briefly in London to meet with Willie. She arrived in St. Louis on Thanksgiving Day and I went to Union Station alongside Carolina and Caine to welcome her and take her home.

The moment Star stepped from the train, I was stunned by how physically attractive she had become, and she had lost her naïveté completely. She always possessed an inner confidence. Now there was a maturity and grace in her movements and expressions that had not been present before. She still looked like Carolina's twin, with freckles across her nose and cheeks and tiny gold flecks in her blue-gray eyes, but she had surpassed her mother in sheer beauty. She wore a long fur coat and her hair was cut short and "bobbed" in the style of the day. Except for a small amount of lipstick, she wore no makeup, and yet, Star could easily have launched a thousand ships. And there was no doubt about her love for her son. She picked up Caine, who ran to her the instant he saw her, and held him as close and tight as she could, spinning in a circle, kissing him, repeating over and over, "Mama loves you, Mama loves you."

During the drive to Carolina's, Star noticed Sailor's ancient lapis lazuli hanging from a necklace Caine now wore around his neck. "Why is he wearing the blue stone?" Star asked her mother, who deferred to me.

"Sailor said he should have it with him at all times," I said. "He didn't tell me why, but after the air show, I think I know why—as a talisman for protection."

Star nodded and held Caine closer, only letting go when he finally said, "You're squeezin' me, Mama."

On Christmas Eve, Mitchell Ithaca Coates returned to St. Louis, bringing along at least a dozen presents for Caine and a half dozen for everyone else. He had been living in the city for which he was named, Ithaca, New York, through the summer and fall of 1923. He went there to be with his long estranged father, who was dying of lung cancer. He stayed by his father's side until the end, which came sometime during the night of December 10. After settling affairs in Ithaca, Mitch headed straight for St. Louis and Carolina's home. He was slightly thinner than the last time I had seen him, but otherwise seemed the same. His easy smile and buoyant spirit were still intact and he was wearing his familiar black tuxedo and black tie. He looked handsome and prosperous, which he was. Carolina said he had made a fortune in the first two years following Prohibition, then got out of the business completely when he learned his father was sick, well before he had made any serious enemies, or been arrested, or lost his money. Now he was the semiretired co-owner of two businesses: the St. Louis Stars, a charter member of the Negro National League, and a nightclub on West Pine called Chauffer's Club, one of the hottest spots in town for black musicians. Mitch didn't expect me to be at Carolina's, but he handed me two presents anyway and said, "Merry Christmas, Z. I missed you, man."

"Me, too, Mitch," I said. "Me, too."

A deep snow fell on New Year's Day and we celebrated by having a small feast. Ciela made a huge pot of Cuban-style black-eyed peas with onions and peppers and chunks of smoked ham throughout, served with cornbread and great quantities of sweetened iced tea. It had been a long time since I had seen snow and I stood by the window watching the snow fall all day on the big oaks and maples, covering them and silencing the whole neighborhood. Nothing moved except the snowflakes. I watched them falling, drifting, piling up like white time. All I saw were seconds, minutes, hours, years . . . years and years. At one point, I heard a voice nearly as silent as the snow and turned around. No one was there. Less than a whisper, the voice sounded like Opari, but it was not. It was another. She spoke to me as if we had already been engaged in conversation. She said, "Is it innocence we are compelled to save and keep from harm's way at all costs? No! It is experience. We must protect it, preserve it, and shepherd it from hill to hill, heart to heart, like fire in a frozen world. Experience alone is our power, the source of our magic, our deep knowledge. We can only learn in increments, degrees, drops, and small pebbles of truth, often random in meaning, backward and forward in time. Eventually, one by one, these pebbles will be collected and a path shall be revealed. Then we must ask the obvious: to where? The answer awaits us at the Remembering. All hands shall be extended, unasked and unannounced, and the Window will open."

Through the window and to no one and nothing, I asked, "But where? Where is the Remembering?"

The snow was silent. I felt a presence approaching from behind. "Z? Are you all right?" It was Owen Bramley. He had his glasses off and was walking toward me, cleaning them with a handkerchief.

I blinked twice. "What? Oh, yeah, sure," I said. "I was . . . thinking out loud."

"You were speaking to someone, asking questions."

"Was I? Well, it's nothing." I turned and stared again at the white world outside. "There's no one there."

Owen made no comment. A few moments passed while we both looked through the glass. "I appreciate your vigilance, Z. We all do. I want you to know there was nothing you could have done differently at the air show. You were there for our protection, for Caine and Carolina, and I want you to know I am trying to do the same for your people. We need your protection from a madman and a madwoman, but soon you and your people will need protection from *us*."

"Us?" I asked. "Who is *'us'*?"

"The United States of America, the world, mankind . . . they're not ready yet, Z. They're not ready for you. Solomon was right. They will eat you alive for possession of your secrets."

I let several seconds pass. Outside, a large clump of snow suddenly broke free from the roof and fell, exploding into the snow below. The collision never made a sound.

"We know," I said, looking back at Owen. "We have always known."

Music is the most mystical of all elements of consciousness. According to Sailor, the Meq once used singing as their only form of communication. Painters often feel as if they are playing an instrument rather than painting, and when a painting works, it never feels like work, it feels like playing music. Families know this and use it. If a son is in danger, or a daughter missing, it can become a voice, a bridge, and a silent smile between them. Few things can do this. Music is one.

The winter slipped by quickly. With fireplaces blazing at both ends of Carolina's living room, music became our passion. On the radio, on the phonograph, in concerts and in clubs such as Mitch's Chauffer's Club, the "Jazz Age" was healthy and active in St. Louis, and we talked of little else. Many brilliant musicians passed through and touched our lives. At Carolina's request, Mitch always invited his favorite players to her house for a good home-cooked meal and a few relaxed hours away from the road life. Each of their talents and personalities were unique, but their hearty enjoyment and appreciation for Ciela's cooking was universal.

One man I remember well was a young black guitar player from Memphis named Furry Lewis. He told wonderful stories, mostly about characters he knew from the streets, and he had a droll, sly sense of humor. Late one night in the kitchen, I became his mark and unwitting straight man. We were eating pulled pork sandwiches with coleslaw and black beans with rice. "You got to come down to Memphis and see me, kid," he said, then wiped his mouth carefully, slowly, stretching the pause, never meeting my eyes. Finally, I said, "Well, sure, Mr. Lewis, I'd love to. Where do you live?" He looked at me and smiled. "Oh, don't worry, kid, you can't miss it. It's the first little red house painted green."

In the spring of 1924, we welcomed back baseball and our long, slow walks in Forest Park, then farther to the south along Hawthorne and Longfellow Streets, and all through the cultured, diverse beauty of Shaw's Garden. Except for an enigmatic postcard from Geaxi, we heard little from Europe or anywhere else. The adage "no news is good news" became our maxim and comfort. Geaxi's note on the postcard was written in Basque and transitional Meq. Translated, it read:

> NOVA WITH ME—VISIONS AND VOICES DAILY—R.
> AND O. OFF TO FIND THE PEARL—I MAY HAVE FOUND
> SOMETHING BIGGER—EGIBIZIRIK BILATU—G.

I knew the Pearl referred to Zuriaa, and the news about Nova was worrisome, but not unexpected. However, the "something bigger" was a mystery. Sailor sent no word, nor did Ray or Opari, which was not unusual, but still caused a few unsettling dreams.

Solomon Jack Flowers turned eighteen in April and made the startling announcement he was not attending college in the fall. Instead, he was going directly to work as a staff writer for *The Sporting News.* He had already published a few articles under his current pseudonym, Solomon Jack. He said the name made him sound wise. Carolina stifled a laugh, rolled her eyes, and simply wished him well.

The Cardinals had another so-so season, but Sunny Jim had a good year along with arguably the best right-handed hitter of all time, Rogers Hornsby, the Cardinals shortstop. He hit .424 that year, an amazing batting average. He was a difficult man, however; blunt, brutally honest, and gray eyes cold as stone. "The Rajah," he was called. Sunny Jim had another name for him— "Jolly Rogers"—because Hornsby had smiled twice all season, on and off the field.

Late in the year we got to watch what became Nova Gastelu's final screen performance. The film was Erich von Stroheim's *Greed*. In the original, unedited version, Nova plays a waif and street urchin in a dozen scenes and is completely convincing. She truly is an actress. Unfortunately, no one will ever know. Owen Bramley, through various contacts and transfers of favors and money, had arranged for all of us to see a private screening of the original version in St. Louis. We entered the theater at ten in the morning and exited just in time for dinner, eight hours and fifty reels later. The film the public saw was only twenty percent that length. The rest was cut and disappeared from Hollywood forever, and so did Nova. After hearing about Zuriaa, she became convinced by Geaxi to end her life as a Giza "movie star."

In January of 1925, on the night of the twenty-third, I experienced a Walking Dream unlike any I had ever dreamed before. In total darkness, I rose from my bed and discovered dozens of tiny handprints glowing on the door of my bedroom. I walked toward them and the door swung open by itself. No one was there, but I saw more handprints on the walls of the hall outside. I followed them to the stairs and down to the first floor and through the living room. Eventually, they led to the small room where Georgia's old upright piano still stood. The handprints covered the piano, glowing white, yellow, orange, and red. A large book lay open where the sheet music usually sat. The handprints were bright enough to illuminate the text. It was *The Odyssey* by Homer. Odysseus was on his return home to take vengeance on the suitors of Penelope. It was at the failing of the old moon and the coming of the new. My eyes focused on one line. It read, "The sun vanished out of heaven and an evil gloom had covered all things about the hour of the midday meal, during the celebration of new moon." I closed the book and instantly the handprints disappeared. At that moment, I became aware of where I was and rubbed my eyes, which were watering. When I reopened them, the book had also disappeared.

The next day, Mitch dropped by in the afternoon for a sandwich. It was cold and snow still covered the ground. In the kitchen, he took off his coat and muffler and blew into his hands, saying, "Guess what happened in Ithaca today, Z."

"Ithaca?" I asked.

"Yeah . . . Ithaca, New York, where my father lived."

"What happened?"

"A total eclipse of the sun." He paused and blew into his hands again, then shook his head. "Man," he said, "I sure would like to see one of those."

I looked past him, through the kitchen window in the direction of Carolina's "Honeycircle," which was blanketed in snow.

I walked over to the window and blew on it. I pressed my hand against it, then took it away, leaving a perfect handprint on the frosted glass. "Yes," I said, "they are dreams in the sky."

On March 18 of that year, Carolina, Mitch, and Jack were nearly killed, not by Zuriaa or the Fleur-du-Mal, but by something just as unpredictable and deadly—a tornado. The storm is still called the Great Tri-State Tornado because it was the most powerful, destructive tornado in American history.

Mitch had instigated the trip, a scouting trip to Carbondale, Illinois, where he planned on meeting a young black ballplayer named Caleb Bellows, whom Mitch thought might make an excellent center fielder for the St. Louis Stars. Carolina and Jack simply went along for the drive. By two o'clock in the afternoon, they had passed through Perryville on Highway 61 and were heading south. Suddenly, on the horizon to the southwest, a huge black cloud appeared. It was moving at a rate of sixty miles per hour. Mitch decided to stop and pull over on the side of the road. They each got out of the car and stared as it roared by in the distance. The funnel cloud seemed already obscured by flying debris and the giant tornado had only begun its swath of devastation. It crossed the Mississippi and charged through Illinois and Indiana, lasting a record three and a half hours on the ground, with the funnel averaging a quarter mile in width and occasionally growing as wide as a mile. An estimated 690 people were killed. If Mitch had not stopped when he did, the number would surely have been 693.

On May 30, Rogers Hornsby replaced Branch Rickey and became a player-manager. Rickey remained as vice president and continued to develop his ingenious farm system. St. Louis lost the next two games, a doubleheader in Pittsburgh, even though Hornsby hit two home runs in the second game. The summer passed and the Cardinals again could only look forward to next year.

The pace of life at Carolina's was fast, but full and peaceful. I neither heard nor felt danger. There were no surprises, no real worries, but also no word from Opari, Ray, Geaxi, Nova, or Sailor. I carried the Stone with me at all times, as always, and never used it. More like a rare coin or a lucky charm, the Stone of Dreams was only something slightly heavy in my pocket. I did receive one long letter from Willie Croft in November. It was sent from a town in Wales that was eighteen letters long and unpronounceable. He said he missed St. Louis dearly, but he went on and on about Caitlin's Ruby, saying he finally had found someone he could trust to live there permanently. Through Mowsel and with the full approval of Pello Txopitea, his son Koldo would become caretaker and overseer. Arrosa, now Koldo's wife, would accompany him. I let Star read the letter and she smiled as she read it, laughing to herself. I could tell she wanted to see Willie again. As she handed it back to me, she said, "I can hear his voice."

The early months of 1926 flew by and another premier musician became a close friend of our family. He was from Davenport, Iowa, and his name was Leon Bismarck Beiderbecke, better known to everyone as Bix. He played the cornet and he played with fire and precision, as well as being a brilliant composer. He played with black players at the Chauffer's Club and with white players at the Tremps Bar on Delmar and the Arcadia Ballroom on Olive. His musical influences, abilities, and interests were as diverse and complex as his playing. Many times he attended concerts of the St. Louis Symphony with Carolina, Owen, and their mutual friend, the jazz pianist Bud Hassler. Bix left St. Louis that summer and only lived a few more years, unfortunately. He died young during an alcoholic seizure at the age of twenty-eight. I still think he is one of the best horn players ever.

Jack was working more and more, traveling to sporting events and publishing funny vignettes taken mostly from baseball; hilarious characters based loosely on real players Sunny Jim had known. Jack also discovered a young writer and a new book that changed his destiny, if there is such a thing. The writer's name was Hemingway. He had been born in Chicago, but now lived in Paris. The book was *The Sun Also Rises.* Jack knew instinctively the writing was new and good; however, it was Spain, the Pyrenees, and Basque country that captured Jack's heart and imagination.

Caine and I made numerous trips to Forest Park and the Zoo, especially the bear pits, where we rarely spoke and watched for hours. I always acted as his older brother. He was only eight years old, but he was approaching my height at an alarming rate. He called me Zianno now instead of Zano, and I missed hearing it.

In October, one of the most competitive and magical seasons in the history of Cardinals baseball concluded with a National League Pennant and a chance to play the Yankees in the World Series. Carolina had box seats and season tickets, and because of it we were offered the first opportunity to buy tickets to all home games, which we did without hesitation. The Yankees were considered the most feared team in baseball, with a lineup called "Murderers' Row," consisting of Babe Ruth, Bob Meusel, Lou Gehrig, and Tony Lazzeri. They had hitting, pitching, and depth, but it made no difference. The Cardinals were led by a perfect mix of talented young players like Sunny Jim Bottomley, as well as experienced veterans, such as Rogers Hornsby and the grizzled Grover Cleveland Alexander. He was broken down and alcoholic and near the end of his career, but at one time he had been considered one of the greatest pitchers in baseball. Mitch asked Sunny Jim about him in June, the day the Cardinals purchased Alexander from the Cubs. He said, "Now I'm not saying I'm a bettin' man, Sunny Jim, but let's pretend I was. What I'm askin' is . . . uh . . . well, how bad is he?" Sunny Jim scratched his head, then laughed. "Mitch, I'll just say one thing about it. You can smell him long before you ever see him."

On the afternoon of October 10 with the series tied 3–3, we gathered around the big radio in Carolina's living room and turned up the volume. In the bottom of the seventh inning, the Cardinals were trying to hold a 3–2 lead. There were two men out and the bases were loaded with Tony Lazzeri batting. Hornsby stopped the action and called for Grover Cleveland Alexander in the bullpen. Drunk and still half-asleep, Alexander walked to the pitching mound. He got Lazzeri to strike out, but not before Lazzeri hit a long fly ball, barely foul in the left field stands. The Cardinals were out of the inning with their lead intact. In the ninth Babe Ruth was thrown out at second base to end the game and the Cardinals won the World Series of 1926. Much later, Grover Cleveland Alexander described it this way: "Less than a foot made the difference between a hero and a bum."

On a cold, gray day in December, the Cardinals' owner, Sam Breadon, surprised everyone by trading the manager and second baseman, Rogers Hornsby. "The Rajah" had asked for a three-year contract since the Cardinals won the World Series and they traded him instead. Sunny Jim said, "It's going to be hard filling his shoes, no matter who takes his place." There was no irony in his voice. I could tell he meant what he said, regardless of how he felt about Hornsby the man. Then he added, "That's baseball."

I had hoped to hear news from Opari and Ray by the New Year, but none came. Geaxi, Nova, all remained silent. Most of my time during the winter of 1927 was spent in the kitchen, talking with Ciela about Cuban cooking and discussing the subtleties of the shortstop position with Biscuit. On March 2, I was working on a crossword puzzle when Jack burst into the kitchen and threw a newspaper down on the table, then walked over to the stove to see what Ciela was cooking. I picked up the newspaper and began to browse through the pages. On the third page, I recognized a name in a column about a young airmail pilot, currently living in St. Louis. The name was Charles Lindbergh and I remembered the tall, skinny barnstormer whose timely actions had saved Geaxi's life. He had just begun construction in San Diego on a single-engine, custom-built airplane he planned on flying nonstop from New York to Paris, alone. At stake was the Orteig Prize of $25,000, originally offered in 1919 to the first one who could accomplish the transatlantic feat. In the years since, several good pilots and their aircraft had exploded or disappeared in failed attempts. Lindbergh would be the first to try it solo. He said his plane would be ready in sixty days and would be called the *Spirit of St. Louis*. Investors in the project were all local St. Louis businessmen, including E. Lansing Ray of the *Globe-Democrat*. The publisher of the rival *Post-Dispatch* had declined to invest, saying, "I want no part of a one-man, quixotic enterprise." The column ended with the writer praising Lindbergh's courage and wishing him luck, referring to him as "the lone eagle." The writer's name was Jack Flowers. In the sports section, I found another short piece about Babe Ruth signing a new three-year contract with the Yankees that paid him an estimated $70,000 per season, a tremendous amount of money for a ballplayer. The piece was informative, incisive, and well written. The writer's name at the bottom: Jack Flowers. I looked up and he was standing by the stove. He was a carbon copy of his father, Nicholas (Nick) Flowers, without the mustache.

"What happened to 'Solomon Jack'?" I asked.

He glanced back, knowing I'd found and read the articles. "He still works for the *Sporting News,*" Jack said, then smiled. "But not for long."

On March 3, Oliver "Biscuit" Bookbinder's life was also about to change. Just before noon, Sunny Jim telephoned long distance from Florida with an offer that Biscuit could not refuse. A team the Cardinals played in exhibition games, a traveling all-star team playing out of Cuba, was missing a shortstop. The regular shortstop had disappeared near Sarasota with a burlesque dancer from Miami. If Biscuit could make it down to Florida in three days, Sunny Jim said he would get the job at shortstop, or at least a shot at it. Sunny Jim told him he was good enough to do it.

"Sunny Jim is right," I said. "You are good enough. Now, go play the game. You will never regret it."

Biscuit did not hesitate. Mitch drove him down in record time, and since Biscuit was still a teenager, Ciela insisted she go along as chaperone. For luck, I gave him a double eagle gold piece on the day he left and he promised never to spend it. The three of them roared away on a Tuesday and Mitch was back less than two weeks later. In a week, Biscuit was offered the position of shortstop for the Havana Habaneros, which he accepted. He was now a professional baseball player. A week after that, he was asked to move to Cuba and play with the team on a permanent basis. It was another offer he could not refuse. On my birthday, May 4, we stood in Carolina's kitchen and toasted the missing Oliver "Biscuit" Bookbinder, along with Ciela, who had decided to go with him to Cuba, though she was reluctant to leave St. Louis and especially Carolina. She telephoned us from Miami the night before they departed. "It is the right thing to do," Ciela said through constant tears and sobs. She had prayed on the matter and asked for guidance. God had spoken to her in a tiny voice. He had whispered, "*Vamos,* Ciela. *Vamos.*"

On May 11, I finally received word from Geaxi. It was a telegram delivered along with Jack shouting the news that Charles Lindbergh had just landed at Lambert Field in the *Spirit of St. Louis,* setting a new nonstop speed record of fifteen hundred miles in fourteen hours, twenty-five minutes. Jack was breathless and laughing and saying, "He's on his way, Z! He's going to Paris!"

"What are you talking about, Jack?" It was Carolina.

"Lindbergh. Charles Lindbergh is on his way to New York, then, when he's ready—nonstop to Paris." Jack paused and remembered something in his hand. "This is for you, Z," he said. "It was addressed to my office for some reason."

"What does it look like?" Carolina asked. She was standing at the far end of the table, peeling potatoes. She tossed one to Jack. "The airplane. What does the *Spirit of St. Louis* look like?"

"It is beautiful . . . silver and sleek and fast. He's going to make it, Mama. I know he will."

I excused myself and went directly to my bedroom. I opened the telegram and read it carefully. Once again, it was written in a hybrid form of Basque and Meq. Translated, it read: "NOVA NOW SEEING VISIONS AND HEARING VOICES OUT OF CONTROL. MAY LOSE HER. TAKING HER DIRECTLY TO RUBY. COME NOW. ALSO HAVE OTHER NEWS—GEAXI."

I left that night on a train for New York, then within a day, on a ship for England, which Owen Bramly booked ahead of me. Mitch asked to accompany me and I welcomed his company. After four days of rough seas, we arrived safely in Southampton on the afternoon of the nineteenth. Willie Croft was there to greet us with open arms and a new limousine, a black and silver Rolls-Royce with huge wheels and reinforced frame. It looked like something made for a duke, which it was. Willie had purchased it from the Duke of Hamilton.

We cleared customs without incident or delay and piled into the Rolls-Royce for the long ride to Cornwall. While Mitch and Willie caught up with each other's lives, I slept behind them on the rear seat. By the time Willie slowed and made the wide turn down to Caitlin's Ruby, I was awake, alert, and anxious to see Nova.

As soon as we came to a stop, I leaped out of the limousine and walked over to the low stone wall alongside one of the paths leading west. I climbed on the wall and faced the setting sun, turning orange and gold behind a thin bank of clouds on the horizon. I breathed in deeply. I felt a familiar breeze brush across my face. It was filled with the smell of wild leeks, Italian cypress, thistle, pine, and the faint, fresh taste of the open sea. It was the scent of Caitlin herself.

"Man, that smells good," I heard Mitch say. I turned and he was referring to the aromas drifting out from the kitchen windows and over the drive.

"Arrosa's bounty," Willie told him. "Come inside, Mitch. Arrosa will serve you something straightaway. It's all Basque, you know, and quite good." Willie looked my way. "You as well, Z—come inside."

"In a minute," I said.

"Oh, damn, I nearly forgot," Willie said, slapping his head. He started walking toward me.

"What?" I asked.

"This," he said, pulling a folded envelope out of his shirt pocket.

I reached down and he handed it to me. It was a telegram from Jack in New York. He must have left St. Louis shortly after us.

"I forgot completely, Z. It came last evening from Falmouth. I apologize."

I opened it on the spot. It had been sent on the nineteenth. Today was May 20. It read: "LONE EAGLE TAKES OFF TOMORROW MORNING FROM ROOSEVELT FIELD. WISH HIM GOOD LUCK. JACK."

That meant Charles Lindbergh was in the sky right now, somewhere between New York and where I stood. He might even fly over Cornwall. That is, if he makes it. If he doesn't crash, veer off course, meet foul weather, run out of gas, or fall asleep.

"Anything wrong?" Willie asked.

"No. I mean, I hope not."

"What are you saying, Z?"

"Where is Geaxi?"

"Why, almost right behind you. Turn around."

I turned and saw Geaxi, still a few hundred feet away, running directly toward me out of the setting sun. She wore her black beret, boots, and leather leggings and vest, tied with leather and bone. She wore no jewelry and I knew the Stone of Will was in her pocket. She closed the gap in seconds and without a sound.

Not even out of breath, she said, "An adequate response time, young Zezen. I am impressed."

"Good to see you, too, Geaxi." I paused. "Where is Nova?"

Geaxi removed her beret and glanced at Willie, who turned and headed for the kitchen. "I will tell Arrosa to keep everything warm," he said.

Geaxi looked at me. Her gaze was steady. Her eyes were black and piercing. She gave nothing away. She nodded in the opposite direction, down the path that led to old Tillman Fadle's stone cottage. "Come with me," she said quietly, turning me with a touch and leading the way.

Inside the cottage, there was little light and no sound. The air felt cool and damp. Tillman Fadle had never completely modernized the dwelling. It was charming and quaint, but full of drafts. Geaxi lit a candle and walked to a small room off the kitchen with its own fireplace. A daybed, pushed against the far wall, took up half the space in the room. There was only one window and a single standing lamp. The curtains on the window were drawn and the lamp turned off. A fire burned and crackled in the fireplace. Nova sat in front of it in a rocking chair, staring into the fire with a frozen gaze. Her face was pale. She wore no eye shadow, no lipstick, and no jewelry. She was dressed in a long white nightgown and wearing Geaxi's ballet shoes for slippers. A beautiful blue and green woolen shawl, covered with dancing reindeer, was draped around her shoulders. Geaxi had kept her clean and brushed her hair, making certain she ate regularly and slept when she could, but Nova was a living ghost. Her mind and soul were not in the room.

"This is the only place where she is at peace," Geaxi said. "She will stay here without wandering off, which became dangerous in Norway."

"What happened?" I asked.

"Her visions increased in content and frequency, even during sleep. She would wake terrified from nightmares of exploding balloons rising two and three miles in the sky. She saw handprints everywhere in vivid colors, while being awake or asleep. She became increasingly consumed with the image of a silver-winged bird, a 'lone eagle,' falling from the sky into the sea. She—"

"Lone eagle?" I interrupted.

"Yes," Geaxi said, "until everything ceased at once." She brushed back Nova's hair with her hand. "We were still in Norway, far to the north near Trondheim. We were having breakfast. I was waiting for a man I had been trying to find for three years. Suddenly Nova lifted her coffee cup and turned to me. 'Geaxi,' she said, then gasped and closed her mouth, as if her breath had been stolen. She has not said a word since that moment. I had to remove the coffee cup from her hand. She had locked in place, then disappeared somewhere inside herself, and there she remains. Trumoi-Meq said he has neither seen nor heard of this state. I have not yet spoken with Sailor."

I looked once at Nova, then gave Geaxi the telegram from Jack.

She read it quickly. "Who is the 'lone eagle'?"

"Lindbergh—he's flying solo to Paris."

"Lindbergh? Charles Lindbergh?"

"Yes."

"He is flying now?"

"Yes."

Geaxi glanced at Nova and adjusted the shawl around her shoulders. She stirred the coals in the fire, then added a log. Finally, she motioned for us to leave. Geaxi ran her hand through Nova's hair once more and I stroked her cheek. Nova made no response. We turned and left the cottage without a word and walked up the gravel path in silence. It was getting dark and a few stars were visible. Halfway to the house, Geaxi stopped and looked to the west.

"Lindbergh will need our help," she said. "He will break down. He will sleep. He will fight it, but his mind will let go. He will not be able to stop it. We must be there with him. We must keep him awake."

"How?" I asked.

" 'The Voice.' It is an ancient practice, long forgotten and rarely used. The Meq understood and used it during the Time of Ice to communicate over great distances. It must be found within, then sent through time and space. It travels more from the heart than the mind; however, its power is significant and Trumoi-Meq is convinced the practice saved many lives." Geaxi looked at me and smiled. "You and I, young Zezen, shall be the ones to do this now."

"Have you done this before?"

"Never."

"How will we know what to do?"

"How did you read the old script in the caves?"

I had no answer.

"The supreme argument does not require speech, Zianno.

Now, let us eat. Arrosa is an excellent cook and we shall need our strength for the vigil. Koldo can look after Nova. She trusts his presence. He will make a good Aita someday."

We stopped at the house long enough for Arrosa to pack a basket full of lamb sandwiches, cheeses, fruits, cider, and a large bag of Catalonian olives. Arrosa wished us luck, but never asked our destination. Geaxi led the way through darkness and drifting ground fog, up the hill and along one of the six paths leading to the ruins of Lullyon Coit. She always referred to the place as "the slabs." The ancient granite stones had stood for millennia as an enigmatic marker or shrine, a mysterious shelter pointed in a precise direction for an unknown purpose. Now, they lay broken and scattered on the ground like pieces of a giant jigsaw puzzle. Using only his mind, Sailor had toppled them all in seconds. He never completely explained his purpose to anyone. I think it was an act of anger and frustration. I think, at that moment, he truly believed there was no purpose, and worse, there might never be. Despair is the most dangerous state of mind for the Meq.

Geaxi and I sat amid the broken stones until dawn, facing west, listening to the darkness. At times, I extended my hyperhearing farther and deeper than I ever had, sometimes miles out to sea. Still, I heard nothing. Should we even listen for him? Should we listen for his plane, his voice, his mind, or his heartbeat? How will we know when to send "the Voice"? Where would we find it? What was it? All through the night we discussed these things and a thousand others. We ate the food, drank the cider, and talked about everything. The olives were delicious and sparked a memory from Geaxi. It was a long, wonderful, funny story about her mama and papa and the famous olive oil her papa made, renowned and prized throughout the Mediterranean and beyond. We also talked about St. Louis and Carolina and her family. She asked several insightful questions about the game of baseball and current American culture and music. I tried to explain what a "flapper" was, but I am certain Geaxi never quite understood it. She suggested we keep talking, share everything, combine our actions and minds, synchronize and prepare. "Always when facing the unknown," Geaxi said, "one should be relaxed and focused." We talked, listened, and waited.

As dawn approached, our conversation gradually decreased and our senses sharpened. The wind blew in gusts from the north and west. It was still pitch-dark to the west. I turned just in time to catch the first rays of light breaking in the east. Something crossed my mind, something Geaxi had not mentioned all night long. I turned back around. "In the telegram," I said. "What was the 'other news'?"

Geaxi never answered. She was facing west, leaning forward. "Listen!" she said. "Do you hear that, Zianno?"

I concentrated as hard as possible, leaning forward and listening, stretching my "ability" far into the North Atlantic. I heard the wind, but nothing else.

"He is slipping away . . . what . . . yes . . . yes . . ." Geaxi mumbled. Her eyes glazed and her pupils dilated. She opened her mouth and began to produce a sound that could not be heard, only felt and understood instinctively. I felt a vibration begin in my stomach and spread to my heart and lungs, then finally to my throat and mouth. In tandem and parallel, as in a chorus, we began making the same soundless sound. It was effortless. It was like swimming in another dimension, a dreamlike highway of spirit and mind.

I looked back as the sun rose and spread light across the broken stones. Every single cat of Caitlin's Ruby had gathered around us. Green eyes danced like stars, staring back in silence. I turned again and Nova was standing just beyond the farthest broken block of stone. She was in her white nightgown and her feet were bare. The shawl had been abandoned. Her eyes were dark and distant. She was staring to the west. Geaxi never turned around. She closed her eyes and increased the volume and intensity of "the Voice." I closed mine. We traveled together as a wave, crashing through space, ahead of the sun, ahead of time . . . west, west . . . west into darkness.

And there it was! A strange silver bird with no eyes, and wheels instead of talons, more albatross than eagle, flying low and straight on the horizon, close to the water. Suddenly and without warning, our wave, our chorus, increased and swelled. Another powerful voice had joined us, sweeping us forward, our "Voice" changing, filling and spilling down, directly through the silver bird and the living mind within. *"A—haz—tu!"* we sang. For a brief moment, the strange bird dipped slightly, then recovered and regained its true and steady course toward the east and the light of dawn.

I opened my eyes. I looked for Nova, but she had shifted position. She now stood to the west of "the slabs," staring back at Geaxi. Neither spoke for several moments. Geaxi searched her eyes. I started to reach for her and Geaxi grabbed my arm, holding me back.

"Are you awake, Nova?" Geaxi asked. She took a tentative step toward Nova, extending a hand. "Do you know where you are?"

Nova stopped staring at Geaxi and glanced at me, then down at her nightgown and bare feet. She seemed puzzled, confused, like a small child who has just awakened from a long dream.

"How did I get here?" Nova asked. "And what are you doing here, Zianno?" She rubbed her eyes and turned in a slow circle, trying to understand.

I laughed and smiled. "You walked," I said. I was simply glad to have her back.

"And you spoke!" Geaxi said.

"Why wouldn't I?" Nova replied.

Geaxi and I exchanged quick glances.

"Who woke me?" Nova asked. "The voice was not you, Geaxi, and it was not Zianno, but it was Meq. I heard it clearly. The three of you were singing, 'A—haz—tu.'"

"That was another?" I asked. "The other voice was not you? I assumed the other voice had been yours."

Nova looked to Geaxi. "Who was it?"

"I do not know," Geaxi said. She paused and looked west again, frowning. "Yet, his voice was completely familiar to me in a way no Meq ever has been."

"He?" I asked.

Geaxi dropped her frown and turned to me. "What?"

"*He*—you said *he* was familiar to you."

"I did? I said that?"

"Yes."

Geaxi shook her head back and forth. Gradually, a small smile appeared. "I do not know who or what it was," she said, "but I have never felt such a thing. Never."

Back at the house, Arrosa was up early and preparing breakfast. She was shocked to see Nova, but not completely surprised. The Meq and their mysteries were not unfamiliar to her.

Later, all of us, including Arrosa, Koldo, Willie, and Mitch, gathered in the courtyard of Caitlin's Ruby to watch the skies. It was Saturday, May 21, 1927. In the thirty-first hour of flight, the *Spirit of St. Louis* was sighted and signaled while flying over Cornwall. We never saw the *Spirit of St. Louis,* but the drone of the big engine could be heard for miles.

Geaxi said, "We shall go to Paris. I must congratulate him."

Mitch said, "I second that! The man has earned it."

Nova continued to look slightly confused. "Who? Who is he?"

"The 'lone eagle,' " I said. "Charles Lindbergh."

At 10:24 P.M. that evening, he landed safely in Paris at Le Bourget airfield. The entire flight had taken thirty-three and one-half hours.

His life would never be the same.

6

ELUR

(SNOW)

Snow is separate from all other phenomena in Nature for one specific reason: when it snows, each tiny six-sided snow crystal, every single snow "flake," is unique and unlike any that has ever fallen before or ever will after. Still, is it not strange that at the end of this miraculous creation and fall, each instantly becomes part of a whole, forever unrecognizable as they were? Punishment or reward? Remember, Nature makes no mistakes.

We left Caitlin's Ruby early in the morning, just as the last remnants of fog were burning off and all of Caitlin's cats were scattering back into obscurity. All except one, a big white male Persian with an enormous tail, who sat staring at us from a stone wall close to the limousine.

"I call him Snow White," Nova said. "He is the only one among them who will not let me near."

Nova took a tentative step toward the wall and Snow White jumped and ran the length of the wall before stopping. He looked back once, then disappeared over the side with the others.

Arrosa sent us away with plenty of food and a letter of introduction to a woman now living in Paris on the Rue d'Ulm in the Rive Gauche, the Left Bank. Geaxi had not been to Paris in several years and had no existing contacts in the city. Also, for various reasons, she did not want to stay in a hotel. I had never been to Paris and neither had Nova. Mitch said he was planning on staying with an old friend from St. Louis—"a surprise visit," he called it. Arrosa assured us her friend could be trusted in every way and would be glad to give us shelter and any assistance we needed. They had first met as dancers in New York and had remained close ever since. Her name was Mercy Whitney and she had been living in Paris throughout the 1920s. Arrosa said she was independent in mind, spirit, and bank account, and loved to laugh.

Geaxi thanked Arrosa and said, "Those are good attributes for anyone."

I loaded what little luggage we were carrying and in minutes we were headed east. Willie did the driving and Mitch sat up front with him. Geaxi, Nova, and I sat in the back.

"First stop—London," Geaxi said. "I must check the mail at Lloyd's, then we are off to Paris."

"The mail?" I asked. "At Lloyd's? What's the joke?"

"I should have said safety deposit box; however, it is still the mail to me. We have used Lloyd's Bank in London for over a century as an occasional message drop, particularly by Trumoi-Meq."

"That sounds much too modern to be Meq," I said. I scratched my head and winked at Nova. "I would have thought it more likely we had a drop at Stonehenge."

Nova laughed, but Geaxi did not. "We do, young Zezen,"

she said evenly, then leaned forward and began talking over the seat with Willie about current experimental aircraft design in Europe.

I laid my head back and let my mind drift. Spring was in full bloom and the English countryside became a rolling kaleidoscope of color and texture. We opened the back windows of the limousine and let the wind rush through. It felt the same way good fresh spring water tastes. I smiled all the way to London.

Once we were in the city, Willie drove with skill and patience through the narrow maze of streets. The noise and traffic seemed to have tripled since the last time I'd been there. Luckily, a block from Lloyd's, we found a place to pull over and park. Geaxi, Mitch, and Willie left for the bank while Nova and I stayed behind.

As soon as we were alone, Nova turned to me. She was wearing her heavy Egyptian mascara and her lips were a deep red. She showed not a trace of the frail and pale ghost she had been only days before. Still, something was troubling her.

"Z," she said, "you are the Stone of Dreams. I know of no one better than you to tell." She paused and stared blankly out the window.

"Tell what, Nova?"

"I have been having a series of dreams, but one in particular. Over and over, more and more horrible each time." She paused again.

"What do you see? What's in the dream?"

"A balloon—a huge, awful, burning balloon. Over and over, rising, burning. I can't make it stop." She turned back to me. "What does it mean, Z?"

I knew she wanted an answer. She was desperate for one, and

I wanted to give her an answer, but there was no answer, no truthful one.

"I don't know what it means, Nova. It is your dream and your balloon." I looked into her eyes closely. "Can you live with this nightmare, Nova? Will you be all right?"

She sighed and smiled slightly, then laughed once. She put her hand over the center of her chest, where the Stone of Silence hung from a necklace underneath her blouse. "Yes, of course, Z. As Geaxi likes to say, after all, we are Meq."

In less than twenty minutes, the others returned. Willie and Mitch jumped in the front seat. Geaxi climbed in back with Nova and me. "To Paris," she said, throwing three London newspapers across the seat. Charles Lindbergh's flight was the headline story in all three. Without delay, Willie put the limousine in gear and we were on our way. He would drop us at the docks, where we would be off to Calais, then on by train for Paris. Geaxi withdrew a letter from her vest, waving it back and forth. "News from Mowsel," she said.

"Where is he?" I asked.

"New Delhi. He is with Sailor. They have found Zeru-Meq. Negotiations are under way to enlist his assistance in finding Susheela the Ninth and stopping the Fleur-du-Mal however possible. No decision yet, and also no sign or rumor of the Fleur-du-Mal himself. I think I know why."

"You?"

"Yes. I do not believe he is anywhere near New Delhi. Quite by accident, I learned of something in Norway. It is the 'other news' I mentioned in my telegram to you."

"What is it?"

"The Fleur-du-Mal has a home."

"A home!"

"Yes—in Norway. I believe he is there now and has been there since you saw him in Egypt. The man I was waiting to meet in Trondheim is the man who sold it to him. Nova was stricken before he arrived and I never got the exact location of the home. However, I know where the man was going from Trondheim. If we are in luck, he is still there."

"Where?"

Geaxi smiled wide. "Paris," she said.

Mercy Whitney's home on the Rue d'Ulm was a sprawling, light-filled, ten-room apartment directly above a small restaurant and café called "La Belle Étoile." The building was old, but clean and well kept, with dark green shutters and wrought-iron balconies. Day and night, delicious aromas and scents drifted up from the kitchen below and filled the air with traces of garlic, fresh-baked bread, or roasted lamb. During our entire stay in Paris, I was constantly hungry. In our first conversation, Mercy Whitney acknowledged the problem.

Geaxi, Nova, and I stood in the hallway outside her apartment door. Mitch had gone his own way at the train station, saying he would stop by the Rue d'Ulm address in a day or two. He never mentioned where he was going or whom he was surprising, but he checked his luggage twice to make certain he had packed his tuxedo.

I knocked on the door. In seconds, I heard footsteps and the door swung open. An attractive black woman in her late twenties, taller than average and dressed in denim overalls, stared back at us. She had reddish brown hair, which was cut short and parted on one side with a dramatic wave plastered across her forehead. She was barefoot and her overalls, hands, face, and feet were splattered with yellow paint. She looked each of us over thoroughly, then spoke to me.

"Am I dreaming?" she asked. "Are you three children for real?"

"I think so," I said. "I've never been asked that before."

"And you speak American English. Are you triplets?"

"No, but we're very close. Maybe this will explain it. It's a letter from Arrosa."

Her eyes lit up. "Arrosa?"

"*Sí,*" I said and handed her Arrosa's letter.

As she read the letter, Mercy Whitney laughed with abandon at every sentence. I couldn't help but smell the wonderful aromas wafting up the stairs. When she finished, she said, "Come on in. I haven't seen that girl since she moved to Cornwall. I need to hear all about her." She saw the hypnotized expression on my face. "Afterward, I'll clean up and we'll go downstairs and eat. You will not be able to stay here without thinking about it, so we better fix that craving right away. What're your names?"

I gave her mine and Nova and Geaxi introduced themselves. As she led the way inside, I told her we were from St. Louis.

"Well, you two sound like you're from St. Louis," she said, nodding toward Nova and me. She looked at Geaxi. "But I cannot place your accent at all. What would you call it?"

"English with a hint of Phoenician," Geaxi said flatly.

A moment passed. Then Mercy Whitney laughed again—a big, generous, lusty laugh. "Of course, of course," she said. "What else could it be?" She turned and waved for us to follow her down the hall, then stopped and winked at Geaxi. "I like the beret and leggings."

"Thank you, Mercy. By the way, is Charles Lindbergh still in Paris?"

"Oh, yes, he's still in Paris, all right. That man is the toast of the town—no, I should say the toast of the world!"

"So it would be difficult to see him, no?"

"Impossible, unless you were asked." She paused and raised one eyebrow. "Do you know Lindbergh?"

"He saved my life once."

"Of course he did." Mercy started to laugh, then stopped. Something else occurred to her. "Wait," she said. "There may be a way and my boss will love it. Three nights from now, she is invited to a gala performance at the Theatre des Champs-Élysées, a benefit for the Airman's Relief Fund. Lindbergh is going to be there. She loves children and you're from St. Louis, her hometown. She would love to take you along, I just know it."

"Who is your boss?" I asked.

"Josephine Baker." Mercy looked at me and waited for a reaction. "You never heard of her?"

"No, I don't think so."

"I have," Nova said with a smile. "She's amazing."

Mercy laughed big and loud, then turned in a pirouette spin even Geaxi could admire and waved for us to follow, saying over her shoulder, "Yes, yes, and yes." She laughed again. "Josephine is amazing. That she surely is."

We were led down a long hallway that both divided and connected the entire apartment. The living room, dining room, and kitchen adjoined each other and all rooms opened onto the hallway. There were five spacious bedrooms and two bathrooms. A dozen huge windows lined the north and west sides. Mercy said we were lucky, we could each have our own room. She often had boarders filling up the place for weeks. She said dancing with Josephine Baker paid well, but not that well, and from time to time she needed extra income to afford the apartment. And she had to live in this apartment because of one room at the end of the hallway—the artist's studio. Dancing paid the majority of her bills, but she was in Paris to live in this apartment and paint in this specific studio.

"Why?" Geaxi asked bluntly.

"Because Rune Balle once lived and painted in this studio. He is my inspiration."

"Rune Balle!" Geaxi almost shouted.

"Yes."

"Who is Rune Balle?" I asked.

"Few have ever seen his work," Geaxi said. "Let alone the man himself. He is more than merely obscure. He and his work are virtually unknown to all but a handful of people. He is also the man I was waiting to meet in Trondheim." Geaxi paused. "How do you know of Rune Balle, Mercy?"

"My father owns a painting of his, done in 1903 shortly after Balle studied with Edvard Munch. It is called *Snowblind*. My father first showed it to me when I was twelve. I've wanted to be a painter ever since."

"I see," Geaxi said. "And how did your father obtain the painting?"

"I'm not sure. I never asked. But did I just hear you correctly? Did you say you were waiting to *meet* Rune Balle?"

"Yes."

"Rune Balle has not been seen or heard from since 1906. He is considered dead, even by his own family."

"True enough," Geaxi said, "until recently. I believe I now know where he has been and where he may be at the moment."

"What—where for God's sake?"

"The Left Bank."

"But, but, that's here, that's where we are!"

"I know," Geaxi said with a smile. "We could use your assistance, Mercy. You are familiar with the area and you know the people. We will have to ask questions. You could make it much easier for us."

"I would be more than happy to help," Mercy said. She shook her head, then broke into another round of boisterous, contagious laughter.

Finally, Geaxi asked, "Mercy, are you all right?"

"Yes, yes, of course. I'm fine," she said. "It's just that I can't help thinking about something Arrosa said in her letter. It's a bit of an understatement."

"What was that?" I asked.

"She told me to 'expect the unexpected.' "

Two days passed in a blur of activity. From early morning until late at night we combed the streets, shops, cafés, and bars of the fifth, sixth, and seventh arrondissements. We made countless strolls up and down Saint Germain and Saint Michel, asking questions, searching, hoping to find a connection to Rune Balle. No one seemed to know him, which was not odd since he had been considered dead for twenty years. Lindbergh's name, however, was everywhere and on everyone's lips. Mercy accompanied us during the day, but at night she was working at Chez Josephine. We spent both nights in Montmartre, high up on rue Florentine, loitering near two clubs across the street from each other, Bricktop's and Zelli's. Geaxi said they were the kind of places Rune Balle had preferred in his youth. We watched the traffic and never saw a sign of him, but Nova became completely absorbed and fascinated with Parisian street life—the personalities, hairstyles, conversation, and especially the fashion. Geaxi seemed unaffected by it, telling me, *"Il faut cultiver notre jardin,"* or "We must cultivate our own garden."

By morning of the third day, we still had not heard from Mitch. I worried about it. It was unusual for him not to call or come by. Whatever the reason, if he had fallen down, fallen ill, or fallen in love, it was probably serious. We made our rounds anyway and then headed back to Mercy's apartment for lunch. The telephone rang. Mercy picked up the receiver, laughed, then held out the receiver so we could hear. The voice came through loud and clear. It was Josephine Baker, laughing and shouting and telling Mercy to get those children from St. Louis over to her apartment now, faster than a pig squirms. She wanted to meet us before we went to the benefit that night. She couldn't wait to talk about St. Louis. She was sending over her car and her chauffeur within the hour. From her place we would all go to the Theatre des Champs-Élysées together. She went on and on. Mercy finally stopped her and said we would be waiting on the front steps.

Less than an hour later we were picked up and driven to Josephine Baker's apartment. Her chauffeur opened the door getting in and out, then ushered us inside the apartment. Mercy had warned us that Josephine loved animals, but the reality was bizarre. Between and among a cluttered, exotic, eclectic collection of things and furniture, including a bust of Louis XIV, stacks of letters and magazines, records, clothes, costumes, and furniture, she kept a parakeet, a parrot, three baby rabbits, and a snake. We were led through the apartment into a large kitchen, where half a dozen people were gathered in a small circle, each with a smile on their face and a champagne glass in their hand. In the midst, kneeling and talking rapidly, Josephine Baker was telling a story about Berlin. She was also grooming her pig. The pig's name was Albert and he smelled of perfume. She caught a glimpse of the chauffeur and looked up, first at him, then to Mercy, then over to us. She was at eye level. She was dressed in a full-length silver gown with sequins sewn in an intricate design, platinum loop earrings, and a string of pearls around her neck. Her short hair was styled similar to Mercy's, only the wave across her forehead ended in a spit curl. She wore heavy eye makeup and oxblood lipstick. On her head she wore a lacy skullcap covered in sequins. She was a beautiful, stunning, brown-skinned girl of only twenty-one—the rage of Paris— and yet, she looked familiar. I was certain I knew her, I had seen her before, but I couldn't place it. Then she smiled. It was a great, wide grin, which took me back instantly to the night I met Arrosa at Mitch's club in St. Louis. I remembered a young girl backstage, trying to sneak in and watch the dancers. Mitch called her "Tumpy," but he said her real name was Josephine. For a second that night, the girl and I caught each other's eye and she smiled, just before Mitch pushed her out the door.

Josephine Baker's smile faded and she stared at me. I saw in her eyes the gradual recognition of our mutual memory, followed by the puzzling paradox that comes with it.

"I remember you," she said. "It was St. Louis . . . I was a kid about your size . . . I remember you, but . . ."

"How is it possible that I appear the same now as in your memory?"

"Yes."

"Because the true you chose to remember it that way. If you did not, I would not exist."

Josephine Baker laughed and whistled. "That sounds almost crazy, honey."

"You're not the first girl to say that."

"But that don't explain nothin'," she said.

Nova smiled and said, "Oh, yes it does."

"It could explain everything," Geaxi said.

Josephine Baker stood and waved her arms high in the air and shook her hands as if she were in church or singing in a revival. *"Tout de même,"* she said. "You must be an angel because Mitch needs some hometown cheerin' up and I ain't been able to help him one little bit."

"Is this where he's been staying since he got to Paris?" I asked.

"That's right, and we were havin' a swell time until this mornin'. Then Mitch came down with the blues real bad. He's as sour and mean and quiet as a man can be."

"Where is he?"

"In a church."

"Church?"

"Yes, and I'm worried about him. He's been there for hours. Why don't you talk to him, honey? Cheer him up—talk him into goin' with us tonight." She pointed to a dark-haired man with a thin mustache standing near her. "Pepito will take you there."

"I'll go right away," I said.

Pepito was Josephine Baker's companion and soon-to-be husband. He was an obvious hustler, but he was nice to me and we struck up an easy conversation. He led us through traffic for several blocks until we stopped in front of an old and ornate church, Saint-Paul–Saint-Louis. The facade was three-tiered and rose seven or eight stories, covered in great stone columns and arches with statues in recesses on all three levels. Pepito climbed the steps with me, saying he would wait for me under the massive stone arch of the entrance. I walked inside. My eyes adjusted quickly to the dim light and I found a place to sit near the aisle on the last row of pews. The cavernous cathedral was eerily silent and all the pews were empty, except for two people: a young girl in the front row who seemed to be weeping, and a black man two rows ahead of me. He sat with his head bent forward and his eyes closed. It was Mitch. As always, he was wearing his tuxedo, but the jacket had been removed, the tie loosened, and the collar unbuttoned. I stood and walked down two rows. He kept his eyes closed. I sat and moved over until I was within five feet and waited.

Thirty seconds passed. Almost whispering, I said, "Mitch, are you all right?"

He looked up slowly, not even surprised to see me. There were no tears in his eyes, but there was a deep and true sadness. "Hey, Z," he said. His voice sounded dull and flat. "I been meanin' to call, man. I just . . . I just ain't got around to it."

Another twenty seconds passed. I gazed around the cathedral. "I didn't know you liked churches, Mitch."

He smiled faintly. "I can't say I frequent the joints, Z."

"Any reason you picked this one?"

"It was old."

"Sounds like a good reason to me." I let a few more moments go by. The girl in the front row rose to light a candle at the altar. I heard her mumbling a prayer. I turned to Mitch. "What's wrong, Mitch?"

He took a deep breath and sighed. "Nothin' I won't get over.

Today is May 27, the same day my old man died in Ithaca. It hit me hard this time around." He paused and looked up at the girl by the altar. "I think about him different now than I used to. I miss him."

"I know how you feel. I miss my papa every day."

"No, Z, that ain't what I meant. You miss what you two had together. I miss what we never had until the very end, and then we just ran out of time. I only got to know him those last few months. Inside, I hated him most of my life, but in the end I got to know him. And I forgave him inside. Now I miss him and I can't bring him back. It's not fair, man."

"I agree. There's nothing fair about it."

"And he died confused, Z. That ain't fair either."

"What do you mean, 'confused'?"

"He never got rid of his guilt . . . and his regret."

"Because he left you and your mama?"

"I think so, but you see, he'd done it before. He told me he did it twice in his life—once in Africa, and again a few years later in St. Louis. He spent several years with his family in Africa before he left, but he left St. Louis not long after I was born. He said I got a half sister somewhere. No doubt about it, he had a pile of regret. And you know what the saddest part is, Z? He never knew why. 'I have searched my soul,' he told me, 'and I have never known why I did it—either time.' "

"That is sad, though he must have been happy to finally have you with him."

"Yeah, he loved it. He had a hell of a life, Z. He was an engineer, a gambler, a preacher, and a professor. He quoted Walt Whitman all the time, and the Bible. He survived a shipwreck off West Africa and being captured by a desert warlord named

El Heiba, then escaping with the daughter of a shaman. She was being held as a slave because El Heiba believed she had some kind of voodoo power. They made it out of the desert and cross-country all the way back to her village, where he lived with her and her people for years as man and wife. Wild stuff, man, but he lived it."

Suddenly, I got a chill up my spine, not because of the story but because I'd heard it before—in Africa! The coincidence was too startling to be an accident. "Mitch, did your papa ever tell you the name of your half sister?"

"Yeah, he said it out loud one time. He whispered it. He called her 'Emme.' " Before I could say anything, Mitch added, "I got a picture of him right here, Z. I took it myself about a week after I got to Ithaca." He reached for his tuxedo jacket and withdrew a photograph from the inside pocket. "Here he is," Mitch said, "that's Cayuga Falls in the background."

I looked at the snapshot and another strange coincidence occurred. I had seen the face in the photograph before. I had met the man in 1919, just as we were preparing to dock in New York. It was when we were bringing Star home, finally, after all those years in Africa, along with the bodies of Nicholas and Eder. I was walking the deck alone when a thin old black man asked me to watch his things while he stepped inside. I remembered the books he carried with him, *Leaves of Grass* and the Bible. His bookmark in the Bible was a train ticket to Ithaca, New York. Mitch's father was the same man. I almost laughed out loud at the recognition, then realized where we were.

"Mitch," I said, "you are not going to believe a couple of things I have to tell you."

Just then, the wide doors behind us opened and I heard

Josephine Baker's voice saying, "*Merveilleux! Merveilleux!* What a church!"

Mitch and I both turned around. Mitch said, "Tumpy, what are you doin' here?"

She wore her long silver gown with sequins and they sparkled in the half-light and shadows. She marched over to Mitch, speaking in exaggerated whispers. "Because, Mitch honey, we have decided that you need a night out and we won't take no for an answer." She stopped and looked down at Mitch in the pew. Pepito followed close behind her. She glanced his way. "Ain't that so, Pepito? We all agreed, right?"

"*Sí, sí,* we all agreed," Pepito said. He started to say more, but decided to light a cigarette instead. Josephine grabbed the cigarette out of his mouth before he could light it and stuffed it in his coat pocket without saying a word. She turned back to Mitch and flashed her biggest, widest grin. "Come on, you got to go, honey. What do you say?"

Mitch answered slowly and without much emotion. "Josephine, don't take this personally, but I believe I'll pass on this one."

Josephine almost stamped her feet in frustration, then glanced at me for help.

"I think she's right, Mitch," I said. The sadness still filled his eyes.

Mitch looked away, toward the altar. "I just don't feel like it, man. I just . . . I don't know . . . I just . . ."

I heard the doors swing open behind us. I turned and Mercy Whitney walked through, dressed in an elegant crimson dress and wearing a skullcap similar to Josephine's. She smiled when she saw us and hurried over. Ruby earrings dangled from her ears. Her lips were the same color as the rubies. "What a beautiful old church," Mercy said. Mitch suddenly looked startled, as if a bell had rung. He turned in his pew instantly. His eyes found Mercy's and Mercy's found his. The exchange was and is one of the rarest moments in life and I was witness to it. I recognized it because I had experienced the same moment in China when Opari and I first looked into each other's eyes. It is a split second of wonder, mystery, and magic. It is love at first sight. Unexpected and unprepared, and in the dim light of the church of Saint-Paul-Saint-Louis, Mitchell Ithaca Coates and Mercy Whitney were given the flower of that moment. It came to them unasked and unannounced and in full bloom. I couldn't help myself and laughed out loud with joy, despite where we were. Josephine Baker had also seen the exchange and joined in, understanding immediately what she had seen. Mitch and Mercy ignored us. Their eyes were locked. I watched Mitch's eyes. I have never seen such a sincere and heartfelt sadness disappear so quickly. Finally, Mitch smiled and said, "I just changed my mind, Tumpy."

"I can see that, honey," Josephine said.

I noticed an older priest walking up the aisle from the altar. He was not pleased or amused. "I think it's time to leave," I said, nodding in his direction.

"Time indeed, the car is waitin' for us," Josephine added.

Outside, there were two limousines lined up against the curb. We climbed in the open door of the lead car and were welcomed by Geaxi. She said Nova was in the second car with the rest of Josephine's entourage. The lights of Paris were shining all around us. Josephine told her chauffeur, "Theatre des Champs-Élysées, Etienne, *s'il vous plaît*." We pulled into traffic and in moments the church of Saint-Paul-Saint-Louis became a memory, but the moment inside was alive and well in the front seat, where Mitch and Mercy were only beginning a conversation that would last the rest of their lives.

After waiting in a long line of limousines on avenue Montaigne, we arrived at the gala event. When Josephine stepped out, she was more than welcomed, she was practically worshipped. Shouts of "La Perle Noir!" and "Our Fifine!" surrounded us. She rushed past, waving at everyone and throwing kisses. The presence of children in her entourage was nothing unusual. The people of Paris knew she loved animals and children and often took them with her wherever she pleased.

We were met inside by one of the managers. Josephine was currently dancing with the *Folies Bergere,* but I was told she had become famous at the Theatre des Champs-Élysées, where she performed her outrageous Banana Dance in *La Revue Negre.* The manager accompanied us to a private box reserved especially for Josephine. Whistles and scattered applause greeted her as she appeared, waved, and took her seat. It was nothing compared to the thunderous, hysterical standing ovation a few minutes later as Charles Lindbergh made his entrance. He waved from a private box on the opposite side of the hall, along with local dignitaries and a few aviators. He was taller than all of them and looked half their age and half their weight, but he was the reason they were there. He was the reason everyone was there. Even Josephine clapped and whistled, shouting his name with abandon.

Geaxi, Nova, and I took our seats behind Josephine, Pepito, and a half dozen others. Mitch and Mercy sat off to one side, completely oblivious to everyone and everything. They spoke rapidly and never stopped staring in each other's eyes. The diva,

Mary Garden, dressed as Lady Liberty, sang the Amercan national anthem and the show began.

Geaxi kept her attention focused on Lindbergh's box throughout the first two acts, then turned to me. She winked and said, "I think I shall take a stroll, young Zezen." She slipped on her beret and gracefully exited unnoticed into the hall behind us.

Nova enjoyed everything about the show and the performers. She wanted to know each of their names and was constantly asking Josephine about costumes, sets, jewelry, and makeup. She was fascinated with the theater and the people who lived the life of the theater. She told me she loved the "illusion of it all." She watched every act with anticipation and joy, laughing and clapping, sometimes jumping up and down, exactly like an excited twelve-year-old girl—the best illusion in the room.

Occasionally, I glanced at Lindbergh's box, fully expecting Geaxi to suddenly appear, but she never did. Mitch and Mercy continued falling in love, oblivious to most of the show and the people around them. At one point, I saw Mitch touch Mercy's lips and trace the outline with his fingers. I remembered doing the same thing with Opari and for several minutes I was lost in a kind of dream, thinking only of Opari, longing for her, aching for her.

It was Geaxi who broke the reverie. "Zianno, come quickly!" I turned and she was standing directly behind me. She motioned for me to follow. "Quickly!" she repeated. I rose and left without a word to anyone.

Once we were in the hall, I asked Geaxi, "Did you get to see Lindbergh?"

"No," she said, pulling me aside. The hallway corridor was

crowded and she wanted privacy. Geaxi acted calm, though her black eyes burned bright with energy. "I just met someone," she said. "I was, in fact, near Lindbergh's box, observing the security, which was extensive. To devise a plan, I found a seat on a small bench against the wall of the hallway. As I was thinking, a black woman approached me directly. I remained silent and she sat down on the bench. 'Do not be alarmed,' she said, then smiled. I smiled back." Geaxi paused.

"So, that's not unusual," I said.

"Yes, but then she asked, 'Do you know Zianno Zezen?' I did not answer right away. Instead, I looked in her eyes. She was aware that I was Meq and she was completely comfortable, even respectful. I examined her closer and realized she must be a shaman's daughter. She had been deliberately scarred as a child with three raised lines on both temples."

"Emme Ya Ambala!" I shouted.

"Yes. We spoke at length. She recounted your time together in Africa and said her grandfather's last words contained your name. She then asked what we were doing in Paris. I trusted her intuitively and told her the truth—we were searching for a man named Rune Balle." Geaxi's eyes brightened again. "Without hesitation, the woman said she could help. 'If Rune Balle is in Paris,' she told me, 'my husband will find him.' "

"I know him," I said, "and she's right, he is the perfect man to help us."

"She is waiting. She wishes to see you, young Zezen."

I burst out laughing.

"What is so humorous?" Geaxi asked.

I turned to run back to Josephine's box. "Stay here," I said, "there is someone else she needs to see."

In less than a minute, I returned with Mitch and Mercy in tow. Geaxi seemed puzzled, but she spun in an effortless motion and led the way toward Lindbergh's box.

We hurried through the crowd, which was an assortment of the Parisian elite dressed in jewels, gowns, and tuxedos, along with World War I aviators in full uniform, most missing an arm, or leg, or wearing an eye patch. As we got closer to Lindbergh's box, photographers and reporters gathered and filled the hallway, all waiting and hoping to get a picture or a quote from "Lucky Lindy." Then I saw her. Apart from the crowd, on a small bench against the wall, sat a black woman in her late thirties. Her skin was dark chocolate and her hair was cropped close to her head, like Geaxi's. She wore a dress covered in the bright colors and designs I had first seen in Senegal. She was very attractive and very pregnant.

I tapped Geaxi on the shoulder. "You never told me she was pregnant."

"As Sailor would surely point out, young Zezen, you never asked."

I glanced back at Mitch. I had not yet explained where we were going or why. I had simply grabbed him and said, "Follow me."

Captain Antoine Boutrain stood next to her. His hair was streaked with silver and his face was beginning to show the weathering from years at sea, but other than that, he looked well and healthy. Emme smiled broadly and reached for his hand as we approached. She stared up at me in silence, then we embraced for several moments. As we separated, she said, "I knew we would see each other again. I am thankful it has finally come to pass, Zianno Zezen."

"I agree, Emme. And there is something you need to see. Mitch," I said over my shoulder, "show this woman the picture inside your jacket."

"What?" he asked.

"Just do it. Let her see the picture."

Mitch gave Emme the photograph of his father and she looked at me, then studied the picture. For a full minute she said nothing, then she spoke. *"I am not to speak to you, I am to think of you when I sit alone or wake at night alone, I am to wait, I do not doubt I am to meet you again, I am to see to it that I do not lose you."*

Behind me, Mitch said, "That's Walt Whitman, man."

Emme glanced at Mitch. "Why, yes it is."

"I think you should meet someone," I told her. "Someone you never knew existed." I pulled Mitch toward me. "Mitch," I said, "this woman is from Mali in West Africa. She is the grand-daughter of a Dogon shaman and holy man. She speaks perfect American English, which she learned from her father a few years before you were born. He was a black engineer from the United States . . . from Ithaca, New York."

Mitch gazed at me in disbelief as the truth came to him. "Emme?" he said, stunned.

Emme looked at Mitch, then to me with a baffled expression.

"Emme Ya Ambala," I said, "I would like to introduce you to your half brother, Mitchell Ithaca Coates of St. Louis, Missouri." I looked at Mitch standing with Mercy. "Mitch, my friend, this is definitely your lucky day."

Emme glanced down at her father smiling in the photograph, then back to Mitch's face. She smiled and Mitch smiled back. All three had the same smile. "Is he still . . . ?"

"Alive?" Mitch asked.

"Yes."

Mitch said nothing, then shook his head slowly back and forth. Mercy had her arm wrapped in his and she seemed to hold him a little tighter. Antoine Boutrain placed his hand on Emme's shoulder. Emme nodded and started to speak, but never got the chance. Without warning, two photographers rushed right through us, one of them almost clipping Mercy with his camera as he ran. Charles Lindbergh had decided to leave early and every photographer in the hallway was scrambling for a shot.

Geaxi said, "I shall be back shortly," and headed directly into the crowd. For some reason, I felt compelled to follow. "We won't be long," I said, and sprinted to catch up.

Geaxi moved as smooth as a pickpocket, slipping by and around and squeezing through the onlookers, reporters, photographers, city officials, and security people. Still, we could get no closer than fifteen feet from where Lindbergh would make his exit. The crowd pushed and pressed together and we had to think of some way to get a better view. Geaxi said it was not necessary that we get any nearer, only that she be able to see him clearly.

"What do you want to do?" I asked.

Geaxi adjusted her beret and we both fought to keep our place. "Do you still carry those gold coins, those double eagles?" she asked.

"Yes, it's a habit now. I have two in my pocket."

"Give them to me."

I handed her the double eagles and she turned and spoke in French to two reporters pushing against us from the back. In ten seconds, a deal had been struck. Geaxi gave one of the men one of the coins, then turned and said, "Follow me, young Zezen, and hop on." The first reporter bent down enough to let Geaxi straddle his shoulders, then stood up. "Excellent view!" Geaxi said. The second reporter kneeled and I climbed on, the same as I had when I first rode on my papa's shoulders to watch a baseball game, fifty-two years earlier. The man stood at the exact moment Lindbergh appeared in the hallway, surrounded by dignitaries and security. They helped him through the mass of reporters and photographers. Lindbergh walked quickly. The crowd kept shouting his name from all directions. He looked like a boy to me—a tall, shy boy caught in the middle of something he never imagined. He tried to thank the people as he passed, but there were too many. Shouts, praises, and questions from reporters filled the hallway and drowned everything else out.

I glanced at Geaxi. She was smiling. Lindbergh was thirty feet away now, almost out of sight. Geaxi closed her eyes, then opened her mouth and used "the Voice." Without making a sound, she whispered, "*Alegeratu!* Congratulations, Slim. Good luck."

Lindbergh stopped abruptly and turned, looking back over the crowd. The people around him urged him on and kept him moving, but he glanced back twice before disappearing down the stairs and out of sight.

I looked at Geaxi. "Can you do that whenever you want?"

She grinned. "Yes," she said. "However, until now I was not aware of it." She tapped the reporter on the shoulder to let her down. I did the same. Geaxi gave the men the other double eagle and shook their hands, thanking them in medieval French. They seemed confused, but pleased about the money, and left speaking rapidly back and forth. Once they were gone, she said, "Tomorrow, young Zezen, we begin our search for Rune Balle."

"I'm surprised you didn't say *'tonight.'* "

"You are attempting to be humorous, no?"

"*Sí, un poco,*" I said. Inside the huge hall, the show went on in high spirits. A duet was singing *Me and My Shadow.* "It has been a long day, Geaxi. That was the best I could do."

A month to the day passed and no sign of Rune Balle's presence in Paris could be found, even though Captain B, or Antoine as he preferred to be called, had his extensive underground network combing every district in the city. Geaxi, Nova, and I usually went with him when he would rendezvous with informants. They all wondered if he had suddenly adopted grandchildren, but Antoine ignored their comments. Mitch and Mercy stayed with Emme while we made our rounds. Mitch and Emme had long discussions, sharing their separate memories of their father. By the end of the month, Mitch began talking about opening a club in Paris with Josephine as a partner. He even said he was going to learn to speak French. I reminded him that they didn't play baseball in Paris and Mitch solved the problem by saying he would come home in the summers. Mercy and Emme became close friends and Mercy helped her with all the household chores. Emme was going to have her baby at any time and Mercy promised to stay with her through the ordeal. Antoine seemed nervous about becoming a father, but his happiness was self-evident. Emme never complained about anything and couldn't wait to be a mother. Her eyes would dance and sparkle with delight at the thought of it. One night while we were sitting at the kitchen table, I told her I wished PoPo could be there with us. She rubbed her swollen belly and said, "Oh, but he is, Zianno, he is."

On June 27, Geaxi and I were having lunch at a café in Montparnasse. Antoine and Nova had gone to see a stained-glass artist who lived a few blocks away and had once known Rune Balle.

"Before Nova returns, there is something we must discuss," Geaxi said.

"What is it?"

"It is time for Nova to experience the Bitxileiho, the Strange Window. There is to be a total solar eclipse not far from Caitlin's Ruby in two days. The path of the eclipse crosses Wales and northern England. I shall take Nova, but you should stay here to continue our search for Balle. If all goes well, we will be back in Paris by the first of August."

I hadn't thought of the Bitxileiho in years. I remembered the helplessness, the inability to move, and the cold terror of the infinite. The experience is unique to the Meq, but necessary for our "maturity." It is also the place and state of mind where we cross in the Zeharkatu. However, because of her "visions," for Nova the experience might prove dangerous or harmful.

"Do you think she'll be . . . all right?" I asked.

"I do not know," Geaxi answered. "It is a chance we must take. We may not have another opportunity for years." Geaxi paused, then asked, "Do you agree, young Zezen?"

I didn't like it, but I also knew its importance. "Yes, I agree. Have you contacted Willie?"

"Yes, he will be waiting for us in London. From there, we head straight for Giggleswick in northern England."

I studied Geaxi's eyes. She gave nothing away, as always, but I could tell she didn't look forward to the event. "Good luck," I said.

"Yes, well, let us hope we shall not need it."

Antoine and Nova returned fifteen minutes later. They sat

down with disappointed looks on their faces. The man they had gone to see was in Chartres and would not be back until August 1.

Geaxi turned to me and said, "Perfect." Then she looked at Nova and said, "Nova, we need to talk."

Early in the morning on June 29, a total eclipse of the sun passed through Wales and swept across North Yorkshire. There was only one place along its path where it was visible from the ground—Giggleswick. The weather before the eclipse had been miserable, but a sudden break in the clouds allowed witnesses there to experience twenty-four seconds of totality. Geaxi, Nova, and Willie observed and experienced it from the school grounds in Giggleswick, along with dozens of astronomers and photographers. In Paris, at about the same time, I was still asleep—and dreaming.

It was winter in St. Louis. I was in Sportsman's Park, standing at home plate. The grandstands were empty and the entire field was covered in snow. Dressed in black, the umpire stood on the mound with his back to me, facing center field. I felt the bat in my hands, but I couldn't see it. The umpire turned and stared at me. He wore a mask, which he removed slowly with one hand. But one mask only revealed another. A chill ran through me. He seemed to smile beneath the mask and threw the pitch at high velocity. I saw a sphere racing toward me. It was white, but it was not a baseball. It was a snowball, which then became a snowflake, spinning through space like a wheel with six spokes. I swung and everything went white. I woke up breathing hard and fast, as if I had been sprinting for my life.

When Geaxi and Nova returned to Paris two days later, I knew the instant I looked into Nova's eyes that twenty-four seconds of totality had been enough time to affect her deeply. There was calmness, resolve, and wisdom in her I had never seen before. Nova had changed completely. I saw a new purpose, or direction. She reminded me a great deal of her papa. She and Geaxi were standing just inside the door of Antoine and Emme's apartment. Antoine was out, and Emme and Mercy were in the kitchen.

"You've seen your papa, haven't you?"

"Yes," she said, slightly startled. "How did you know, Zianno?"

"I can see him in your eyes."

"He came directly through the Window, Zianno. He was like a star as bright and blue as Sirius. He spoke in a way that was similar to 'the Voice,' but not quite the same. He told me there was no longer any need to fear my visions. He said I could learn from them . . . we could all learn from them."

"He's right," I said.

"I know that now. Somehow, in some way, my papa has released me, Zianno. It sounds naïve, silly almost, but I finally, firmly realized I am not losing my mind."

I told her I once felt the same way about my dreams. Then I turned and asked Geaxi if the Bitxileiho had been a pleasant experience for her.

"I assume that is another one of your attempts at humor and irony, no?" She had one eyebrow raised and was glaring at me. "The Bitxileiho is never *fun,* young Zezen. Nor is it a 'pleasant experience,' at least not for me. I could easily pass an eternity without experiencing another."

Before I could respond, Antoine burst through the door and ran into Geaxi. She tumbled forward in one graceful somersault, then leaped to her feet and spun in a quick pirouette to see who or what had hit her. Antoine apologized immediately, then went on to say he had heard from the stained-glass artist. The man had contacted Antoine and informed him that Rune Balle was currently in Chartres, repairing and restoring the ancient stained-glass windows high above the clerestory in Chartres Cathedral. The man had seen Balle and spoken with him only a week ago. Geaxi suggested we leave on the spot and Nova agreed. I looked at Antoine. Chartres was very near Paris; however, I could tell he was reluctant to leave Emme, even for a day. She might go into labor at any moment.

Geaxi noticed his anxiety and said, "This time, Antoine, you should stay here."

He smiled gratefully. "*Oui,* mademoiselle. This is the choice I prefer. *Merci.*"

Geaxi and Nova took baths and changed clothes while I waited for them in the kitchen. I watched Emme talking with Mercy. Her belly was big and round as a giant, prize-winning melon, which she was massaging gently with her fingertips. I knew she would probably have her baby before we returned. Emme seemed to sense what I was thinking and said, "Zianno, I would like your blessing before I go into the hospital."

"You have it, Emme, but you won't need it. Everything will be fine. You're an expert. I've seen you deliver a baby before. Remember?"

She laughed. "I could never forget," she said.

Half an hour later, we were in the street and on our way to catch a train for Chartres. Emme sent along roast lamb sandwiches and cucumbers, and we ate them on the train as the sun set in the west. A faint mist and drizzle caused the light coming through the glass of the window to fracture and dance in patterns and shades of gold, pink, and tangerine.

"Do you enjoy that effect, Zianno?" Geaxi asked.

"Yes," I answered, "yes, I do."

Geaxi took a large bite from her sandwich and stared out the window as she ate. A full minute passed. Quietly and without elaboration, she said, "Then you shall likely enjoy Rune Balle."

Sudden violence, or the nearness of it, when felt or sensed in advance, gives any warrior, hunter, or shepherd a primary advantage in any conflict—the element of surprise. The Meq have always had this ability, especially when traveling together. As we approached the gothic Chartres Cathedral, I noticed its twin spires rising into the night sky like two black blades. Nova, Geaxi, and I each sensed an imminent danger within.

We raced to the three massive front doors. They were all locked. Geaxi led the way around the corner and along the south wall, stopping suddenly in front of a small doorway almost hidden from view. The door was open. Geaxi seemed to know it would be there.

"How . . . ?"

"Never mind," she said. "Follow me."

Without hesitation, I reached for the Stone in my pocket. Simultaneously, Geaxi and Nova reached for their Stones. Geaxi also carried hers in her pocket. Nova wore hers on a leather necklace, which she removed and held in her palm. Even in the darkness the gems sparkled bright and brilliant around the Stone of Silence. My Stone and Geaxi's were no more than heavy, pitted oval rocks—two black eggs, but regardless of their appearance, we would need all three.

We entered a narrow hall and moved quickly until we came to a small opening, which led to another opening covered by a thick curtain. Geaxi parted the curtain, revealing the vast interior of the great cathedral. There were no lights on, but a few candles were burning on top of scaffolding erected along the far wall and extending out into the church, ending forty feet in the air above the inlaid stones of the Chartres Labyrinth. On the highest platform a struggle was taking place, causing the scaffolding to shake and sound as if it might be coming apart. The two Maori assassins we had interrupted in St. Louis were about to murder or torture a man they were holding between them. They had torn open the man's shirt and they held him in the air with one hand apiece. Each had pearl-handled daggers in the other hand. The captured man had wild gray hair and a ragged beard. He was screaming at the Maoris in Norwegian. It was Rune Balle. He yelled, *"Morder! Morder! Snikmorder! Din mor liv inn helvete!"*

Geaxi began climbing the scaffolding without taking her eyes off the Maoris. Nova and I tried to keep pace. Geaxi climbed silently and quickly. In seconds we were over the top. The Maoris stood ten feet away. They had their daggers poised. Rune Balle screamed something, then spit in their faces. The daggers started forward.

"Hear ye, hear ye now, Giza!" Geaxi droned, holding the Stone out and pointing in their direction. Nova and I joined her. *"Lo geltitu, lo geltitu, Ahaztu!"* we said in unison. The Maoris dropped their daggers instantly and stood with their arms at their sides. Their tattooed faces went blank, their eyes dulled. Almost automatically, we added, "Turn and go now, Giza, go like lambs. *Ahaztu!*"

It was an ill-fated command for the Maoris. We had unintentionally sent them to their deaths. They turned with puzzled expressions and calmly walked in the opposite direction, off the scaffolding and into thin air, falling forty feet and landing head-first and dead center on the six-petaled rosette at the heart of the Chartres Labyrinth.

Rune Balle had dropped to his knees. He rubbed his chest where the daggers would have pierced his heart. He crawled to the edge of the platform and stared down at the Maoris and the blood spreading across the stone floor. From the height of the platform, their blood looked black instead of red. He turned to us and said something in Norwegian, then in French.

Geaxi said, "In English, Rune, speak in English, please. Your nephew said you speak English fluently."

Rune looked down at the Maoris. He let out a long sigh, then took in a few deep breaths. He rubbed his chest again and spit twice, watching the spit fall until it hit their bodies. Geaxi let him gather himself. He looked up at her. "Do I know you?" he asked.

"No, however, we were scheduled to meet not long ago through your nephew. Unfortunately, circumstances prevented it."

"Do you mean my nephew Knut? In Trondheim?"

"Yes."

Rune Balle ran his eyes over the three of us, studying us carefully from head to toe. His eyes were pale blue and piercing. Sharp features, tangled long hair, and scruffy beard, along with his shirt being ripped to shreds, gave him the look of a captured Viking. He focused on the Stones we still held in our hands, particularly Nova's with the embedded gems. "I have heard of those," he said, rubbing his chest. "He told me of them once in the mountains . . . and what they could do. I thought it was a fable."

"He?" All three of us practically shouted.

"Who is '*he*'?" I added.

Rune Balle stood and looked down into my eyes. He was at least a foot taller. "Your eyes are dark, each of you. His were green." He paused, then went on. "Other than that, the boy resembled all three of you."

"Is he the one who bought your property?" Geaxi asked.

"No. A man the boy referred to as 'Uncle Raza' purchased the farm. I believe the man was Hindu. His name was Raza Vejahashala. The boy was the strangest boy I ever met. They requested a tour of the farm and all the surrounding mountains. I had several unusual structures on the farm. One was a greenhouse, where I maintained a rose garden year round. The boy seemed overjoyed with it, but his joy was expressed in a bitter, haunting laugh that has echoed in my mind ever since."

I glanced at Geaxi and Nova again. It was the Fleur-du-Mal without a doubt. Then another thought came to me—Zuriaa! Searching for her presence, I turned in a slow circle. The cathedral was vast and the light dim, but Zuriaa was nowhere near. Geaxi, Nova, and I all wondered the same thing—who sent the Maoris, and why? It didn't make sense.

Nova picked up an old red sweater lying on the platform between two trays of stained glass. "Yours?" she said, handing it to Rune Balle.

He removed what was left of his torn shirt and pulled on the sweater. "*Takk*. Thank you," he said.

"Could you tell us where to find your farm?" she asked. "We will be glad to pay for the information."

"There is no need," he said, "I will take you there myself." He gazed down at the two dead men lying on the cathedral floor in the center of the labyrinth. "My work here is finished."

We would have left Paris the next day, except Emme decided to have a beautiful baby girl at ten after ten in the morning. The baby weighed eight pounds, two ounces and was twenty inches long. Her skin was the color of milk and coffee, her eyes were dark, and tiny black curls covered her head. She was given the name Antoinette PoPo Boutrain. A day later, Emme would sign a paper naming Antoinette's godparents—Mercy Whitney and Zianno Zezen. I couldn't have been more proud. Geaxi and Nova agreed to delay our departure another day in order for us to visit Emme and Antoinette in the hospital. By that time, the police had informed Rune Balle he should not leave Chartres until the investigation was complete. Rune was not suspected of any wrongdoing, but the Maoris carried no papers or identification on their persons. Along with tattooed faces and expensive dark suits, the Maoris were a mystery and their strange deaths warranted further study. After two weeks of futile investigation, Rune Balle was told he was free to travel at will. The police had found no clues whatsoever and the Maoris were simply filed away and forgotten.

During that time, Antoine had been listening to some of our discussions about where we were going and why. Antoine believed we would need assistance in eliminating the Fleur-du-Mal, though he never mentioned him by name. He said he had known many assassins, but none as cruel or invisible as our "friend." I reminded Antoine he had just become a father and he ought to remain in Paris. He still insisted on going. Geaxi, Nova, and I all said no, and I was surprised when Emme said he should go. Through PoPo and me, she had learned long ago of the Fleur-du-Mal and his infamy. He needed to be stopped and Antoine could help. She said Mitch and Mercy would give her all the assistance she needed, while Antoinette would give her more than enough love, and all of them would pray for our safe and swift return. Still, we said no.

I cabled Owen Bramley and Carolina in St. Louis, asking if all was well and if they had heard from anyone, meaning any of the Meq. Carolina cabled back within a day saying Owen Bramley was on an extended trip to Hawaii and Japan. She assured me that all was well, then chastised me for being gone so long. She said Charles Lindbergh had returned to St. Louis and was greeted by a huge crowd and Mayor Miller. She added that she had not heard from anyone else.

We packed lightly and left Paris the next day by train, deciding to purchase anything we might need in Norway. Rune Balle had arranged for us to stay in Bergen with his sister, Penelope, and his nephew, Knut. They lived in a large three-storied home his family had owned since the 1840s. I asked him if Penelope was a common name in Norway. He laughed and told me his father's favorite work of literature was *The Odyssey,* which he used to read to them as a bedtime story when they were children. "My sister," he said, "was named for the wife of Odysseus. She may be the only Penelope in Bergen." I asked if his farm was near Bergen. "Relatively near—less than one hundred kilometers, but isolated," he answered, then added, "no, not isolated, *protected.*"

London was our first stop after ferrying from Le Havre. Geaxi wanted to check our deposit box at Lloyd's for messages. There were none. I telephoned Caitlin's Ruby and spoke with Arrosa and Willie. Neither had heard from anyone. It was as if every Meq except Geaxi, Nova, and me had disappeared. Geaxi assured me it was nothing unusual, there had been centuries of absence and silence in the past. It was common for the Meq. That was true; however, it failed to relieve the anxiety of not knowing. She then reminded me there were other Meq in the world I had never met. Did I ever wonder where they were or worry about them? I had no answer.

"Aside from that, young Zezen, I suspect there is only one you are truly concerned about, no?"

I said nothing because we both knew the answer.

We caught a late train for Newcastle, where we spent the night and then early the next morning boarded a ferry for Bergen. Halfway across the North Sea, we encountered rough seas, which gave Nova a bout of seasickness. It was highly unusual. Geaxi said she had never heard of one of the Meq experiencing seasickness. Nova recovered quickly, but she seemed bewildered and alarmed by what had happened. She said she had never been seasick before and it might portend some ill will for us. Geaxi tried to assure her there was nothing to be concerned about. But once we reached the outer islands and approached the Vagen harbor of Bergen, all our spirits lifted, including Nova's.

Bergen is a thousand-year-old port city. Surrounded by mountains, the city has long been called "the town between seven mountains." As we entered the inner harbor, the sun was setting behind us. Two of the peaks, Floyen and Ulriken, were golden in the last rays of light. Green pines covered the hillsides and ships and sailboats were everywhere. I had never seen a more beautiful town and harbor. Geaxi remarked that she had first visited Bergen in 1350 on a Hansa ship, only a year after the Black Plague had appeared and spread throughout Norway. She said at that time the harbor was equally beautiful, but a miserable destination.

Rune told me to enjoy the clear air and colorful sunset because in the past he had seen it rain in Bergen for twenty days in a row on several occasions. I replied that rain could not dampen the beauty of Bergen. Rune grunted and said I might make a good Norwegian.

After disembarking with the other passengers, Rune escorted Geaxi, Nova, and me through customs. We walked along the quay, then up narrow streets and steep hills to Rune's family home. With the sun down, the air cooled dramatically and by the time we arrived, I could see my breath. It was the middle of September. The days were getting shorter and colder. The Fleur-du-Mal might or might not stay the winter in Norway. I hoped silently we were not too late.

Penelope and Knut welcomed us inside the large entry hall. She was a stunning woman, probably in her mid-forties, with coal black hair and ice blue eyes. She made me think of how Caitlin Fadle must have looked. Knut was a young man in his early twenties and had the same features as Penelope. They were both clearly ecstatic to see Rune. I could tell Knut idolized his uncle. Rune then asked if someone named Svein was still alive. Knut said he was. Rune looked relieved, glancing at Geaxi and saying, "Roses . . . Svein takes care of the roses."

Rune was right about the weather. The next morning we not only had to buy rain gear, but sweaters, wool caps, boots, jackets, and gloves. Rain fell cold and steady and the temperature dropped twenty degrees. By midday we were finally outfitted properly and on our way to Voss, an ancient town on the northern edge of Vangs Lake, and only an hour by train from Bergen. In Voss, we leased a small fishing boat from a man Rune knew and trusted. We launched immediately, with Rune behind the wheel. Our destination was the farmstead of Rune's old friend and confidant since childhood, Svein Stigen, gardener and caretaker for the Fleur-du-Mal.

When Geaxi first told me the Fleur-du-Mal had purchased a home in Norway, I thought it was a joke. This would be the last place, I thought, where he would consider living. Norway was too remote for his international tastes and habits. Why had he chosen it?

Rune slowed the engines and veered to our starboard side. Suddenly, an almost invisible inlet appeared between two headlands, two promontories of sheer rock, rising 150 feet above the lake.

"Through this channel lies Askenfada," Rune said. "It used to be uninhabited during the winter months because of heavy snowfall and the danger of avalanches."

"Askenfada?" Geaxi asked.

"Yes."

"Do you know what that word means?"

"No," Rune said. "No one seems to know the source of it. The word is not Norwegian. This place has always been called by that name."

Geaxi turned to Nova and me. "The word is an old Meq word," she said.

"What does it mean?" Nova asked.

Geaxi stared up at the steep cliffs as we passed through the narrow channel. The rock faces were streaked black and gray in the rain and they seemed to disappear into a fog hanging over the channel. She looked away and said, "The word means 'final enclosure.' "

The cliffs ended abruptly and the channel opened onto a wide, tear-shaped cove and harbor, surrounded by two green valleys connected at the far end of the cove by a slim strip of land beneath a wall of rock. At least three waterfalls fell from the cliffs. Both valleys were dotted with firs, pines, paths, pastures, stone buildings, barns, and farmhouses. Mountains with snow-covered peaks encircled and towered over everything. The place was an idyll, a fortress—a naturally protected world within a world.

What happened next is difficult to explain to anyone but the Meq. Geaxi, Nova, and I all felt it at once. I can only liken it to a chill or shudder running up and down your spine simultaneously. However, it is not a chill or shudder and it runs through Time. It is a sudden recognition of an intense Meq experience. The memory of the experience inhabits a particular place or space. This one came from the Time of Ice and it was a warning or beacon of great danger. Something terrible had happened here.

"Geaxi, do you know of this place?" I whispered.

"No," she said calmly. "Nor does Sailor or Trumoi-Meq or anyone else. The Fleur-du-Mal has discovered something . . . unusual."

Rune made a turn toward a small dock on the shore of the southern valley. Nova asked him why he ever sold such a property. Rune explained there had been no choice. The family fortune had dwindled and Penelope's husband had vanished, leaving behind a mountain of debt. About that time, the tall Indian man called Raza appeared and offered Rune enough money to ensure Penelope and Knut would be well taken care of for the rest of their lives. Rune took the offer without hesitation, but insisted his friend Svein be allowed to stay and live in his farmhouse. The Stigen family had lived in this cove for over two hundred years and Svein was the last of them. His terms were accepted and Rune soon left for Paris to work in Chartres. "You know the rest," he added.

"Is there no other way in or out than through the channel?" Geaxi asked.

"No," Rune answered. "A tunnel was begun once in the 1860s. It was never completed. Svein and I explored it together as children."

He eased the fishing boat into position along the dock and we tied off, then hurried through the rain and up a steep path to a large, rambling old stone and timber farmhouse. Svein Stigen was standing in the open doorway with his arms spread wide. He wore a bright red and gold sweater and a big gap-toothed grin. He greeted Rune in Norwegian and the two men embraced warmly. Svein had the same wild gray hair and scraggly beard as Rune. It looked like a reunion of two unrepentant Vikings.

He seemed a little surprised to see Rune, but especially surprised to see us. "Who are these children?" he asked Rune in Norwegian.

"In English, Svein, old friend. Speak in English."

"Ah! English it is then," he said, and quickly led the way inside. "Come stand by the fire and warm yourselves."

An hour later we were well fed, warm, dry, and sadly informed that we had missed the Fleur-du-Mal by three days. Using a speedboat, he and Raza had left in a hurry. They did not say where they were going or when they might return, only that it would be sometime before the end of the year. Svein was to watch over everything in their absence, especially the greenhouse and precious rose garden. We were disappointed but not dispirited. We still had the element of surprise in our favor. All we had to do was wait. We knew we could do that well.

Two and a half months passed. During that time we had ample opportunity to explore Askenfada and the surrounding landscape with Svein and Rune as our guides. The Fleur-du-Mal's residence and most of the larger buildings lined the hillsides of the valley opposite to Svein's farmstead. By water, the distance was less than a mile and the crossing took only a few minutes. Walking around the teardrop cove and across a narrow strip of soil and loose rock at the base of a wall of cliffs took half the morning. As the temperature dropped and the weather deteriorated, our journeys by land ceased completely. Snow came early and often. Firs and pines along both valleys were blanketed white for weeks at a time. Constantly, wind whipped at the mounting snow on the surrounding peaks. Svein said we must all be vigilant for avalanches. In the infinite silence of Askenfada, they were commonplace. And there was no sign of the Fleur-du-Mal.

Most of the buildings and structures were open and accessible to Svein, but even he was locked out of the Fleur-du-Mal's private residence. The large stone and timber building attached directly to the greenhouse and rose garden. Its heavy wooden doors were locked securely and every window barred. Svein's entrance to the greenhouse was completely separate. Rune said that once he sold the property to Raza, extensive reconstruction began all around Askenfada. Svein was not allowed to live here during this period. Nevertheless, the entire place had remained beautiful in its starkness and simplicity.

We rarely left the cove, except for supply trips to Voss. Occasionally, Rune would leave for Bergen to visit his sister and nephew. Geaxi, Nova, and I made no attempt to contact anyone, Meq or Giza. Silence was necessary to keep our presence at Askenfada completely unknown.

For the last seven days of November through the first five days in December, snow fell day and night. We were essentially snowbound. We played chess, watched the falling snow, and ate meal after meal of Svein's cooking. On December 6, the storm finally broke. Rune announced a visit to his sister's home and asked if anyone wanted to join him. I said I would love to go, but hesitated to say yes. The Fleur-du-Mal could appear at any moment. I think Geaxi saw the cabin fever in my eyes and told me to go along. "If the Fleur-du-Mal arrives, we shall wait for your return before taking action. Go, young Zezen, enjoy yourself."

Rune and I left for Voss, then boarded a train for Bergen. As we looked for seats on the crowded train, Rune said, "In Bergen I will take you to the Fisketorget, the Fish Market. It is the best in Norway. We will find something special for my sister to cook tonight, eh!"

"Good idea," I said. "Svein Stigen is a fine man and a true friend indeed, Rune. But he is a terrible cook."

Suddenly our compartment went dark. We had entered the mouth of a tunnel, the first of many to come. In the darkness, Rune and I laughed all the way through.

Penelope did prepare a delicious meal that evening, a baked cod dish she said she first learned from a Basque fisherman. Afterward, we gathered around a well-used upright piano and Rune entertained us with Parisian cabaret tunes. He was off-key, his French was bad, and Knut continually begged him to stop, but Rune would have none of it and sang for two hours. Outside, the night sky was crystal clear and the lights of Bergen burned all around the harbor. Finally, after we had finished the last of the champagne and Rune's voice began to fade, we said good night and I fell into a long, dreamless sleep.

When I woke in the morning it was a different world. Snow was falling thick and heavy. At least a foot and a half had already fallen. I dressed quickly and woke Rune with a rap on his door. "Time to go," I said. A raspy voice inside asked, "Where?" "Look outside," I said. "We don't want to get snowbound in Bergen." A few moments later the voice said, "Give me twenty minutes."

With a basket of fresh rolls from Penelope, we caught the morning train for Voss, then settled into our seats. The train was crowded but quiet. We shared rolls and coffee and watched the snow through the window. The hour-long ride passed mostly in silence. My thoughts drifted and I daydreamed until we pulled to a stop at the station in Voss. Slightly unfocused, I gathered my cap and muffler and stepped from the train onto the platform. In the next second I felt the presence of Meq more intensely than I ever had in my life. My mind sharpened in an instant and I took in a shallow breath. It was overwhelming. I turned to Rune. "Wait for me," I said and walked toward the source of what I felt.

Everyone in the noisy crowd wore big coats, caps, and boots. All were in a hurry to get home. I was bumped hard several times and never looked up or said a word. I walked in a straight line until I saw them, all of them, huddled together in a corner of the station on two benches. They looked like children waiting for their parents. They each wore boots and heavy coats like everyone else, except they were not like everyone else and never had been. They were in the middle of a rapid and fierce conversation, which allowed me to notice them before they noticed me. One of them, a girl, an ancient girl with beautiful black eyes, turned and stared at me with a look of total surprise. "Zianno!" she shouted, then smiled and whispered, "my love."

It was Opari. Ray Ytuarte sat next to her. Trumoi-Meq, in his tattered navy jacket, sat next to Ray. Sailor sat on the second bench. Zeru-Meq, whom I had not seen since China, sat next to him. They all looked up at once.

"Can this be true?" Sailor asked. His "ghost eye" swirled like the snow outside the station.

I walked the few feet between us and stared down at him, then looked at Opari. Her eyes flashed up at me. "Oh, it's true, all right," I said.

Ray said, "Damn, Z!" He moved over next to Sailor and I sat down next to Opari. I took her hand and she laced her fingers in mine. I glanced back at Sailor. "But why are all of you here, Sailor?"

He nodded toward Zeru-Meq and Mowsel. "The three of us were closing in on Susheela the Ninth. We tracked her from New Delhi to Berlin, then to Oslo. We lost her trail here in Voss. She vanished again. Yesterday, Opari and Ray appeared without warning. They were following Zuriaa's trail and a single clue—an old Meq word—'Askenfada.' "

"We followed the trail from Reykjavik to Trondheim to Voss," Opari said.

"We lost it, Z," Ray added, "right here in this station."

"Now, why are you here, Zianno?" Sailor asked.

I was just as confused as they were. I looked around the station. "The Fleur-du-Mal lives near here," I answered. "A hidden cove called 'Askenfada.' Geaxi and Nova are there now, waiting for his return."

"The Fleur-du-Mal has a *home*?" Ray asked.

"It's a little more than that."

Trumoi-Meq leaned forward and grinned, exposing his missing tooth. He looked everyone in the eye, one by one, until he stopped at Zeru-Meq. He said, "It would seem we have a coincidence beyond proportion."

Sailor interrupted, as if something had just occurred to him. "All five Stones have been together only once since the time of Those-Who-Fled!"

Zeru-Meq turned to Sailor. His bright green eyes sparkled. He was the uncle of the Fleur-du-Mal and the only one among us who knew his true history. "Yes, old one," he said, then glanced at Mowsel, "and the occasion is no coincidence."

"What are you saying?" Opari asked.

"Today is the seventh day of December, no?"

"Yes."

"We have been tricked, Opari, tricked and manipulated into being here for a celebration—a very wicked one, I imagine."

"What does that mean?" I asked.

"Xanti Otso, my only nephew, bless him, was born on December 7. There is something he wants all of us to see together and he was clever enough to arrange the event on his own birthday. His arrogance is boundless."

"And his madness," Sailor said. He was turning the star sapphire around his forefinger in frustration. "What are the intentions and involvement of Susheela the Ninth and Zuriaa in this ridiculous scheme?"

No one said a word. Behind us, the crowd was thinning. I turned and glanced through the windows of the train station. It was still snowing.

Ray broke the silence with the truth. "There's only one way to find out," he said.

"What is it?" I asked.

"Let's go to the party!"

Rune was standing near the exit doors, staring out through the windows and peacefully smoking a pipe. His wild, tangled hair seemed to fly out in every direction. I tapped him on the shoulder. He turned and the pipe fell from his mouth. Rune had gotten used to seeing three of us together, but to see me with five others was almost too much for him. Staring each of them in the face, Rune said, "*Illusjon! Magisk! Umulig!* Impossible!"

"We must hurry, Rune," I told him. "I'll try to explain later."

He looked at me and laughed. "There is an explanation?"

"It's complicated," I said, then we turned to leave for the docks. The cabin of the fishing boat was cramped, but we managed to fit inside, protected from the wind and cold and snow, which fell all the way to Askenfada.

Rune cut the engines to a low drone as we entered the hidden inlet behind the headlands. Once we passed into the channel between the cliffs, the silence around us became total. Slowly, we cleared the channel and drifted into the secret cove and harbor. Fog and snow made it impossible to see the ring of surrounding mountain peaks, but both valleys were visible.

"Damn," Ray said. "You'd never know this was here."

"Precisely," Zeru-Meq said.

"Is the channel the only entry?" Sailor asked.

"The only entry and the only exit," I answered.

"I now know why this place carries the name Askenfada," Mowsel said, amazed by the silent beauty and extreme isolation of the ancient cove. "The Meq have been here long before Xanti Otso."

"Yes," Opari said quietly. "I can hear them."

"No," Sailor whispered, "not *them*—just one . . . a very old one of us."

I glanced at Sailor. It was strange. For a split second, his "ghost eye" had stopped swirling and cleared completely.

Barely audible, Ray said, "Susheela the Ninth."

Rune stared straight ahead, toward Svein waiting for us on the tiny dock below his farmstead. All of us, all the Meq inside the cabin, stared across the cove to the other side. We looked up the valley toward the shadowy maze of stone and timber structures dotting the hillsides. The complex was almost invisible through the falling snow, but in the greenhouse and in the private residence of the Fleur-du-Mal, the lights were on.

Rune turned and caught us staring. He sensed our concern and unease.

I realized at that moment how completely we had been deceived. The element of surprise was exposed and lost. The irony is that we never had it. The Fleur-du-Mal had it all along. Now he was waiting for us.

Sailor must have been thinking the same thing. "An obvious trap," he said. "He will be expecting us by water. Is there no other way across?"

"Yes," I answered, "one—but in the snow and this late in the day, the trip would be impossible."

Sailor turned the star sapphire on his forefinger round and round and glared at the lights across the cove. "He knew it would be this way. There is no longer any reason for stealth. As Ray said, 'Let's go to the party' and see what this mad child has in mind."

After docking, we stepped from the fishing boat one by one. Oddly, Svein showed no surprise whatsoever at the number of us. "This way," he said, "there is warmth inside." Svein's voice was the only thing I heard and it cut through the profound still-ness surrounding us. Snow fell in large, soft flakes, and our foot-steps landed in silence.

Geaxi opened the wide front door, expecting to see me, but not what trailed behind. Once she saw the others, she let out the high, trilling sound she and Opari make when something ex-traordinary occurs. Even in the frigid cold, the sound gave me chills.

Sailor paused as he passed by Geaxi. The two of them stared at each other without expression. Sailor smiled first. "You seem well, Geaxi."

"And you, Sailor," Geaxi said flatly. She turned to go inside before he could see her smile. Opari gave me a wink.

Sailor also stopped when he saw Nova. He noticed the change in her instantly. "Aha!" he said. "It has happened! You once proclaimed or predicted 'the shift is soon.' I see clearly, Nova, there has been a shift." Sailor gave his niece a long and warm embrace, the first time I had seen him do so. Briefly, he introduced her to Zeru-Meq, then said to all of us, "We must talk now."

Rune and Svein disappeared into the kitchen while we gathered in the living room. In minutes, we were out of our heavy
coats, gloves, and caps, standing in a semicircle in front of a
crackling fire, warming our hands and sipping hot cider.

Sailor said, "I will begin. I will tell everything Zeru-Meq,
Mowsel, and I have learned to this point. Opari will follow and
speak for her and Ray, then you, Zianno—tell us what you
know." He paused and looked hard at each of us. "We must be
brief and do this quickly. Perhaps we can solve this riddle. Only
then should we discuss our purpose for being here, regardless of
the Fleur-du-Mal's purpose."

"What is that?" I asked.

"The same as yours, Zianno," Mowsel said. "We are here to
assassinate the assassin. We are here to kill the Fleur-du-Mal."

I glanced at Sailor and looked at Zeru-Meq. Xanti Otso was
an evil, amoral being, but he was also related to Zeru-Meq. I
wondered how Zeru-Meq felt about plotting to kill his own
nephew. He saw my concern and said, "The Fleur-du-Mal,
poor soul, shall die the way he prefers to kill—by the blade." He
reached down and withdrew a long dagger from inside his boot.
The knife blade glinted in the firelight. There was silence in the
room, then Sailor, in his measured voice, began to talk.

Thirty minutes passed. Sailor spoke and Opari spoke and I
spoke, accurately recounting the events leading each of us to
Norway and Askenfada. We were seeking an answer or a clue as
to why this elaborate rendezvous had been orchestrated. Why
was Zuriaa here? Was Susheela the Ninth involved or had she
also been tricked and lured to this "final enclosure"? Was the
Octopus with her? The Fleur-du-Mal most likely knew what
we wanted, but what did he want? All was still a mystery.

Trumoi-Meq suggested there was no need to wait any longer. Rune and Antoine would ferry us across the cove and accompany us the rest of the way from a distance. Svein would stay here. Once there, we would act on instinct. We should remain apart and approach the residence with extreme caution. We must be vigilant and ready to act at any moment.

We all agreed without saying a word. In a mock toast, Sailor held out his mug of cider toward the fire, which popped and crackled at almost the same instant. *"Egibizirik bilatu,"* he said bitterly. "Let us hope this is a proper course of action." Sailor set his mug down on the hearth. He reached for his heavy coat and removed a small leather satchel from an inside pocket. He opened the satchel and handed out five daggers to Geaxi, Nova, Ray, Opari, and me.

"The 'Knives of Caesar'?" Geaxi asked.

"Yes," Sailor answered.

I looked down at my dagger, which had an ivory handle engraved with a Latin inscription. "These aren't—"

"Yes," Sailor interrupted. "These are a few of the knives used to murder Caesar. I have always carried them, but never used them. Now is the perfect time."

Svein advised us to have one cup of soup before we left, which we did. After collecting our coats, gloves, caps, and mufflers, we made our way down to the fishing boat and climbed aboard. Rune started the engines and we pushed off. There was no other sound in the cove. The snow on the peaks of the mountains looked heavier and deeper than ever.

As we made the crossing, I began to experience something strange, yet I was certain I had experienced it before. It was not déjà vu; it was an echo through time from someone shouting in a language I did not understand. It felt like a warning or signal of distress. It was old. Opari squeezed my arm. I knew she also heard it or felt it. We were huddled together, standing in the stern of the fishing boat. Everyone else stood packed inside the cabin with Rune. Ahead of us, the long dock on the opposite shore slowly came into view. The speedboat was anchored there inside a covered slip. Beyond the dock and up the steep slope, I could see the hothouse lights of the expanded greenhouse. Through the swirling snow and against the dark background of cliffs and peaks that surrounded the compound, the powerful electric lights burned like a cluster of fuzzy stars.

Rune cut the engines and docked the fishing boat with barely a sound. We stepped carefully onto the dock and Mowsel turned to Rune. He asked him to follow at a safe distance, but Rune refused and insisted on going with us. He had his own personal reasons and would not even consider staying behind. No more was said about it and we set out for the nearest stone path leading up the slope toward the greenhouse and the home of the Fleur-du-Mal. We walked in three groups. Rune, Sailor, and Zeru-Meq led the way, followed by Geaxi, Nova, and Ray. Trumoi-Meq, Opari, and I were last.

Our progress up the hillside was slow. The complex of buildings had changed since Rune owned the property. After two days and nights of continuous snowfall, he was deliberate about choosing our route. Everything in Askenfada was built on a series of connecting terraces. The Fleur-du-Mal's residence and greenhouse were on the highest terrace, virtually at the foot of the massive cliffs and overhangs, and there were several ways to approach. No one spoke as we climbed steadily higher and closer. Tall firs, their limbs heavy with snow, were scattered between the stone paths and buildings. One by one, we climbed the terraces, each one slightly steeper than the last. I glanced up at what I could see of the sky. We probably had more than an hour of daylight left, but it was already getting hard to see. On the terrace just below the greenhouse, Sailor motioned for everyone to stop with a wave of his arm. In silence, we each looked up at the bright lights shining through the foggy windows of the greenhouse. Every other building in the complex was dark, including the Fleur-du-Mal's private residence. The greenhouse was the most reconstructed and renovated structure on the property. A new wing now stretched a hundred feet from the residence itself to the building that was once the entrance to the abandoned tunnel and now housed a generator for the hothouse lights. Directly behind everything, a rock overhang rose fifty feet in the air. I noticed huge snowdrifts piled high on the ridge above the overhang. Opari tugged at my sleeve and pointed out three entrances to the greenhouse, spaced about thirty feet apart. Three stone stairways led down from the doors to our terrace. Sailor was thinking the same thing and waved for each group to cover one of the doors. Without a word, we spread out and climbed the final set of steps to the upper terrace.

On the top step, we paused and stared at the amazing structure Rune had begun and the Fleur-du-Mal had completed. Made of iron, stone, and glass, the long greenhouse glowed like a warm lamp against the frozen background of rock and snow. Then we heard the music, barely audible and coming from inside the greenhouse. It was a recording. The melody was haunting, spare, and beautiful. I looked at Opari and Mowsel. Mowsel whispered, "Mozart—Piano Concerto Number 23 in A—Adagio. My favorite."

The entrance itself was recessed in the wall and the door was in shadow. On either side, the glass windows were fogged over, but only the lower panes. Opari stood watch inside the recess while I climbed on Mowsel's shoulders and peered into a higher window. I looked inside. The rose garden was directly beneath me. Dozens and dozens of rosebushes, all in red, were planted in perfect rows. All had been tended immaculately. Bright lights shone down at certain angles, capable of creating the illusion of different times of day and seasons. The soil in which the roses were planted was dark and rich. Svein had said the foundation was three meters deep and could be heated from below, if needed. Deep within the garden, a space had been cleared. In the center of the space stood a rare Ming Dynasty three-panel screen. It was positioned behind the phonograph playing the music. Six feet away a boy was snipping and trimming a rose-bush while Mozart played. He wore leather boots laced to the knees. His dark hair was pulled back in a ponytail and tied with a green ribbon. He had his back to me. He worked carefully on the roses and made each cut with precision. Suddenly he stopped and laid down his scissors. A second passed—two, three, a dozen—finally, slowly, his head turned in my direction. Then I saw it, there in his pierced ear. This boy was not wearing the ruby earrings of the Fleur-du-Mal. He was wearing Usoa's blue diamond. It was Zuriaa!

She knew exactly where I was and looked in my eyes. A cruel smile crossed her face. She laughed and walked over to the standing screen. She folded back two of the panels, revealing a girl, a black girl, gagged with a red scarf and bound to a chair with rope. Her skin was the color of coffee beans, rich and dark. Her hair was black, silky, and cropped close to her head. Susheela the Ninth. In her lap was a small black box made of onyx, inlaid on top with a unique design in serpentine and lapis lazuli—the Octopus. She glared up at Zuriaa with fury in her green eyes. Zuriaa walked behind her and withdrew a curved dagger from her boot. She jerked back Susheela the Ninth's chin with one hand and lightly traced the long knife blade across her throat, smiling at me as she did it.

I stood down from Mowsel's shoulders and started to tell him what I'd seen. He shook his head and nodded toward the recess in the wall. I turned.

"Bonsoir, mon petit," a soft, familiar voice said from the shadows. My heart froze, but I said nothing.

"You are late," he said. "What kept you, pray tell?"

I took a deep breath and glanced at Mowsel. "Yes, well . . . it snowed."

I heard a rustling sound and a gasp from Opari. He pushed her forward and they came into the light. The Fleur-du-Mal was standing behind Opari. He was dressed in black and silver fur and leather. He held Opari's head at an angle with one hand and a dagger to her throat with the other. Her eyes stared into mine. I saw anger and concern, but no fear. I told myself to calm down. Inside the greenhouse, the music had stopped playing.

"What do you think of Askenfada?" he asked, smiling.

"I think it's lonely."

His smile faded. "You are like your pitiful grandfather, Zezen, and all the others—you know nothing of true beauty!" He forced Opari forward slightly, pressing the knife harder against her throat and bringing a trace of blood. "Do you still think of this ancient girl as *beauty*?" he asked, holding Opari's head at a severe angle, then licking her on the cheek and neck. He looked me in the eyes. "Shall I kill her now, *mon petit*?"

Rune saw me start forward and held me back.

The Fleur-du-Mal laughed sarcastically. "You make me sick to my stomach!" He spit at the ground.

I said nothing. Absolute silence surrounded us. Our breathing was the only sound I could hear. Several seconds passed. "Call the others," he said finally. "I tire of this charade. I know where they are." He nodded toward each of the entrances. "It is time."

"Time for what?"

"I have a surprise for all of you," he said. "Do it!" he whispered through clenched white teeth. He pulled Opari's head back again with a jerk of her hair, baring her throat to the light. He pressed the knife down even harder, drawing more blood. "And please, Zezen, do not yell. It could prove dangerous."

I wasn't sure what he meant, but I didn't hesitate to do what he said. I stood clear of the entrance and waved to Sailor, ninety feet away, and Geaxi, thirty feet closer. They were barely visible through the falling snow.

Before they approached, the Fleur-du-Mal backed Opari into the shadows of the entrance. As they came closer, he whispered their names, even Nova and Rune. The last to appear was Zeru-Meq. "Well, well, well," he said, "I never expected you, Uncle."

Quietly, cautiously, Sailor passed the others and walked up to me. He looked once at Mowsel, then asked, "What have you seen, Zianno?"

I didn't answer.

In a soft snarl from the shadows, the Fleur-du-Mal said, "The Holy Grail, Sailor . . . Zezen has seen the Holy Grail."

All the others stopped in their tracks when they heard his voice. He prodded Opari forward into the light. Sailor glanced at Opari and the dagger at her throat, but showed no emotion or reaction. In his own calm voice, he asked, "What do you mean, 'the Holy Grail'?"

"The very thing you seek, Umla-Meq, possibly more than me—the Octopus and the old one who stole it."

Zeru-Meq took a few steps forward. "Happy Birthday, Xanti," he said.

"Stop there, Uncle! Go no farther or I will take Opari's life in an instant!" the Fleur-du-Mal snapped. "None of you move," he said to the rest. Gradually, his smile returned. He looked at Mowsel. "You," he said, "raise Sailor on your shoulders as you did Zezen. I want Sailor especially to see for himself."

Mowsel glanced at me, then put his hands on his knees and squatted down, letting Sailor climb onto his shoulders. He stood upright and Sailor leaned against the glass window and gazed inside. When his eyes found Zuriaa and Susheela the Ninth with the Octopus in her lap, he almost lost his balance, then he seemed lost in something else. He stared in frozen silence for thirty seconds. He seemed to be listening more than watching. Slowly, he turned his head, looking at the Fleur-du-Mal with ultimate contempt. Sailor was furious, but his voice remained calm. "What is this about, you madman?"

"Get down now, Umla-Meq, and go stand with the others. You do the same, Uncle."

Sailor surveyed everything around him with his eyes. He looked once at Opari, then hopped down with barely a sound and took a few steps toward the others. He stopped suddenly and said to the Fleur-du-Mal, "By the way, would there happen to be a Sixth Stone inside the little box? I was just curious, but you are not obligated to answer, of course."

The Fleur-du-Mal laughed bitterly. "At the moment, the Stone is elsewhere. The ancient black witch refuses to tell me where it is, poor thing. She will surely regret that decision, just as she will surely lead me to it." He paused. "She is not *obligated,* of course." He laughed again, a hollow sound, and no one laughed with him.

"I see Zuriaa does your bidding," I said. "I thought you told me she was insane and hated you."

"Oh, make no mistake, *mon petit,* Zuriaa is quite insane. I simply found I could use her skills and easily directed her hatred to fear and then into worship, of a sort. As long as she continues to be able to function and be of value, she will be used." He paused again. Sailor had stopped next to Zeru-Meq and Rune. "Enough of this chatter," the Fleur-du-Mal said. "Zezen, you stand with the others. The moment is at hand."

"Why are we here?" Geaxi asked.

"Ah, my dear Geaxi, you have surely noticed by now that all five Stones are present, have you not? It occurred to me once I had found the black girl, the other five Stones were no longer relevant, nor the Meq who carried them. I threw some crumbs out and each of you came eagerly, like blind mice. But I digress. To answer your query, Geaxi, you are here to die. It is unfortunate about Uncle being present, but *c'est la vie.*"

Zeru-Meq spoke. "You and I both know why you want the Sixth Stone, Xanti, and why you are obsessed with these roses. You cannot erase it or make it go away. The Stone will make no difference."

"Silence!" the Fleur-du-Mal screamed. "You know nothing!"

"I saw what I saw," Zeru-Meq said.

"You saw what you wanted to see. You always have, Uncle.

And now, sadly, you shall have to die with the others. Raza, come into the light!"

The tall Indian man named Raza Vejahashala walked quietly from the shadows, opening the greenhouse door behind him as he stepped forward. The light from inside framed the Fleur-du-Mal and Opari in silhouette. The dagger was still at her throat.

Raza wore a long, full-length fur coat. Before anyone knew exactly what he was doing, he withdrew a coiled black bullwhip from his coat, which he unwound and held at arm's length. The Fleur-du-Mal said, *"Gjensyn, mon petit."* Raza raised his arm in a quick, fluid motion, then cracked the whip as hard as he could. The crack sounded like a high-powered rifle shot. It echoed off the rock overhang surrounding the greenhouse, then rose up the steep ridge above. The stillness afterward lasted ten seconds before we heard something faint and far away. It sounded like a waterfall high in the mountains. In moments, I realized it was not a waterfall—it was snow, a wall of snow dislodged from the ridge by the crack of the bullwhip and falling fast. We had seconds to escape. I looked in Opari's eyes. She was staring back at me.

In that same instant, the Fleur-du-Mal released Opari, giving her a boot in the back, which sent her lunging toward me. He laughed as loud as he could, telling Opari, "Go die with the others!" He and Raza ducked back into the greenhouse and closed the door. I caught Opari and the two of us turned in one motion and started running for the edge of the terrace. There was no time to take the stone stairway. I glanced once at the others. Everyone was running. Rune stumbled and fell. Zeru-Meq tried to help him and was knocked down. I thought I saw Sailor turning back to help them both. We ran for the edge and bounded into the air, falling twenty-five feet to the next terrace.

We tumbled over and over, then regained our footing and ran to the edge of that terrace and jumped again. We landed, ran, and jumped again. Small clumps of snow and rock hit us from behind and above as we ran. I could hear the roar as the avalanche came thundering down from the overhang, burying the greenhouse and everything around it.

Finally, luckily, on the fourth terrace down from the top, we were safe. I was certain I had broken my ankle, but I knew it would heal within hours. Opari had only a few cuts and bruises. Geaxi, Nova, Ray, and Trumoi-Meq all made it without serious injury. Sailor and Zeru-Meq had been partially buried on the third terrace down, but they survived and crawled to safety.

Rune had not been so lucky. He did not possess our speed and was caught and buried under a wall of snow. In seconds, the greenhouse and all the roses inside had disappeared forever. I looked up the steep slope to where they had been moments earlier. Now there was only a giant swirling cloud of snow rising in the silence. The Fleur-du-Mal destroyed his own creation in order to destroy all of us. Except for Rune Balle, his plan failed. But where was the Fleur-du-Mal? It was too late in the day to find the answer or search for Rune's body. We had been fooled, trapped, and nearly killed. I was the only one with broken bones, but everyone was bruised or bleeding somewhere. We got our bearings and Sailor led the way down to the dock. We found the fishing boat and climbed on board. Ray started the engines. As we pulled out in the cove, I looked down to the covered slip where the speedboat had been anchored when we arrived. The slip was empty.

As we stepped from the boat onto Svein's dock, Sailor grabbed my arm and pulled me aside. His "ghost eye" was filled with clouds. "She spoke to me, Zianno," he whispered.

I said nothing at first, then I understood.

"Did she speak to you, Zianno?"

"No, she was bound and gagged," I said. "How did she speak?"

"From inside with a voice I recognized in my heart of hearts. I heard her clearly."

Sailor looked across the cove. It was nearly dark. He squinted and stared up the slope to where the greenhouse had been. Then he shook his head back and forth.

"What?" I asked.

"She told me over and over there is no Sixth Stone—the Octopus is an empty box! She remains alive only because the Fleur-du-Mal thinks she has hidden it from him."

I followed Sailor's gaze across the cove. I thought about what he said. I had no doubt Susheela the Ninth was capable of speaking with her mind. I knew the instant I looked in her eyes she was older than all of us beyond measure. "Do you believe her?"

"Yes."

I turned and looked at Sailor. As he stared up the slope his "ghost eye" cleared. He seemed frozen again, detached, more listening than watching. "It was Deza's voice I heard." He turned his head and looked deep in my eyes. "She spoke in Deza's voice, Zianno." Deza, Sailor's Ameq, had been decapitated by the Phoenicians in Carthage almost three thousand years earlier. Sailor never imagined he would hear her voice again, but Susheela the Ninth had somehow found what was deepest in his heart and mind and spoken to him in the same voice.

An hour later, after we changed clothes and warmed ourselves around Svein's roaring fire, we gathered in the kitchen to discuss how we might recover Rune's body. Svein said he could hire a crew in Voss the next day. The snow must be removed before it built up on the ridge again. Mowsel suggested the rest of us stay out of sight until the crew finished the job, in order to avoid any unnecessary questions. I kept thinking of Penelope and Knut. I knew how this would break their hearts, but I also knew I must be the one to tell them. We would find Rune's body and I would take him home to them. Opari sensed what I was thinking and held my hand in hers. Together, all of us decided not to discuss anything further that evening. We each knew how lucky we were to be alive. It was time to rest.

As Opari and I climbed into bed, she asked, "What does she look like?"

"Susheela the Ninth?"

"Yes."

"Except for green eyes and black skin, she looks like you, Opari . . . she could be your twin."

Early the next morning Svein left for Voss. He returned soon after with a full crew and they set to work immediately. The weather improved. The sky never cleared completely but snowfall was limited to occasional flurries. By the end of the day the crew had found and recovered Rune's body. He had been caught on the second terrace down and buried under fifteen feet of snow. Svein and his crew also discovered how the Fleur-du-Mal escaped the avalanche. During his reconstruction of Askenfada, he had completed the abandoned tunnel Svein and Rune had played in as children. By extending and expanding the greenhouse, he disguised the entrance and the tunnel became his secret passageway, not through the mountain, but down the slope and exiting onto the terrace nearest the dock, just above the covered slip and the waiting speedboat.

I hated the Fleur-du-Mal. I hated him for many reasons, all of them personal and fundamental. He was an abomination and an aberration as a living being. He was a murderer, not merely an assassin, and he had nearly killed us all. He was complex, devious, and unpredictable. He was a psychopath with no boundaries and without moral conscience, and he was still a mystery to me. He seemed to have no weakness, no vulnerability, and he only acted with calculated malice. Did he have a Bihazanu, a heartfear? If so, what was it? I had questions for Zeru-Meq. I wanted to know what he meant when confronting the Fleur-du-Mal, he said, "You and I both know why you want the Sixth Stone" and "I saw what I saw." But I was sick of the Fleur-du-Mal and decided I would ask these questions another time. Sailor, who had never personally pursued the Fleur-du-Mal before, announced that he and Zeru-Meq would leave immediately for India and attempt to find any information they could about Raza or his family. "We must find a way to stop the Fleur-du-Mal once and for all. There is too much at stake," Sailor said. "And we must do it now. There is no other option. He has crossed a line I never thought he would cross. Zeru-Meq agrees. When we find him, we will send word."

No one spoke much after that. Even Opari and I said little to each other. We sat together for hours by the kitchen window, drinking tea and watching Svein and his crew far across the cove and high up the hillside, digging in the snow. Once, without looking at me, she took my hand and wove her fingers through mine. In the softest voice in the world, she said, "We are Meq, my love. We go on."

Later that night, long after Svein's crew had gone, Opari and I walked outside and down the stone stairs to the small dock. Snow was still falling, but only in great, single, floating flakes. We walked to the end of the dock. Slowly, the sky began to clear. I saw a star, then two, then a three-quarter moon appeared, sending faint shafts of light across the cove. I turned to Opari. She was looking up. One of the last snowflakes in the sky spun down through the light and landed like a frozen butterfly on her cheek. Instantly, it became a tear.

PART III

Time is the reef on which
all our frail mystic ships are wrecked.

—NOEL COWARD

7

PIXKANAKA

(LITTLE BY LITTLE)

According to a strange fable long told at sea by Basque whalers and fishermen, there was once an old man in the mountains who one day set out walking, along with a young boy who rarely spoke. The old man had lost much of his memory and nearly all of his eyesight, so he took the boy with him, but the boy had no idea where they were going. They kept climbing and climbing, walking on and on until they were nowhere really, halfway between heaven and earth, alone together and completely uncertain if they were anywhere at all. The old man rubbed and scrubbed his eyes, frantically trying to regain his vision. The boy seemed unconcerned. Finally, after finding nothing at all familiar or recognizable, the old man turned to the boy and asked, "How did we get here?" Without hesitation or even blinking an eye, the boy replied, "Little by little, sir . . . little by little."

Rune Balle was laid to rest on New Year's Day. The air felt frigid but the sky was crystal clear and deep blue. Svein Stigen accompanied Penelope and Knut, along with Opari and me, to a small stone church and cemetery less than a mile from where Rune was born. We buried him in a grave adjacent to his father and grandfather. Penelope and Knut had taken Rune's death hard. Opari and I promised to stay as long as we were needed or could be of some comfort. Also, I wired Owen Bramley and Carolina to send a substantial transfer of funds to Bergen in Penelope and Knut's name. I felt extreme guilt about everything, even though it had been the Fleur-du-Mal who had done the killing. The truth of it is that Rune should not have died. Little by little, he had been drawn in and used, by all of us, not just the Fleur-du-Mal. We had to make it up to them in some way. Money would be a start. Long ago, Solomon had made sure we had it. We could do the same for Penelope and Knut.

Sailor and Zeru-Meq left Bergen almost as soon as we arrived. They bought tickets for the train to Oslo, and from there would begin their long trip to India. Sailor paused to remind me of what Susheela the Ninth had revealed. He said it meant we now knew something the Fleur-du-Mal did not—there is no Sixth Stone. We could use this against him. "It is a significant weakness," Sailor whispered with a wink of his "ghost eye." "And I shall exploit it."

Mowsel stayed behind with the rest of us, but before Sailor and Zeru-Meq had gone, he suggested we all meet in Spain in ten years' time, which they agreed to do. Zeru-Meq casually mentioned he had not been back to Spain in a thousand years. "Then it is time, my friend," Sailor said. "The Gogorati is less than ninety years from now." He turned and looked each of us in the eye. "All Meq should see Spain again." Both Zeru-Meq and Sailor wore similar clothing, including leather boots laced to the knees. They were the same height and weight. Each had dark hair, though Sailor wore a braid behind his left ear and Zeru-Meq did not. As they walked away in close conversation, they looked like brothers, possibly twins, yet they had been antagonists to one another for centuries. The chase for the Fleur-du-Mal had something to do with bringing them together, but that couldn't have been the sole reason. I asked Mowsel what happened, what brought about the change? He said, "I do not know what either of them would tell you; however, I believe the answer is quite simple. Sailor had to abandon the question, 'Why us?' and Zeru-Meq had to abandon his position, 'Why anything?' "

Nova and Ray wanted to spend more time together, as did Opari and I. They had not been apart since the avalanche. Though he never said so, Ray had wanted to be with Nova for decades. She was Egizahar and he was Egipurdiko. Mowsel said a true union between the two had never taken place, but there was no doubt when I looked in their eyes they were each other's Ameq and always had been. Ray said quietly, "I say we oughta get back to St. Louis, Z. Maybe spend a little time there. I don't know what to do about Zuriaa. I'm gonna have to think on it awhile."

Mowsel announced he was taking Geaxi to France. "There is a man in the Dordogne," he said. "He wishes to show us a cave his son discovered. I am intrigued."

"Do you think about the Remembering often, Mowsel?" I asked.

"Often?" He opened his mouth, displaying his gap. "Constantly, Zianno. Sailor is correct. We must all be vigilant for signs. We are running out of time, and we must never be as ignorant and vulnerable as we were here again. We cannot afford it."

When he and Geaxi departed Bergen, I told him, "*Egibizirik bilatu,* Trumoi-Meq. And you, too, Geaxi. In ten years' time," I added.

Geaxi said, "Five winds, young Zezen." She threw on her black beret and adjusted the angle.

"One direction," I said back.

Mowsel raised the collar of his old and tattered navy coat and he and Geaxi disappeared up the ramp and onto a ship sailing south for the Mediterranean.

On January 3, Opari, Nova, Ray, and I said farewell to Penelope and Knut and boarded a Norwegian ship bound for Reykjavik, Halifax, and New York. It wasn't necessary, but to be discreet we boarded separately. The crossing was cold and wet. It made no difference to me. One port at a time, I was going home again. I knew it for certain once we had passed through customs in New York. Ray said he wanted, in order, a roast beef sandwich, a root beer, a copy of *The New York Times,* and a shoeshine. Opari and Nova laughed, but he was serious and did all four. A kid about our size polished his boots, and Ray gave him pointers from start to finish, along with a short lecture on the various techniques of brushing and slapping the rag. Afterward, Ray tipped the boy a double eagle, leaped out of the chair, and shoved the sports page in my face. He jabbed at a picture and the caption underneath.

"Remember him?" Ray asked.

I recognized the big man in the picture immediately. Anybody would, though the last time I had actually seen him play was in St. Louis as a lanky pitcher with the Boston Red Sox. That day he hit a grand slam to win the ball game. His name was Babe Ruth. Now he was the most famous baseball player in America.

"He hit sixty home runs last season, Z. Sixty!" Ray shook his head, rolled the newspaper in his hands, turned, and took an imaginary swing for the fences. "Damn," he said. "Welcome home."

★   ★   ★

Early in the morning just before arriving in St. Louis, I had an unusual dream. The dream was strange throughout, though it began in a familiar place—Sportsman's Park. I was standing on the pitching mound. The field and the grandstands were completely empty, except for Mama and Papa, who sat together with faint smiles on their faces. The odd thing was that I could see them at all. It was night and huge, bright lights attached to standards rose over the ballpark, lighting the whole field and grandstands. But lights, light standards, and night games had not yet occurred in reality. They were several years away. I didn't have time to ponder it because, one by one, they began going out. Opari stood next to me. She wore Mama's glove on one hand. In the other, she held Papa's baseball with the Stone of Dreams still stitched inside. She turned and handed me the ball. The lights kept going out—right field, center field, left field. I looked to home plate. There was no hitter, no catcher, only the umpire. He took one step toward me and stopped. He removed his mask. I could see his eyes. I knew what was inside them. It is what I see when I look in the eyes of all Meq. The umpire's eyes were Meq, but there was something not quite the same, something . . . more than Meq. "Throw the ball," my papa yelled from the stands. "Throw the ball, Zianno." I hesitated for a split second, then turned and threw the ball to the umpire. I couldn't see him catch it, but I heard it hit his bare hand and knew he had. Then he spoke, or tried to speak. His voice was unlike any Meq I had ever known. All I could understand was the word "union." What did it mean?

"Union Station."

"What?" I asked, rubbing my eyes.

"Union Station," Opari said. "We are in St. Louis. Wake up, my love."

The Meq, especially old ones, begin to notice change in the world and in the Giza, change in the way they look at life and live it, long before the Giza recognize it in themselves. Old ones also are acutely aware of populations, migrations, and population growth. For Opari, in just a few short years of the twentieth century, the Giza had changed the world dramatically and irreversibly, and they were everywhere. It was no longer the world she had known for three thousand years and never would be again. Yet, she lived in the moment completely, as do all old ones, letting each day appear and disappear equally.

"This city looks beautiful in the fog," Opari said. "I have always loved cities in the fog."

The four of us were in a taxi on Lindell Boulevard, headed for Carolina's house. Patches of snow from a recent snowfall covered rooftops, sidewalks, tree limbs, and in the early morning light, buildings and people seemed ghostlike as we passed. Traffic was sparse because of the hour, but I could tell St. Louis had grown and thrived in our absence. And Opari was right—it was beautiful in the fog.

Ray tipped the driver and we walked up the long drive and under the stone arch to the kitchen entrance of Carolina's big house. We hadn't telephoned or sent word ahead that we were on the way, so I expected to surprise someone. I knocked lightly on the door, but there was no response. I heard noises inside and turned the doorknob. It was open.

Star stood at the kitchen counter. She was in her late twenties and looked to be the exact replica of Carolina at her age— strawberry blond hair pulled back, loose strands hanging in her face, blue-gray eyes flecked with gold, and freckles across her cheeks and nose. She wore a long robe and slippers and was furiously scrambling eggs in a large bowl. Behind her, Caine was standing at the stove frying bacon. He was almost ten years old with dark hair and piercing dark eyes. He had already grown to my height and was beginning to resemble his father, Jisil al-Sadi. Star smiled wide when she saw me and dropped her whisk in the bowl when she saw Nova. Years earlier, they had become friends as close as sisters and both ran to embrace the other. Caine didn't know quite what to do. He seemed startled and mumbled, "Hey, Z."

I laughed and said, "Hey, Caine."

"Where is everybody?" Ray asked.

"Grandma and Owen and Jack went to Cuba."

"What?" I asked.

Star explained. "They went to visit Ciela, Z. Mama said she missed her and worried about her. Owen suggested they go down for the winter and pay her a visit. They've been gone since Christmas. I'm glad you're here, Z." Star gave Nova another hug and said, "I'm glad all of you are here. Caine and I were getting lonely."

"When are they coming back?" I asked.

"Not until sometime in the spring. In her last letter, Mama said they haven't decided. She said she and Ciela were busy with 'a project,' whatever that means."

"Spend the winter in Cuba . . ." Ray said. "Sounds nice, don't it, Z?"

For Nova, Ray, Opari, and me, it had already been a long winter and there was more to come. The idea did sound good and I knew what Ray was really saying—"Let's go down there now." But Star meant it when she said she and Caine were lonely. I could see it in her eyes. "Maybe next year, Ray," I said. "Let's have some breakfast." He winked back, understanding. I looked at Star. "Have you got enough for us?"

"Always, Z, always," Star said.

For the next three months, we lived slow and quiet lives. Opari and I settled into our old room on the second floor and Ray and Nova moved into Owen Bramley's room across the hall. Two weeks before they left for Cuba, Star said Owen had moved in with Carolina in her carriage house above the "Honeycircle." Carolina told Star she was "simply too old for the comedy of pretense." Owen Bramley had always said Carolina was remarkable. I knew, as did everyone else, his true feelings ran much deeper, and for that reason the news came as no surprise. Knowing Carolina's fierce sense of independence, it probably took her this long to admit she felt the same. Owen Bramley had been her ally for years—now he was her partner. It was good news.

Opari and I spent many hours with Star and Caine. Star still possessed her natural exuberance and joy, but she had matured and become more introspective. Though she was completely at home in St. Louis, she experienced the times in which she lived from a slight distance. Star admitted missing Willie Croft and talked about him often. She said she also had been dreaming of Jisil, explaining that the dreams began the night after she and Carolina had taken Caine horseback riding for the first time. Caine was a natural and instinctive rider and took to it instantly. It was in his blood. All of his family were expert horsemen and had been for centuries. And for the first time Caine asked about his father. Star had no answer and that night the dreams began, including images of Jisil, his murdering brother, Mulai, and the Fleur-du-Mal.

"Are we in danger again, Z . . . from the evil one?"

"I wish I could say no, Star, but I can't. You must always be vigilant for Caine. We all must."

Carolina, Owen, and Jack returned on the eve of the first home game of the year for the Cardinals. They were completely surprised to see us, and Carolina insisted we all go to the game the next day to celebrate. She said they had been watching baseball all winter in Cuba. Oliver "Biscuit" Bookbinder had begun his career in the Cuban League and Carolina and Ciela attended several games in several towns. All the ballparks were rough. Carolina longed for Major League baseball and Sportsman's Park. She was nearly sixty years old now and finally beginning to show her age. Lines around her eyes and mouth had deepened, but her beauty remained and she seemed extraordinarily healthy. Even though she was fair-skinned and freckled, she had a suntan. Owen and Jack were equally tan and robust. I remarked on it and asked what they'd been doing to radiate such health. Carolina answered with one word that was unfamiliar to me. "Snorkeling," she said. Jack had discovered the recreation through a friend and Carolina fell in love with it. They all did. After she explained what it entailed, I understood her fascination and told her I'd like to try it. I asked about Ciela and Carolina said together they had opened a home for underage girls, whom they quietly rescued from the brothels of Havana, where absolutely anything or anybody, including children, could be bought and used for pleasure. Carolina said Ciela was determined to make the refuge a permanent home and Owen Bramley had given her the money to ensure she could do it without financial burden.

Owen Bramley was a few years older than Carolina and also just beginning to show his years. He still wore his wire-rimmed glasses, which he would often wipe clean on his white shirt. Owen rarely wore any other color of shirt than white. And he continued to construct his Chinese kites for Caine, teaching him how to make them fly in Forest Park.

"My God, Z," Owen said. "What have you been doing?"

"I'll tell you all about it later, Owen. It may take a while."

"It always does, Z. Are you all right? Is everyone healthy?"

"Everyone is fine."

"Of course, of course." He paused and wiped his glasses. "My God, it's good to see you. It's damn good to see all of you, isn't it, Carolina?"

"Yes, it is, Owen," Carolina said, looking at me eye to eye. "It always is."

I don't know whether it was because of the return of spring, or baseball, or simply being together, but within two days, Carolina's house had transformed into a busy, bustling home again, full of voices and stories and every kind of activity. It felt like it always had, except that Caine was now the only child among us, at least the only real child.

The Cardinals had a pennant-winning season that year. Opari and I went to nearly every home game during the summer, taking turns occasionally with the others because there were only so many seats in Carolina's box. All the players knew Carolina and many stopped by to say something before each game. Some even made a ritual out of it. Just for luck, they each made sure Carolina blessed their bat. It must have worked. By the end of the season, every player in the lineup was doing it, and the manager, Bill McKechnie, never forgot to tip his cap to Carolina just before the first pitch. The Cardinals set an attendance record and won ninety-five games, finishing ahead of the New York Giants by two games, but then losing the World Series to the mighty Yankees in four straight. Our longtime friend, Sunny Jim Bottomley, had a fantastic year. He batted .325 and led the league in home runs and RBIs. Jack followed the season closely and wrote about it in the *Post-Dispatch*. His writing was passionate, accurate, and insightful. He always touched on something beyond the facts. Jack wrote about the human inside the uniform, mentioning nuances and aspects of the game missed by other reporters. Jack was twenty-two years old and now resembled his father, Nicholas, more than ever. Carolina was proud of him, and rightly so. I liked him a lot. He had become a realist and a dreamer, an absolutely necessary combination for a reporter who writes beyond the facts.

Caine adored his uncle Jack, though he never called him by that name. They were twelve years apart in age and yet they acted as brothers, or more aptly a young father and son. Jack had taught Caine how to care for Mama's glove, how to choose the best oil and rub it in softly with the proper technique. Caine had another glove he used for playing catch, but he always kept Mama's glove oiled and well protected. And after losing an entire childhood together, Jack and Star had been allowed to be a real brother and sister and became close friends.

The next year was the end of the decade and the Cardinals' season went down with it. By July they were essentially out of contention. In the fall, there were two events that occurred a month apart and both would affect and impact America and the world for the rest of the century. One of them affected things instantly, the other was not as obvious and took a while. In October, the Stock Market crashed on what was called Black Tuesday, and in November, Ray, Caine, and I went to the movies. We saw Mickey Mouse for the first time in *Steamboat Willie.*

Mitch Coates never did come back from Paris. The freedom and complete lack of discrimination he felt was much stronger than his love for baseball. However, it is my guess his love for Mercy Whitney was the true reason. He kept in touch with postcards and occasional long letters, mostly about nightlife in Paris and the continuing troubles and adventures of Josephine Baker. He said he and Mercy had become as close as family with Antoine, Emme, and my goddaughter, Antoinette. In a letter dated January 1, 1930, Mitch gave Owen Bramley instructions to liquidate all his business interests in St. Louis, including his stake in the St. Louis Stars, keeping only his home, which he asked Carolina to look after until he returned.

News from Sailor and Zeru-Meq was nonexistent, but Mowsel sent word that he and Geaxi were on their way to pay an extended visit to Malta, Geaxi's *jaioterri,* or place of birth. The Cardinals won it all that year and again the next, beating the Athletics both times in the World Series. During this period, Ray, Nova, Opari, and I never left St. Louis or stayed anywhere but Carolina's home. The city changed and grew around us, yet our lives were insulated—insulated but not invisible. Staying unnoticed, unknown, and most important unremembered has always been essential to our survival. We were becoming careless. I was made aware of it twice in October. On the seventh, after Wild Bill Hallahan pitched the Cardinals to victory in Philadelphia, Opari, Caine, and I went for a long walk in Forest Park. Caine was growing up quickly. He was already several inches taller than Opari and me. As we walked our usual path, we passed an older couple we had seen for years along the same route.

Having seen Caine come of age and rise to our height and beyond while we remained unchanged had frightened them. They no longer were glad to see us and turned away as we approached. We were not normal, not at all like other children and they could sense it. They didn't know what we were, but they knew what we were not. We had been recognized and remembered.

"It may be wise to leave this city, my love," Opari whispered.

"Maybe," I said.

Three days later, on the tenth, the lefty Wild Bill Hallahan beat the Athletics again to win the World Series for the Cardinals. Ray and I witnessed the whole game from Carolina's box seats. Two boxes down from ours, the commissioner of Major League baseball, Kenesaw Mountain Landis, sat with various dignitaries and celebrities, as well as several local St. Louis politicians. His bony face and snow white hair stood out among the others. When he wasn't talking to someone, he observed the game and the players with piercing concentration. After the game and the celebrations on the field, he and the other men turned to leave. We were still in our seats as he passed by. He glanced at me, then stopped abruptly when he saw Ray and stared down at him like a hawk. His eyes narrowed and his thin lips tightened. Then the commissioner of baseball spoke to Ray. "I never forget a face," he said. "I have seen you before, son, and either my mind is playing tricks on me, or else I want to know who you are."

Ray looked him in the eye. "I don't believe we ever met, Judge."

"Perhaps not, but I have seen you before, son. Cincinnati it was, I am certain." He paused and leaned over slightly, so that only Ray could hear him clearly. "That was over thirty years ago, which is impossible."

Ray waited a heartbeat, then winked at him. "Damn, Judge," Ray said, "you got a hellava memory."

The others began urging the commissioner forward. "I want to know who you are, son. Do you hear me?" But he never had a chance to find out. The press and photographers were shouting to him and the other men pulled him on, then Kenesaw Mountain Landis disappeared into the crowd.

Ray turned to me. "It's about time we got lost, Z."

The encounters with the older couple and the commissioner were unlikely, rare, and probably harmless, but I agreed with Ray, it was time to get lost for a while.

Ray and Nova left for New Orleans a week later. Ray said he wanted to see his "old stompin' grounds." Nova was all for the adventure and they both looked forward to spending more time with each other. Opari and I couldn't decide where to go. Our decision was made in an instant on the afternoon of Carolina's annual Thanksgiving Day feast, which she calls only a "fancy lunch." As the garlic and rosemary mashed potatoes were being passed around the table, a telegram arrived from Ciela in Cuba. In it she said Biscuit Bookbinder had been selected to start as shortstop for the Cuban All-Star game in November. Before we finished the meal, arrangements had been made and within three days, Opari and I were on our way to Havana, accompanied by Owen Bramley and Carolina, who couldn't wait to teach us how to "snorkel."

The train ride to Florida allowed Carolina and Owen a chance to speak with Opari and me in a different manner than they would at home. With Caine, Jack, and Star, they maintained a

more maternal and paternal attitude, even though it wasn't necessary. I think it was unconscious and instinctual on their part
and they couldn't help themselves. But alone with Opari and
me and away from St. Louis, they both became candid and re-
flective in their remarks. Their own mortality, or a reference to
it, crept in at the edge of many conversations. It was light-
hearted and casual, but it was still there.

"I'm falling apart piece by piece, Z," Carolina said somewhere in Alabama.

"I don't think so, Carolina," I said and meant it. "You look as
healthy as ever."

"Illusions, illusions," she said, laughing.

Carolina truly did look in top health, but Owen Bramley
seemed a little less energetic and long-winded than he'd always
been. He was a few pounds thinner and his reddish hair had
turned light gold and silver. Red and brown blotches were now
mixed among the freckles on his skin. He removed his glasses,
wiping them clean on his shirtsleeve and talking about the state
of the economy with weary eyes. The world was headed for a
deep depression and Owen Bramley saw it approaching. He
stared out at the passing soybean fields and spoke without his
usual optimism.

"We won't be able to feed them, Z, there will be so many un-
employed. The whole damn thing is going to collapse."

"What about you?" I asked, then followed the thought.
"What about Carolina, what about us? Will we be all right?"

"We're the fortunate ones, Z. Solomon made sure we had
enough money and I made sure all our investments were diverse
and secure. Everything we own is paid for and we've got plenty
of cash reserves. We're set, but that will not stop the collapse, Z.

One big collapse—worldwide." He wiped his glasses one more time and shook his head back and forth slowly. "It's a damn shame."

By the time we reached central Florida, the skies had cleared and the temperature had climbed twenty degrees. At the first stop, Opari and I opened our window and breathed in the overpowering smell of countless ripe oranges. Miles of orange groves lined both sides of the train tracks. St. Louis and the coming winter suddenly became a distant memory. All my thoughts turned to Cuba.

I asked Carolina about the home she and Ciela had started. I was told it was not really a home at all, but an old resort and tobacco farm called "Finca Maria." And it was nowhere near Havana as I assumed, but in the hills north of the small town of Vinales. All of the girls living there came from the streets, brothels, and bars of Havana. Ciela found them and gave them a chance for a new life in a completely different environment. Some rejected it and returned to the life they had always known within weeks, unable to adapt or accept the change. Most welcomed the chance and willingly began to transform themselves under Ciela's guidance and endless generosity. Carolina said even the girls who left respected Ciela and her work. The pimps and bar owners despised her, which made her work clandestine and dangerous. Carolina remarked that Havana was probably the most corrupt and wide-open city she had ever seen. Owen Bramley agreed, but added that Ciela was not being foolish, only fearless. He admired her a great deal and made certain she had anything she needed. He also hired a few men he could trust to silently watch over Finca Maria as a kind of discreet security force. "You just never know about those characters in Havana," Owen said.

We boarded a small passenger boat in Miami on a balmy Sunday morning and sailed south for the Straits of Florida and the old Havana harbor.

On the crossing, I told Opari a few true tales from my time as a smuggler with Captain Woodget. On several occasions the captain found quick and safe refuge in the port and harbor of Havana. I also told her about the countless number of slave ships that passed in and out of the same port.

Ciela and Biscuit were waiting for us. Owen slipped us easily through customs. Opari and I held new passports that Owen had procured. They weren't forgeries, either. They were genuine United States passports and I have no idea how he got them. When I thanked him, he waved it off, saying it was nothing, he only had to know one man—the right one.

Ciela had gained weight and her hair was streaked with silver, but she looked healthy and she was overjoyed to see us. Her skin had turned a dark brown from the Cuban sun and her wide smile was exactly the same. She gave everyone a great hug and a shower of greetings in rapid Spanish. Biscuit waited patiently, then wrapped his arms around Carolina, embracing her without a word. His arms had become the arms of a young man in his early twenties. He stood slightly shorter than Owen and wore a thin mustache on his upper lip.

Carolina looked him over carefully and frowned in mock disapproval. "Biscuit," she said, "I believe I will have to call you Oliver now instead of Biscuit. You are much too handsome for a name like Biscuit."

He owed his life to Carolina and he knew it. "You can call me anything you want, Carolina, for any reason."

"Does that go for me, as well, Oliver?" I asked.

"No chance, Z. You'll have to call me Biscuit."

"What was your batting average last year, All Star?"

".336."

"Not bad. How many errors?"

"One."

"What happened?" I asked, knowing full well only one error in a whole season for a shortstop was phenomenal.

"It was a bad hop, Z," he said with a tiny smile, then turned to Owen Bramley. "Jorge Fuentes is waiting for you in Cojimar. I'll take you there."

We squeezed into a maroon and black DeSoto sedan Owen had purchased for Ciela to use. The heat and humidity were stifling. We kept the windows open and drove east. Cojimar was only six miles down the coast. We stopped alongside a promenade that nearly ran the length of the small fishing village. It was late in the day, but there were still a few hours of light remaining. White clouds swelled and spilled over the horizon to the west. Carolina and Opari took their shoes off and walked barefoot.

Biscuit led us to a lazy, open-air restaurant called La Terraza. We found a table where two Cuban men were engaged in quiet conversation. They were each about thirty years old and both men rose to their feet as we approached. Jorge Fuentes greeted Owen in English and shook his hand warmly, then introduced his cousin, Gregorio Fuentes. After exchanging pleasantries, Gregorio excused himself and left. There were only four or five other fishermen sitting on the open terrace. Owen put his arm around Jorge and said to the rest of us, "Jorge is the best damn fishing guide on the island."

"No, please, señor," Jorge replied. "This is a grand exaggeration."

"Well, say what you like," Owen said, giving Carolina a wink. "It's the truth, is it not, Carolina?"

"It is the gospel truth," Carolina answered. "And diving guide, I might add."

"Indeed," Owen said.

"You are too kind, señor."

While Owen and Jorge made arrangements to rendezvous in La Coloma in one week, Opari and I walked to the other side of the terrace and let the light ocean breeze blow across our faces. The water and sky were both deep blue, with high cirrus clouds in feathered rows stretching west until they merged with the clouds on the horizon. Half a dozen fishing boats and a small yacht were moored nearby. Nothing seemed to move, and if it did, it moved slowly. The only sounds except the sea were the voices of Owen, Carolina, and Jorge. Opari took my hand in hers and whispered, "This destination is *jator,* my love, the very best choice."

Biscuit still had several road games to play before the All-Star game itself and was unable to go on to Finca Maria. We decided to spend the night in Havana with Biscuit, then Owen drove the hundred or so miles to Vinales. The roads were rough but the scenery was beautiful and changing constantly. After turning north in Pinar del Rio, we entered the Sierra de los Organos and the Vinales Valley where huge masses or buttes of limestone called *mogotes* rise out of the green tobacco fields like silent guardians. Opari said they reminded her of the odd limestone hills of Quilin in southern China.

Winding up into the sierra, we reached the small tobacco town of Vinales. A few miles higher up, the buildings and fields of Finca Maria spread out from the narrow road. All the buildings were painted in pastels—pinks, yellows, pale blues, and greens. All had red tile roofs and open beam ceilings. The surrounding fields and gardens were lush and well manicured, and even though Owen had hired workmen to renovate everything when Carolina and Ciela bought the property, the whole place still had the feel of the Spanish Colonial era.

Six girls approximately between the ages of thirteen and eighteen came running out to meet us. They each wore simple cotton dresses and some were barefoot. They all were smiling. None of them looked like they'd ever heard of Havana, let alone lived there as virtual slaves in the bars and brothels of the poorest neighborhoods. It was clear that whatever Ciela was doing was working. They had been given their lives back.

Opari and I were given our own room in a large rambling ranch house that had served as a resort near the turn of the century. One by one, Ciela's girls fell in love with Opari, each wanting to adopt her as a little sister. Opari spoke fluent Spanish with them and they all were impressed by her facility with languages. Ciela's first condition on living at Finca Maria was that every girl must learn to read, write, and speak English. She also taught them basic skills in cooking, cleaning, manners, hygiene, and personal grooming. Her intention was to assure each girl a chance at living and working anywhere she wished, including America. Owen had already assisted in the emigration of two girls to Miami, where they both found good-paying jobs in the front office of a Miami hotel.

In the short week that followed, we took three long bicycle rides and hikes through the Vinales Valley and among the *mogotes*. Our guide was "the best damn guide in the valley" according to Owen Bramley. His nickname was "Indio" and he led us to several limestone caves and underground rivers inside the *mogotes* themselves. The entire Vinales Valley was spectacular and time went quickly. On a clear Sunday morning, Owen, Carolina, Opari, and I said good-bye to Ciela and the girls, then left to meet Jorge in La Coloma. It was Indio who drove us south in the big DeSoto. He had a younger brother living in La Coloma, and when he mentioned that his brother had been born mute, Carolina thought of Georgia and insisted Indio accompany us.

On the trip, Owen and Indio discussed the current political and social situation in Cuba. "This dictator Machado," Indio said, looking out at the poverty in each passing village, "he must exit, he must be removed. The end is near. There will come revolution, señor." Owen nodded and agreed with Indio, but quietly and without passion, which was unlike Owen, and he was sweating profusely. Opari noticed the same thing. Carolina never mentioned it and kept her conversation limited to where we were going and what we might see while we were snorkeling. Then she heard Indio say Machado had closed all the schools indefinitely and her attention shifted. She could not believe he would deny the children of Cuba an education. To Carolina, it was an intolerable and criminal act of involuntary starvation. Owen said he would "have a chat with a fellow in Washington" and see what could be done about it.

But I never got to find out who the fellow was and we never went snorkeling. Just as we arrived in the small coastal town of La Coloma, Owen turned white and his breathing became rapid and shallow. Indio asked if he was all right and Owen couldn't answer. Indio sped to the home of his brother, Luis, and we rushed Owen up the steps and through the door. Inside, there was a couch piled high with rubber fins, rubber goggles with glass lenses, nautical maps, nets, and two spear guns. Indio and Luis cleared the couch with one motion and we laid Owen Bramley down.

Carolina removed Owen's wire-rimmed glasses and wiped his face and neck with her handkerchief. Indio found a wet towel and Opari laid it across his forehead. His eyes were closed and he was barely conscious. Luis set a small electric fan on an end table and positioned it to blow on Owen's face. Then he asked Indio a question by signing with his right hand. Indio answered, *"Sí, sí, rapido!"* Luis turned and ran. I assumed he left to find a doctor.

A few minutes passed. Owen's eyes fluttered for a moment, then opened suddenly. "My God," he whispered and focused on me with great difficulty. "I am going out like Solomon, Z."

"You are not going anywhere just yet, Owen Bramley. Do you hear me?" It was Carolina. She took one of his freckled hands in hers and kissed it. "You'll be fine. We'll rest here and then I'll take you back to Finca Maria when you can travel. You only need a little rest, Owen. Just a little rest."

I glanced at Opari. She was staring at me, shaking her head back and forth. That was when I knew Owen was right, he was dying like Solomon. Opari had seen it a thousand times in a hundred different countries. She would not be wrong.

Luis had to travel to Las Canas to find the doctor. By the time they returned the sun had set and Owen Bramley had died in Carolina's arms. He slipped into unconsciousness shortly after speaking to me and woke once, just as he was about to take his last breath. He opened his eyes and mumbled, "Kites . . . kites."

Carolina cried silently but openly. All of us did. Luis's front door was standing ajar and Carolina sat motionless, staring out across the asphalt road toward the sea a half mile away. She said nothing. She let her tears swell and roll down her cheeks without wiping them away. I thought back to that unknown crossroads somewhere in the depths of China. A train was under repair and on the other side of the train in a wide field full of laughing children, I saw kites rising into the air, one by one. Owen Bramley was making them. Maybe that's where he was now.

Carolina closed his eyes and kissed his eyelids. "Good-bye, Owen, good-bye," she whispered.

Beside me, in a low, mournful drone, Opari chanted, *"Lo egin bake, lo egin bake."*

Solomon used to say Owen was "one of those damn Scottish men; he will pay you no mind and get the job done and done right." That was true and much more. In all the years I knew him, Owen had never once asked who or what the Meq were, yet he devoted most of his life to helping us. He was "remarkable," as Owen himself might say. I reached for his wire-rimmed glasses on the end table and carefully fit them over his ears and nose. He looked as he always had to me. I would miss him for many reasons and many years.

In the time that passed before Luis arrived with the doctor, Carolina talked about Owen Bramley. Carolina talked and Opari and I listened. We walked out of the house and across the road to a narrow strip of beach between two outcroppings of rock. The sea broke hard against the jutting rocks, then lapped up gently onto the beach. We took off our shoes and let the water come up to our knees. Carolina said Owen had always loved her for the very best of reasons, never the easy ones. Opari smiled and said, "Carolina, you are a wise woman."

When Luis and the doctor returned, the doctor conducted an examination of Owen and confirmed he had died of a heart attack. He then asked Carolina what she wished to do with the body. Indio interrupted, saying he would be honored and pleased to take care of the arrangements, whatever she wished

to do. He added that it was the least he could do for Señor
Bramley, a fine man. Carolina did not hesitate. She said Owen
had been as happy here in Cuba as he ever had, and she would
bury him at Finca Maria.

Before Indio and the doctor took him to the mortician,
Carolina washed Owen's face and smoothed his hair. For burial
dress, she told Indio where to find clean clothes in the DeSoto.
Indio mentioned that Jorge Fuentes was anchored in La Coloma
awaiting word from Señor Bramley. He said he would give Jorge
the sad news instead. The doctor and Luis carried Owen out to
the car, laying him down carefully across the backseat. Indio
started the engine. The doctor climbed in and the big sedan
pulled out onto the road and sped away. The three of us were
left standing on the steps with Luis. No one said a word until the
DeSoto was completely out of sight.

Carolina turned slowly and asked Luis a question, not with
words, but by signing with her hands. She and Georgia had
never needed the skill, but Carolina had since learned to do it
on her own.

Opari leaned over and said, "I must learn this language of the
hands."

Luis answered in rapid movements and fingering, then Carolina thanked him with spoken words in Spanish. She looked at
Opari. "Luis has given me directions to a nice beach only a mile
or two from here. Would you walk with me? You're welcome to
go along, Z, if you like?"

I looked in her eyes. I knew them well. "Maybe later, Carolina," I said. "I think you need to be with Opari now more
than me."

Carolina smiled faintly. Then she and Opari removed their
shoes and walked away. Opari reached for Carolina's hand and

they kept walking, an older red-haired woman and a dark-haired little girl. Luis and I watched them. They didn't speak. It wasn't necessary. We watched until they disappeared in the distance, across the road and through a line of palm trees. They were still holding hands. Often, the best and longest-lasting gift is in the smallest package. I loved them both at that moment more than ever before.

Luis tapped me on the shoulder and crooked his finger, motioning for me to follow, but before we turned to go he touched his heart and pointed in the direction of Carolina and Opari. I stared into his eyes. They were dark brown and he had the same smooth, broad face as his brother, Indio. Luis was only in his mid-twenties and looked even younger, yet he already possessed the poise and awareness of a much older man. He knew instinctively there was something curious or odd about Opari and me, and he respected it. To Luis, we were simply another mystery in the world.

"*Sí, Luis, sí,*" I answered, touching my heart.

He smiled, then turned and led me through his small home to a courtyard in the rear, which was larger in area than the house itself. White stucco walls enclosed the space on three sides. Inside the walls, several fully mature orange trees provided shade at all times of the day. Dozens of stone sculptures and pre-Columbian stone heads, some of them Olmec, were scattered throughout the courtyard. Luis led me to a few cane chairs covered with bright-colored cushions. The chairs were clustered around a long, low table made of oak slabs and in the middle of the table sat a solid stone ball, perfectly round and about a foot and a half in diameter. The ball was gray-black speckled granite and must have weighed two hundred pounds. It was slightly cracked and missing chunks of stone on one side. The surface had been ground, sanded smooth, and polished. The stone was old and had been worked by experts. There were strange markings carved at five intervals in a broken line around the ball. The ball was unique, I had never seen anything like it, but it was what covered the top that stunned me. A handprint, a small hand, wider than mine and with shorter fingers, but a child's hand for certain, had been carved across the top of the ball. I glanced at Luis, then looked closer at the markings. Suddenly I recognized one of them. It was the symbol in Meq script for the word "is." I had seen it in the Meq cave in Africa, in the center of an "X" that translated, "Where Time is under Water— Where Water is under Time." The symbol appeared in the palm of the handprint and at all five intervals in the broken line around the ball. My heart jumped.

"Where did this come from, Luis?" I asked, then remembered he was mute and I didn't know how to sign.

Luis motioned for me to wait where I was and turned to go inside. He was back within thirty seconds carrying an old photograph and a map of Cuba. He pointed to the photograph and put his finger on one of two boys who were standing on both sides of a man wearing a fishing hat and grinning ear to ear. They were standing on a pier with an enormous blue marlin hanging upside down behind them. The big fish must have been twelve feet long and weighed six hundred pounds. Luis touched the man's face in the photograph, then touched his heart, and I knew the boys were Luis and Indio and the man was their father. Then Luis ran his finger along the entire southern coast and western tip of Cuba. He pointed at the stone ball, then the map, and then to his father, and I got my answer. Luis's father had found or purchased the ball on the southern coast of Cuba when Luis was a boy. But I had many more questions and decided to wait for Carolina before I asked them.

Opari and Carolina were separated by over three thousand years in age, one being Meq and one being Giza, and yet I could tell the instant they returned that the walk along the beach had served its purpose. Carolina loved Owen in a different way than she had Nicholas, perhaps not as intensely, but just as deeply and for a much longer time. Opari helped Carolina cope with the suddenness of losing Owen, though she never mentioned him by name. She told me later they talked only of their sisters, Georgia and Deza, and how little time they had been allowed to spend with them, and how much they missed them still. There was sadness in Carolina's eyes, but she seemed resigned to what had happened.

The three of us had a quiet conversation about informing Star and Jack in St. Louis and Willie Croft at Caitlin's Ruby in Cornwall. We discussed whether to wait for a burial and Carolina made the decision there would be no funeral or formal service. We would bury Owen at Finca Maria ourselves, simply and privately, just as Owen preferred to live.

Indio was due back soon and Luis was waiting for us in the courtyard. I told Carolina and Opari I wanted them to see something and led them through the house and out to the long low table with the perfect granite sphere resting in the middle. Opari made her haunting trilling sound when I showed her the handprint on top of the ball. She ran her fingers slowly over the stone, marveling at the expertise of the workmanship and the smoothness of the surface. She commented on the age of the stone, wondering aloud how old it might be. "Old," I told her, then I showed her the Meq word "is" among the strange markings at the intervals, and especially in the palm of the handprint.

Opari gasped. "Where did this ball come from, Z?"

"Right here. Right here in Cuba!"

"Where in Cuba? How does Luis come to have this?"

I turned to Carolina and looked in her eyes. "That's what I'd like to find out," I said. "If you're up to it, Carolina, I could use your help with Luis. I need you to sign for me so I can ask him some questions."

"This ball is important, isn't it, Z?" Carolina asked.

"It could be, but if you don't feel like it, I understand. We can always do it later."

"Don't be silly," she said, "let's do it now. God knows Owen would."

Indio returned two hours later and in that time we learned everything Luis knew about the stone ball. His father had discovered it while diving after a major hurricane passed over western Cuba and rearranged miles of coastline, exposing features previously unknown and unseen. The ball was on the floor of a cave nearly thirty-five feet below the surface. Luis said his father was able to dive and hold his breath for five minutes or more at a time. Even so, it took two men two days to get the ball into the boat. Luis said his father kept the location of the cave secret, not telling Indio or Luis where it was for fear that being young they might be tempted to tell someone. He said his father and the other man both died within the next few years before ever revealing the exact location. Luis only knew that it was somewhere from La Coloma west to Playa Maria La Gorda, or along the southern coast of Isla de Pinas. I asked Luis why keeping the location secret had been so important to his father and the other man. When Carolina told me what he said, I wasn't expecting it. "The answer is why I live in La Coloma," Luis signed, "and why I am also a diver and still search for this cave. My father said there were more stone balls in the cave. I want to find them."

I glanced at Opari. A tiny window of curiosity opened in our minds that neither of us could close. "I'd like to come back sometime, Luis, maybe next year. You can teach me to dive. I'd like to help you look for that cave."

Luis signed that we were welcome anytime and he would be glad to teach me to dive, although he wasn't sure I could go that deep.

"You might be surprised," I said.

We spent the night in La Coloma, then said farewell to Luis and started early for Finca Maria. It was a long, hot, and difficult journey. Carolina remained quiet along the way, while Opari and I kept our conversation limited. Finally, rising up into the hills above Vinales, the air became a little cooler and drier. Ciela was waiting for us. She gave Carolina a warm and silent embrace the moment she stepped from the car. Biscuit was absent, but Ciela said he had been informed.

Carolina filled the next day by driving with Indio to Pinar del Rio and taking care of legal matters. Owen Bramley's casket arrived the following day in a separate vehicle driven by a mortician. He was resting inside a simple but elegant coffin of hardwood and brass. We buried him at sunset under a sky of pale gold with fiery layers of orange and red. The gravesite had a clear view of three massive *mogotes* in the distance. They looked like great elephants forever frozen in place, perhaps as sentries. Carolina said a prayer, one that she had composed herself, and

Ciela said one in Spanish, crossing herself at least a dozen times. Not far away, the girls of Finca Maria each released a Chinese kite in his honor. Opari finished by singing a prayer in Meq, a droning lament, which allowed all of us to shed our tears. Then, with Indio's help, we gently lowered Owen Bramley into the earth.

On our walk back to the house, Carolina turned to me and said, "Z, I've been thinking about something and yesterday in Pinar del Rio I finally said, 'Why not?' "

"Why not what?" I asked.

"Why not stay here?"

I looked in her eyes. I had seen the same expression many times in her life, the first being when she told me she was going to place a whorehouse in the most exclusive neighborhood in town.

"I've thought it through," she said. "I could send for Star and Caine, they will love it here, and Jack can take care of the house. The work I've been doing here with Ciela is more important and rewarding than anything I could do in St. Louis." She paused. "I need to get away from St. Louis for a while, Z." She glanced at Opari. I could tell they had discussed this on their walk. "And you and Opari want to find Luis's cave, don't you?" She paused again. "Well, don't you?"

"Yes," I answered.

"Why wait for next year? Do it now. We will all go diving."

I reached for Opari's hand. "What do you think?"

Without hesitating, Opari said, "I believe it is an excellent plan, Carolina. I could not have thought of a better one myself."

The decision had been made. Carolina telephoned St. Louis and relayed her plans to stay in Cuba and the reason why. The unexpected news about Owen shocked Jack, Star, and Caine, who had grown to be like a son to Owen. Jack understood and agreed to watch the house in St. Louis. After traveling by train to Miami, Star and Caine arrived at Finca Maria on the last day of December 1931. All the girls were bewitched by Caine, who was starting to enter puberty and acted embarrassed by the whistles from the girls and the teasing he received. But he didn't run from the attention. Caine already possessed the dark good looks of his father. Star embraced the life at Finca Maria. She relished the food and slower pace of life and became close to all the girls. By February we had settled into a routine that we followed week after week, then month after month, and eventually year after year. While the rest of the world plunged deeper into the Great Depression, in western Cuba, little by little, we began our Great Obsession. Each Friday at noon, Carolina, Opari, Caine, and I loaded the DeSoto with supplies and Carolina drove from Finca Maria to La Coloma. We stayed in a bungalow Carolina purchased for almost nothing. It was close to Luis and near the marina where his boat was anchored. The bungalow was small and simple, and after Carolina had improved the wiring and plumbing, and redecorated, she named it "Pequeno Maria." Every Saturday and Sunday, we sailed and explored with Luis, covering miles of coastline, sometimes fishing, but mostly diving, and always searching for the lost underwater cave with the stone spheres inside.

At first it was fun, a game, an adventure like treasure hunting. We had some difficulty finding equipment small enough for Opari and me to use, but once we did Carolina and Luis taught us all about rubber goggles, fins, and snorkeling, and Opari taught me a method of breath control she learned from Chinese pearl divers during the Ming Dynasty. Within weeks, Opari and I were able to dive with Luis, going down thirty to forty feet and staying down four to five minutes, while Carolina and Caine patrolled above in the boat. Luis called it "skin diving." Opari and I fell in love with it. The more we did it, the more we wanted to do it, and the more I studied the stone ball in Luis's house, the more I wanted to see the others. It was the same for Opari. Quickly, diving was no longer just "fun." We became obsessed with finding the cave.

Luis's father left behind a journal and several notebooks filled with detailed drawings of underwater landscapes and odd formations he had observed surrounding the cave. The problem was that all his notes pertaining to location were written in a personal code only he understood. Luis continued to use the notes as reference, but not for guidance. Instead, he carried out a systematic search based on grids he had drawn over nautical maps, coastal maps, and geological surveys. He was exploring each grid one at a time and there were hundreds remaining.

Usually, we drove back on Monday and our life at Finca Maria occupied our weekdays. However, during exceptionally good diving conditions Opari and I would stay through the week and continue diving with Luis until Carolina returned the following weekend. Many times early on, I thought we had found the cave or at least a landscape to match the drawings, but it was never the right one.

Our time at Pequeno Maria became completely isolated and we rarely talked of anything other than diving and the search. The area was extremely remote and the population sparse. At Finca Maria, though there were many of us living on the sprawling farm, the surrounding country was rural and news mainly concerned local events. Biscuit brought us baseball news when he visited and Indio kept us abreast of current events in Cuba, particularly the opposition to Gerardo Machado and his secret police, the "Porro." Jack kept us informed about the world at large through long letters and telephone calls, which Carolina made from Pinar del Rio every week. On May 12, she spoke with Jack and learned that the kidnapped baby of Charles Lindbergh had been found dead. The sudden news saddened all of us and Carolina became depressed and melancholy for days. She said she missed planting flowers in spring and tending to her "Honeycircle," and she missed Owen more than ever. Then she decided to plant a "Honeycircle" at Finca Maria in his honor. She placed honeysuckle bushes and wildflowers in a wide ring around his grave, and planted fragrant white mariposas throughout. Whenever she felt the need, she spent the whole day tending to the "Honeycircle." It worked. She would always return with a smile, refreshed in mind and spirit.

Our life was basic, simple, and our routine changed little. Days were slow and full, yet time seemed not to exist. The days and months ran together like small streams into a river. In the evenings at Finca Maria, kitchen scents of cumin, sour oranges, onion, and garlic mingled with echoes of distant mockingbirds, and on weekends the scent of sea spray and salt. Four years slipped by and I barely took notice. Even though I was Meq and understood our unique perspective on Time, this "detached" feeling was brand-new to me, so I mentioned it to Opari. She told me not to worry. "It is common," she said. "You are experiencing what the old ones learn to do gradually as segments of time become longer. I have felt two hundred years pass in the state of mind you are experiencing. It is said that before the Time of Ice, this state was given a name. It is called 'denbora dantza egin,' or 'timedancing.' You will come to know this delicate balance intuitively and how to extend it or contract it. You must learn this well, my love."

I continued in the same exquisite balance and strange state of being here/not here for another year, learning the nuances and shadings, and learning how to "extend or contract" as Opari had said I would. There were odd "side effects," which Opari said were normal. One I welcomed and one was a trade-off that frightened me. When I thought about Opari living in this state for two hundred years or more, I gained new respect for her and all the old ones. I welcomed the fact that while I was in this state I had not one thought or dream concerning the Fleur-du-Mal. He simply was not relevant. What frightened me was that I also began to lose my ability to *feel* beauty of any kind, in anything, from Opari's beautiful face to pink and golden Cuban sunsets in the Vinales Valley. I *saw* the beauty in things, but I was unaffected, empty, and numb to it. Beauty, like the Fleur-du-Mal, was not relevant. I now knew old Meq had to endure long stretches of time without one of the true joys in life. There are many trade-offs in extreme longevity, but that was one bargain I wasn't sure I could accept. I also realized I had no choice.

Only Opari knew of my curious state of mind. I showed no outward signs or symptoms and to others I seemed no different. I was able to watch Biscuit play baseball in crowded Havana ballparks or talk politics on the veranda at Finca Maria with Indio. I ate well, I laughed, and I explored. I welcomed Willie Croft, who came for a short visit in 1934 and decided to stay at the request of Star. Carolina even taught me the skill of signing, which enabled me to have endless conversations with Luis about the cave and the stone balls. We heard nothing from Sailor and Zeru-Meq, or Geaxi and Mowsel, and the Fleur-du-Mal was not only out of mind, he was out of sight, silent, and his presence was never felt. Then, in March 1937, I began to return to my normal state of mind. Each day felt as if I were walking through a large house from one small room to another. In weeks I was outside and in the open air. My mind was once again clear and focused, and my love of Cuban sunsets returned, along with an active and palpable hatred for the Fleur-du-Mal.

On the last day of the month Opari and I went diving with Luis. The day was overcast and colder than usual. We were exploring a small rocky inlet near Cabo Corrientes. On our first dive of the day, Opari, who was not wearing her rubber fins, slashed her feet severely on a patch of coral none of us had seen. Blood streamed from the wounds and spread through the water around us. Luis and I each grabbed one of her hands and swam for the surface. Once we were on the boat he tried to clean the wounds, but she continued bleeding profusely. Each gash was a half inch to an inch deep. Opari remained conscious and calm. She said when she stepped on the coral it felt as though she had stepped on a bed of razor blades. Luis went to get fresh towels and bandages. When he returned, he dropped the bandages where he stood and stared at Opari and her feet. Her wounds had all closed and the bleeding had ceased completely. In minutes, several deep open cuts had become a few jagged red lines, which would also disappear within an hour and leave no scars or even a trace of one.

"What are you?" Luis signed. "You must tell me. This is magic I have witnessed—magic or a miracle!"

Opari spelled out the answer. "We are called the Meq."

"What are the Meq?" he asked.

Opari glanced at me and smiled. *"Dendantzi,"* she said out loud, then signed "Timedancers."

★   ★   ★

In early April, Jack arrived for a visit and a celebration of his birthday later in the month. He was going to be thirty-one years old and was now a well-respected reporter and correspondent whose columns covered everything from Dizzy Dean to Mohandas Gandhi. He resembled Nicholas more than ever. Before he said hello he handed me a letter from Geaxi. It had been sent from Malta and he received it a week earlier. I opened it immediately. It was a strange letter with only two enigmatic sentences, one in Basque and one in Phoenician. I could read the Basque, but Opari had to translate the Phoenician. The letter read: (Basque) "Have found something UNDERWATER—we are on our way to Pello's." (Phoenician) "Many Ports, One True Harbor." Neither Opari nor I knew what she meant, but the word "underwater" intrigued me.

We had already planned a big fiesta for Jack's birthday, but Ciela saw no reason why we should wait. Within an hour she and the girls had prepared a delicious *ajiaco,* which they served outside, along with the American beer that Jack brought with him. As the celebrations were beginning, we had two surprise guests, a boy and a girl who arrived in a taxi all the way from Havana. The boy wore an old red beret and grinned at me with dazzling white teeth. The girl wore heavy black eye makeup, reminiscent of Cleopatra. It was Ray and Nova.

Nova went straight to Carolina and gave her a long and warm embrace. Ray looked at Carolina, Ciela, and all the girls, then glanced at Willie Croft, Jack, Star, and finally Caine, who was now nearly eighteen and stood a foot taller than Ray. He turned to me, taking off his beret and fanning his face with it. "Damn, Z, I thought this was supposed to be Cuba." He waved his beret in the direction of Carolina, the girls, and everybody else. "This ain't nothin' but South St. Louis."

I laughed out loud. It was always good to see Ray. "How was New Orleans?"

"We only spent a few weeks down there, Z, then took off for Mexico. New Orleans has lost its charm if you ask me. We were in Veracruz until last week. I called Jack and he said he was goin' to Cuba. When he told me about Owen, I thought we ought to come for a little visit." Ray glanced at Carolina. "I know it's been a while now. How's she doin', Z?"

"She's all right, no, she's better than that—she's remarkable. We buried him over there," I said and pointed to the "Honey-circle."

Ray looked off in the distance at the surrounding hills and the three *mogotes* standing guard on the horizon.

"Damn good spot," Ray said. "Owen's gonna like it here."

Jack brought us all up-to-date on current events everywhere, including the state of Major League baseball in America, the Depression, FDR, fascism in Europe, the Spanish Civil War, and several long and hilarious tales involving his most recent girlfriends. Carolina was prompted to say he should be ashamed of himself. Of course, Caine loved these stories best and begged Jack for more. Opari and I were concerned with what Jack told us about the war in Spain. We learned that as recently as March 30, the Nationalists had opened an offensive in the Basque region. The Nationalists had also enlisted the help of the Italians and the German Luftwaffe. The fighting was bitter and bloody and Spain itself was being torn apart. Jack said this was only the beginning—it would get much worse for Spain, the Basque, and their homelands. Opari had not seen her homeland in over twenty-eight hundred years, but she thought this news to be especially foreboding. My first thoughts were of Pello and his family and tribe. If the war came to them I knew they would fight, and fight to the death. What I couldn't understand was why Geaxi and Mowsel were traveling directly into a civil war. The Meq have never involved themselves in Giza politics or war and try to avoid all war zones, even in their homeland.

Two weeks later, Willie Croft received a cable from Arrosa in Cornwall. In it she said Koldo had left Caitlin's Ruby for Spain. He was headed for Pello's compound of small estates and *caserios* only a few miles outside Guernica. Opari told me the town of Guernica was considered an ancestral and symbolic home for all the Basque. On Jack's birthday, the twenty-sixth of April, before Willie could cable Arrosa an answer, we heard the shocking news of the bombing of Guernica and all the nearby towns and villages. It was the first known aerial bombardment of civilians with the intent of total annihilation. Squadrons of German planes dropped bomb after bomb starting about four o'clock in the afternoon on market day and continuing until darkness, creating a firestorm that burned the town into oblivion. Men, women, and children died by the thousands under the bombs, bullets, and falling buildings. Many were gunned down in the surrounding fields while trying to flee.

"So this is the twentieth century," Opari said, barely in a whisper. Her eyes were the most beautiful and sad I'd ever seen. "The Modern Age, no?"

We waited for word from Spain or from Arrosa and heard nothing for three days. Finally, Willie Croft made the decision to leave immediately for Caitlin's Ruby. Star surprised no one by announcing she was leaving with him. Star and Willie had been living together as a true couple for months. It was Caine who surprised everyone, particularly Carolina, when he announced he was going along. He said he'd always wondered about Caitlin's Ruby and he wanted a chance at attending Cambridge. Caine had been home-schooled in Cuba, but he also had amassed a large library at Finca Maria and read voraciously. I thought he had a decent chance and wished him well. Carolina beamed with pride and I think Star saw, possibly for the first time, a little bit of Jisil come clearly into focus through Caine's eyes. Willie gave Caine a wink and said, "I know just the man to reach. He'll make certain you get a damn good crack at it."

Carolina and Indio drove Willie, Star, and Caine to Havana where they would catch a ferry to Miami, then sail for England. The rest of us said our farewells to them at Finca Maria. Star leaned in close to me as she turned to leave and whispered, "Should Caine and I still worry about the evil one?" There was no true answer, but I didn't want Star or Caine living in fear, even if that fear was justified. I also knew they were powerless against the Fleur-du-Mal. He had proven it over and over again. So I lied and answered, "No." That same night, rain began to fall throughout the Vinales Valley and most of western Cuba. It rained for six long days and nights. The temperature never fell below eighty degrees and the humidity soared. On the afternoon of May 4, my birthday, a taxi arrived from Pinar del Rio. Inside, there appeared to be two children in the backseat, a boy and a girl about twelve years old. They both got out slowly. The girl wore a black vest held together with leather strips attached to bone, ballet slippers for shoes, and she carried a black beret in her hand. I saw a profound weariness in her eyes. The boy seemed to need assistance from the girl and placed his hand on her arm for guidance. Once outside, he jerked his head back and breathed deeply, taking in the heavy, humid air and filling his lungs, straining to catch the rich, sweet scents of Carolina's "Honeycircle" in the distance. The boy's hair was dark and it curled around his ears and over his collar. He wore a white cotton shirt, loose black trousers, and despite the heat, leather boots laced to the knees. His eyes rolled back in his head and he grinned wide, revealing the gap of a missing front tooth. It was Trumoi-Meq and he was blind.

I walked out to meet them. "*Buenos dias,* young Zezen," Geaxi said. She paused and looked around, stopping to stare at the *mogotes,* three humps of gray-black stone and green vegetation barely visible on the horizon. "I assume this is Finca Maria," she said softly. Her voice was as weary as her eyes.

No one spoke of Trumoi-Meq's blindness or asked Geaxi the reason for their sudden appearance. Opari and I simply welcomed them to Finca Maria and everyone, including Ray, embraced, then Carolina led us all inside. Mowsel walked beside Geaxi, sensing her movement more than touching her, and moving with equal grace. His blindness seemed almost undetectable or somehow irrelevant.

Ciela prepared a simple meal of black beans and rice, which we ate in the kitchen, pulling up chairs around the table or sitting on countertops. We limited our conversation to local gossip and the latest news from Biscuit in Havana. Indio and Jack discussed politics and Cuba's current dictator, Fulgencio Batista, but the civil war in Spain and the massacre at Guernica were never mentioned. Everyone respected Geaxi's and Mowsel's silence. We each knew they would take us there eventually, when the time was right and they were ready.

After dinner, it was Jack who suggested coffee and sweets on the veranda. Carolina, Ciela, and Indio stayed inside while Jack and the rest of us sat outside on wicker chairs facing west. The sun had just disappeared behind the *mogotes* and the rain had finally ceased. Two dogs barked in ragged dialogue somewhere far in the distance, however I might have been the only one who heard them. Geaxi and Mowsel sat quietly. Ray glanced at me once, saying nothing. Nova never spoke and held Ray's hand, as Opari held mine. Jack broke the silence, lighting a cigar and saying, "Z, I think we ought to take everybody down to La Coloma tomorrow. I think you ought to go skin diving."

I looked at Jack and smiled and thanked him with my eyes. I knew instantly going to La Coloma was exactly what we should do. Opari squeezed my hand, thinking the same thing. "Yes," I said without hesitation. "Let's go to La Coloma. Tomorrow!"

We rose early and packed what we needed into the old DeSoto, then headed south. Jack had the wheel and he handled the rough Cuban roads as best he could. Geaxi remained attentive, but spoke rarely. Mowsel was more animated and asked question after question about the Cuban landscape and climate. Ray asked Mowsel if he'd ever been to Mexico. To my surprise, after such a long life and countless journeys, Trumoi-Meq answered, "No, I have not."

Approaching La Coloma, I decided to bring up something Geaxi had said in her letter from Malta, before she and Mowsel left for Spain. She was staring out the window. I leaned over and tapped her on the knee to get her attention. She turned her head toward me slowly. "You said you found something on Malta, something underwater," I said. "What was it, Geaxi?"

"Why do you ask?"

"Because where we are going, there is something unusual that was found here and it was also found underwater."

Geaxi glanced at Mowsel. His eyes were focused elsewhere, but his head was turned and tilted in my direction. "What is it, young Zezen?" she asked.

"A sphere or ball. A perfectly round, solid granite ball."

Mowsel opened his mouth in surprise. "With engraved markings and symbols?" he asked.

"Yes."

"And a strange, small handprint engraved on top?"

"Yes."

"This sphere, it was found by a diver?" Geaxi asked.

"Yes, in an underwater cave by the father of the man who lives here. His name is Luis and his father died before Luis could learn the location of the cave. He still searches for the others."

"Others?" Mowsel asked, tilting his head in the opposite direction.

"Yes. His father said there were other stone balls in the cave. That's what we have been doing here all this time—searching for the cave."

Just then, Jack came to a halt in front of Luis's home a mile or so west of town. Luis was gone, probably at sea, however his door was never locked. Everyone in the tiny community knew and loved "the nice man who spoke with his hands." Jack said he was going for supplies and would be back within the hour. He left in the direction of La Coloma and we hurried inside. I led everyone through the house and out into the courtyard and the shade of the orange trees. Mowsel followed easily, and without touching anyone or anything. Nova mentioned the many sculptures and admired the Olmec heads scattered throughout.

Ray said he liked the orange trees. As we neared the low oak table, Geaxi saw the stone ball resting in the middle and stopped dead in her tracks. "It is the same," she said in a hushed voice.

Mowsel reached his hand out. "Where is it, Zianno? Let me touch it."

I took his hand and leaned over, placing his fingers directly on one of the markings, the old Meq symbol for "is." "Do you recognize this?" I asked.

He said nothing for a moment, then smiled wide, exposing his gap in front. "This was in the cave in Africa!"

"Yes, it was."

"What does this symbol mean?"

"It is the old word for 'is.' "

"What do the other markings mean? Can you read them, Zianno?"

"No . . . not yet."

Geaxi looked at Opari. "What do you make of this?" she asked. "Had you ever heard of these spheres, or seen them before?"

"Never. Zianno and I have debated the possible meaning for years. Nothing has been revealed. We are certain the sphere is old, very old, from before the Time of Ice, however its purpose remains an enigma." Opari looked once at me. "And now we know there are other spheres in other parts of the world. What can this mean? Does this have anything to do with the Gogorati, the Remembering? If it does, we must decipher it."

Mowsel had both hands on the stone ball and his fingers traced over the markings again and again, furiously following the lines and curves of the carved symbols. At times, his eyes rolled back in his head as he concentrated. Suddenly he asked, "How deep was this cave?"

"Thirty-five feet at least," I answered. "Why?"

"Because the cave on Malta was approximately the same depth. This is important, do you see?"

"No."

"Think, Zianno. With the melting of the ice, sea levels have risen since the world of the stone spheres existed! The face of the Earth itself has altered. Perhaps . . . just perhaps, the Meq have as well." Suddenly he laughed out loud. "Yes, Opari," he said, tilting his head and searching for her scent and presence. "These spheres have everything to do with the Remembering."

"Then why am I unable to read this writing, except for one word?" I asked.

"Because the spheres have nothing to do with *our* Remembering."

I looked at him blankly. I didn't understand, nor did anyone else.

"Do you not see, Zianno? The answer is as simple as it is mystifying." He paused again, staring into space.

"What do you mean?" I asked.

"There has been another, earlier Gogorati. Ours will not be the first!" He laughed again. "Who is to say, perhaps there have been many?"

The thought raced through each of our minds and instantly, intuitively, we knew Trumoi-Meq was right. The idea was outrageous and mind-numbing to think of the expanse of time involved, but somehow we knew that it was true. And that made the Gogorati seem more confusing and fearful than ever. What was it?

★　　★　　★

Jack came back sooner than expected, saying he had hit the jackpot in La Coloma. He opened the trunk of the DeSoto and displayed two wooden crates full of lobster and shrimp, harvested that morning by a local fisherman. Jack bought the fisherman's entire catch plus rubber fins and masks his children no longer used. "Enough for everybody," Jack said, then asked if I would mind picking up some fresh fruit at a little stand he saw not a mile from Luis's house. Geaxi decided to accompany me and we set out walking under a brilliant blue sky with towering white cumulus clouds building to the south.

Two children, a boy and a girl, ran the fruit stand. There wasn't much to buy in the stand, but what they had looked delicious—coconuts, ripe bananas, lemons, limes, and a Cuban passion fruit called *guerito.* Ciela served it often, by itself or mixed with other fruits. Geaxi held one of the apple-shaped fruits in her hand and asked the children in Spanish if they knew where the fruit got its name. The children said no and Geaxi told them the name came from its flower, which was known as "*flor de las lagas,* or flower of the five wounds." At first the children showed no understanding, then they beamed, smiling and saying in unison, "*Ah, sí, sí, Pasion de Cristo!*" I paid for our fruit and turned to leave, but Geaxi lingered, talking and laughing with the children. I watched her carefully. When we returned to Luis's house, it seemed as if she had been partially renewed, in a manner similar to the way our bodies heal, only this was a wound that could not be seen. Ten minutes later, without anyone asking, she gave us a full account of what happened in Guernica and to whom. She started talking and didn't stop until the awful tale was told.

Geaxi and Mowsel entered Basque country on the night of April 25 from the north, through the Pyrenees using secret trails and hidden routes they had known for centuries. Pello and several Basque compatriots met them outside Pamplona. The men all wore berets and most carried rifles. Geaxi said their faces each reflected the stress of war and their eyes knew death at close range. In stolen trucks, the men drove through the night, arriving at Pello's compound of *caserios* before dawn. After sleeping through the morning, Pello suggested going into nearby Guernica for market day. War or no war, Pello wanted to have a feast to celebrate Geaxi and Mowsel's arrival. In Pello's tribe, the ritual was older than the country of Spain itself and he had no intention of letting a few fascists from Madrid break the tradition. A group of twenty or so men, women, and children, along with Geaxi and Mowsel, piled into two open trucks and started through the hills for Guernica. At that time, Guernica was an open town far behind the lines of fighting and Pello felt there was nothing to fear.

Geaxi said the sky was a clear, soft blue and the market was full. Peasants crowded in from the countryside and all the neighboring villages. The women shopped and gossiped, the men smoked and relaxed, and the children spilled out in five directions. The afternoon passed. At 4:30 P.M. a church bell rang the alarm for approaching airplanes. Five minutes later a single German bomber dropped three or four bombs in the center of town. Fifteen minutes later came another bomber, then more and more, wave after wave of bombers followed by fighters demolishing Guernica and murdering innocent people indiscriminately and without mercy, killing anyone, even machine-gunning children trying to run away through the fields. Geaxi and Mowsel were trapped in the town along with everyone else. She saw Pello trying hard to get his people to safety, but there was too much chaos and they were too scattered. Building after building began collapsing. Geaxi said she and Mowsel took refuge in a sewer, standing six inches deep in water until the attacks subsided. People screamed with pain everywhere. Most were missing arms or legs or both. Blood pooled and ran in the streets and people were dying all over the crumbling town in piles and heaps. Geaxi and Mowsel waited, then made their break for safety. As they were running past the church of St. John, Mowsel saw a girl wandering aimlessly, in shock and completely oblivious to everything. Just then, the incendiary bombs began to fall. Mowsel stopped and tried to get the girl to take his hand, but she only stared at him, then backed off in horror. He tried again. Suddenly she turned to run into the church and Mowsel reached out and grabbed her just in time. The church of St. John exploded and stone, glass, and splintered wood knocked them all back ten feet. The girl was left unconscious, but alive, and Geaxi was unhurt, except for several cuts and bruises. Mowsel had taken the blow directly in his face. Hundreds of tiny shards of glass ripped into both eyes and destroyed the optic nerve. Instantly, he was blinded and probably beyond normal Meq restoration and repair. He was also bleeding. Geaxi quickly tore her shirt into strips and wrapped a temporary patch around his head. With Mowsel holding on from behind, Geaxi carried the girl to safety in the hills, where they stayed the night. Geaxi said she never slept, and all night long she watched the most ancient town in Basque country become an inferno.

The next day, after finding a home for the girl, they learned Pello Txopitea and twenty-three of his closest family and friends had perished. His son, Koldo, alone survived, but only by pure chance. Earlier in the afternoon, he had experienced an upset stomach and decided to leave Guernica and return to the compound. When Geaxi and Mowsel finally made it back, they asked Koldo if there was some way they could help. Koldo thanked them but told them they should probably leave Spain as soon as possible. He said there was nothing Geaxi and Mowsel could do. This was a Basque tragedy—the tragedy was theirs, the war was theirs, and it was only the beginning. Geaxi and Mowsel stayed long enough to say their farewells to Koldo and the remainder of his tribe, then walked out of Spain and began their journey to Cuba and Finca Maria.

"Why did you go to Spain in the first place?" I asked.

Mowsel answered. "There was a man in Pello's tribe who contacted me on Malta. While blowing a bridge for the Republicans, he said he had exposed a cave in the rocks underneath. Something unique was found inside; however, he did not say what it was in the letter. Geaxi and I were too curious to stay away."

"I only wish we had," Geaxi whispered, "things might have been different."

"You must put that thought out of your mind," Opari said.

We were in Luis's courtyard, sitting in the cane chairs around the oak table. Jack and Luis were grilling the lobster and shrimp not far away. Geaxi glanced at Trumoi-Meq, sitting proud and blind, tilting his head toward the drifting smoke, then leaning forward and caressing the stone sphere with his fingers, still feeling for the truth behind the symbols.

"What do you think, young Zezen? It is ironic, no?" Geaxi asked.

"I'm not sure I know what you mean, Geaxi."

"As we learn more about the Remembering . . . little by little, we are falling apart."

8

PUXIKA

(BALLOON)

When is childhood truly left behind? Is there a certain place, or place in time where this occurs? Is it inevitable? Is it in the mind, body, or both? Is it gradual, as the apple ripens, or is it in the moment the apple falls? Perhaps the answer lies with a grand balloon seen rising silently to the top of the sky; a terrible balloon that is not a balloon at all and shall never, ever be a toy.

We spent two continuous weeks in La Coloma under fair skies and on calm seas. We found no trace of the cave, but Ray and Nova fell in love with the underwater world of skin diving. I discovered Ray to be an excellent swimmer and faster below the water than any of us, including Luis. Geaxi said she had been diving since she was a child, but never with rubber fins and goggles. Mowsel always insisted on going along, though he stayed in the boat with Jack while we were underwater. Each day we sailed the coastline and every night we ate fresh fish and drank Cuban beer in the courtyard with Luis and Jack. It was a good and healthy two weeks for all of us. As we were preparing to leave, I asked Mowsel where he thought Sailor and Zeru-Meq might be. I was certain that wherever they were, they would have heard about the Spanish Civil War and realized our planned rendezvous in Spain in 1937 was out of the question. Mowsel said he had no idea and I should not hold my breath while waiting to find out. Sailor might inform us from time to time, if it suited him, but Zeru-Meq had never informed anyone of his whereabouts at any time. But that was before we returned to Finca Maria. The moment Jack pulled the old DeSoto to a stop, Carolina handed me a letter from Star. In the letter, Star said Arrosa was alive, well, and staying in Paris with Mitch Coates and Mercy Whitney. She had attempted to reach Spain after the bombings, but Koldo insisted she go back to England until the war was over. She fled to Paris instead. Arrosa had been devastated after learning of the deaths of Pello and the others. The only good news lay in the fact that she was now safe and out of harm's way. Also, folded inside Star's letter there was another letter, a one-page note and envelope postmarked six weeks earlier. The letter was addressed to me and had been mailed to Caitlin's Ruby from Singapore. Opari translated for me because it was written in Chinese and in a style I didn't recognize. She said the peculiar technique had gained popularity only during the T'ang Dynasty. I did recognize the signature at the bottom. The letter was from Zeru-Meq.

The literal translation was this:

The old one and this one assume no meeting in the home-land. The old one sails for the northern islands. All treasures need maps. Where two great rivers marry, in the city of the Saint, the "List" lies hidden in the wall. The old one requires the names. Meet this one in the city on the eighth day of the sixth month.

Zeru-Meq

I asked Opari to read it again. I knew "the old one" referred to Sailor, "the city of the Saint" was St. Louis, and the date was the eighth of June. The rest was a complete mystery to me. "Does anyone know what this means?"

"I only know Zeru-Meq has never written to us, nor has he ever been to America," Mowsel said, bobbing his head back. "This 'List' must be of extreme importance. *Que es,* Geaxi?"

"No se," Geaxi answered, then glanced at Opari. "Have you ever heard of a 'List'?"

"No," Opari said. "I am unfamiliar with this."

I looked at Ray and Nova. "Do either of you know anything about a 'List' hidden in a wall?"

"Ain't got a clue, Z," Ray said.

"Neither do I, Zianno," Nova added.

I looked at Jack. He was listening, still sitting in the driver's seat of the DeSoto with the door open. To him, it was all gibberish and riddles. He shrugged his shoulders. Carolina stood a few feet away from the car, shielding her eyes from the sun. "I know what it is," she said suddenly.

All heads turned to Carolina. She was staring at me, but her eyes were in the past.

Quietly I asked, "What is the 'List,' Carolina?"

"It was 1904," she said, "just before the World's Fair. Solomon had helped many diverse people from the Far East, people he

had met and befriended in his travels before his eventual encounter with Sailor."

"Yes," I said, "at Solomon's 'remembering' . . . all of them
were there."

"That's right, Z, but there were some among them with
something else in common besides Solomon, something you
did not know."

"What?"

One at a time, Carolina glanced at Ray, Nova, Geaxi, Mowsel,
Opari, and then back to me. "Some had knowledge of you . . .
of the Meq. Solomon said the names of these people were written on a list, a special list, which he gave to me to keep in my
safe in Georgia's room."

"And Sailor . . . did he know about the 'List'?"

"Yes, but . . ."

"But what?"

"Solomon told me there were a few names on the List he
thought Sailor did not know about."

Geaxi interrupted bluntly. "Who were they?"

Carolina glanced at Geaxi. "That I don't know. I never read
it. I simply locked it in the safe and forgot about it." She turned
back to me. "Until now."

"We must leave soon," Opari said. "Zeru-Meq will not be
late; however, he may be early. It is an old pattern of his. I know
it well."

"I agree," Geaxi said, "as soon as possible."

I looked at Carolina. "They're right . . . we've got to go." I
watched her. She still held her hand up, shielding her eyes. "Are
you ready to go home, Carolina?"

"No, Z . . . not yet. I'll give Jack the combination to the safe."
She dropped her hand and took hold of Opari's hand, then

mine, and the three of us turned and started walking into the house. "I believe I'll stay here with Ciela a little longer," she said.

By making a single telephone call to Washington, D.C., Jack made it possible for all of us to travel together and still pass through United States Customs without suspicion or delay. The customs agent in Miami was waiting for our entourage and ushered us quickly through a separate entrance with only a quiet smile and a wish that we "have a nice stay." I asked Jack the identity of the man in Washington and Jack said he had never been told his real name, but Owen assured him the man could be trusted implicitly. Owen gave Jack the number in confidence five years earlier, along with instructions not to use it unless absolutely necessary. Owen called the man "Cardinal" and told Jack to always say the password "sunrise" when the man answered. Mowsel and Geaxi appreciated the assistance of "Cardinal," as we all did; however, Mowsel expressed concern about not knowing the man's true identity, while Geaxi wondered out loud if Owen had compiled a "List" of his own. Jack said he was not aware of one, but opening Carolina's safe might answer the question. In five years, this was the first time Jack had called the number. It would not be the last.

Winding through the Deep South, our train passed through parts of Georgia, Alabama, Tennessee, and Kentucky. Life in the rural areas seemed much the same as it always had, but when we slowed down, weaving our way through cities and towns, the effects of the Great Depression could be seen in each one. Whole blocks of buildings and businesses were closed, boarded up, and abandoned. In every city of any size, I witnessed men, women, and families on the move with little to eat and nowhere to go.

Jack said, "Believe it or not, Z, things are better now than they were a few years ago." As we crossed the Mississippi River and entered St. Louis, I saw the same effects. Still, it was midday June 1, the sun was shining, the city was bustling with more traffic than ever, and it felt good to be there. I turned to Opari. Before I could say a word, she whispered, "Welcome home, my love."

Outside Union Station, Jack hailed a taxi and we loaded what little luggage we had into the trunk. Jack sat in front with the driver, while the driver watched the six of us in his rearview mirror, piling into the back, including a blind Mowsel in a beret, who grinned wide when he felt the man staring at him. He tilted his head in the man's direction and removed his beret. "I smell the scent of the great river," Mowsel said, "but tell me, sir, how is the baseball team faring, the one named for the Cardinal? I have heard much about them." The driver continued to stare at Mowsel in silence for several moments, then turned to Jack. "Where to, mister? And is that kid for real?" Jack gave the driver Carolina's address, then looked straight ahead and smiled. "You'll have to ask him," he said, "but as far as I can tell, they're all for real."

It was a tight squeeze for us on the ride to Carolina's house, even with Opari sitting on my lap. I sat on the far right side and Mowsel sat on the far left with Geaxi to his right. Whispering in his ear, Geaxi described for Mowsel the people, automobiles, buildings, churches, trees and parks, anything and everything we passed, while he leaned his head out the open window to catch the changing scents and sounds along the way. Mowsel wanted to remember it, but more as a guide and internal map than an aesthetic experience. Ray sat in the middle and Nova sat pinched in next to me. At the intersection of Olive and Grand,

I felt something prodding my right side and lower back. I asked Opari if she could reach down behind me and find what was causing it. She did and pulled out an old *Post-Dispatch* newspaper, rolled up and wedged between the seat and door. Opari unrolled it and read the date—May 7, 1937. The front page was covered with an enlarged photograph of the German zeppelin, *Hindenburg,* burning in the sky over Lakehurst, New Jersey, on the previous night. We had heard of the event in Cuba, but none of us had yet seen a photograph of it. In the photograph, underneath a massive ball of fire exploding above them, people could be seen running for their lives. None of us spoke. The photograph itself defined the horror of the tragedy. Opari began to roll the newspaper back the way it was, but Nova reached out and grabbed the newspaper and kept staring at the image and the photograph. She didn't say a word or make a move. She didn't even blink. She was frozen. Finally, Ray glanced at me, then ripped the newspaper from Nova's hands and threw it out the window, which prompted the driver to yell something back at Ray. Ray ignored him and gently lowered Nova's eyelids with his fingertips, then held his hand in place over her eyes. Gently, he pressed her head down on his shoulder and she relaxed, falling asleep the rest of the way.

"She has done this before, no?" Opari asked Ray.

Ray looked up at Opari and nodded, then whispered, "More than once."

"Is she also having visions again?"

"No . . . not visions."

"What then?" Opari whispered.

Ray turned his head as far to the right as he could and looked at me. "Dreams," he said.

Carolina's neighborhood was in full bloom. Overhanging

trees and thick green hedges made her house barely visible until we turned into the long driveway. The driver let us out under the stone arch and Jack unlocked the big house first, then the carriage house above the garage and swung the louvered windows out wide. He told Ray to let Nova rest in Carolina's room overlooking the "Honeycircle." Jack said a soft breeze filled with the scent of honeysuckle might be just what she could use.

Geaxi, Opari, and I opened all the windows of the big house, letting the fresh air circulate. Jack had closed everything tight when he left for Cuba, nearly two months earlier. As I walked from room to room the hot, slightly musty air made the house seem old for the first time. In Caine's room, I paused, then remembered something. I looked in his closet. I was fairly certain it would be there. I reached up and pulled down the shoe box where I knew he kept it, along with neat's-foot oil and a clean cotton cloth. I took the lid off the shoe box and picked it up. It was small, made for a child, and old, a relic by modern standards, but the stitching still held and the leather was soft. I put one hand inside and pounded the pocket with the other. It was Mama's glove and it fit me perfectly. I rubbed the pocket slowly with my fingers and thought about Mama. I could see her cutting and stitching the leather. She'd laughed at my first dream, which was baseball, but she'd also created with her own hands and imagination the means to pursue it. Mama gave me her glove and Papa gave me his baseball and they both gave me what was inside—the Stone of Dreams. Unconsciously, I reached down and felt for the ancient egg-shaped black rock. I took it out and held it in my palm, staring at it, wondering what it truly was, what it truly meant.

"Z . . . where are you?" It was Opari and she was standing in the doorway, but she didn't see me in the closet. I walked out, holding the Stone and still wearing Mama's glove. She glanced down at my hands. "Zianno, what are you doing?"

I paused, then slid the Stone back in my pocket, placed the glove back in the shoe box, and put the shoe box back on the shelf. I turned and walked over to Opari and took her hands in mine. I held them up to my lips and kissed her palms. I looked in her eyes and they were black as coal, just like Mama's. "I suppose I was dreaming," I said.

Opari smiled and kissed the back of my hands. "Then I must wake you," she said, leading me toward the door. "Come, my love. Jack is about to open Carolina's safe."

We hurried downstairs and through the alcove leading to the little room Carolina called Georgia's room. It was her sanctuary in the big house and always had been. Books filled the oak shelves and Georgia's piano still sat in its place against the wall. Carolina's beautiful cherrywood desk and Tiffany lamp rested in front of the only window in the room. Her desktop was crowded with photographs of Jack, Star and Caine, Owen Bramley in various parts of the world, and one picture each of Nicholas and Solomon. As we entered, Jack was opening the window for fresh air. Mowsel sat on Georgia's piano bench, staring somewhere beyond the little room, and Geaxi sat next to him.

"Where's Ray?" I asked.

"He stays with Nova," Geaxi answered.

Just then, Ray burst through the door. "You ain't opened it yet, have you? I love to open safes. You never know what you might find."

I looked at him. "How's Nova?"

"Asleep," he said. "She'll be fine in a while."

I glanced at Opari and her expression said differently. She was concerned for Nova.

Ray walked over and ran his fingers along the edge of Carolina's desk, admiring the grain and color of the wood. He sat down on the corner of the desk. "Where's she hide it, Jack? No, don't tell me. Don't even move. Let me look around first and I'll tell you where it is."

Jack laughed and said, "All right, Ray—where is it?"

Ray had his beret in one hand. He placed it at the proper angle on his head and scanned every wall of the little room, then took three steps over to a space between the bookshelves where an oval mirror in a white frame hung on the wall. He grinned at the rest of us and gently pulled on the bottom of the frame. The mirror swung out on its hinges without a sound, revealing a square wall safe with a black combination lock. "Sometimes, it's obvious," Ray said. He removed his beret and took a deep bow, waving his beret in front of him.

We all laughed, including Mowsel, though I'm not sure he knew why, then Geaxi said, "Open the safe, Jack. Let us see what this 'List' contains."

Jack read the numbers Carolina had given him and turned the lock four times, twice right and twice left, and the door opened. He shuffled through a few papers, mumbling to himself, "Deeds . . . contracts . . . property." He took out the papers, along with pieces of jewelry and a few other things belonging to Carolina, and set them on the desk. He looked in the safe again and removed two items that were behind the papers. One of them I recognized. I'd seen it once before on the day it was put in the safe, the day of Solomon's "remembering" in 1904. Scott Joplin had surprised Carolina and me in the little room and requested a favor. He had written an opera especially for Lily Marchand to sing, but she had disappeared. He wanted Carolina to keep the manuscript for him until she was found. Unfortunately, I was the one who found her two years later, butchered and murdered by the Fleur-du-Mal during a hurricane. Scott Joplin died a decade later without ever knowing what happened to Lily. Jack read the title of the piece, *"A Guest of Honor—an Opera."* He also read an attached handwritten note that said, "This one's for Lily, and only Lily—Scott."

The other item was an elegant black lacquered box, probably Chinese, with the initials S.J.B. painted on top in crimson red. The box was old, yet still in excellent condition. Jack unfastened the tiny latch on the front and lifted the lid. He looked inside. "It's a letter," he said. Jack took the envelope out gently and laid it on Carolina's desk. The paper was yellowed and fragile, but the ink of the writing was visible and clear. The letter was addressed to Solomon J. Birnbaum, Hotel de Mondego, in Macao. It was stamped and dated September 1, 1885. Jack handed the letter to me. "You knew him best, Z. You should read it."

I took the two-page letter out of the envelope and unfolded it carefully, making sure not to tear the paper at the creases. The first page read:

Monsieur Birnbaum,

Please excuse my English. Within this letter you will find the names of all the men I have met in the Orient who have done business with the Magic Child you seek by the name of Sailor. I have also included five names of men I know who knew another, only this one is not familiar to me. His name is Xanti Otso. Beware, these men are of doubtful and dangerous character. I now consider my debt to you, sir, to be paid in full. Adieu and God bless.

Capt. Antoine Boutrain, Bourdes Co.
Shanghai, 1885

The second page of the letter was filled with three columns of names. The first two listed the Giza who had known Sailor and the third listed the five who had "done business" with Xanti Otso. The names were in a dozen different languages and beside each name Captain Boutrain had written the man's country of origin or the port where they had met. I read the lists out loud to everyone and no one recognized any of the names. Silently, I read over the lists again to myself. Suddenly one of the names looked familiar, then a face to match the name came to mind. It was the face of an old Ainu man I'd first met on the train to St. Louis, then again at Solomon's "remembering." There, through his granddaughter Shutratek, he asked me, "What do you keep alive?" It was an unusual question to ask and I never knew why he asked it. Still, I answered with the truth. I told him, "The Meq is what I keep alive." My answer seemed to please him, but it definitely did not surprise him. Now I knew why. Sangea Hiramura was his name and I started to speak the name aloud and tell the others. I never got the chance.

Before I could say a word, Nova came stumbling in the room wearing only a torn cotton nightshirt. She was barefoot and covered with bleeding scratches on her arms and legs. She fell into Mowsel and Geaxi on the piano bench, sending them all to the floor. Ray rushed over to help Nova, while Geaxi got up on her own, pulling Mowsel up with her. Nova was conscious, but her eyes looked glazed and vacant, and her face was ghost white, except for ruby red lipstick smeared across her mouth. Tears mixed with heavy black eyeliner ran down her cheeks in black streams.

"Nova," Ray said softly, holding her by the shoulders. "Come back, Nova . . . come on back to us . . . you can do it . . . you're safe, Nova, you're safe . . . come back now, darlin' . . . please . . . come back, baby."

Nova's knees buckled and she collapsed, but Ray held her shoulders and knelt to the floor with her slowly, letting Nova's head come to rest in his lap. Opari hurried over to check her breathing and take her pulse. Jack said he'd get some water and a wet cloth from the kitchen and left the room. Mowsel asked Ray if Nova was conscious. Ray said, "I don't know . . . maybe . . . her eyes won't focus." Ray was worried. This was much worse than anything Nova had been experiencing recently.

"Kiss her," Geaxi said suddenly, almost laughing.

Everyone turned and looked at Geaxi. Mowsel angled his head sharply to the right and gradually, as he understood what Geaxi had said, opened his mouth in a wide grin and nodded his head up and down.

"What did you say?" I asked.

Geaxi looked at me, raising one eyebrow slightly. "I told Ray to kiss Nova, young Zezen. Was I not clear?"

"Yes, but . . . I don't understand."

"Geaxi is right," Opari said. She looked up at me and smiled. "This is something you should know, my love, and I had nearly forgotten. It is older than all of us." She looked back to Ray. "Kiss Nova on the lips, Ray, and she will wake, and wake as herself because she is your Ameq. This ancient gift is yours now, Ray," Opari said. She reached out for my hand. "And ours, Zianno, if we should need it."

"You got to be kiddin' me," Ray said. "Somethin' that simple?" He didn't hesitate and kissed Nova with passion. Nova's smeared lips responded and she moaned once, as if she were being pulled from some other place. Ray held her close and after a few more seconds, backed away and looked in her eyes. She blinked several times, then focused and found Ray's eyes. She lifted one hand and ran her fingers back and forth over Ray's lips. No one spoke or moved. Slowly, deliberately, Nova turned her head to see where she was and who was in the room. She gazed down at her bare feet and felt the scratches on her arms and legs. Then she stared directly at me.

"What happened, Nova?" I asked.

"I had a dream, Zianno."

"What about?"

Nova turned and glanced at Opari, Geaxi, and Mowsel. She touched Ray's lips again and smiled, only it was a timid, fearful smile. She looked up at me and started to laugh, then stopped herself. "A balloon," she said.

"A balloon?" I glanced once at Opari, then back to Nova. "What kind of balloon?"

Just then Jack ran into the little room with a glass of water in one hand and a dampened towel in the other. Nova looked up at him from the floor. "Nova!" Jack shouted. He was surprised to see her conscious. "Here," he said, handing her the glass and giving the towel to Ray, who wiped Nova's eyes, cheeks, and mouth clean, then helped her to her feet and into Carolina's chair behind the desk. Nova took several sips of water and thanked Jack twice. He asked if she was all right, if she needed anything else? Nova said no, she was fine, and sat back in the chair. The faint scent of honeysuckle drifted in through the open window and across her face. Nova turned her head toward the scent and breathed in deeply. She closed her eyes once, then turned back to the rest of us, completely awake and alert.

"Tell us your dream, Nova . . . if you wish," a voice said gently. It was Mowsel's voice and even though he was blind, he knew Nova was herself again.

She turned to me. "It happened so fast, Zianno, it was terrifying . . . and it didn't feel like a dream . . . it felt real."

"Where were you?"

"In the dream, I awoke as I would in this world, except I was standing by a gate at the entrance to a castle. I don't know where I was, but I was waiting for someone. It was late morning on a beautiful summer day and the castle was deep in the hills. I could see the coastline of a large bay in the distance to the west. The only sound I could hear was the sound of wind blowing through pine trees. Then the gate opened and an old woman walked out. She was no taller than me and kept her head bowed. Her hair was elaborately braided and she wore a blue silk kimono covered with embroidered pink and white cherry blossoms and birds of every color. 'I am Murasaki Shikibu,' she said. 'I see you have found me.' She raised her head and smiled, staring at me with green eyes. She had brilliant white teeth and her smile was bitter and sardonic. 'Look to the west, Nova,' the woman said, and I knew who she really was. I turned and far to the west across the bay I thought I saw a balloon rising high in the air and changing colors like a kaleidoscope. Yet, somehow, I also knew it wasn't a balloon; it was something else, something evil beyond description. The old woman turned to me and threw off her kimono and wig, laughing long and loud. It was the Fleur-du-Mal. He looked me in the eye and inside I felt the deaths of a hundred thousand souls passing through me at once. I screamed and tried to run away, but I don't remember where I ran. I just ran and ran." Nova looked down at the scratches on her arms and legs. They were already healing. "I must have jumped out of Carolina's room into the honeysuckle bushes. The next thing I remember is waking to Ray's kiss."

For a moment no one spoke. I glanced from face to face to see if anyone knew what the dream might mean or portend. Geaxi asked Nova if she had dreamed of the Fleur-du-Mal before. Nova said, "Never." Mowsel leaned forward and asked if she had ever been to Japan. "Never." Opari asked the central question: "If the balloon was not a balloon, what was it?" Nova couldn't answer; she only knew it was unspeakable. I asked, "Who is Murasaki Shikibu?" Nova shook her head back and forth. "I've never heard of her, Zianno."

"I have," Jack said. He was standing by Carolina's bookshelves. He scanned the shelves until he found a certain book and tossed it to me. "*The Tale of Genji* by Lady Murasaki," Jack said. "Her full name was Murasaki Shikibu. Most people think it's the first novel ever written. She wrote it almost a thousand years ago."

I looked at Nova. "Have you read this book?"

"Never."

A few seconds passed in silence. No one knew what any of it meant, but we were all in agreement that the appearance of the Fleur-du-Mal in Nova's dream must not be ignored. Geaxi said, "Zeru-Meq is due to arrive soon. Perhaps what he has to say will shed some light."

Ray walked over to the open window and looked up through the trees, surveying the sky. It was cloudless and bright blue. "Well, I just hope he don't come tomorrow. He won't like it."

"Why not?" Jack asked.

"There's gonna be thunder, rain, and lightnin' all day long, maybe worse."

"How do you know that? Today's a perfect day."

Ray swiveled his head and grinned at Jack, but didn't say a word.

I said, "Because he's the Weatherman, Jack," and Ray gave me a wink.

Ray was right, of course. Just before dawn, booming thunder woke us all and by the end of the day three separate storm systems had moved through St. Louis from the west. Ray grinned every time he saw Jack that day. On the sixth of June, the Cardinals played a doubleheader against the Phillies at Sportsman's Park. Jack, Opari, Ray, and I went early and took our seats in Carolina's box. Opari had become an avid fan of baseball. She even wore a Cardinals' ball cap to the game, but took it off when she overheard someone behind her say, "What a cute little girl!" The Cardinals won the first game 7–2 and the umpire, "Ziggy" Sears, ended the second game early by calling a forfeit in the fifth inning and giving the win to the Cardinals. The Phillies had gone into a stall, trying to slow the game down until the Sunday curfew would cancel the game. The fans booed the Phillies off the field. On the way home, Opari asked about the unusual event. I told her in the game of baseball, the Phillies had tried a tactic that was more cheating than strategy, and such a play was against the rules. And in baseball, the umpire starts the game and can end the game, if necessary. On the field of play, he is the final authority.

"Zeru-Meq will find this game amusing," Opari said. "He will like these odd nuances."

"Speaking of Zeru-Meq, I thought he liked to arrive earlier than expected. Where is he?"

"I said he may arrive early, it has been one of his patterns, but nothing about Zeru-Meq is expected or predictable, my love. Zeru-Meq is his own umpire."

"Yes, I know," I said, groaning slightly. "I remember China."

June 8 passed uneventfully and without a word or sign from Zeru-Meq. No one expressed concern. On June 13, the Browns played the Yankees in a doubleheader. Ray and I decided to go, even though we rarely attended Browns' games. Both of us were anxious to see the second-year center fielder for the Yankees, Joe DiMaggio. Jack was covering the doubleheader for the *Post-Dispatch* and let Ray and me sit with him in the press box. In the second game, Joe DiMaggio smacked three home runs and made several great defensive plays. DiMaggio's third home run towered over the center field fence and was caught by a kid who made a spectacular bare-handed catch. The kid waved the ball high in the air, then removed his cap and took several deep bows, which drew laughter from the big crowd. I couldn't see the kid's face clearly, so I borrowed Jack's binoculars and focused on the center field bleachers, but the kid had already disappeared somewhere among the fans.

That night, long after dinner, Opari, Ray, and I walked the short distance to Carolina's "Honeycircle" to have a quiet conversation about Nova. While we talked, Ray was catching lightning bugs and then letting them go. Opari stood by Baju's sundial and I was sitting on the grass next to her. At one point, out of the corner of my eye, I saw a shadow moving silently into the opening of the "Honeycircle." I turned my head slowly. In the darkness, I could see the dark figure of a boy, standing with his legs spread wide and his hands on his hips. I panicked at first, remembering the Fleur-du-Mal's figure standing over me in almost the exact same place the night he slashed every tendon in my knees and shoulders. I jumped to my feet and faced him. There was just enough moonlight to see he was wearing boots laced to the knees and some sort of gem on one hand because it sparkled in the faint light. He started toward me and I knew he wasn't the Fleur-du-Mal.

"Zeru-Meq?" I asked.

The boy took another step. "I should think not," he said, and kept walking until we could all see his face easily.

Opari laughed and said, "Hello, Sailor."

Sailor tossed a baseball he was holding to me. When I caught it, he asked, "Did you see the catch, Zianno?"

I didn't understand until I glanced at the ball. It was an authentic Major League baseball. "That was you today, the kid in the center field bleachers?"

Sailor didn't answer, but asked if I was aware of the fact that the stitching on a baseball was remarkably similar to an ancient design for infinity. Then he asked, "Did you find the 'List'?"

"Yes," I said. "What about—"

Sailor cut me off. "I will explain later, Zianno."

"But the letter from Zeru-Meq?"

"A necessary ruse," Sailor said, glancing over at Baju's Roman sundial. He stood in silence for a few moments admiring the ancient timepiece before he spoke. "Last week, on the eighth of June, in the Pacific and on the coast of Peru, there was a Bitxileiho. Totality exceeded seven minutes. The last time this occurred was over eight hundred years ago." He paused. "Baju and I were there," he said, then looked away quickly. He offered

his arm to Opari and she smiled, folding her arm in his. "Shall
we go inside?" Sailor asked, and started walking toward the big
house before Ray or I could move.

"Damn," Ray said.

"I suppose that means yes," Sailor said over his shoulder.

I was surprised Sailor didn't ask to see the "List" the moment we
stepped inside. Instead, he suggested tea in the kitchen. Geaxi
and Mowsel had gone for a walk in Forest Park. Nova was washing dishes and Jack was sitting at the table writing a letter to
Carolina and Star. The popular song "My Funny Valentine" was
playing on the radio in the next room. Sailor greeted Jack
warmly, then walked over to Nova and embraced her. "How is
my niece?" he asked quietly. I had never heard Sailor address
Nova as "niece" and he seemed to be acutely aware of her recent fragile state of mind. Nova assured him she was fine. Jack
left to turn the radio off and the rest of us took our seats around
the table. Except for his boots, Sailor was dressed like any other
kid in America. He even had a floppy, snap-brimmed cap exactly like the caddies at the golf course in Forest Park. He said
he wanted to hear everything that had happened to Pello and his
tribe in Spain. He knew there had been many deaths, but he
wanted to know the extent. Opari prepared the tea while I tried
to relate some of what Geaxi had told us about the bombing
of Guernica. Sailor listened without moving. His "ghost eye"
glazed and clouded and swirled. He was horrified. I hadn't yet
told him of Mowsel's blindness when the kitchen door burst
open and in walked Mowsel himself, followed by Geaxi.

Mowsel almost bumped the table. He stopped short and felt
his way to an empty chair. He was mumbling something about

glass greenhouses and light. Geaxi saw Sailor instantly and stood still in the doorway. Sailor watched Mowsel without saying a word. Then Mowsel suddenly fell silent and turned his head toward Sailor, but his eyes focused somewhere on the ceiling. He grinned and said, "Do I smell the sea or is that merely the scent of an old mariner?"

Sailor made no response. He glanced once at Geaxi, who said nothing. He moved his chair closer to Mowsel and held his hand up in front of Mowsel's face. Mowsel continued to stare at the ceiling. Sailor leaned even closer. "How long have you been blind, old friend?"

Without hesitation, Mowsel answered, "Since Guernica."

Sailor paused. "Do you think it is permanent?"

Mowsel dropped his grin and angled his head in the opposite direction. He seemed to be remembering something, maybe Guernica. "It is possible," he said.

Sailor looked up to see if Jack was in the room. He wasn't. Sailor's jaw was set tight with anger and he twirled the blue sapphire on his forefinger round and round. I hadn't seen him that way since northern Africa when he told me about the Greeks who traded and sold the bones of the Meq who had been slaughtered in Phoenician temples. Sailor turned to me. "These Giza . . ." he said bitterly, "they will kill us yet."

Opari leaned forward and laid her hands on the table. "We cannot change the Giza, Umla-Meq."

"No, we cannot, but the Giza are changing everything else!"

Opari waited for Sailor to look at her. When he did, she pressed one hand against her chest, over her heart and over the Stone of Blood hanging from a leather necklace beneath her blouse. "We will survive, Sailor. We are Meq . . . we must."

Mowsel reached out and found Sailor's face with his right

hand. He gave him a gentle slap on the cheek and grinned. "Do not worry, Umla-Meq, I am well, and Opari is correct—we must survive."

Sailor started to respond just as Jack entered the kitchen. Jack looked at me and said, "I thought you might want to use Georgia's room, so I opened the safe."

Sailor glanced over at me. "The 'List'?"

"Yes."

He stood and motioned for me to lead the way. "Shall we, then?"

As we left the kitchen, Mowsel fell in behind Geaxi, never touching her and matching her step for step without running into anything. Sailor watched his longtime friend with admiration and affection. I even saw the hint of a smile cross his lips.

With all of us in Georgia's room at once, it quickly became close and crowded. Sailor stood by the Tiffany lamp and read Antoine Boutrain's letter without reaction or expression, except for a single nod of his head, as if confirming something. When he was finished, Geaxi asked him bluntly, "What is this about, Sailor?"

Jack had left as we entered and there were only Meq in the tiny room. I realized for the second time in my life, all five Stones had gathered in the same place. The last time had not gone well.

"Zianno," Sailor said. "Do you recall our final conversation in Norway? I told you the Fleur-du-Mal now had a significant weakness because we knew something he did not."

"That there is no Sixth Stone?"

"Precisely, and I said we could exploit his obsession."

"Yes."

"Our opportunity has arrived and we must act soon." Sailor's "ghost eye" swirled. He looked around the room from face to face.

"I'm confused," I said, pointing at the letter. "What does the 'List' have to do with it?"

"Zeru-Meq and I recently became aware of this 'List' in Singapore, quite by accident through a family he has known and trusted for centuries. The family had once conducted several clandestine affairs with Captain Antoine Boutrain. I knew nothing of this 'List' and I am certain the Fleur-du-Mal is unaware of its existence. Someone on the third list, the list of five names who associated with Xanti Otso, has a descendant we must find and find soon."

"Why?"

"He or she will likely know the exact location of the castle where Susheela the Ninth is imprisoned. Zuriaa is there. The Fleur-du-Mal is not. He seems to be working again, and at fever pitch, as well as searching for the Sixth Stone."

"Now I am confused, old one," Mowsel said, leaning his head to one side.

"I concur," Geaxi added. "Make yourself clear, Sailor."

Sailor rubbed the blue sapphire on his forefinger. "Yes, yes, of course, you are right. I shall begin where it began, which was India six months after leaving Norway. However, I suggest we do this in another room. This room is charming, Zianno, but not for seven of us on a summer night in this city."

"It should be cool in the 'Honeycircle,'" Nova suggested.

"Indeed," Geaxi said, starting for the door with Mowsel a step or two behind.

On the way out, I whispered to Sailor, "I recognized one of the names on the list of five names. I met him briefly in 1904 . . . and he knew I was Meq, I'm sure of it."

Sailor stopped walking, completely surprised. He still held Antoine Boutrain's letter in his hand. "Who is it?"

"Sangea Hiramura."

"Japanese?"

"Yes and no. He was Ainu."

"Is he still alive?"

"I doubt it. He was at least seventy-five then."

"Tell me about him," Sailor said. His "ghost eye" almost glowed.

"I will . . . after you tell the rest of your tale. I want to know what's going on."

Sailor nodded once. "Agreed," he said.

"There's something else. Opari and I discovered an unusual object in Cuba, as did Geaxi on Malta, almost simultaneously. They are old, Sailor, very old, and I know they have something to do with us, maybe the Remembering, or at least one Remembering. They were found *underwater*."

Sailor gave me a quick glance. He seemed intrigued, but turned and started out of the tiny room. "Later," he said.

We walked to the "Honeycircle" in silence. Overhead, only a few stars were visible through a dark haze of clouds. Traffic could be heard faintly in the distance, but Carolina's neighborhood was still one of the most quiet neighborhoods in the city.

Everyone sat in a loose ring around Baju's sundial. Sailor sat on the sundial's stone base, while the rest of us were sitting on the grass, or in Ray's case, lying on the grass. Lamps inside the carriage house shone through louvered shutters and cast long bars of light across Sailor's face. "As I was saying," he began.

"Six months after leaving Norway, Zeru-Meq and I arrived in Madras. We had not yet seen, heard, nor felt a trace of the Fleur-du-Mal. In Madras, we were hoping to find the family of his Indian accomplice, Raza. In that effort we were unsuccessful. However, while we were there, on a whim, Zeru-Meq attended a Hindi gathering at which the pacifist leader, Gandhi, gave a passionate speech. When he returned he told me he felt the presence of his nephew at the event.

"Why the Fleur-du-Mal was present is still a mystery, but finally Zeru-Meq had a trail to track. Zeru-Meq has several unique abilities he has learned through meditation; however, I also learned Zeru-Meq has an innate ability to follow the Fleur-du-Mal without seeing him. We are not certain how or why this occurs, perhaps the reason is because he is the uncle of Xanti Otso. Whatever the answer, he is only able to sustain this ability at a certain distance, which is always difficult to predict. The Fleur-du-Mal moves rapidly, as we all know, and particularly so when he is working. Nevertheless, we followed his 'trail' to Goa." Sailor paused for a moment, stroking the star sapphire on his forefinger. Then, suddenly, he asked Mowsel if he remembered their first voyage to Goa in the late 1500s. "Was the year 1581 or 1591?"

Mowsel angled his head toward Sailor's voice and frowned. "It is you who are the Stone of Memory, Umla-Meq . . . you tease me, no? It was during the winter and spring of 1591. A magnificent voyage; we discovered a great deal."

"Yes, yes, of course," Sailor said quickly, all the time twirling the star sapphire as he spoke. He continued to talk and he talked for half an hour. When he finished, Sailor had revealed more about the Fleur-du-Mal, his activities, his motives, methods, moods, and madness than we'd ever known before, even how he began to establish bases of operation in India, Ceylon, Singapore, China, and Japan going as far back as the 1550s. It was as if Sailor had been corresponding with him—intimately, psychologically. We also learned Zeru-Meq was not and had not been in Singapore. Sailor wanted the Fleur-du-Mal to think the opposite, thus the "necessary ruse." The Fleur-du-Mal had discovered he was being followed. The false letter Sailor wrote had enough veracity in it to be believable and was purposely allowed to fall into the Fleur-du-Mal's hands. Meanwhile, Zeru-Meq continued his surveillance and Sailor was able to make his way to St. Louis. He also told us the Fleur-du-Mal had been working covertly for a Giza government, assassinating several political and social figures, though Sailor didn't know which government or what country. The assassinations had occurred throughout Southeast Asia and along the coast of China and were becoming more frequent. The Fleur-du-Mal no longer took the time to carve roses into the backs of his victims, Sailor said. The kill itself, however, was the same—a quick and clean slash of the throat from ear to ear.

I wanted to ask the obvious question, but Geaxi beat me to it. "How do you know what you know, Sailor? You seem to have acquired a great deal of knowledge about the Fleur-du-Mal. No, you seem to know more than a great deal. How did you learn these things?"

Sailor hesitated. "She tells me."

"She?"

"Susheela the Ninth," Sailor said, and turned to me. "Through dreams, Zianno. She tells me through dreams, though they are infrequent and irregular." Sailor looked at Opari. "She speaks in Deza's voice, Opari. She uses Deza's voice, but she is not Deza." He looked back to Geaxi and glanced once at Mowsel. "She is . . . *denbora dantza egin* . . . like no other among us."

"What the hell is that?" Ray asked.

"Timedancing," Opari answered. She winked at me and smiled. "Ask Z about it, Ray."

"What is it, Z?"

"Uh . . . well . . . it's hard to describe, Ray. It's kind of a strange balance you keep inside, like a weightless walking dream or a dance through time. You're here, but you're not here. It's like a waltz with what's real and what's not."

Ray stared at me, squinting, then he said, "Hell, I do that all the time."

"What do you mean, 'like no other'?" Geaxi asked Sailor.

"She goes deeper, much deeper, farther, and for as long as she desires. It is effortless for her. She is a master at it and this infuriates the Fleur-du-Mal. He has imprisoned her for it and vowed to keep her imprisoned until she tells him what she has done with the Sixth Stone."

"Why?"

"Zeru-Meq says it is simply envy and jealousy. He calls his nephew 'a sad and dangerous pilgrim who chases magic instead of truth.' The Fleur-du-Mal is obsessed with powers he does not possess, particularly the 'ability' of timedancing. He has never been able to do it and knows he never will. He must endure his madness and his pain alone and in real time."

"Why is that? Why can't he do it?" Nova asked. She sat cross-legged with Ray's head in her lap. Ray sat up when she spoke.

Sailor looked down at Nova, then at Ray. The long braid behind his ear fell forward into a shaft of light. The tassel on the end was weighted with an oval piece of polished onyx. "Because, like Ray, he was born with green eyes. He is Egipurdiko and the Fleur-du-Mal is fully aware that only Egizahar are able to cultivate this 'ability.' It is the one and only *true* difference between the 'diko' and the Egizahar."

"Damn," Ray said under his breath.

As Sailor spoke, I noticed whenever he mentioned Susheela the Ninth, his "ghost eye" cleared completely. He also stopped twirling and stroking the sapphire on his finger.

"What about the 'List,' Sailor," I asked.

"A few decades before the Fleur-du-Mal found and purchased Askenfada in Norway with the assistance of Raza, he did the same in the Far East. One of the names on the list of five was the man or woman who acted as broker for Xanti Otso, finding and purchasing a well-fortified medieval castle somewhere on the Pacific rim in China or Japan. The descendants of this Giza will likely know of the castle and its location. We must find the castle while the Fleur-du-Mal is working and I am certain we do not have long. The Far East is quickly being usurped and occupied by the Japanese. Soon, travel may be difficult, even for us."

Mowsel had not said a word. He kept his head bowed, listening to every word Sailor said without showing any emotion or expression. Slowly, he raised his head and leaned forward. "Will there be war in the East, Umla-Meq?"

Sailor looked at Mowsel and stood up on the stone pedestal of the sundial. He reached one hand out and ran his fingers along the edge of the bronze gnomon. In the darkness, the gnomon cast no shadow and told no time or season. "It is inevitable," he said evenly. "And from what I read, and also what

Zianno has told me of the German bombers in Guernica, there will be war in Europe as well." Sailor paused and turned to face Mowsel. "It seems this time, old friend, these Giza are determined to slaughter each other by the millions."

"What do you propose, Sailor?" Opari asked.

"Tomorrow," he said, holding up Captain Antoine Boutrain's letter between his thumb and forefinger like a winning card in a poker game, "we shall divide the names on the list of five among us and begin our search for each of them and their descendants."

"This ain't gonna be easy, Sailor," Ray said. "Not if what you say about the Japanese bein' everywhere is right. The word 'difficult' won't be close to what we'll run into. We're gonna need some help."

"He is correct, Sailor," Geaxi said. She stood and began to pace the "Honeycircle." Her steps made little or no sound in the grass.

Opari turned to me. "Jack," she whispered and I knew immediately what she meant.

"Sailor," I said, "give me a day or so. I think Jack might know someone who can help us."

"Who is it?" Sailor asked.

"I can't tell you."

"Why?"

"Because I don't know who it is."

"Then why should he help us?"

"Owen Bramley knew the man. Owen left Jack a number to call in Washington if we ever truly needed help. When we wanted to leave Cuba together, and quickly, Jack contacted the man and the next day in Florida we were whisked through customs without being asked a single question."

"And you do not know his name or identity?"

"Jack was only given the name 'Cardinal' and a password, 'sunrise.' "

Sailor looked at Opari, Geaxi, and down at Mowsel. "Do you trust this *elkarte,* Trumoi-Meq, this *association?*"

"No, Umla-Meq, I do not. I believe it is Giza *joku*—adult games—they play. However, we must respect and trust the judgment of Owen Bramley. This has been proven many times." Mowsel leaned his head in the opposite direction. "And we have no option, old one. If you think we should make haste in finding these names, Ray is correct, we will require help."

Sailor looked at me. With no hesitation, he said, "Talk to Jack, Zianno. Find out what he can do, and soon."

Nearby, within twelve feet but completely invisible in the darkness, Geaxi asked, "Sailor, why do we not pursue the Fleur-du-Mal before finding the castle? Is it not logical?"

A few seconds of silence followed. "We shall need Susheela the Ninth alive, Geaxi," Sailor said. "We cannot eliminate the Fleur-du-Mal once and for all without her."

A few more seconds passed. From the dark, Geaxi said, "I see."

Sailor stepped down from the stone pedestal and took hold of Nova's hand, pulling her upright and folding her arm in his. He started walking, leading both of them and us toward the opening in the "Honeycircle" and back to the big house. Somewhere in the distance, I heard a cat squeal, followed by a barking dog. "In the morning, Nova," Sailor said, "I want to walk with you in Forest Park and tell you the story of your father and his wonderful sundial."

*   *   *

I spoke with Jack the next day and told him our problem. He understood and agreed we should call "Cardinal." He dialed the number in Washington and someone picked up the receiver after one ring, but said nothing. Jack used the password "sunrise." Ten seconds later, "Cardinal" was on the line and Jack wasted no time in telling him exactly what we needed and gave him the list of five names. On the spur of the moment, Jack added that we could also use seven diplomatic passports. To everyone's surprise, and without hesitation or even asking a single question, "Cardinal" said it would all be arranged. A week later, a plain brown package appeared one morning in Carolina's driveway, lying alongside the *Post-Dispatch*. Jack opened the package on the kitchen table and spread the contents out. Five separate folders contained long dossiers on each of the five names plus dossiers on their descendants and their current addresses, except for Sangea Hiramura. His dossier contained a single sheet of paper with no information on him and only the names and history of three sons and one daughter, Shutratek, the same woman I spoke with on the train to St. Louis and again at Solomon's "remembering." The dossier said Shutratek had returned from the World's Fair in 1904 and was still living in Hokkaido. Two of the sons had remained in Japan during the Fair. One son eventually moved to Tokyo and the other moved to Anchorage, Alaska, in 1915, where he disappeared. The fate of the third son, the one who had accompanied Sangea and Shutratek to St. Louis, was unknown. Along with dossiers, the package contained seven brand-new diplomatic passports for seven children from the same family in Brazil. The children looked remarkably like us. Jack laughed once, then dealt the passports out like playing cards to Nova, Ray, Geaxi, Mowsel, Sailor, Opari, and me.

Sailor mumbled under his breath, "I should like to meet this 'Cardinal' one day."

"I think not," Mowsel said, leaning his head toward Sailor. "Before you meet him, old one, I think we should know more about him than he seems to know about us."

"Trumoi-Meq is correct," Opari said.

"Agreed," Geaxi added.

Sailor glanced once at Mowsel and turned to Jack. "If possible, try to find out who 'Cardinal' truly is, Jack."

Jack said, "I'll do my best, Sailor."

All that day and night we discussed the names on the "List" and their dossiers. Sailor informed everyone of my connection to Sangea Hiramura and it was decided that Sailor and I should be the ones to find and track down his descendants. Among the five names, there was one other Japanese name. His descendants were now living in Manila and Nova and Ray would go there. Two of the remaining three names were Chinese, one of them a woman from Nanking and the other a merchant from Hong Kong. Opari chose to investigate the woman, saying the woman herself was not familiar, but the name was well known. Opari said the family had been a powerful and infamous force in the region since the Ming Dynasty. Geaxi and Mowsel chose the other Chinese name, mainly so Geaxi could fly across the Pacific in Pan American Airlines' flying boat, the China Clipper. The last name on the "List" was American and his descendants now lived in Honolulu. Since there were no more of us to do it, Jack suggested he investigate the American and his family.

"The China Clipper leaves for Hong Kong from San Francisco," he said. "She makes her first stop in Honolulu." Jack paused and looked at each of us one by one. "Why not me?"

No one said a word for a moment or two, and it wasn't me, or Opari, or Geaxi, Ray, Nova, or even Sailor who answered. It was Mowsel. He grinned wide, exposing his gap and tilting his head in Jack's general direction. "Why not, indeed!" he said.

The Egizahar Meq may be able to use and develop various forms of dealing with time and the passage of time, including the elegant, bewitching, difficult, and conscious/unconscious art of timedancing. Most if not all of these skills and "abilities" involve the illusion of time slowing down. According to Sailor, Mowsel, and Opari, this has always been so. In a similar, but external and practical manner, all Meq possess the ability to mobilize and simply leave—anytime, anywhere, and for whatever length of time is necessary. This is not illusion. The Meq can and must be able to *move.* Our survival depends upon it.

Jack wasted no time in wiring Carolina and telling her he was closing the big house and going on the road for several weeks, maybe months. He kept his destination vague and said he would stay in touch. Then he informed the *Post-Dispatch* that he would be unavailable and out of the country until further notification, bought our train tickets, and by the end of June we were leaving Union Station and heading west. In San Francisco, on the Fourth of July, along with the rest of America, we celebrated Ray's birthday. We spent the whole day taking long taxi rides back and forth across the new and beautiful Golden Gate Bridge.

We had made reservations on the China Clipper before we

left St. Louis. Our departure date was set for the sixth. On the fifth, Jack picked up our tickets and itineraries for the long flight and brought them back to the hotel. In the package along with the tickets, there was an unmarked envelope with a neatly typed, two-page letter inside. It was unsigned, although there was little doubt who wrote the letter. It was from "Cardinal" and included a short, but comprehensive dossier on the third son of Sangea Hiramura, the one who had supposedly disappeared years earlier in Alaska. His name was Tomizo, though he was often called Sak or "strong wind." The dossier listed an address in Juneau where he had lived as recently as 1935. "Cardinal" suggested we begin our search there. Since this was more information than we had on the other sons or Shutratek, Sailor and I changed our plans. Instead of flying to Hong Kong and sailing to Japan, we were going to Alaska. Sailor welcomed the new information, saying "Cardinal" seemed to have exquisite timing, then he turned to Jack with a wry smile. "I cannot help wondering, Jack," Sailor said, giving me a quick glance, "are we being led, followed, or simply *anticipated*?"

"I can't answer that," Jack said. "But I can stop this thing right now, Sailor . . . if you want. You tell me and I'll tell him and it'll be over."

"I do not think it would be that easy at this point," Sailor said. "No, we must play it out. We must find the castle. If 'Cardinal' can help us in this, then so be it. We have no choice."

"We always have choice, Sailor," Geaxi remarked.

Without looking at her, Sailor said, "Not this time, Geaxi."

The morning of July 6 began cold and foggy. In our hotel room, Opari and I woke early and stayed in bed all morning, holding each other and talking, telling stories, and laughing. We had spent the last few years being together almost every day. I would miss her more in this parting than ever before and she felt the same. I was learning once again the Itxaron, the Wait, only intensifies with time. Any and all partings and farewells become more difficult as the Wait lengthens. Both of us were learning to spend the precious hours and moments before departure, not by sharing our thoughts of separation, but our dreams of return.

Just before noon, the seven of us, plus Jack, met for a quick meal and Sailor outlined his plan. He suggested we relay all information concerning the castle through Jack in St. Louis. Sailor seemed to think Jack would be home in weeks and none of us would be searching longer than six or seven months. Mowsel didn't agree, but we all agreed to relay our information through Jack. By one o'clock, the skies had cleared. An hour later, Sailor and I watched from the dock as the giant, luxurious, and graceful seaplane, the China Clipper, lifted out of the water of San Francisco Bay, circled in a wide arc, and flew directly above the Golden Gate Bridge, then disappeared over the horizon. Before the big plane was out of sight, I thought I caught a glimpse of Ray tipping his beret to us through his passenger window.

Sailor and I left the next day. On an impulse, we went shopping for new clothes. We packed them in our suitcases along with our Brazilian passports and boarded a train for Seattle. Though we didn't know it at the time, that same day on the other side of the Pacific, Japanese forces were invading China at the Battle of Lugou Bridge, also known as Marco Polo Bridge. Once we were in Seattle, we booked passage on a small passenger ship, the *Sophia,* whose course north, according to their itinerary, "followed the whales to Alaska." To Sailor and me, that sounded good enough.

On the beautiful trip up the coast, the weather held and most passengers roamed the decks of the ship constantly. Sailing inside Queen Charlotte Sound, the *Sophia* followed Hecate Strait, staying on the inside passages, stopping in Ketchikan, then on to Petersburg and beyond to Stephens Passage. The rugged, green coastline was visible nearly every day of the voyage. As Sailor and I became a common presence on deck, several of the women passengers commented on our comportment and good manners. They were impressed with Sailor's English and the fact that two children could be traveling alone and without a chaperone. Sailor usually answered, "Brazil is very far away, madam. We have learned quickly." Our story was a simple one: we were on our way to visit our uncle for a year. No one ever doubted the story and we raised no suspicions with the captain or crew. Ten days after leaving Seattle, the *Sophia* anchored in Juneau on the only bad weather day of the journey. The captain said he'd never seen such good weather hold for so long. In Juneau, a steady rain was falling, and it continued to fall. During the next four months, there were three clear days in Juneau.

On the first day there, we found the address "Cardinal" had given us. It was a boardinghouse a half mile up the hill from the docks on the north end of town. The tenants seemed to be mainly fishermen and longshoremen. Tomizo Hiramura was nowhere to be found, but he was remembered affectionately by the landlord, who even showed us a unique piece of sculpture he once received from Tomizo in lieu of rent. He handed the piece to Sailor for him to examine. It was part of an antler, hand-carved and sculpted into the shape of a hunter at sea, alone in his kayak. Tiny geometric shapes and symbols were etched into the kayak, and the whole piece was polished to a high sheen. Sailor ran his finger lightly over the shapes and glanced at me. "Ainu," he said. The bottom of the kayak had been flattened so the piece could sit on a mantel or table. Sailor turned it over and carved into the base was the name Sak. The landlord said he'd heard the odd man was still in Juneau; however, he hadn't seen him.

A little over four months later, we were still in Juneau ourselves, searching, asking questions, and coming up empty. It occurred to me that every time Sailor and I had ever gone searching for something or someone, they always became impossible to find. In December, another worry clouded my mind. We learned from the newspapers that the Japanese had taken over Nanking and a massacre of the civilian population was rumored to be taking place. My singular thought and worry was Opari. I knew she was in extreme danger and I could do nothing about it. Sailor reminded me Opari was much more acquainted than were the Japanese with the people and landscape around Nanking. She would be able to intuit who to see and where to go well ahead of the Japanese. "And do not forget, Zianno, she carries one of these," Sailor said. He reached inside his shirt and slowly extracted the Stone, which hung from a leather necklace. I knew he was right, and tried to put it out of my mind, but my dreams became continually more restless and filled with horrific images for weeks.

On a tip from a salmon fisherman, we flew by bush plane to the town of Sitka, where we spent the rest of the winter. The days were short, wet, cold, and dark. We traveled on to Valdez on another tip, but found no current or reliable information on Tomizo Hiramura, though many people had recollections of him. From Valdez, we followed leads to several small coastal towns and a few villages. By the end of summer, we were staying in Seward. We had no luck in Seward either; however, they did have an excellent local semipro baseball team and I went to every home game. We lived the better part of the next year on, in, and around Kodiak Island, one of the most beautiful and isolated places we'd been. We met fishermen from all over the world, including Russians, Norwegians, Japanese, and native Aleuts. Tomizo was not among them.

Moving around Alaska at that time was not too difficult for two twelve-year-olds on their own. Alaska was still a territory and not yet a state, which meant most things were a little more wide open. Sailor and I often drew stares, but never a question. Most Alaskans had seen stranger things than the two of us.

The country is so big and so wild it is difficult to describe in any language. It must be experienced. Mountains and coast, coast and mountains, Alaska seems to never end. From Kodiak Island we went to Kenai, based on a conversation we had with a potter. He showed us a beautiful bowl he had been given. It was decorated in an ancient style the potter called *jomon*. I turned to Sailor and asked, "Ainu?" Sailor nodded yes. The bowl also had "Sak" etched into the base.

That same night, there was a display in the skies over Kenai like I had never seen before, even in Norway. The northern lights shimmered and danced above us in five, six, seven shades of blue and no other color—only infinite folding curtains of blue, opening and closing all night long across the sky. Sailor and I walked along the shoreline, watching and talking about the Meq. Sailor spoke at length of missing friends and family. He shared memories of Eder, Baju, Unai, Usoa, and also related several adventures he'd had with my own mama and papa, Xamurra and Yaldi. We discussed Nova's dreams and Sailor showed deep concern for Nova. We talked again about the stone spheres and Sailor asked a few questions about where they'd been found and by whom. At some point, I brought up the Fleur-du-Mal.

"Why does he do it, Sailor?"

"Do what, Zianno?"

"All of it . . . every despicable act! Murder, torture—name it. Why does he hate so much and so many? What happened to him? And why is he so obsessed with the Sixth Stone? Why doesn't he believe Susheela the Ninth and just let her go?"

"Firstly, he cannot let anything go. There lies his true problem. Secondly, you have asked two questions, Zianno. It is ironic both questions seem to have the identical answer."

"I don't understand."

"Do you recall in Norway when Zeru-Meq confronted his nephew?"

"Yes. Zeru-Meq told him he knew why Xanti wanted the Sixth Stone and he 'saw what he saw.' I have always wondered what he meant and what it was Zeru-Meq 'saw.' "

Sailor paused and looked up again at the northern lights. He turned his star sapphire between his thumb and forefinger. "I also wondered these things. Once we left Norway, I confronted him directly and asked him to tell me what he had 'seen.' If Zeru-Meq had not been the one to tell me, I never would have believed it. But, alas, Zeru-Meq never lies."

"What did he see?"

"And Xanti was only twenty-two months old at the time."

"Sailor, what did Zeru-Meq see?"

"In my opinion, he saw nothing less than the birth of the Fleur-du-Mal!"

I looked at Sailor dumbfounded. "I'm lost. Please . . . start at the beginning."

"Yes, of course," he said, glancing up at the sky once more. Dawn was at least an hour away and the northern lights still danced above us, but we both knew a fog bank would soon be creeping into Cook Inlet and within thirty minutes everything would be obscured. "I suggest we return to the hotel room," Sailor said. "I shall relate exactly what Zeru-Meq witnessed and then you divine its meaning. I tell you, Zianno, this incident explains everything."

An hour later, Sailor had finished talking. He was sitting in the one chair the room had to offer and I sat on the edge of my bed. Like Sailor when he had heard the story, I could barely believe it. It sounded impossible, especially for a twenty-two-month-old Xanti Otso. The incident had occurred 2,128 years ago in Sabratha, Xanti's birthplace. His father's name was Matai and he was on the run from the invading Romans. Matai was Meq, but he had also been a known assassin for Hannibal and other Carthaginian generals. Hilargi, Xanti's mother and Zeru-Meq's sister, had asked to leave Sabratha and escape to Spain as soon as possible. Zeru-Meq was to assist them down the coast to a small village where he had arranged a clandestine crossing to Spain with a Basque fisherman. Hoping to surprise his sister, he arrived in Sabratha a day earlier than expected. As he approached the small house, he heard a woman screaming. It was Hilargi. Zeru-Meq rushed inside to see Matai standing over Hilargi, who was on the floor, bleeding and dying with a knife plunged deep in her throat. Rose stems and rose petals were scattered around her. Matai's face and hands were covered with scratches. Xanti sat on the floor ten feet away. In his hands, he held two wooden toy blocks Zeru-Meq had made for him. He was staring without emotion at Matai. In the next instant, a kitchen knife came flying through the air and plunged into Matai's throat. He fell to his knees, then looked once at Xanti and collapsed on top of Hilargi, rolling over and gagging. He died within seconds. Zeru-Meq glanced down at his nephew, but Xanti said nothing and did nothing. He simply stared at Matai. No one had thrown the knife. Zeru-Meq is confident there is only one explanation—Xanti did it with his mind. For what reason, he never found out. The boy never said a word then and he has never used telekinesis again, but Zeru-Meq thinks Xanti has been driven ever since by an insatiable desire to regain this ability and power. Zeru-Meq says Xanti believes the Sixth Stone will give it to him.

"Do you not see the pattern, Zianno?" Sailor asked. "The Fleur-du-Mal seeks dominion over everything and everyone. He has developed acute abilities and skills which no other Egipurdiko Meq has ever possessed, before or since. He flaunts all things Meq simply because he can, as well as curses and spells, such as the one in Mali—the 'Lie' and the 'Prophesy.' However, all this aberrant and perverse ambition is driven by his true desire and obsession for the one 'ability' he craves more than all others—telekinesis. It is because he has *lost* this 'ability' and cannot regain it that his madness was born, thus the Fleur-du-Mal."

I let a moment or two pass and thought about what Zeru-Meq had seen and Sailor's theory about what it meant. I wasn't sure if the theory was the correct one or not. There were so many contradictory facts concerning the Fleur-du-Mal. Sailor's theory seemed too simple and predictable for Xanti Otso. I'd looked in his green eyes many times and each time there were more heads than one on the beast inside.

"Did you know Matai Otso, Sailor?"

"No, I did not. He had an unsavory reputation to say the least, yet he was never said to be unstable or particularly vicious. He was merely known as a reliable and efficient killer."

"Did you know Hilargi?"

"Yes, I knew her well. She and Zeru-Meq had a bond as close as twins although she was five years his junior. Hilargi had a pure heart, a warm smile, and a quick wit. I shall never understand why she crossed in the Zeharkatu, nor shall Zeru-Meq." Sailor paused and sat forward in his chair. "Zianno, regardless of the Fleur-du-Mal's motives, we must free Susheela the Ninth. This is imperative!" Sailor's "ghost eye" cleared instantly.

I hadn't heard him mention Susheela the Ninth in some time. "Have you heard . . . the voice recently? In your dreams?"

"Do you mean Deza or Susheela the Ninth?" Sailor asked, raising one eyebrow.

"Either . . . both."

Sailor remained silent for a full ten seconds. "No," he said finally.

Sailor and I left Kenai for Anchorage soon after, where we lived through the winter and spring, the "long season" I called it because of the many short days and long, dark nights. In Anchorage, I was able to contact St. Louis. I was surprised but pleased to hear Carolina's voice. She had returned to St. Louis earlier in the year when Jack told her he would be away from St. Louis for an extended length of time. I asked if she knew where he was going. Carolina said Jack told her he was "on assignment." "For whom, the *Post-Dispatch*?" I asked. "He never said," Carolina answered. She also mentioned she had been in touch with Star, Willie, and Caine in Cornwall, and Mitch in Paris. They all feared war was inevitable in Europe. Caine was in his second year at Cambridge and Carolina was worried. I asked if she'd heard anything from one of us. "Not a word," she said, then added, "Z, are you all right?" I assured her I was fine and so was Sailor and I promised to write a long letter. It would be over two years before I did, and under much different circumstances.

During that spring in Anchorage, Sailor found and befriended a local taxidermist who had met with Tomizo Hiramura the previous year concerning various methods of mounting large birds of prey, such as hawks and eagles. This was puzzling information, but it was our first lead in months. The taxidermist believed Tomizo had relocated to the interior, possibly to Fairbanks.

After paying too much for a bush pilot and a flight to Fairbanks, our frustrations only began to multiply. Not one person we spoke with had ever heard of Tomizo, and life for two boys traveling alone became more difficult daily. It was much harder to remain anonymous in Fairbanks. We left two months later with nothing but a piece of advice, which Sailor construed to be a good clue—the best place to watch eagles. An old man in Fairbanks had told him to go to Homer where the eagles were "thick as crows." We reached the little town of Homer at the far end of the Kenai Peninsula in six days, one day after war had been declared in Europe.

It was four o'clock in the afternoon. The sun was already a faded, pale yellow far to the west. Low, broken clouds spread across the sky. Sailor and I walked the length and breadth of Homer in twenty minutes. Sailor said he felt an odd sensation, but didn't elaborate. At the south end of town, jutting out on a spit of land and rock, was a restaurant and saloon with its own sizable dock and direct access to the sea. As we approached, we detoured down to the water's edge and made our way toward the dock. Suddenly Sailor stopped in his tracks, holding me back and pointing to a lone figure of a man squatting on the dock, staring up at the forest of pines and boulders in the hills above the restaurant. We followed the man's gaze with our eyes. "Eagles," Sailor said, and he was right. I could see at least fifty or sixty bald eagles perched in the tops of trees and maybe twenty more in the air, circling and soaring. We walked the ten paces separating us, stopping just short of the dock. The man had his back to us. He was wearing baggy trousers and a heavy, plaid shirt. His hair was dark and thick.

Sailor said, "Sak?"

The man turned in one motion and stared at both of us without saying a word or showing any expression. Gradually, a trace of a smile crossed his face and he reached inside his pocket, fumbling for something. He found it and extended his arm with a closed fist toward Sailor. Then the man surprised us more than we had surprised him. He turned his hand over and opened his palm, offering Sailor a small cube of salt and uttering the oldest of Meq greetings. *"Egibizirik bilatu,"* he said. "I am Sak."

Sailor glanced once at me and turned back to Tomizo Hiramura, saying something I had never heard him say to a Giza. "I am Umla-Meq," he said, "Egizahar Meq, through the tribe of Berones, protectors of the Stone of Memory." After that, he introduced me in the same manner.

Sailor then dropped his formal speech, but continued talking. Once again I was amazed by his facility with languages. Speaking to Sak in the same even tone he always used, he spoke for twenty minutes. There was nothing unusual about that, except it was in fluent Ainu, a language I had never heard, nor had many others. I had no idea what Sailor said; however, I heard him mention the Fleur-du-Mal twice. He finished abruptly. He bowed his head once, saying in English, "I thank you for listening to the foolish tale of a foolish traveler."

Silence followed for a moment with Sak and Sailor staring at each other. Sak was only a few inches taller than Sailor and me. He had a wide, square jaw with a thick beard and thick eyebrows over dark eyes, and looked to be about forty to forty-five years old. He and Sailor stood on the dock nearly eye level with each other. In the late light, the only eagles visible were the few still in the air.

A hint of a smile appeared again on Sak's face. In a deep and clear voice he said, "What do you wish of me, *akor ak*?"

Within twenty-four hours the three of us were in Anchorage and booking passage to Nome. In that short span of time, Sailor had learned that Sak did know of a *casi,* or mountain castle, purchased around the turn of the century in Japan by his father and sold to a Meq known to the family only as Xanti. The location of the castle was kept secret, even from Sak, but he said his brother, Nozomi, could find out. I wondered how Sak had known the oldest of Meq greetings, *"Egibizirik bilatu,"* which roughly translated means "the long-living truth, well-searched for." I learned from Sailor the ancestors of Pello and the ancestors of Sak were part of the same great clan of Giza who were seafarers and travelers during and after the Time of Ice. Using reindeer hides for sails they navigated the world's oceans and seas for millennia, migrating immense distances, trading knowledge of the sea, sailing techniques and technologies, culture, and most of all—language. Sailor believed the Ainu tongue, at its root, is the only language on the planet similar to Basque. Sak agreed to help us and even lead us to someone he called "the Russian cousin," who would take us into Japan without being noticed. Sak seemed more perplexed at how we became aware of his existence at all, let alone found him. Sailor didn't tell him about "Cardinal," but he did mention Solomon, whom Sak had heard his father and sister speak of many times and always with great respect.

Landing in Nome, we disembarked just as the first winter winds swept in from Siberia. Sak led us to a small hotel in an older part of the historic town. Nome and the small hotel had both seen better days. A devastating fire in 1934, combined with the Great Depression, had taken its toll on Nome.

The storm that followed the winds gave Sailor and me time to get better acquainted with the odd, middle-aged Ainu, Tomizo Hiramura, or Sak as he preferred to be called. Sak had a keen mind and wit. He spoke English well, with only a slight accent, but he had a habit of incorporating slang terms and certain expressions that were purely his. For example, he called everyone "son" in the same way Mitch might use "man" to address someone, and every so often for no apparent reason, he would shout out the phrase "Holy Coyote!" None of this affected his efficiency, however. After the weather cleared, we traveled up the Seward Peninsula to the home of "the Russian cousin." The man's face was lined heavily and burned dark from years at sea. His name was Isipo and Sak introduced him as "the last of the Kuril Ainu." Isipo owned a fishing trawler, which regularly sailed the coasts of Alaska and Russia, fishing mostly for salmon and trading with the native populations, and caring little for international laws and regulations. He could easily get us to the Russian port of Petropavlovsk in Kamchatka. From there, we could make our way through the Kuril Islands and into Hokkaido. Once we were safely in Japan, we could find Sak's brother in Tokyo. Isipo assured us we could make the run before the weather got too rough. The plan sounded risky, but good, and Sailor and I put our complete trust in the two Ainu men, two of the strangest characters we'd met in years.

It took Isipo a mere four days to prepare the trawler and gather enough false papers and certificates of commerce to cover us if we happened to be stopped or boarded. Isipo set the time of departure for dawn the next day. Sailor and I used the time to shop for new clothes and footwear more suited for life at sea in rough, cold waters. In Nome, finding them in boys' sizes wasn't easy.

Sailor thought we should not send word to St. Louis about what we'd learned or where we were going. "What purpose would it serve?" he asked. "Even if Geaxi or Opari or any one of the others were to receive the information, it would be too late."

"Too late?"

"Yes. If . . . no, I should say *when* the Japanese are finally at war with the West, the Fleur-du-Mal will surely return to his castle and Zuriaa, and especially Susheela the Ninth. He will not lose her nor take the chance of it. I have no doubt."

"How do you know the Japanese will be at war with the West?"

"I have seen countless wars begin, Zianno. Except in scale, this one is no different. Believe me, another world war is coming. It is simply a matter of time."

Luck was with us crossing the Bering Strait and sailing south to the fishing lanes along the coast of Russia. Isipo handled the trawler skillfully, while navigating our way through wild and turbulent seas. Many times, the troughs between waves sank twenty to thirty feet deep. Nevertheless, in a month, we were preparing to enter Avacha Bay and the city of Petropavlovsk. It was bitterly cold, but clear, and the majestic, snow-covered peaks of three separate volcanoes rose up behind and around the old port.

"Koryaksky, Avachinsky, and Kozelsky," Isipo said, waving at each of them one by one. "Most beautiful," he added with a grin.

There was a sizable Soviet naval force stationed in Petropavlovsk, as well as an extensive coast guard. Isipo was stopped by a small patrol boat and asked a few questions. Gratefully, we were cleared and told to proceed into port. We made repairs and restocked supplies, then set out for the Kurils the next day.

In three weeks, we'd snaked our way south as far as Kunashir Island, where we were surprised just after dawn by a Japanese naval patrol. While Sailor and I stayed silent and unseen in the background, Isipo showed the young lieutenant his false papers. The lieutenant scanned the papers and gave Isipo and Sak a hard, vicious look, followed by an expression of disgust. He turned and ordered his first officer to draw his pistol and arrest Isipo. Sailor and I glanced at each other. We hadn't used the Stones in years, but we had no choice. Without hesitating, Sailor and I withdrew our Stones and held them out toward the two sailors.

"*Lo geltitu, lo geltitu,*" we droned in unison. "*Ahaztu! Ahaztu!*"

The lieutenant's face suddenly clouded over with confusion and he instantly went blank. His first officer dropped his pistol on the deck and stared at it, as if the gun had no meaning whatsoever.

"Go like lambs, now, Giza. You will forget," Sailor said in perfect Japanese. "*Ahaztu!*" he repeated.

The two sailors climbed slowly back into their patrol boat and the lieutenant walked numbly toward the bow and pointed with a weak finger in the direction of the port of Yuzhno-Kurilsk. In minutes, the patrol boat was over the horizon and Isipo headed the trawler south to Hokkaido. He and Sak never said a word about what they'd witnessed. They both seemed to have *expected* it. By the time the sun set, we'd cleared the straits and rounded the eastern coast of Hokkaido and were slipping into Kushiro as just another fishing boat, coming in a little late. After all that time in Alaska, we were finally in Japan. It was the last day of January 1940. That same night, Sailor's dreams began again.

We said farewell to Isipo from the docks in Kushiro. He was going to return to Petropavlovsk and spend a few weeks, depending on the weather, and eventually sail home to Alaska and the Seward Peninsula. Sailor thanked him in Ainu and in Meq. Isipo nodded and shook our hands. His hands were strong and sinewy as rope. He told Sak to come home in one piece, then said good-bye.

We turned and disappeared fast. We had no legitimate identification, and wouldn't have until we reached Sapporo and the home of Sak's sister, Shutratek. It helped that Sak was an Ainu and he and Sailor spoke Japanese, but none of us were legal. We decided in case we were asked for identification, Sailor and I would pose as Portuguese orphans abandoned in Macao and rescued by Sak. Luckily, we had no confrontations because the story would never hold up to someone like the naval lieutenant we had encountered at sea. Neither Sailor nor I wanted to use the Stones again unless absolutely necessary.

We followed several lonely, wintry roads to Obihiro, catching short rides where we could. There weren't many. Along the way, we exchanged our Western clothes, piece by piece, until we were indistinguishable in a crowd. In Obihiro, we obtained seats on the only bus traveling through the mountains to Sapporo. It was a long, beautiful, treacherous journey, and cold. Sailor seemed to doze and sleep often on the trip, much more than usual. Every time he woke he muttered a name under his breath. He said the name slowly, with his eyes closed and a faint smile on his lips. In a low whisper, he breathed, "Su . . . shee . . . la." He said it with such quiet reverence, I could think of only one thing. I knew it didn't make sense, but it sounded as if he was in love.

As we approached the outskirts of Sapporo, Sak seemed bewildered by how much the city had changed and grown since he'd last seen it. I asked how long it had been and he paused before answering. He was anxious and agitated. I knew something or someone had driven him from Sapporo and his family years earlier, but he'd never given a reason and I'd never asked. Sak said, "Thirty years next month." His anxiety was understandable. He also had no gift to give his sister, and this seemed to upset him more than anything else. Sailor solved the problem by removing the piece of onyx hanging on the tassle of the small braid behind his ear. "This should suffice," Sailor said. "It is very old and from very far away—Ethiopia." He handed Sak the polished black stone. Sak accepted it humbly and thanked Sailor for saving him profound embarrassment.

Shutratek lived in a large complex of houses and buildings, all clinging to and around the sides of a steep hill. A wide veranda circled the house on three sides and made the view even better. Birch trees and scrub pine crowded the hillside. Falling snow kept the neighborhood quiet and traffic was light. Sak knocked once on the door.

When their eyes met Shutratek and Sak both began to cry. Neither made a sound. He presented her the stone and they held each other in silence and let the tears roll down their faces. Shutratek was in her mid-sixties; a short, stout woman with steel gray eyes and silver hair pulled back and tied in a bun at the back of her head. "My brother," she said finally in Ainu. She looked once at Sailor, then over to me and smiled. I wondered if she remembered. "You have very old eyes for one so young," she said. I laughed then, recalling what her father, Sangea, had told her to tell me on the train.

"I wasn't sure if you'd remember," I said.

Shutratek laughed along with me, a big hearty laugh for such a small woman. "Nineteen-oh-four," she said. "Seems like yesterday."

Shutratek served us a delicious fish and onion soup with noodles and she warmed her best sake. She smiled each time she looked in Sak's eyes, but their reunion was bittersweet. Sak learned their father and his older brother, Nozomi, had been murdered only three years after Sak left Sapporo. He also learned his eldest brother, Bikki, the one who remained in the United States at the conclusion of the World's Fair, had never come home. Shutratek and Sak were now each other's last living relative. When Shutratek learned our purpose and the reason for Sak's return was to find Xanti Otso and his fortress/prison, she gasped and covered her mouth with her hand.

"This one you seek," she said, "he have green eyes, wear ruby earrings?"

"Yes!" Sailor interrupted. "Yes, he does."

Shutratek turned and put both hands on her brother's face. "This is same one who kill father and Nozomi," she said. Waiting a moment, then speaking in Ainu, she said, "He carve roses in their backs, Tomizo."

Sak was shocked, but I wasn't, nor was Sailor. It made perfect sense in the Fleur-du-Mal's mind to eliminate anyone who had assisted him in finding his fortress, then leave his grotesque signature and calling card behind for much darker reasons.

"Shutratek," Sailor said, "do you know the location of this place?"

"No," she answered. Shutratek saw the disappointment spread across Sailor's face. "I never learn . . . they never tell," she said.

I looked over at Sailor and he looked at me. His "ghost eye" clouded over and swirled. We were in Japan all right, but it felt like we were back at the beginning.

"We'll find it, Sailor," I said. "And we'll find *her.*"

"I will go with you," Sak said. There was a fury in his eyes I understood well.

"And so I," Shutratek said, taking Sak's hand in hers.

By April, our search was under way. We traveled together posing as grandparents and grandchildren. Sak and Shutratek played their parts well. Sailor and I darkened our faces and all of us dressed simply. We were rarely stopped and both Sak and Shutratek could ask our questions and make our inquiries. We used buses and trains, crisscrossing the landscape and following whatever information we could uncover, which was little or none. The hardest part of the puzzle was in knowing and defining exactly what we were seeking. The medieval castle of Japan is called a *shiro* and there were less than a hundred not in ruins.

But as Sailor pointed out, the Fleur-du-Mal would prize the location of the fortress more than condition. He would have it renovated to his specifications regardless of its physical state. This made the number of possible locations increase tenfold. The entire northern island and province of Hokkaido was eliminated from the search because of its isolation. Tokyo was taken from the list for the opposite reason—it was too convenient and likely to be bombed first if war broke out. We thought it more probable the Fleur-du-Mal would choose somewhere in the mountains or along the coast. Therefore, we ignored the plains-type castles and fortresses and concentrated on the mountain castles, which are a different type of structure and all located in central and southern Honshu or on the island provinces of Shikoku and Kyushu.

That first summer and fall, Sailor remained patient in our search, although his dreams continued nightly. He didn't talk about them, but gradually his eyes showed concern, frustration, and alarm. The military presence and increasing numbers of soldiers everywhere, combined with the fanatic actions, attitudes, and speeches of their leaders, made him feel certain war with the West was imminent. Sailor said he agreed with Zeru-Meq, who loved all of Japan and Japanese culture, but hated the Japanese Empire.

We pushed on through the winter and spring and into the following summer. The fall of 1941 found us in and around the ancient capital of Nara. By December, we had moved to Kyoto and were staying as guests of a Sumi-e master Sailor and Sak had befriended. On the eighth of December, Shutratek and I awoke early and walked down to the open market. As we entered, the smell of daikon was everywhere, overpowering and masking the other fresh scents in the market. Music was blaring through a loudspeaker directly above the daikon stand. At seven o'clock, the Japan Broadcasting Corporation began their first news broadcast of the day. The local population usually paid little attention to the radio, but that morning they all stopped precisely where they were standing and every one of them acted stunned by what they heard. I asked Shutratek what the man had said. She blinked once, as if waking herself, then translated literally: "The Army and Navy divisions of Imperial Headquarters jointly announced at six o'clock this morning, December 8, that the Imperial Army and Navy forces have begun hostilities against the American and British forces in the Pacific at dawn today." World War II had finally erupted. From that moment on, I could not smell daikon without thinking of war.

That evening, Sailor and I discussed our plight and tried to speculate on where Opari, Geaxi, Mowsel, Ray, and Nova might be, or more accurately, where they got caught, because from now on it would be impossible to move at will. We also assumed we had missed our chance to find Susheela the Ninth before the Fleur-du-Mal returned. Sailor was certain the Fleur-du-Mal was already in Japan, or would be shortly. Once he returned, there was no predicting what he might have in mind for Susheela the Ninth. This thought upset Sailor visibly. His face tightened and his "ghost eye" clouded and blackened like a thunderstorm. Much later that night, Sailor shook me awake and held me by the shoulders, staring at me. His "ghost eye" was completely clear.

"She is awake," he said through gritted teeth.

"Who? Who is awake?" I asked. Sailor looked furious. I had never seen him so angry.

"Susheela the Ninth is awake. She is no longer *denbora dantza egin* . . . timedancing."

"Is that bad?"

Sailor spit out his answer in a bitter, low voice. "Zuriaa is torturing her, Zianno!"

From that moment on, World War II became agony for Sailor. Every day he sank deeper in despair because every night he heard the sighs and screams of Susheela the Ninth. I also began having another series of dreams about Opari. In the dreams, she was always alone, but I couldn't quite reach her, and she was always standing among bodies, always the broken bodies. I would wake in a sweat, knowing she was on the planet somewhere. I ached inside to know where. News from anywhere other than Japan was unknown. I worried constantly for Arrosa, Koldo, Willie, Caine, and Star, who were probably in Europe and in harm's way. Many times I wondered where Jack was and what he could be doing. I knew Carolina would be in St. Louis, waiting . . . waiting for all of us.

Still, we persisted. As Sailor put it, "Our war is with Time, not the Japanese." The war did make everything we did and everywhere we went a dangerous activity. Strangers, even Ainus, asking strange questions on the home front during a war will only arouse suspicion and make people reluctant to answer. Sak and Shutratek never seemed to lose their resolve and their belief that we would surely find the fortress in the next town, near the next city, over the next hill. And we kept on, despite the war. We traveled to Osaka, Nagoya, Okayama, Kobe, and back to Kyoto. We saw the castles of Hamamatsu-Jo, Matsue-Jo, Odawara-Jo, and dozens of others, some completely intact and some completely in ruins. None had any connection to the Fleur-du-Mal, past or present. The years of 1942 and 1943 became a blur. We had no true idea of how the war was going. The Japanese only spoke of great and glorious victories for the Emperor, never defeats. But by the end of 1944, conditions had spiraled downward rapidly. Food shortages and clothing shortages were critical. There was little or no gasoline and oil. Bicycles and carts hauled most people and things around, and we even heard rumors Japan might be losing.

All this time, we were never once stopped or interrogated. Sak and Shutratek became good and close friends to Sailor and me. Shutratek had tremendous stamina for a woman in her mid-sixties, yet I could see in her face that our constant travel was taking its toll. Sak seemed to only get stronger as time went by. His clear obsession to avenge his father and brother drove him on like fuel.

In May, we learned of Germany's surrender and Sailor and I believed an invasion of Japan could not be far away. Sailor feared the chaos of an invasion would be worse than existing conditions. Then the fire bombing of Tokyo and other cities increased and intensified and women and children were being evacuated from all the cities to anywhere available. Trains and roads became clogged or shut down, but by August, we were on the island province of Kyushu in the city of Kitakyushu. On the fifth, Sak and Shutratek visited Kokura Castle and met with the family of the staff who served under Mori Ogai at the turn of the twentieth century. Within minutes, we had our break. Not one, but two fortresses in the Nagasaki prefecture had been purchased and restored extensively during that time by the same buyer. One castle was in Nagasaki itself and the other fifteen miles away in the hills above Oomura Bay, northeast of the old Portuguese properties.

"There it is!" Sailor almost shouted. "There is our answer and I should have known it. The Fleur-du-Mal first came to Japanese shores with the Portuguese ships in the sixteenth century. He is familiar with this coast and these ports. This is the place and Susheela the Ninth is in one of those castles." Sailor paused and looked at me. He was more excited than I'd seen him in four years. "We have found her, Zianno."

Taking the train south on the morning of the sixth, I asked Sailor if the Fleur-du-Mal was in Japan, where was Zeru-Meq? Sailor said there was no way to know, then he reminded me that the Meq assume survival and Zeru-Meq had seen many wars in many places and always survived.

"This war is different, Sailor."

"I am aware of that, Zianno, but so is Zeru-Meq."

Unknown to us, an hour earlier on the island of Shikoku, the city of Hiroshima and a hundred thousand lives had been obliterated in an instant by an atomic bomb nicknamed Little Boy.

Sak and Shutratek had only been given the districts where the castles were sold, not their exact locations. However, they were said to be so distinctive, neither could be missed—massive five-story structures of stone, wood, and tile, surrounded by moats and gardens and stone walls seven feet thick. It was Sailor's plan to go to Nagasaki, then decide which castle to seek first. We stepped off the train in Nagasaki Station at three o'clock. The station was crowded as usual with soldiers. We walked through quickly and then out into a sprawling port city on a beautiful summer day. Finding a place to stay was difficult, but in an hour or so, Sak had found decent lodgings. It wasn't until the next morning that the first full reports from Hiroshima began to surface. When we heard the number of estimated dead, we didn't believe it. It was impossible, too many to imagine. A few reports mentioned a "super-bomb" and a "white light brighter than the sun." None of us knew what that meant, but Sailor thought it was only the beginning.

"The invasion is upon us," Sailor said. "This horrendous event means we must find the castles immediately." The map of the entire Nagasaki prefecture was laid out on the table in front of him. Sailor looked down at the map, then at me. "We should divide into two parties," he said. "Zianno, you and Shutratek search for the castle in the hills to the northeast of Oomura, while Sak and I search for the one in Nagasaki. Do not try to enter the castle if you find it." Sailor looked hard at Sak and Shutratek and told them the Fleur-du-Mal was dangerous, extremely dangerous, and should never be taken on alone. "We shall meet back here in two days. If one of us has found the castle, then we return together. Agreed?" No one said a word, but we all agreed.

Shutratek and I left for Nagasaki Station and transferred to Oomura. From Oomura, we walked up sloping, winding streets to the district where the castle might be located. We passed dozens of Western-style buildings and residential areas, asking questions along the way, describing the castle as it was described to us. The day was warm and we walked miles without learning anything. The next day went the same and Shutratek and I both fell into a deep sleep not long after sunset and didn't wake until after dawn. I had a dream just before waking and the sound I heard in the dream was one of the strangest I'd ever heard. I heard the sound of an entire forest falling.

On the morning of August 9, we dressed and left for a breakfast of rice cakes and miso, then began canvassing higher in the hills of the district. About ten o'clock, we stopped at a newspaper stand to read about Hiroshima. I mentioned the castle to the old vendor at the stand and asked if he knew its location. We got lucky. He told us where the castle was and how to get there. I had one 1906 double eagle American gold piece in my trousers that I'd always kept with me. I gave it to the vendor and Shutratek and I walked farther up into the hills toward the castle. After a long climb of nearly an hour, we rounded a corner and suddenly saw the ancient stone walls rising and the castle beyond the walls. A canopy of trees hung over the castle. There was only one gate and it was in the wall on the south side. It looked as if a drawbridge had been in its place at some time in the past. We crept closer to the gate. Shutratek looked at her watch. She was sweating heavily. The time was eleven o'clock and we were supposed to meet Sailor and Sak in Nagasaki at noon. But we couldn't leave now. We had to get closer. About twenty feet from the gate, I noticed the gate was open slightly, maybe the width of a hand. I couldn't resist; I had to look inside. I took a step.

Then it happened. A white light flashed everywhere at once for a split second. It was as if God had taken a snapshot with a flashbulb. Several seconds later, the ground rolled beneath us and we heard the distant blast. We turned to see something rising over Urakami Valley, a ball rising, changing colors from pink to purple to gold—a balloon! I saw Nova's awful balloon rising over a city that Shutratek and I knew no longer existed.

Shutratek shouted, "Sak!" then fell at my feet unconscious and dying. She'd had a massive heart attack. I bent to pick her up. I held her head and tried to make her breathe in, but she never did. She never breathed and she never awoke. I closed her eyes with my hand and laid her down. I looked up again at the balloon, climbing ten thousand, twenty thousand feet in the sky and trailing a long tail of white and black smoke.

"Sailor," I said, "Sailor."

A moment later, from somewhere above and behind me on top of the stone wall, I heard a voice. I knew the voice well.

"Bonjour, mon petit," he said.

Open the curtain
only the width of a hand
and your world will change.

—Trumoi-Meq

END OF
BOOK TWO

STEVE CASH lives in Springfield, Missouri, where he was born and raised and educated. After an attempt at gaining a college degree, he lived on the west coast, in Berkeley, California, and elsewhere. He returned to Springfield to become an original member of the band the Ozark Mountain Daredevils. He is the co-author of the seventies pop hits "Jackie Blue" and "If You Wanna Get to Heaven." For the last thirty-three years he has played harmonica, written songs, perfomed with the band, helped in the raising of his children, and read books. He is writing the final novel in the Meq trilogy.